Caffeine Nig

HEART SWARM

Allan Watson

Fiction aimed at the heart and the head...

Published by Caffeine Nights Publishing 2017

CONDITIONS OF SALE

Published in Great Britain by
Caffeine Nights Publishing
4 Eton Close
Walderslade
Chatham
Kent
ME5 9AT

www.caffeinenights.com

British Library Cataloguing in Publication Data.
A CIP catalogue record for this book is available from the British Library

ISBN: 978-1-910720-81-3

Also available as an eBook

Cover design by
Mark (Wills) Williams

Everything else by
Default, Luck and Accident

Heart Swarm

For

Gary – 'Who Grabbed Life By'

and

Agnes – Our lost songbird

Acknowledgements

As the old saying goes - nothing ever happens in a vacuum – but that's only if you don't count comets crashing into planets and the odd supernova. Likewise, writing a novel is rarely completed in isolation. So, many thanks to those who helped along the way. Julie Adams who worked tirelessly winkling out the worst of my continuity errors and typos. Claire Robertson for patiently answering my police related questions instead of whipping out the handcuffs when confronted with some of my stranger enquiries. Phil Rickman for telling me the right way to do it. Not his fault I didn't always listen. John Smith, Laura Fopp, Margaret Walker, Fiona Johnson, Teri Rowan and Caroline Gleeson for taking the time and trouble to read through an earlier draft of the book and provide me with priceless feedback. Graham Smith and Col Bury for pointing me in the right direction after a few beers at Harrogate.

And not forgetting the usual suspects – Caitlin Sagan, Anne Holt, Tom Young, Gordon Davidson, Linda Moore, Arne Keller, Linda Smith and Jani Coyne for years of encouragement and immoral support.

Also hugs and kisses to my wife, Angela, and my special girls, Joanna and Rosie.

A special big thank you to Darren Laws at Caffeine Nights for making this book happen.

Chapter 1

The phone rang at twelve thirty a.m. on Christmas morning. Harlan's first thought was to ignore the intrusion and let the call go to voicemail. It wasn't going to be anyone wishing him a merry Christmas. There was also the fact he was sprawled in bed with Cara McAullay. She was propped on one elbow, her small breasts challenging him to prepare for another skirmish. She poked him in the ribs with a knuckle.

'You going to answer that?'

His gaze stayed fixed on her breasts. 'Thinking about it. You realise it probably means a shit start to Christmas Day.'

'You mean it could get worse?'

He hoped she was joking. With Cara it was never obvious. Reaching for the phone, he checked the caller display before swiping at the screen. 'This had better be good, Pete.'

Pete Cooper, a detective constable who had drawn the short straw to work over Christmas, sounded nervous. 'Sorry to disturb you at this time of night, sir, but it might be best if you come out for this.'

Harlan blinked. When was the last time he'd been requested to attend anything other than a routine burglary, or a drunken domestic where the combatants had to be physically restrained from killing each other with the contents of the cutlery drawer?

'You realise I'm not back on duty until Monday. Scanlon's supposed to be holding the fort.'

'Yes, sir. It was DI Scanlon who said to call you.'

It wasn't like Scanlon to ask for another DI's assistance, far less his own. Harlan was yesterday's man; so marginalised these days he was in danger of slipping off the page altogether.

'What's so important that Scanlon needs me polluting his crime scene?'

For a few moments he thought Cooper wasn't going to answer. He heard the DC take a deep breath. 'We've got ourselves a dead girl in Brackenbrae. Hanging from a tree in the woods.' Another pause. 'Same tree as last time.'

For a long heartbeat Harlan's universe slipped out of sync, the past overlapping with the present. Five years ago he'd taken an almost identical call on Christmas Eve. In his mind he saw a naked child, her thighs smeared with blood, dangling from a rope braided with green Christmas tinsel. Debbie Fletcher was nine years old when she was raped and strangled, then strung up like plucked game in a poacher's larder. It had been a watershed case for him. The pressure of the investigation finished his already rocky marriage and brought his career trajectory to a crashing halt.

The sensation of layered time became so strong he wondered who he would see in bed beside him if he turned his head, Cara, or Steph, his embittered ex-wife.

'Sir? You still there?' Cooper had a note of concern in his voice.

Harlan breathed out slowly, the gravitational pull of the present dispelling the ghost of Christmas past. 'I'll be there,' he said, and hung up.

As he pushed himself up in bed, Cara asked, 'We got a case?'

He nodded, no longer distracted by her breasts. 'Brackenbrae. A young girl.'

Cara's expression was unreadable. She had been there, still in uniform at the time. She knew what it meant to him. 'Give me five minutes to scrub up.'

'No. Best leave it tonight. It'll look suspicious if I turn up with you in tow. Wagging tongues and all that. Besides, they probably won't let me get involved. Not after last time.'

Cara glared back, but didn't argue. That look of controlled intensity, the one she wore as a mask during working hours, sliding smoothly into place. She dressed hurriedly, tight anger in every rasp of cotton yanked over bare skin, raking fingers through dark tangled hair, wrenching at tugs. Harlan was still trying to find his socks when she paused in the doorway of his hotel room, her nostrils flaring as if under assault from the ripe stench of a month-old murder victim.

'A bit of advice, *sir*. I'd shower first if I were you.'

It took him ten minutes to shower, dress, then hurry down the spiral stairwell of the Cathedral House Hotel, leaving by the side door. After the hot, musky atmosphere of the room, the freezing air outside felt harsh in his lungs. The pavement was treacherous with frost, making navigation of the double-cambered corner difficult as he half walked, half slid past the hotel's main entrance, catching a glimpse of a stony-faced Cara sitting at the bar waiting for a taxi home.

He eased into the Astra parked in the walled yard belonging to the hotel, turning the ignition key and feeling the engine grumble into life. As he waited for the heater to melt the screed of ice on the windscreen, Harlan closed his eyes, his hands gripping hard on the steering wheel to ease the tightness in his fingers.

Was he really doing this? Returning to Brackenbrae? He'd never expected to set foot in that village again in his life, but here he was being reeled back to the scene of his greatest failure on the fifth anniversary of Debbie Fletcher's death – summoned by another young girl found dead in the woods on Christmas Eve.

When the first hint of warmth gusted from the fan heater, he opened his eyes and rolled down the window, filling his lungs with cold air. He knew he shouldn't be driving. He and Cara had spent two hours in the bar drinking gin before heading up to his room. The sex would have burned off some of the alcohol, and Pete Cooper's call had certainly shocked him into sobriety, but he knew he would never pass a breathalyser test. He could request for a car to be sent out which would mean having to admit he was less than sober. Not wise under the circumstances. The other alternative was taking a taxi, but that would mean waiting for Cara to leave first and he wasn't in the mood for another argument at the bar.

Clearing the last of the frost with the windscreen wipers, he let out the clutch and threaded the car through the narrow opening on to John Knox Street, the Astra's headlights sweeping across the granite tombs in the Glasgow Necropolis. Some people might have felt uneasy living next door to a cemetery, but Harlan didn't mind – the dead were harmless; it was the living you didn't want to turn your back on.

The journey to Brackenbrae took just over twenty minutes, heading north-east and crossing the Glasgow city boundary at Bishopbriggs, then continuing out towards Kilsyth and turning off the A303 between Twechar and Queenzieburn. Traffic was almost non-existent apart from late-night taxis making the most of the inflated festive tariff. All too aware of the excess alcohol in his system, he drove carefully, especially wary of the sheen of snow covering the roads as he travelled through exposed sections of countryside.

Brackenbrae had always troubled him, appearing insular and unfriendly to outsiders. The sort of place you could punch your wife in the mouth if she got lippy, and no one thought any less of you. The sort of place where the occupants formed a wall of silence when the police came calling, even when their children were being murdered.

There were more than a few people aimlessly hanging about as Harlan cruised down the main street of the village. Many of them would have attended the midnight church service and hadn't yet gone home, still caught up in the excitement of a body being found. His car drew sharp stares as it passed. Despite the late hour and the poor illumination of the orange streetlights, he knew a few bystanders might have recognised him and already be mentally composing letters of complaint to the Chief Constable.

He was the one who had let the killer slip through everyone's fingers last time. The one who had denied them justice and a proper sense of closure. They definitely wouldn't be rolling out the welcome mat for him.

He had no trouble finding the footpath access into Scaraway Woods. Half a dozen police vehicles were already parked, blue lights flashing, headlamps locked on full beam. A flimsy barrier of crime scene tape held back a group of locals, their ranks swelled by a knot of reporters. Two constables had been stationed to man the barricade, both looking miserable and cold. Harlan had barely noticed the wind in the city centre, but out here, going by the way the blue and white tape whipped and snapped there was a fair gale cutting up. He parked at the end of the line and checked his phone. He had a text from Cara that said – *Don't fuck it up*. He was glad she had calmed down. Cara had a tendency to do stupid things when her anger didn't dissipate fast enough.

Phone stuffed in his coat pocket, he took a deep breath and swung his legs out the car, first making sure he wasn't about to get his feet soaked in a pothole full of muddy slush. Murder scenes were unpleasant enough without damp shoes and wet feet. He made his way past the parked police vehicles to the footpath, flashing his ID to the constables who lifted the tape and let him through with a glum nod. The faces were familiar but he couldn't put a name to either of them. Another sign of spending too much time on the fringes of his job.

Behind him, he heard the reporters chatter excitedly and a flashgun fired causing dark green firs to rear up in the darkness like stark sentinels. He was the last person the press would have expected to put in an appearance tonight. They had performed a hatchet job on him when the last investigation went to shit. Those same newspapers that had once proclaimed him a civic hero turning on him like dogs when selective details of the investigation were leaked to provide a scapegoat. It occurred to him that his bosses were way ahead of the game, already moving him into position to take the fall if this investigation proved to be as embarrassing as last time.

One of the constables at the barrier must have radioed ahead because the bear-like figure of DI John Scanlon came striding along the footpath waving a huge torch like a guiding beacon.

'Harlan. Apologies if I dragged you out of bed, but we thought it best you be here.'

'We?'

Scanlon shrugged inside his bulky parka. 'The DCI. But I fully agreed with him.'

Kyle Kelly had been DCI five years ago and responsible for denouncing Harlan as the idiot who'd let the killer slip away from right under his nose.

'I'd have thought Kelly wouldn't want me within twenty miles of another murder scene in Brackenbrae. Especially a copycat of Debbie Fletcher.'

Scanlon didn't quite meet his stare. 'We don't think it's a copycat. It's more complicated than it seems.'

'Murder scenes are always complicated when schoolgirls are found hanging from trees. Have you identified the girl yet? Is she another local?'

Scanlon's expression was almost pitying. He seemed about to say something else, then half turned and beckoned Harlan to follow. 'Like I said, it's complicated. Best if you come see for yourself.'

Before Scanlon could turn away, Harlan caught his arm, swinging the larger man back to face him. 'Tell me something, Scanlon. If you don't think it's a copycat, does that mean you're already presuming Derek Drake has returned to pick up where he left off?'

Scanlon's open face looked conflicted. 'It's far too early to make any presumptions where Drake is concerned. Let's just say we haven't ruled him out. Now best if…'

'Fuck sake, Scanlon. How many times do I have to say this? Drake was a feeble-minded half-wit who didn't have the brains to plan what he was having for his tea each night, never mind get away with raping and murdering a nine-year-old girl.'

Scanlon ran his hand across his forehead, pushing back his bushy grey hair. 'The evidence was irrefutable, Harlan. You were there. You already know all this.'

'I know the evidence could have been stage-managed. Everything we had would have been picked apart at the seams in court.'

Scanlon blew out a huge white plume of breath. 'Damn you, Harlan. Keep your bloody voice down. There are reporters not twenty yards away and the wind is blowing in their direction. Are you really determined to give them something to write about?'

Harlan bit his lip, he hadn't even realised he was shouting. Obviously not as sober as he hoped he was.

Scanlon gave a fair impression of a man struggling not to lose his patience. 'The only solid leads we had pointed straight to Derek Drake. You do have to admit it looked bad that you'd had him in for questioning and let him walk free.'

Harlan found himself grinding his teeth. The gin from earlier was filling his mouth with a sour acidic taste. Okay, it *had* looked bad that he'd had the slow-witted school janitor sitting across the table from him, and never once did he get the impression the man was capable of anything nastier than forgetting to switch on the school boiler. It looked all the worse when it became evident Drake had scarpered and was in no hurry to be found and sent to trial.

'He wasn't the only suspect though, was he? Remember a certain someone I wasn't allowed to bring in to answer some hard questions.'

Finally, Scanlon's placid demeanour showed a touch of anger. 'And whose fault was that, Harlan? Tell me that, eh?'

Both men stood only feet apart on the footpath glaring at each other, their breath condensing in the cold air. Harlan was the first to lower his head in defeat. Scanlon was right. He only had himself to blame for that fuck-up. Him and no one else. The anger that had fuelled this discussion ebbed away, leaving him feeling empty and tired. Harlan reached out and patted Scanlon on the shoulder. A gesture of surrender. 'Take me to the scene. My feet are fucking freezing.'

He followed Scanlon's broad back along the snow-covered footpath as it twisted through the trees and undergrowth, hearing the scene before it came into view around the last turn. The low growl of an electrical generator, muted conversations, barked instructions and the high-pitched whine of a camera flash unit charging up; the snow absorbing and flattening the sounds like the dead space of a recording booth.

When he and Scanlon reached the crime scene perimeter, Harlan was certain there was a distinct dip in the volume as heads turned in their direction. *DI Will Harlan. The spectre at the feast.* There were maybe fifteen people in attendance, a mixture of white-suited SOCOs, uniformed police, plain-clothed CID, and Jo Haney, the pathologist who looked like she'd come straight from a swanky Christmas party wearing a black cocktail dress beneath a heavy wool coat. She'd swapped her high heels for a pair of mud-streaked wellies, but still managed to look like a society hostess. DC Pete Cooper was talking to someone on his mobile and gave a cautious wave.

Harlan became only half aware of the assembled crowd as he gazed up at the dead girl. From where he stood it looked eerily like the same girl as last time – similar shoulder-length blonde hair, the same shape of face, definitely the same age. And just like Debbie Fletcher, her killer had left the body hanging from a branch of the same tree atop a steep bank of earth.

Around the girl's neck he saw a noose entwined with green Christmas tinsel. Exactly the same signature as five years ago. Two more ropes, also braided with tinsel, tethered the girl's legs to wooden tent pegs hammered into the top of the mound, preventing her body from spinning and swinging in the wind.

Despite being firmly anchored, one sudden gust caused her thin frame to snap violently like bed linen drying on a clothesline.

He heard Scanlon say something, but Harlan couldn't tear his eyes away from the girl. Unlike last time, this girl was clothed in a plain white shift, the cotton looking stiff as card in the sub-zero temperature. There was a terrible vulnerability about the way she hung from the branch, her slender body buffeted by the wind as if she was dancing to a tune only the dead could hear.

Pushing away the feeling of déjà vu at once again being confronted by such a terrible yet so familiar sight, Harlan tried to analyse the scene, looking for any other differences between this time and the last. And then he saw it. He'd been so fixed on the girl that he'd missed it completely. It sat on the snowy ground beneath her feet. A square box wrapped in red shiny paper, a silver bow on top attached to a gift tag that fluttered with the wind.

Scanlon's heavy hand dropped onto his shoulder making him flinch. 'Sorry for putting you through this again, Harlan, but things aren't what they appear to be.'

Harlan flicked his eyes back to the girl, unsure what Scanlon was getting at. How could this be anything other than what it appeared to be? Jo Haney drifted over, her hands wrapped around a steaming Thermos mug of coffee. Because of her public school accent, side-swept frizzy hair and slightly horsey face, the SOCOs often referred to her as Enid Blyton behind her back. Somehow Harlan didn't think *Five Go to the Mortuary* would ever be a commercial success.

Jo Haney gave Scanlon an enquiring look. 'Have you told him yet?'

Scanlon winced and held up his hands like a goalkeeper cradling an invisible ball. Harlan finally dragged his gaze from the dead girl and stared hard at his colleague. Whatever it was that Scanlon had so far failed to mention was the reason he'd been dragged out here.

Scanlon cleared his throat, looking more uncomfortable than ever. 'This is difficult for everyone. Perhaps it's best if Dr Haney explains things seeing as she was one who climbed the ladder to make the identification.'

Jo Haney studied Harlan over the rim of her coffee mug, the tip of her nose bright red from the cold. There was an unmistakable undercurrent of pity in her expression. Harlan trusted her, he'd known the pathologist for years and knew she wouldn't be involved in any subterfuge to further discredit his already crumbling position as a police officer. Her lips, still coated with gloss from whatever Christmas shindig she'd been attending, twisted into a rueful smile.

'I can't be a hundred per cent positive, Will, not until we run the DNA, but I'm almost certain the girl hanging up there is Debbie Fletcher.'

Harlan shook his head, a stupid smile on his face. Of all the things he'd been expecting to hear, this wasn't it. 'Can't be. That's impossible.' Haney offered him her coffee mug and he found his hands were trembling as he brought it to his lips. He felt like he'd been smacked between the eyes with a snowball with a heavy stone concealed inside it.

Once again the past was masquerading as the present, unmooring him from the solid ground underfoot. He cast his gaze to the dead girl suspended from the tree almost expecting her to open her mouth and laugh down at him.

'I know it sounds ridiculous,' Jo Haney continued, 'but I carried out the post-mortem on Debbie Fletcher. You were there, Will, remember? That's my Y-incision beneath her shift. I'd recognise the needlework anywhere.'

Scanlon added, 'And besides, the four girls who discovered the body all recognised her.'

As the coffee went down Harlan's throat he realised it was heavily laced with brandy. He took another large gulp before handing it back. 'Four girls? Out here in the woods?'

'Her friends from back then. Five years ago. It's a yearly ritual for them. They come out here every Christmas Eve after the church midnight service, sing a few carols, leave gifts beneath the tree.'

Harlan felt guilty he hadn't been aware of this. Sometimes it was easy to forget that Debbie Fletcher's murder had messed up a lot more lives than just his own. His ex-wife had often accused him of being too focused on himself to be a good husband and father. She was probably right.

To Scanlon, Harlan said, 'I thought Debbie Fletcher was cremated. So how on earth…?'

'It was a burial. I was asked to attend. You were…'

'Politely requested not to show my face at the funeral to avoid causing further distress to the family.'

Jo Haney said quietly, 'You can see their point, Will. During the investigation you did after all punch the minister in the face.'

'Punched him more than a few times,' added Scanlon, a touch of piety in his tone. 'Broke his nose. And on Christmas Day, too. A respected man of the cloth whose brother happened to be the Minister of Justice at the time.'

Harlan kicked out at a snow-dusted clump of grass, scattering thin powder like a miniature blizzard, earning himself a glare of rebuke from a passing SOCO. 'So if that's Debbie Fletcher, who did they bury?'

Scanlon shrugged. 'I've sent some uniforms over to the cemetery to check if the grave has been disturbed.'

'It won't be.' Harlan stared up again at the dead girl, hating the way the floodlights gave her skin a waxy sheen as if she was nothing but a plastic mannequin. 'There's barely any decomposition. She wouldn't be so well preserved if she'd been in the ground for five years.'

Jo Haney nodded. 'I tend to agree. There is lividity present and early signs of decay. Mottling and discolouration on the skin could indicate she's been frozen and thawed out. Her eyes and mouth are stitched shut. Looks like a mortician's work.'

He held out his hand for her coffee mug but Haney pulled it out of reach. 'Any reason you've left her hanging up there? Or is that just for my benefit?'

'We can't move the body just yet because of the box.' Scanlon pointed to the gaily wrapped cube beneath the girl's feet.

'Something one of her friends left behind? You said they brought gifts.'

'Not that one. Whoever hung the body, also left the box. It's why your presence is needed here tonight, Harlan. It's addressed to you.'

Harlan rubbed at his tired eyes. He was having trouble taking it all in. First Debbie Fletcher's body reappears, then the killer leaves him a gift? The whole situation had taken on a dream-like quality. Maybe he *was* dreaming. If he tried hard enough perhaps he would wake up back in the Cathedral House Hotel with Cara snuggled up beside him in bed. As if sensing his turmoil, the pathologist relented and handed him the brandy-laced coffee. He drained most of it before returning the mug.

Shaking away the sensation of numb confusion, he allowed his anger to resurface. Anger was always a good antidote for when you couldn't get the gears of your brain to engage properly. 'Let me get this straight. You brought me out here to open a Christmas present? I mean, what if it's a fucking bomb?'

Scanlon gave a brittle smile. 'Scene of crime people have already waved their magic wands over it. Gave it a clean bill of health.'

'I still don't see why you need me to open the bloody thing. It's not as if I'm going to complain to the Royal Mail that my post has been tampered with.'

Scanlon pulled his parka tighter around his body, a sure sign he was growing impatient. 'I don't need you to open the damn box, Harlan, I just need to know what the contents signify. It was your investigation. If Derek Drake has returned to taunt us then I'm sure whatever he's left you in that box will have some personal significance. Something between you and him. I thought you'd want to be here when we opened it. If you give me a minute I'll get someone to…'

But Harlan was already striding towards the raised earthen mound, ignoring Scanlon's barked orders to return. He was aware everyone had stopped pretending to be busy and now watching his every move. Before reaching the mound supporting the tree, a SOCO handed him a pair of disposable Nitrile gloves. Harlan gruffly thanked the man, knowing he'd have got a serious bollocking from Scanlon if he'd touched the box without them. Without even thinking properly about what he was doing, he scaled the treacherous hillock, praying he wouldn't slip and fall back down on his arse.

When he made it up safely, he squatted beneath the dead girl to read the gift tag. The message was written in a bold, confident hand with a fountain pen.

For Detective Inspector William Harlan. Merry Xmas.

He teased aside the ribbon holding the wrapping together, careful not to disturb the bow itself, then pulled away the metallic paper from the top, uncovering a plain wooden box. Despite what Scanlon claimed about it not being a bomb, Harlan still winced as he eased the frozen lid away and immediately reeled back from the ripe stench of rotting meat.

Inside the box was a human head in an advanced state of decay, slow-moving maggots visible in the scraggy beard and lank hair. Despite feeling nauseated, Harlan's single true emotion was one of absolute vindication. The killer of Debbie Fletcher may have been mocking him and the police in general, but a gift was still a gift, and the killer had given him a kingly one.

Scanlon was still yelling at him not to disturb the evidence, but Harlan couldn't help himself. Reaching inside the box, he carefully lifted out the head of Derek Drake by the hair, holding it aloft to the gathered throng below. Having a dead girl's feet swaying inches above him, he knew he should really have shown a little more dignity, but the past five years of crippling stagnation and disgrace had taken a heavy toll.

From the top of the mound, he called down loudly to every police officer present, 'Fucking well told you so.'

Chapter 2

'If you think last night is going to act like a magic wand and wipe away the last five years, Harlan, you're badly mistaken. It changes nothing.'

It was seven a.m. and Harlan was sitting in Kyle Kelly's office. The DCI hadn't bothered offering coffee, or even to wish him a merry Christmas. Instead, he was getting a pep talk that definitely wouldn't be nominated for a motivational speech of the year award.

'You were the detective in charge. You were the one who turned the investigation into a farce. Since then your performance has been abysmal. I've twice recommended you be demoted back to a DS, but the chief superintendent won't accept it. He trots out all this baloney about how he thinks you might recapture some of the early promise you showed. In my book, catching one serial killer doesn't entitle you to a job for life.'

Harlan knew Kelly was discomfited over Derek Drake's head turning up. The DCI had signed off on Drake being the killer five years ago and called a halt to the investigation expecting an imminent arrest that never materialised. Casting up Harlan's own failings was Kelly's way of reminding him any resulting fallout from last night's unexpected new developments in the case could still be redirected towards him.

Kelly was sometimes known as *Sieg* Kyle on account his spindle-legged gait that resembled a classic Nazi goose-step when he was in a hurry. It looked especially comedic when he strutted around in his dress uniform. This morning he was dressed casually in golfing trousers and a pale blue woollen cashmere jumper. Harlan wondered if his DCI had been given a new golf clubs as a Christmas present, and maybe planning on trying them out straight after this meeting. His large bald head swivelled towards the office door before glaring down at his watch. The reason for the glare was DI Scanlon, who was also supposed to be in attendance at this early morning meeting, but Scanlon had so far failed to appear.

Kelly turned his attention back to Harlan. 'What I'm saying is this may be your last chance to claw back some of the ground you've lost. Make restitution for last time.' He attempted a sympathetic smile that only made him look like he was suffering from trapped wind. 'Hard to believe you were the blue-eyed poster boy of this department. Now you're simply a sad embarrassment.'

Harlan couldn't deny any of this. He still vaguely remembered being a high-flier with a case clearance rate twice as good as anyone else's, but not because he was such a great detective. What had fuelled his rapid rise through the ranks was the unerring instinct to put the right questions to exactly the right people, knowing intuitively who held a useful piece of the puzzle and who didn't. This inbuilt guidance system had allowed him to focus on the important details, conjuring up a road-map that took him where he needed to be; standing next to the guilty party ready to slap on the handcuffs.

The Debbie Fletcher murder had changed things. He'd suffered a loss of faith; self-doubt and public humiliation choking the life from the intuition he'd been blessed with. These days he simply plodded through the evidence like everyone else did, only much more slowly.

Harlan met Kyle Kelly's stare head-on. 'I appreciate your candid assessment of my abilities, sir, and I'm grateful to be included in the new investigation. It might be stating the obvious, but I'm thinking that Drake's head being left behind at the scene might indicate that someone is emphatically telling us he wasn't the killer.'

'Dear God, Harlan. After all this time you still think Drake was set up? He was a part-time janitor at the girl's school. She knew him well enough that she might easily have got into a car with him.'

Harlan shook his head, already feeling weary of these same old circular arguments. Debbie Fletcher had been abducted on her way home from a Girls' Brigade carol singing rehearsal at Brackenbrae Church. She had walked with her friends until they reached Myrtle Street where Debbie lived, but she never made it to her house. Somewhere on that quiet street, someone was waiting for her.

'Drake didn't own a car and there's no record of him ever holding a driving licence. And why on earth would she have accepted a lift so close to her house? It doesn't make sense.'

Kelly's mouth was a grim slash. 'All the evidence pointed to Drake at the time. You know that.'

'The evidence could easily have been staged. I said so at the time.'

'You mean like the credit card in Drake's name used to access that paedophile website? The laptop with photographs of Debbie Fletcher trussed and bound? For Christ's sake, Harlan, we even found her underwear at his flat with his semen on them. What more do you need? A Facebook selfie posing with the body and a written confession signed in blood?'

Harlan knew how damning it sounded, but he'd never been able to believe Derek Drake was capable of murder. 'That credit card, funny it was the one single card Drake owned, and only ever used for the porn site. And the laptop? Drake's prints all over the casing, but not a single print on the keys. As for semen on the girl's knickers, even that could have been simulated by someone with the right motivation. And don't you find it odd we got the anonymous tip-off about Drake's porn site transaction at the exact same time Drake vanished like a puff of smoke?'

The DCI shook his head sadly. 'If you really think Drake's head turning up in a box proves his innocence then you're as much a fool now as you were five years ago.'

Harlan rubbed at his eyes, trying to banish the hot dry itch caused by lack of sleep. Locking horns with Kelly at this early stage was stupid and could see him kicked off the case before it even got started. Even so, he wasn't going to sit here and be called a fool by a man who wore golfing trousers to work. As he lined up another crunching defensive block, he was saved from himself by heavy footsteps out in the corridor followed by three sharp raps on the door.

Scanlon pushed his way into the office, full of apologies. 'Sorry, sir. Had a bit of a row with the wife over not being there for when the children open their Christmas presents. I did suggest we might wait until after the church service, but then I realised I might not be back in time for that either…' He left the sentence open as if hoping Kelly would grant him dispensation to attend church with his family, but Kelly was in no mood to let Scanlon off the hook.

'I'm sure God will understand why you won't be singing His praises this morning, Scanlon. We all have to make sacrifices for the job.'

Harlan thought the only thing Kelly would possibly be sacrificing this morning was a round of golf. Scanlon on the other hand was one of the few practicing Christians he knew of in the police force. Missing church on Christmas Day would be a real blow to him. Harlan decided to show a bit of support to his fellow detective inspector.

'Just thinking, Scanlon. If you were a Muslim, you could lodge a complaint over religious discrimination. You know, being denied the right to worship on special holy days.'

Kelly threw Harlan a furious sideways look, then snapped at Scanlon, 'Not planning on raising a complaint on the grounds of religious discrimination are you, Scanlon?'

The big DI looked flustered and shook his head. 'No, sir. Not at all,' he muttered, casting Harlan an accusatory frown as if he'd tried to get him into trouble instead of merely demonstrating solidarity with a fellow officer. Hanging up his jacket, Scanlon sat in the empty seat in front of Kelly's desk. The DCI reached across the desk and offered Scanlon his hand.

'Merry Christmas, DI Scanlon.'

'A Merry Christmas to you too, sir.'

Kelly's eyes flicked to Harlan, realising he hadn't wished his least favourite detective inspector the compliments of the season, and maybe wondering if he should now do so, but after a brief moment's hesitation he settled back in his seat.

'So, give me the worst of it.'

Scanlon looked unhappy to be the bearer of bad news. 'Until a DNA test proves otherwise, we have to assume the young girl discovered hanging in Scaraway Woods is Debbie Fletcher. Her friends who found the body made a visual identification, and Dr Haney backs them up. She performed the original autopsy and she's certain it's the same girl.'

Kelly shook his head. 'Wouldn't there be… deterioration to the body? Five years? There should only be bones left.'

'Dr Haney thinks the girl has been frozen and stored somewhere. It's the only explanation.'

'Frozen?' Huge wrinkles appeared on Kelly's head like sand dunes. 'But they buried her. We were both there, Scanlon. Don't tell me the bastard actually dug her up again after the funeral.'

Harlan didn't like the way the two men were already excluding him from the conversation and decided to stick his oar in. 'Not necessarily. He could have switched her body for something else at the last minute. Which means we should be paying a visit to the funeral director to find out who had access to the deceased prior to the burial.'

He expected Scanlon or Kelly to rubbish this suggestion, but Scanlon nodded in agreement. He had the air of a man preoccupied by other concerns. That argument with his wife must have been more serious than he'd made out and weighing heavily upon him. Harlan could sympathise with him. He'd been there himself.

'That's a good point, Harlan,' said Scanlon, rubbing at his double chin. 'Obviously the funeral parlour won't be open today or tomorrow. I'll ask the parents who they had organise the service and contact the owner directly.'

Harlan put on his most helpful smile. 'No need for that. It was Hughes and Sons. The business is run by the youngest son, Tim. When Hughes the elder passed on ten years back, Tim bought out his brother and runs the business on his own.'

Scanlon looked impressed, but Kelly only gave him a calculating look. 'And how the hell do you know that?'

Harlan shrugged, not wanting to admit he'd been up most of the night poring over his old notebooks and copies of the case files. 'I spoke to him last time. Hughes lives with his elderly mother in the new estate at Brackenbrae Meadows. Or least he did five years ago. Never struck me as the marrying type, so he's probably still there. I'll have his home number and address in one of my old notebooks.'

'Was he ever was a suspect for the killing?' asked Scanlon.

'Just a routine chat. I spoke with lots of the locals.' He didn't mention that Hughes had caused his internal alarm bells to ring loudly, and not just because he was a middle-aged man who lived with his mother. He always felt there was something morbidly unhealthy about Hughes' brash enthusiasm with regard to making Debbie Fletcher look like a 'little angel'.

Scanlon said, 'Having you assist this investigation will save us a lot of time, Harlan. Means we can hit the ground running.'

'Just as long as DI Harlan remembers that assisting is all he's doing. Not running the whole bloody show,' growled Kelly with a distinctly sour look on his face.

Harlan smiled back at the DCI. 'Always happy to oblige, sir.'

'You cheating little cow! You rung up those mince pies twice. I want to see the manager.'

Moira felt her face flush deep red like it always did at the slightest hint of conflict. Christmas Day was already semi-ruined by having to work a morning shift at Mike's Mini-Market without having a run-in with crazy Stella Wilson.

'I... I didn't.' Moira pointed at the electronic display listing the scanned goods. 'See for yourself.'

Stella thrust her pit-bull face towards the screen, bottom jaw jutting out aggressively as if she was planning on savaging it with her teeth. 'Doesn't prove nothing,' she spat. 'You probably deleted it again when you knew I'd caught you. It definitely beeped twice. Didn't it, Thom?'

Stella's browbeaten husband shuffled awkwardly behind her, gazing at his feet, looking lost. 'I'm not sure. It might have.'

Stella's voice shifted up an octave. '*Might have?* My fucking tits. It beeped twice, I'm telling you.'

Moira was grateful the only other person in the queue was Sadie Goldridge who looked as if she was on medication of some sort, gazing around her with a dreamy sort of smile on her face. Stella definitely wasn't smiling. Despite the cold snap, she wore only a skimpy denim jacket and a T-shirt with a plunging V-shaped neckline. When she tucked her meaty forearms beneath her bosom in that age-old battleaxe stance, Moira feared the woman's breasts would come tumbling out like uncooked Christmas puddings and add further turmoil to an already tense situation.

Thankfully, Mike, the mini-market owner, chose that moment to emerge from the back shop carrying a box of tinned peas. He was wearing a Santa hat over his balding head, and had a flashing reindeer badge pinned to his white dustcoat. Sensing a problem, he put down the box and made his way to the till, trying to look amiable and full of good cheer. Moira thought the false smile made him look like a child molester.

'Problem, ladies? Anything I can help with?'

Stella was straight in there, eyes bulging, finger pointing. 'This little cow charged me twice for the mince pies.'

Moira looked helplessly at her manager. 'I didn't. Honestly. Look at the screen.'

Mike peered at the display, the fake smile never leaving his face.

'She's covered her tracks. Probably got a little footswitch down below to delete things if the customer catches on.'

Mike continued smiling pleasantly, but Moira knew he found Stella as intimidating as everyone else in the village. 'Tell you what, Stella,' he said. 'Obviously there's been a misunderstanding, but seeing how it's Christmas Day, the mince pies are yours free of charge. Take them off the bill, Moira.'

Stella flashed a triumphant look. 'Well, no need to take things further then.' She nudged her husband with her elbow. 'Thom, what are you waiting for? Get packing.'

Thom Wilson limped past his wife, silently mouthing, '*Sorry*,' to Moira behind Stella's back as he began stuffing groceries into a plastic bag. It was difficult to fathom how Stella had managed to snare Thom Wilson as a husband. He was such a nice unassuming bloke, always had a smile for everyone. Even though he walked with a bad limp, he was happy to lend a hand when volunteers were needed to paint the village hall or repair fencing at the kiddies' playground. Moira had been told he'd got shot in the leg while in the army. Iraq or Afghanistan or someplace like that. She felt sorry for him. He was actually quite good-looking and could have done much better than horrible Stella.

When the Wilsons finally left, Stella directing one last victorious smirk at Moira, Mike casually said, 'By the way those mince pies will be coming out your wages.'

'What? That's not fair. I didn't scan them twice. She made that up.'

Mike looked unconcerned. 'Customers are important. Got to keep them happy.'

'Yeah? And what about keeping your staff happy?'

Her manager finally let his fake smile drop. 'I can always get new staff, Moira. Plenty of kids out there desperate for a decent part-time job so close to home.'

Moira bit her lip, feeling tears of frustration prick against the back of her eyelids. Mike's smile was back as he ushered Sadie Goldridge up to the till. All the old woman had in her basket was a box of cat biscuits. Mike put the biscuits on the conveyor belt. 'Merry Christmas, Sadie. What's this? Got yourself a cat?'

Sadie smiled sweetly. 'Oh no. Those are for me. They're very crunchy and full of vitamins.'

'Oh,' said Mike, rolling his eyes and twirling his finger at the side of his head. 'Well don't go eating too many and giving yourself a tummy ache. The vet's surgery is closed today.' He smirked, pleased with his joke, and then drifted back down the store.

Moira scanned the cat biscuits, half inclined to tell Sadie that Mike had been making a fool of her, but she knew the old woman would just smile and appear not to care. Moira's mum said Sadie Goldridge once used to be a famous medium. Had people coming from all over the place to get messages from dead relatives. She was a sweet old lady, there was no question about that, but it always creeped Moira out seeing her walking around the village muttering to herself, or maybe to the ghosts that still trailed along in her wake. Moira bagged the cat biscuits and gave Sadie her change.

The old woman smiled at her with brilliant white dentures, her eyes as dark and piercing as a starling's. 'You know, dear, I was just speaking with your grandmother. She says she likes what you've done with your hair.'

Moira felt a shiver run through her. Her grandmother was dead and in the ground two years now. She tried to think of something to say but all that came out was, 'Oh, um... that was nice of her.'

Sadie Goldridge beamed back, dentures now clenched like a sprung trap. 'And she also said for you to keep your knickers pulled up tight or you might be next one swinging from a rope in Scaraway Woods. Bye, bye, dear. Have a nice Christmas.'

By ten o'clock Brackenbrae was under siege by a miserable bunch of uniformed police officers, most dragged from the warm embrace of their families for doorstepping duty. Harlan thought it was a pointless exercise as whoever had strung up Debbie Fletcher's body almost certainly didn't enter the woods by way of the village footpath. A mile south from where the body was found, Scaraway Woods brushed against a quiet country road with many convenient lay-bys. That had to be the best bet for carrying the dead body of a child into the woods without being noticed. The public however expected to see police activity of some sort, and the doorstepping at least served as a visible demonstration of due diligence by Police Scotland. He and Scanlon had sixteen uniforms at their disposal, and had paired them off to wander around the village and the council estate asking if anyone had seen anything suspicious the previous evening.

He remembered Brackenbrae was a place composed of three distinct tribes. It had been a former mining village slipping into slow decay until the 1990s when a council-built housing estate was thrown up alongside it to accommodate overspill from Kirkintilloch and Milton of Campsie. Ten years later, private developers purchased adjacent farmland on a long slope overlooking the village and built a few dozen detached homes within a landscaped oasis that instantly became fair game for the opportunist thieves from the village and the council estate. The old village inhabitants sneered at the council estate incomers, while the incomers snarled right back – and both groups despised those who lived in the private housing estate.

DS Cara McAullay accompanied Harlan as he worked his way along Main Street, made up mostly of terraced cottages and a few shops. As they moved on to yet another door in desperate need of painting, Cara said, 'Remind me again why we're doing this instead of hauling in the most obvious arsehole and slapping him about until he talks.'

'Think on it as a public relations exercise, Cara. We wouldn't want the press to think we're lacking in moral fortitude and a steely determination to track down the villain. Anyway, stop moaning, you'll get overtime for this.'

Cara shivered and pulled her black leather jacket tighter around her slender body. Her dark corkscrew hair was pulled back this morning, held with a scrunchie the same shade of red as her woollen scarf. Her long legs were concealed with grey pinstriped trousers, and on her feet she wore her usual Doc Martens. Harlan noticed she'd applied a touch of colour to her thin lips.

'I get that, but why are *we* doing this? This is uniform work. Shouldn't we at least be talking to the creepy funeral parlour guy you told me about?'

'Because Scanlon is running the show. At best I'm only involved on sufferance because of my extensive background knowledge. Kelly wants me to fill in the gaps while not actually being handed any responsibility. Anyway, our creepy funeral parlour guy has agreed to speak with Scanlon later today. Claims he has to take care of his elderly mother who suffers from dementia, and it would upset her routine if the police barged in first thing in the morning.'

Harlan rang the doorbell and it was answered by an unshaven man wearing a shabby dressing gown. In the background he could hear children yelling at one another, probably arguing over a new electronic gizmo that would be consigned to the back of the toy cupboard once the batteries ran down.

'Yeah?' the man asked.

Harlan showed his warrant card. 'Sorry to bother you this morning, sir. Just wondering if you noticed any unusual activity in the village last night.'

'Like what?' the man replied, his tone surly.

Harlan shrugged. It was unlikely anyone was going to say they'd seen a man dragging a dead child down Main Street. 'Maybe a strange vehicle trawling the area. Or anyone acting in a suspicious manner?'

The man stroked his bristly chin looking thoughtful. 'Come to think of it there was something.'

Cara pulled out her notebook, holding her pen ready.

'I did see this odd-looking bloke park a sleigh on the roof across the street. He was carrying a big bag full of stuff. And then he disappeared down the chimney. That unusual enough for you?'

Harlan was about to thank the man for his time and move on, but Cara took a step forward forcing the man to back off. 'You think this is funny? A dead child hanging from a tree and you want to act like a smart-arse? Maybe you won't find it so funny when we charge you with wasting police time.'

The man looked surprised. 'Look, hang on a minute…'

Cara stepped closer, now actually inside the house, her finger jabbing at the man's chest. 'You've got kids, yeah? Imagine how you would feel if one of your children was raped and strung up, and your neighbours thought all it merited was a flippant remark.' She glanced at the nameplate on the door and made a point of scribbling the name into her notebook. 'Just so you know, Mr Houston, we'll be speaking to the dead girl's parents later on, and I'll be sure to make a point of mentioning how amusing you find this.'

The man's cocky manner was gone completely. 'Look, I wasn't disrespecting no one, I just wasn't expecting the police knocking on my door on Christmas morning. I never saw anything, okay.'

The sound of raised voices had caused three tousled-head children between the ages of seven and twelve to peer around the living room door, as well as summoning his wife from the kitchen. Harlan took Cara by the elbow and eased her back. 'Thank you for your time, sir. Happy Christmas.'

As the door slammed closed, he could hear the man's wife giving him grief. Cara was grinning.

'Was that really necessary?'

'I hate jizz-bags like him. Think they can mouth off to the police with no comeback. Hopefully it'll cause a huge row and there'll be no festive shagging on the menu for him tonight.'

'You can be a vindictive cow at times, you know that?'

Cara's smile was cold. 'Well, if I'm not getting any until this is over why should anyone else?'

When Harlan started sleeping with Cara, they had made a strict rule that if both were working on a major investigation together, sex was off-limits. He tried to look as if he was considering the logic of her argument. 'Fair enough. If it helps I'll send you a dirty text.'

Cara wasn't impressed. 'No thanks, granddad. If I want vintage pornography I'll go read *Lady Chatterley's Lover.*'

'Hey, less of the granddad shit, if you don't mind. I'm only thirty-eight.'

Cara's dark eyebrows arched. 'Try thirty-nine, Harlan.'

'I am? Are you sure?'

'You're twelve years older than me. It's why you're such a crap shag.'

Harlan was struggling to reply when a man's voice behind him said, 'Detective Inspector Harlan. Is it true what everyone is claiming? That the body found in Scaraway Woods is none other than the same girl supposedly buried five years ago?'

He spun round and saw a sallow-faced man with sandy hair and protruding teeth grinning at him. Guy Noonan was the journalist who'd had more to say than most when the knives were brandished five years ago. Before Harlan could even say 'No comment,' Noonan was holding up a silver Dictaphone. 'And before you say anything you might regret, this thing is recording. So how about a quote?'

Harlan wasn't surprised word had gotten around so quickly about the identity of the body. The carol singers and their parents would have quickly spread the word. Thankfully Noonan didn't know anything about Derek Drake's head being left in the box. That bit of information would be suppressed as long as possible, but professional nose-pokers like Noonan had contacts within the police who'd spill their guts for a few extra quid all because they didn't get the promotion they expected, or simply realised that after thirty years in the job they'd wasted their life filling in paperwork.

He decided the best way to handle things was to ignore Noonan, walking on without speaking. Cara, however, plucked the Dictaphone from the journalist's hand and tossed it on to the roof of the terraced cottage where it sank into the thin layer of snow covering the slates.

The look on the Noonan's face was priceless. Cara inclined her head upwards. 'Want a quote? Suck my tits.'

Noonan called after her, 'I'd suck them if you had any, you skinny bitch.'

Harlan grabbed Cara's arm and pulled her away before she did something stupid like yanking Noonan's trousers down and throwing them on the roof to join the Dictaphone. As she allowed herself to be led away, she pointed a finger at Noonan. 'Later, Bugs Bunny.'

He decided it was time for a coffee break. They were passing a mini-market that had one of those serve-yourself Costa Coffee machines inside, and he hauled Cara towards the door just as an old lady came out clutching a pink plastic bag. The old lady smiled at them with gleaming white dentures and wished them both a Merry Christmas. Then she said something that caused Cara's jaw to drop open.

'Hello, Cara. Susan sends her best wishes and says to watch your step.'

And with that, the old lady walked off swinging her plastic bag and singing 'God Rest Ye Merry Gentlemen' in a brittle, quavering voice.

Chapter 3

Harlan fed the Costa Coffee machine with a handful of coins and managed to fill two cardboard cups with coffee without scalding his hand. A sign stuck to the cup dispenser claimed the cups were made from sustainable wood pulp; even the plastic lids were produced from recycled material. He wondered if anyone really cared, and if the whole eco-friendly guilt trip was a direct replacement for religion in an ever-increasingly secular society. Who needed confession and atonement when you had multi-coloured wheelie bins and catalytic converters?

Cara was leaning against the shelf holding the sugar and napkins, a black scowl on her face. She scowled a lot at the best of times, but this was a real thunderstorm of a pout, the type that made him wish he had a storm cellar to hide in. Harlan could almost feel the barometric pressure dropping within a ten feet radius of his detective sergeant. He laid the coffees on the shelf, adding a couple of sugars to his own, then stirring the liquid with a strip of plastic so flimsy it barely caused a ripple on the steaming surface of the coffee.

'So, who is Susan?'

Cara sipped at the coffee, refusing to meet his eyes.

'What that woman said sounded like a threat. You know I have to ask.'

Cara glowered down at her Doc Martens.

'You know that old woman from somewhere?'

An almost imperceptible shake of the head.

'But you do know who Susan is, right?'

Cara finally looked him straight in the eye. 'Mind your own fucking business, Harlan. I'll see you outside.'

He watched her stiff back as she strode from the shop, not knowing what to make of the entire incident. If any other officer had spoken to him like she did, he'd have no hesitation in slapping them down hard, but Cara got more leeway than most – and not just because of the sex. Ever since she'd started working under him as a detective constable, Harlan instinctively knew they shared a common bond. They were both damaged in their own way. His own personal fault-lines splitting apart in the seismic shift of the original Debbie Fletcher investigation. As for Cara? Who knew?

You didn't ask about that sort of thing, didn't pick at another person's internal scabs. He sensed Cara's outward hard shell was protecting something thin and brittle inside. Something that could break under the right sort of pressure. It made her appear vulnerable to him.

To everyone else she was a nightmare, she was too unapproachable, too aggressive; had forged herself into a barrier people couldn't push past. Behind her back she was the butt of plenty of jokes. Some smart-arse had once drawn a Roger Hargreaves style caricature of *Little Miss Frosty Fud* and pinned it up in the canteen. Even Harlan had to admit it was funny, but he'd torn it down before Cara had a chance to see it. She'd only have tracked down the stupidly brave artist and tasered him in the balls, causing Harlan no end of reports to fill in.

A bespectacled man wearing a Santa hat wandered past the checkout lane where a pretty, blonde teenager sat staring glumly into space. The man gave Harlan a questioning look, eyebrows raised comically. There was a flashing reindeer badge pinned to his white dustcoat. 'Everything okay there?' the man asked cheerfully. It was obvious he'd witnessed Harlan's tense exchange of words with Cara.

When the man continued staring, Harlan said, 'It's fine. I'm just in for a coffee.'

The man held out his hand, 'Mike McBrearty. I run this place. Mike's Mini-Market. You're with the police, aren't you?'

Not wanting to appear rude Harlan took the man's hand and shook it. 'Is it that obvious?'

McBrearty laughed. 'Not really. It's just I remember you from last time. DI Harlan isn't it?'

'That's me. I don't remember this shop being here last time.' Harlan took a tentative sip from the coffee and decided it needed more sugar.

Mike McBrearty beamed back. 'No, not back then. This used to be a Co-op. When they closed down I took it over. Doing good business. Open every day of the year, early till late. Learned that business tip from the Pakis.'

He grinned again and Harlan wondered if McBrearty was hoping he'd react to the racist term. Some people were like that. Loved to draw you into a conflict. When Harlan stayed silent,

McBrearty continued, 'Just thought I should introduce myself. If you guys are going to be camped here for the next few weeks it's always good to know there's a local shop you can depend upon for ciggies, chewing gum, snacks, soft drinks, that sort of thing.'

Harlan nodded, slightly taken aback by McBrearty's brazen sales pitch. 'Sure. I'll do that.'

'Excellent. You need anything else today? Chocolate, crisps, pork pies?'

'There is something you could help me with. When I came in there was an elderly lady leaving the shop. You know who I'm talking about?'

McBrearty brayed with laughter. 'Oh, you've met Psychic Sadie?' He twirled his finger beside his head, a gesture that drew a disgusted look from the checkout girl now openly earwigging into the conversation. 'Sadie Goldridge used to be one of those mediums. Held séances and talked to the dead.' He made a mock-frightened face and wiggled his fingers. 'Whoo. Spooky, eh? Now she's got bats in the belfry. A few letters short of a Ouija board, you could say. She's always passing messages on from the other side whether anyone asks her to or not. I imagine they'll stick her in an old folks' home soon. Then she can talk all day to the walking dead.'

Harlan took another sip of the coffee wondering if Cara had a dead relative or friend named Susan, and if that was why she had reacted so badly. 'So this Sadie Goldridge. Is she any good? You think she'll solve our case for us?'

McBrearty actually slapped at his thigh and once again laughed like a jackass. 'I can see we're going to get on like a house on fire, DI Harlan.'

Behind him the checkout girl was rolling her eyes as Harlan added another sachet of sugar to the coffee and fitted a lid to the cup. 'Got to get moving, Mr McBrearty. Villains to apprehend, crooks to catch, you know how it is.' He made a half turn as if to leave then stopped dead before slowly turning back in time-honoured fashion. 'There is one thing you could help me with.'

McBrearty plastered that annoying grin back on his face. 'Sure. Anything.'

'For a start you could tell me where were you were between ten o'clock and midnight last night.'

By the time Harlan walked out the mini-market, Cara was back to her normal sullen self. He decided not to make any mention of Psychic Sadie.

'Looked like you found a new best friend in there,' she said.

'That's mini-market Mike. He thought so too, until I disabused him of the notion. At least we can scrub him off our long list of suspects as he was working in the shop till eleven-thirty.'

'The Santa hat was a nice touch. If only all men had such good taste in headwear.'

'Never mind the hat, that flashing reindeer badge could trigger an epileptic fit.'

They walked on in silence, nursing their drinks. Harlan thought drinking coffee in cold weather was always a catch-22 situation. The more coffee he drank to warm his insides, the less there was to heat his hands, and by the time he made up his mind to do one thing or the other, the coffee was tepid and useless for both functions. At least the pavements were mainly clear of snow, although the gutters were still hidden under miniature mountain ranges of dirty slush. Above him the sun was breaking through the clouds like a shrivelled apricot.

Brackenbrae Church was situated at the junction where a spur road, unimaginatively named, New Road, led up the hill past the cemetery to the council flats, and beyond that to the more affluent Brackenbrae Meadow estate. They halted outside the church, sitting on the low wall, backs against the iron railings. Cars were already parking in ones and twos along New Road, the occupants smartly dressed for the Christmas Day service. Harlan guessed most of them couldn't wait to gossip about the dead girl in the woods. They would sit on the pews, whispering to each other, trying hard to appear distressed, but underneath the facade they would revel in the gory details. As the parishioners neared the church gate they stared at Harlan and Cara, marking them for what they were: interfering outsiders. Probably thought they were being disrespectful by sitting down on the job. Harlan didn't care.

The church itself was built from grey stone and had a stained glass feature window that showed Christ leading several small children by the hand. Beneath the figures was the age-old scripture, *Suffer the little children, and forbid them not, to come unto me.*

Considering Harlan's personal suspicions regarding the Reverend Simon Dolman, it was horribly ironic.

His phone warbled. It was Scanlon, telling him that he and DS Adam Brock were just leaving the Fletcher house and would meet them outside the church in five minutes. Kyle Kelly had ordered both DIs to attend the church service, the idea being they could scope out the congregation for kiddie-fiddlers. Harlan imagined Scanlon was secretly pleased to put in an appearance at church on Christmas Day so he wouldn't have to wear a hair shirt for the next month.

Cara inclined her head towards the church behind them. 'So this is the guy whose nose you broke, yeah?'

'Who? Jesus? Even I would draw the line before lamping him.'

'I meant the minister, you twat. Not the hippy in the window.'

Harlan had never discussed the assault with Cara, but imagined she would have heard all the stories about that particular incident and saw no point in soft-soaping the facts. 'The Reverend Dolman was involved, or least knew something about Debbie Fletcher's murder. It was written all over his face. The bastard goaded me. It was as if he thought he had some sort of protection, and as it turned out that protection was me. I was under pressure, lack of sleep, problems at home, I lashed out. He made a complaint, but didn't press charges. When the case was closed, I was disciplined and suspended. End of story.'

Cara came as close as she ever would to a genuine smile. 'Wish I'd seen that. I hate these holier-than-thou sanctimonious bastards. Always going on about turning the other cheek, but when someone does punch their lights out, they shout blue murder. Fucking hypocrites.'

'Scanlon's a devout Christian. He's okay. Except when he comes round rattling his collection tin during Christian Aid week.'

Cara shook her head. 'He gave me a little Bible once. Said it might provide some inner calm.'

'And did it?'

'Not really, but I enjoyed the look on his face when I chucked it in the bin while he was still standing there. Anyway, this Dolman – did he actually admit anything? And if he did, why didn't you just haul him in for questioning?'

Harlan sighed. 'No, he didn't exactly confess to murdering or abducting the girl. He just kept making these comments about how paedophiles are only obeying their God-given nature, and how love, any kind of love, can't be such a bad thing. Fucker was smirking at me the whole time, like he was hoping I'd smack him one – and like a stupid bastard I did exactly what he wanted. Thing is, I was on my own. Pete Cooper was supposed to be with me, but he was late, and I got fed up waiting around. Stupid really. What made it worse was that Dolman's brother was Justice Minister at the time. Heavy political fallout. Me throwing a few punches basically put the good Reverend off limits as far as the investigation was concerned.'

Cara finished her coffee and tossed her cup over the railings where it landed on the grass, earning a look of rebuke from a middle-aged woman and her husband entering the church grounds. The woman looked as if she might actually march over and cause a fuss, but when she saw Cara's answering glower she let her husband lead her towards the church doors. When they had vanished inside, Cara asked, 'So, you got anything special planned for Dolman this morning? Going to sit at the back and heckle? Boo and hiss when he invites us all to pray?'

Harlan stood up and brushed down his coat, then made a point of putting his coffee cup in a nearby rubbish bin. 'No, I'm planning on singing hymns badly out of tune, just for the hell of it.'

Harlan watched as Scanlon drove his car slowly down New Road, searching in vain for a parking place before realising he either had to turn back or drive further down Main Street. After pausing at the junction for a few moments, he accelerated past and parked outside the *Golden Oak* public house a hundred yards down the road. Cara waited until Scanlon and DS Brock were only a few yards away before bothering to stand up.

Scanlon already looked tired and worn out. He couldn't have had much more sleep than Harlan, and he'd also borne the brunt of organising the investigation this morning; recruiting warm bodies for the door-to-door enquiries, assigning individual tasks, and then he had the horrible job of talking to the parents of the dead girl. On top of that his wife wasn't talking to him. Harlan couldn't help but feel a little sympathy for the man.

Adam Brock on the other hand looked fresh and full of eager zeal. He had cropped his thinning blonde hair to a severe buzz cut, accentuating a gaunt face full of sharp angles. His cheeks were always flushed deep red as if he spent all his spare time slapping at his own face to spare everyone else the effort. It was common knowledge that Brock was Kyle Kelly's man, a constant carrier of gossip and rumour to the DCI's office.

Harlan ignored Brock, despite the detective sergeant's sly nod of acknowledgement, asking Scanlon, 'So how did it go with the Fletchers? They must be taking it badly.'

'Devastated. It's like it's happening all over again for them. Probably even worse this time around as we can now add desecration to the list of crimes against their daughter.'

'Any word of when the exhumation will go ahead? Be interesting to see who or what got buried instead of Debbie Fletcher.'

Scanlon pulled off his woolly hat and scratched his head. 'Looks like the 27th. No one is willing to work on Christmas or Boxing Day, especially when it's such a gory task as digging up a child's coffin.'

Brock butted in, 'I'd be more than happy to do it tonight if I got triple time like those blood-sucking council gravediggers get for a bank holiday.'

Even Scanlon thought this was a bit much. 'Show a bit of respect for the dead if you will, Adam. Especially when standing outside a church. Besides, it won't be the council gravediggers. We use a specialised firm for that sort of work.'

Brock nodded and lowered his head slightly, his cheeks flushing a deeper shade of crimson. 'Sorry, sir. I'll be on my best behaviour.' His eyes lifted and looked directly at Harlan. 'I certainly wouldn't like to be the cause of any embarrassment to Police Scotland where the church is concerned.'

Harlan stared Brock down, keeping his voice low so no one passing on their way into church would hear. 'Brock, you might think being the DCI's pet sneak gives you special dispensation to make sarcastic comments to a superior officer, even one as seemingly dead in the water as me. But disrespect me like that one more time and I'll demonstrate, very forcibly, how badly you've miscalculated the situation.'

'Gentlemen. Gentlemen.' Scanlon wormed his bulk between them. 'No fighting on Christmas Day please. We have a job to do here.'

Harlan continued eyeballing Brock, waiting for a response, but Brock surprised him by lowering his gaze and saying, 'Sorry, DI Harlan. That was uncalled for.'

Scanlon beamed at Brock, then swivelled to Harlan. 'See? All sorted out. Easy as that.'

It actually worried Harlan that Brock had apologised so quickly. It meant the bastard was working up to something and wanted to keep his powder dry.

Scanlon checked his watch. 'The service starts in ten minutes. I suppose we should go in and take our seats. Not that I expect we'll learn much about who placed the girl's body in the woods, although there's always a valuable lesson to be learned from the teachings of the good book.'

Seeing Harlan share a smirk with Cara, he said, 'I take it you disagree, DI Harlan?'

'I've always thought a good book is something you read on holiday.'

Scanlon shrugged, he was well used to his religious beliefs not being shared by his colleagues. 'Each to their own, I suppose.'

As he walked on, Harlan took his arm and stopped him. 'Hang about. Do all church services on Christmas Day start at the same time?'

'What do you mean?'

'Are they synchronised? Like football matches. A three o'clock kick-off sort of thing.'

Scanlon laughed. 'Like football matches? What an absurd comparison, but no, it depends on the individual church. My church, for instance holds its service half an hour later than here in Brackenbrae. What are you getting at?'

'Well, look, both of us know this is a huge waste of time. I was thinking you could nip back to your own church and enjoy the service with your family. It might help keep the peace later on. I'm something of an expert on the subject when it comes to marital spats.'

Scanlon shook his head. 'No, I can't possibly do that. The DCI would be furious if I skipped off.'

'But he's not going to know, is he? Hell, it's only for an hour or so, and you're due a break. You've been on duty since seven a.m.'

Scanlon looked thoughtful. 'I suppose if the DCI doesn't hear about it…'

'He won't be hearing anything from either DS McAullay or myself, I can assure you of that. Not sure about your man though.'

Scanlon gave a sharp glance at Brock who was holding out his hands as if protesting his innocence. 'I won't say anything, sir. Honest.'

'I suppose it has been a harrowing morning,' Scanlon mused, almost to himself. Then he straightened up. 'You're right. I am due a short break, and it's not as though I'll be missing anything crucial to the case. But, to be on the safe side, not a word to Kyle Kelly, eh?'

Harlan clapped Scanlon on the back. 'You better scarper while you still have time. See you around noon.'

As Scanlon hurried off, Harlan turned and headed for the church gates, Cara taking her place beside him. He wasn't just being altruistic and wanting to help Scanlon smooth out his troubled domestic situation, his absence meant Harlan could score a few petty points at Brock's expense. As the DS trailed along behind them, no doubt looking forward to sitting inside the warm church, Harlan turned and said, 'Where do you think you're going?'

Brock looked confused. 'Into the church. That's what DCI Kelly instructed.'

Harlan rubbed his cold hands together. 'Doesn't take three police officers to do that. You can stay out here and keep an eye on the door in case the killer makes a break for it.'

Brock's face was a picture as he realised they were leaving him out in the cold. He was about to argue the point before thinking better of it. 'Yes, sir,' he said in a voice that was far too meek for Harlan's liking. As he and Cara strolled up the concrete steps leading into the church, Harlan turned suddenly and caught Brock with a tight little smile on his face. It quickly vanished to be replaced with a look of indifference so quickly that Harlan wondered if he'd imagined it. With the slightest nod of his head,

Brock turned away. Whatever he was up to, Harlan guessed he would find out in good time.

After the policeman departed the mini-market, Mike McBrearty hurried towards his office at the back of the store, taking a moment to glower at Moira sitting primly at her checkout as if butter wouldn't melt in her mouth. He knew the dumb little bitch had been smirking behind his back when that arsehole of a detective quizzed on him on where he'd been the night before. So much for gratitude. Mike had gone out his way to be pleasant and helpful and what did he get for his trouble? Some washed-up wanker of a copper humiliating him in front of his staff. The only saving grace was that no new customers had chanced in while he was explaining his whereabouts.

He entered the small office, slamming shut the door behind him and throwing his Santa hat onto the already cluttered desk. He ran his hand over his damp balding head then wiped his palms on his white dustcoat leaving a dark smear. Mike loved wearing the hat, but it didn't half make his head sweat. He clicked on the kettle for a cup of tea then slumped into the wheelie chair in front of his desk and switching off the flashing reindeer badge. No point in running down the batteries if no one was actually there to admire it. Mike loved Christmas. It was his favourite time of year.

As the kettle hissed into life he leaned back in the chair. *Fucking DI Harlan.* Mike remembered him from five years ago. Swanning around as if he owned the place, thinking he was some kind of detective superstar, then making himself a laughing stock when he failed to make a single arrest. The bastard was so arrogant he thought he could beat up the Reverend Dolman right after the Christmas Day service. Yes, Mike remembered DI Harlan all right. How the police had the nerve to send that clueless twat back again was unbelievable.

He thought again of Harlan demanding to know his movements on Christmas Eve. Luckily he had a good alibi. He'd been working in the shop till midnight, in plain view of anyone who happened to be passing in the street, running the till, stacking the shelves, checking stock. Except for the few times he'd nipped into his office for a cuppa, keeping an eye on the mini-market from the split-screen video monitor taking up most of the desk space. Mike glanced at the monitor showing the interior of the store from four different angles. With the flick of the control stick he adjusted the camera angle so he could get a better view of Moira's legs. Pity he couldn't afford a colour display that actually zoomed in and had high definition image quality.

The kettle switched itself off in a splutter of steam and Mike poured the boiling water into his mug, dropping in a tea bag then stirring vigorously until the liquid looked dark enough to stain wood. He poured in a splash of milk from a carton on the desk and added four sugars. He knew at his age so much sugar was courting diabetes, but he needed the instant rush. Running a mini-market wasn't so easy as many people thought. You needed tons of energy to keep on top of things, juggle the bills and VAT invoices while skimming a bit off the top for a rainy day. Mike sipped his tea, feeling the sugar flood into his bloodstream, calming him, making him feel steady and in charge. DI Harlan and his nosy-fucking-parker questions had made him nervous. As he'd told the detective – it was hard not to account for his whereabouts when you were working in a brightly lit shop behind a plate glass window.

But he hadn't been exactly honest with Harlan. There had been that half hour where he'd locked up and slipped out through the back door into the lane running behind the shop. His little favour for a friend was none of Harlan's business. And if anyone had tried to gain entrance during that time and mentioned it to the detective, Mike would simply claim to have been in the toilet having a shit. Fucking hell, as far as he knew it wasn't yet against the law to have a shit in your own shop. Well, as long as it wasn't in full view of the public. The thought made him grin. Maybe one of these days he would yank down his trousers and squat in front of the shop window to lay down a giant turd. Give the fuckers something to talk about.

Mike had another look at Moira's exposed legs on the monitor. She might be a mouthy little cunt but she did have good legs. Sometimes he got lucky and caught her just as she crossed her legs, getting himself a tantalising glimpse of her knickers. Not today though. His employee's smooth thighs remained primly locked together, unlike some of his other middle-aged part-time help who perched behind the till like they were expecting an examination from their gynaecologist. Those old slappers with their flabby thighs and over-stuffed gussets held no interest for him although he knew a few who got off big-time on that sort of thing.

When his tea was finished, Mike got up and put the Santa hat back on then activated the flashing badge. He was back in control and thinking straight once again. He doubted if DI fucking Harlan would be back with a search warrant, but just to be safe, Mike made a mental note to get rid of some incriminating packages of meat from his stockroom freezer while he still had the chance to do so.

The inside of Brackenbrae Church was far easier on the eye than its dismal exterior. Serious money had been spent refurbishing the building since Harlan last set foot in here. The walls, once hidden behind dark wooden panelling had been stripped back, sanded smooth and painted a soft white colour. The faded red carpet was gone, replaced by light-coloured hardwood flooring; this same wood also providing a suspended ceiling, concealing the old rafters, except for the area directly above the chancel. Even the pews looked new and expensive, buffed to a high sheen and fitted with blue cushions.

Centre stage was a huge Christmas tree, decorated with glass baubles and twinkling white lights, dwarfing the pulpit set off to the side. Best of all, as far as Harlan was concerned, it was warm. He could feel hot air softly rising from vents beneath the pews, and as he wriggled his toes inside his shoes, he wondered how a church in a struggling village like Brackenbrae managed to raise the funds for such a renovation. Perhaps Dolman had leaned on his politician brother to wangle some sort of government grant, which would be soaked up the unassuming taxpayers.

He and Cara sat on the back pew nearest the entrance. There were perhaps fifty or so people in the church, a mixture of old folk and families with young children. As he'd expected, no one stood out from the pack as a conspicuous child-rapist-killer. The congregation's murmuring was accompanied by unobtrusive organ music that drifted through the church from a speaker system displaying the distinctive *Bose* logo. Yet another sign of a healthy church fund.

At exactly eleven a.m. the music swelled in volume and the congregation stood with much shuffling of feet as the Reverend Simon Dolman entered the church and walked up the central aisle holding his Bible. He was dressed much the same as the last time Harlan had laid eyes on him; well-cut black suit and a charcoal-coloured clerical shirt. He was a tall man and cut an imposing figure as he strode towards the pulpit. Harlan thought his mane of wavy brown hair slightly too long for a man in his early fifties.

Climbing the pulpit, Dolman placed the Bible on the lectern and reached down to a hidden shelf, retrieving a slim wireless headset microphone, which he slipped on his head, adjusting the position of the tiny mouthpiece so it nestled neatly beside his mouth.

Smiling at the congregation, Dolman said, 'Let us pray,' and bowed his head.

As the minister droned on for a few minutes, thanking Almighty God for this and that, Harlan found himself drifting back five years to when he had interviewed the man. The Reverend Dolman must have been one of the last people to see Debbie Fletcher before she vanished and that certainly warranted an informal chat.

It was easy now to look back and see how easy it had been for Dolman to manipulate him the way he did. Like he had told Cara, he had been without sleep for almost thirty-six hours, spending the entire previous night in Scaraway Woods, then holding an early morning briefing session before going to talk with Debbie Fletcher's distraught parents, much like Scanlon had done this morning. On top of that he'd had Steph screaming down the phone over what a lousy father he was for missing Holly opening her presents. He'd been stressed out, not thinking straight.

He'd found Dolman sitting on the front pew, apparently engaged in silent contemplation until Harlan realised he was reading a magazine. The moment Harlan looked into Dolman's eyes, his radar had pinged loud and clear. This man was a threat. Simon Dolman carefully closed his magazine and laid it beside him on the pew. 'Ah, you must be Detective Inspector Will Harlan. The man who single-handedly brought the notorious serial killer, Howie Danks, to justice. How many girls was it Danks strangled? Nine? Ten?'

'Ten that we know of,' Harlan replied, taken aback by this reference to Danks.

The minister smiled and Harlan saw he'd had surgery to correct a harelip, the procedure leaving behind a small white scar on his top lip running up to just beneath his nose. 'Made you quite a celebrity arresting Danks, didn't it? And now here you are to apprehend whoever disposed of poor little Debbie Fletcher. I wish you luck with that.'

It wasn't often that anyone managed to wrong-foot Harlan so quickly, but Simon Dolman had done just that. It wasn't exactly what he said, but the way he said it. He gave the impression of a man at his ease, unconcerned by the fact a young member of his church had been murdered; her naked body left hanging from a tree. Dolman's challenging smile and air of disengagement, told Harlan he was being mocked.

'You don't exactly sound grieved or even shocked by the girl's death. A strange attitude for man in your line of work.'

Dolman continued smiling. He stretched his arm out so it was resting on the back of the pew and very deliberately extended his legs, crossing one foot over the other; the actions of a man completely relaxed and peace with himself. He could have easily been sitting at home reading a book or watching football on the TV with a cup of tea in his hand.

'Why should I be shocked, Mr Harlan? A young girl being raped and murdered is hardly uncommon these days. Sadly, it's the way of the world.'

Harlan's blood pressure surged. Who was this jackass to sit there and casually philosophise about the destruction of a child? He wanted to haul him to his feet and slap some sense into Dolman.

'As far as I know, the pathologist has yet to establish evidence of any sexual interference.'

Dolman rolled his eyes as if dealing with an imbecile. 'But they will. I think we can take that as a given.' Then unbelievably, he winked at Harlan, and said, 'After all, she was a very pretty girl.'

Harlan couldn't believe his ears. Not only was this man of the cloth rationalising the murder as a trivial, every-day occurrence, but actually finding it a source of amusement. Even the serial killer Howie Danks hadn't acted with such a blatant disregard for his victims.

His consternation must have shown on his face as Dolman twirled his hand and said, 'What you fail to see, Mr Harlan, is that what happened to Debbie Fletcher was an act of love. Most paedophiles fall in love with their chosen sexual partners. If it was merely base lust, they would find an alternative outlet like pornography, but falling in love compels them to act upon their desires. As a devout Christian, I find I cannot condemn any act of love, no matter how misguided.'

That was when Harlan punched Simon Dolman in the face. Twice. Or maybe it was three times. He would have continued punching him if not for Pete Cooper finally showing up and dragging him away.

Chapter 4

Sadie Goldridge poured herself a cup of tea, dropped a handful of cat biscuits into a cereal bowl and carried them through to her living room where the television was showing a cartoon featuring an ugly green ogre who spoke with a fake Scottish accent. It was all a bit too frantic for her to understand as characters from old fairy tales appeared and then quickly disappeared just as quickly again. She munched on the cat biscuits, enjoying the way they crunched noisily between her dentures, then blew on her tea and sipped from the cup.

Her husband, George, sat in the opposite armchair watching the telly. He obviously found it easier to follow, as now and again he snorted with laughter. Sadie hadn't bothered making her husband a cup of tea. George had passed on more than ten years ago, suffering a massive coronary while cutting the grass. He never had anything to say, but that was all right by her. In the years before George's death they had spent most of the time in companionable silence anyway. He probably wouldn't stay long, he never did, but Sadie appreciated him popping by on Christmas Day.

Laying her cup on the side-table, Sadie rested her head against the intricate crochet-work of the antimacassar draped over the back of the armchair. Everything was slipping away from her these days. She would be eighty-six in February and realised the ever-increasing periods of confusion where time seemed to slip backwards and deposit her somewhere far in the past weren't merely a temporary indisposition like a summer cold, or a chilblain. Dementia had come calling and intended to stay. She hoped that she would pass over to the other side before things got so bad she was bundled into a care home where some hard-faced nurse would tear away the last shreds of her dignity.

Sadie had no fear of death, not after the life she had led. A life that straddled the borders of the veil itself. Her grandmother had been a famous medium and held regular séances in her front parlour, charging people to pass on messages from the other side. Back then, before the end of the nineteenth century, being a medium was a respected vocation. The Victorians took that sort of thing very seriously. Less so when Sadie's psychic abilities unexpectedly manifested in the 1950s.

Word of her talent soon spread; it was amazing how many people were desperate to receive a few words of comfort from a relative who had recently passed on. As her reputation grew, she found herself saddled with an agent who hired local halls and had her talking to hundreds of people at a time through a microphone that she never fully trusted not to electrocute her. She guessed the agent made far more money that what she was paid, but with George laid off from his job at the munitions factory, what she did earn had kept a roof over their heads and food in the larder.

She had eventually grown tired of the endless succession of spirits wanting to reach out to those they left behind. Even now the dead still popped up when she least expected them and compelled her to pass on their words. Just like this morning when the checkout girl's grandmother gave her such a nasty message, or on the way out the shop, that little girl passing on a message for the angry-looking young woman in the leather jacket.

Not once did a spirit give an inkling of what the afterlife was really like. It was as if they were forbidden to pass on that sort of information. She'd asked George countless times when he came calling, but even he had only smiled sadly and shook his head. As Sadie slipped into a light doze, her last thought was that she'd find out soon enough one way or the other.

It was an hour later when her eyes fluttered open. The television was now showing a church service from some big cathedral, hundreds of people singing 'O Little Town of Bethlehem'. George was gone of course; he'd have left after the cartoon finished. Sitting in his armchair was someone she hadn't seen for a long time. She remembered everyone said he'd done something really wicked, but she'd never believed that. He'd always been nice and polite to Sadie, carried her shopping home, and once fixed a burst pipe when she couldn't get a plumber. She'd heard gossip down at the post office claiming he was living abroad these days, in America or Australia, somewhere the police wouldn't catch up with him.

He was staring at her with an intense expression, his dead eyes full of pain and sorrow. The dead were often like this when they finally managed to break through. Sadie wondered what sort of unfinished business had brought him to her. She tried to remember his name, but her head felt fuzzy as if she was having one of her episodes, like the time she looked out her window and saw a double-decker tram rattle past down the Main Street, which was odd as Brackenbrae was too small a village for trams to run, and the last one in service in Glasgow had been retired in 1962.

She tried again to catch hold of the young man's name from her malfunctioning memory banks, but all that came into her head was a cartoon image of Donald Duck quacking at her. Then she laughed out loud as the visual prompt forced the clanking machinery of her mind to cough out a name.

'Hello, Derek. What can I do for you?'

After the Reverend Dolman's opening prayer, the next twenty minutes were taken up with singing hymns and readings from the Bible. Harlan used the time to answer a few texts, including a terse one from his ex-wife, Steph, demanding to know what time he intended handing over Holly's Christmas present. It should have been this morning, but he'd cancelled. Holly was now fourteen, and it was more difficult each year to think of suitable gifts. Long gone were the days when he could make a last minute dash to the Disney Shop to grab some overpriced movie merchandise.

This year he had plumped for a fifty quid iTunes voucher and a pair of gold earrings. He would have loved to have spent more, but Steph had laid down strict ground-rules regarding him trying to buy his daughter's affections. That was fair enough, but Steph and her new husband didn't exactly hold back when buying gifts for Holly. They'd even bought her a pony for her last birthday. So much for not buying their daughter's affections.

The Reverend Dolman had descended from his pulpit and was standing at the top of the centre aisle. He held up a framed photograph of Debbie Fletcher. Harlan recognised the picture as the same one her parents had given the press. It was a school picture, Debbie wearing a sky-blue blouse and a school tie, smiling cheekily at the camera.

'Debbie Fletcher was murdered five years ago,' Dolman said in a solemn voice, 'and although the police have yet to formally identify the body of a similarly aged child found in Scaraway Woods last night, I can tell you, without any shred of doubt that Debbie is that child.'

Although many of the congregation must have already heard the rumour, they still engaged in an agitated chorus of whispers. Dolman held up his hand for silence. 'Perhaps the police will discover answers to the questions this desecration poses, but I very much doubt it.'

Dolman deliberately caught Harlan's eye at this point, and he could swear the side of Dolman's mouth tugged upwards as if he was stifling a smirk. Harlan stiffened in his seat, feeling Cara lay a hand firmly on his arm perhaps anticipating he might leap up and break the man's nose a second time.

'In fact, I see we have Detective Inspector Harlan present this morning.' Dolman raised his hand in Harlan's direction causing a sea of curious heads to swivel round. 'You might remember DI Harlan from the original investigation into Debbie's murder. Despite his rather heavy-handed interview technique,' Dolman paused for a few inevitable sniggers, 'he never did come close to catching the culprit. Instead, it was only once he was withdrawn from the investigation that certain evidence was found. Evidence that pointed the finger of blame directly at Derek Drake.'

Cold air swirled into the church as the door opened. Harlan saw the journalist, Guy Noonan slip inside, taking a back seat on the opposite side of the aisle. He noticed Noonan had retrieved his Dictaphone. Noonan gave a quick buck-toothed sneer in Harlan's direction before bringing out his phone and begin to video Dolman. This time it was Harlan who placed a hand on Cara's arm in case she took it upon herself to forcibly heave the journalist back out the door.

The Reverend Dolman give Noonan a small nod of recognition, and Harlan began to suspect a set-up. Dolman was staging something. Did he really think he could provoke him into another physical assault with Noonan there to record it? How stupid did Dolman think he was?

'Derek Drake was a troubled lad,' continued Dolman. 'Not the sharpest tool in the box, you'd have to admit, but he was always willing to lend a helping hand.'

'Murdering bastard,' shouted a man in the middle pews.

The Reverend Dolman smiled sadly and held both hands out in a gesture of appeal. 'This is a Christian church, and as such, the pillar of our faith is in the act of forgiveness. Is there any here among you who can find it in their hearts to forgive Derek Drake?'

There was an uncomfortable silence among the congregation. This wasn't what they were expecting.

'Tell me this. If Jesus Christ, our Lord and Saviour, was standing before you and begging forgiveness for the soul of Derek Drake, would you deny Him?' The question was met by more whispers and shaking of heads. Dolman shrugged. 'I understand your reservations. At times like this we lean towards the teachings of the Old Testament. *An eye for an eye. A tooth for a tooth.*'

Dolman stamped his shoe on the hardwood flooring, his voice an angry shout. 'Vengeance! Retribution! We are only weak humans after all. There are limits to our forbearance. But what if I tell you I have conclusive proof Derek Drake could not possibly have committed this crime?'

This time the reaction was yells of outrage and disbelief. Even Harlan was stunned. Had Dolman been tipped off about Drake's head being left in the box at the crime scene? No matter what history lay between them, Harlan was determined Simon Dolman would be in an interview room by the end of the day. For now, he kept quiet, not wanting to miss a word the minister uttered. Scanlon was going to be really pissed at missing this.

Ignoring the clamour, Dolman turned and walked towards the Christmas tree. 'Before I go into all that, I'd first like to make a gesture of tribute to the memory of Debbie Fletcher.' He signalled to the front row and two men scurried behind the tree, dragging out a tall stepladder that had previously been hidden by the tree itself. While the men held the ladder steady, Dolman began to climb. Harlan estimated the tree to be at least twenty feet high, its top branches just short of reaching a cross-beam traversing the church roof above the chancel.

Dolman seemed to have no fear of heights as he ascended the stepladder. Using the cross-beam to steady himself, he stretched across to hook the framed picture on top of the tree. 'Debbie Fletcher,' he called out loudly. 'Forever and always, our sweet little Christmas angel.'

Amazingly, the congregation who only seconds before had been on the verge of mutiny, broke into a round of applause. Dolman grinned like a man possessed, but made no move to climb down from the top of the stepladder. Instead, with his arms outstretched for balance and wobbling precariously, he moved onto the top step, one arm hooked around the cross-beam as the men at the bottom fought to keep the ladder steady. Through the speaker system Harlan could hear Dolman's breathing had changed. There was a ragged edge to it, a pleasurable rasp, like a man enjoying vigorous sex might make on the approach to orgasm. His tongue slowly traced a line around his lips.

'You wish to know why I'm so certain Derek Drake didn't rape and kill Debbie Fletcher?'

Harlan felt his heart thump in his chest. Something was way off here. It was like his long-lost radar had suddenly hitched into life. Simon Dolman was about to do something unthinkable. He could almost feel the heat of Dolman's fever wash across the church. Then he realised exactly what the minster was about to do and did nothing to stop him. It was already too late. He saw Dolman grasp hold of something laid flat on top of the cross-beam. It was a noose braided with a strand of bright green Christmas tinsel.

Reverentially, like a priest donning a stole, Dolman placed the noose around his neck and pulled the knot snugly under his ear. Harlan was dimly aware of Guy Noonan snapping away with a camera, his mobile in his other hand recording the whole thing.

The last few sentences the Reverend Dolman ever spoke on this earth were, 'I killed Debbie Fletcher. I fucked her and then I choked her to death. And it was all so sweet. *I am the face in the darkness. I am the heart of the swarm.*'

Dolman jumped from the ladder, his body falling at least twelve feet before the rope pulled taught. The *Bose* sound system clearly amplified the dry snap of his breaking neck; a distinct sharp crack, carrying with it all the finality of a pistol shot to the head.

Dev sat like a sixth-year schoolboy Buddha in front of his Xbox 360. On screen he was being chased by a giant hammer-wielding psycho whose head was hidden inside an old-time combination safe bound closed with barbed wire and iron padlocks. His finger pushed and toggled automatically on the controller, backing off from the swinging hammer while launching a series of Agony Bolts into the chest of his nemesis. Safe-Head went down, blood pooling like red sludge from the edges of the combination safe door.

His mind was barely on the game. He'd played it half a dozen times and automatically flowed through the moves like a dancer practicing a familiar routine of slick sidesteps and high-kicks. Dev was thinking of more important things. He had the opportunity to make himself a bit of money. A lot of money. Unlike his mates who always got a decent handout from their parents, he never had much spare cash in his pocket. The thought of having a wad to splash around excited him. He thought of what he could do with so much money. New trainers, new games, new clothes – *new Dev*.

On the screen his character died under a crushing blow from the reanimated psycho's hammer. His mouth gaped open in surprise. *How the fuck did that happen?* He could almost play this game with his eyes closed. Tossing aside the controller in disgust he pushed himself off the floor and sat on the bed, opening the lid of his laptop, unable to resist checking out once more the pictures that would earn him serious money.

The images weren't so good, taken on his phone through a gap in the blinds of one of his paper-round customers. Dev delivered *The Evening Times* after school and last week while pushing the paper through the letter box of a house in Brackenbrae Meadows, he thought he heard a faint cry of pain. Squatting beside the letter box he'd listened more closely and realised he was hearing the sound of a woman having sex. It was already dark so he slipped around to the rear of the house spotting bright light leaking from around the edges of a window blind. Unable to help himself, he quietly knelt beneath the window and struck gold when found the blind had rucked up near the bottom, allowing him a slim viewing window into the room.

He'd recognised the woman on the bed, her head thrashing from side to side on the pillow while a naked man pounded away between her thighs. Dev had no idea who the man was, as all he could see was a thrusting arse and a drooping pair of hairy bollocks, but he did know who the third occupant of the room was – the man filming the action with a video recorder mounted on a tripod. Hardly daring to breathe lest he made a noise to alert the occupants in the room to his presence, Dev snapped off half a dozen pictures and made his escape. At the time he hadn't even considered the blackmail scheme, only thinking to send the photos to his mates for a laugh. By the time he'd finished the paper round and walked home, he'd wised up, realising he could do quite nicely from the pictures.

Now once more flicking through the low resolution shots, it occurred to Dev that if he played things right, he might even get enough cash for a flat. *How fucking cool would that be?* Away from shitty Brackenbrae. Away from the no-hopers on his housing estate who thought getting a job in Asda or McDonald's was a proper career plan. Best of all, he'd be away from this house he shared with his mum and stepdad.

Looking at the sordid pictures had given him a hard-on, which considering who the woman was, made him feel a bit weird. He flopped back his bed wondering if he would be committing some kind of sacrilege by having a wank right before Christmas lunch. The only thing stopping him was the thought of his stepdad, Steve, barging in and catching him in the act. Steve was a stealthy bastard. You never heard him when he crept along the hall and pushed the door open without knocking. Dev knew Steve would just love to catch him looking at porn on his laptop or smoking out the window. Steve never missed an opportunity to give Dev grief in front of his mum. It was a territorial thing. The alpha dog keeping the young contender in line. Dev had read about this behaviour in a magazine. The article had been about teenagers coping with the added pressure of living with a step-parent. What the article didn't take into consideration was how to deal with a control-freak stepdad who also happened to be a convicted murderer.

Dev's real dad died in a car crash seven years ago when Dev was ten. He was just getting used to being part of single parent family and all the undivided attention that came with it, when mum met Steve and they were married within six months. Dev wasn't the only one who didn't approve of the relationship. Mum's family practically disowned her when they discovered Steve had recently been released from prison after doing an eight-year stretch for manslaughter.

It was a subject never spoken about, but Dev knew his stepdad had gotten into a few fist-fights in the pub when they first moved to Brackenbrae, the locals deciding to show him how they felt about having a killer in their community. This tailed off when they discovered how handy Steve was in a fight. Dev had asked his mum about it once, but all she'd said was that Steve had accidentally killed his friend in a bit of horseplay that had gone wrong. It had been an accident and Steve should never have gone to jail in the first place.

Not that Steve ever lifted a hand to Dev. Not once. He preferred to impose his authority in different ways when he felt Dev needed some form of discipline. Suspending his crap excuse for an allowance, grounding him, confiscating his mobile and even changing the password on the Wi-Fi to stop him getting online. Worse than that, Dev was convinced Steve went out his way to make sure he could hear him screwing his mum by pounding away on the bed springs more vigorously than usual when he was mad at his stepson. Psychological torture. The bastard.

Sitting on his bed Dev smiled grimly. Soon he'd be out from under Steve's thumb, and all he had to do was to send the email. He logged on to the fake account he'd created and opened the draft email. He read it through once more and then changed his original demand of five hundred pounds to five thousand. Making sure the pictures were attached, he poised the icon over the send button and took a deep breath. If he did this there would be no going back. Dev hit the mouse pad. The email was gone. Too late now to call it back.

He checked his watch, the new Storm model he'd got from his mum and Steve for Christmas, and saw he still had ten minutes before lunch. Maybe he'd have that wank after all.

While the Revered Simon Dolman's body gently swung from the rafter, all hell broke loose inside the church, the congregation stampeding for the doors that led into the small outer reception hall, their panic quickly creating a logjam of bodies pushing against the exit, trapping them inside. Tearing his eyes away from the swinging corpse, Harlan barely managed to grab hold of a young girl before she got trampled in the mad scramble to leave the church. Even as he handed her to safety, a frail-looking man was knocked off his feet and bashed his head against the edge of a pew, the sight of bright red blood on the polished wooden floor causing further hysterical outbursts.

Harlan saw Cara calmly snapping a picture of Dolman with her phone before she finally pitched in to help. A teenage boy took an elbow to the face, his spectacles shattering with the impact, and one middle-aged woman hovering nervously further up the aisle simply collapsed in a dead faint. All Harlan could do was grab bodies from the edge of the scrum and yell at them to stand clear of the door. The main problem was making himself heard as everyone was either shouting or screaming, the ear-splitting clamour further fuelling the congregation's distress; making them stupid, filling them with the overwhelming animal instinct to flee blindly.

He caught a glimpse of Guy Noonan slipping out a fire door at the opposite end of the church, and cursed himself for his own stupidity. He should have noticed there was a second exit. He began to physically haul people back, no longer caring if he caused a few minor bumps and scrapes as he propelled them towards the fire door. Cara followed his lead, and together they managed to clear a way through and finally open the doors properly, ushering the remaining people out into the reception hall a few at time, ensuring no one fell down the concrete steps and broke their stupid necks. It didn't help Harlan's mood to see Noonan now snapping photos from the church gates. The bastard really was covering the scene from all angles.

Once the main exit was clear, DS Brock wandered into the church looking stunned. 'What was all that about? Was there a fire or something?'

Harlan pointed to where the Reverend Dolman's corpse appeared to be levitating halfway up the giant Christmas tree. 'Don't just stand there. Get hold of Scanlon, any way you can. He needs to get back here as quickly as possible. Then guard the entrance with your life. Let no one in who doesn't have any business here.'

Sending Cara to the other end of the church to make certain no reporters slipped in through the fire exit, Harlan phoned for medical aid to attend the injured, after which he put in a call to control, requesting all available uniforms currently on door-to-door duty make their way to the church with all possible haste. The next call he made was to DCI Kyle Kelly, thankfully only getting his voicemail. He left a short message giving the basic facts of Simon Dolman's suicide, and that he and Scanlon were locking down the scene.

After making sure the injured were as comfortable as possible, Harlan moved to the chancel and stared bleakly up at the Reverend Simon Dolman. The minister's face was slack, jaw hanging open in an idiot's gape; bulging eyes still glittering with the joyful malice he'd expressed before stepping from the ladder. Part of Harlan, the vengeful part that harboured the notion all child-killers deserved to die on the end of a rope, was glad Dolman was dead. At the same time, he was filled with a sense of loss he would never find out what had driven Dolman to commit such a terrible crime. And why steal the body and keep it frozen somewhere for five years? It made no sense.

An even bigger question was, why had Dolman made such a public show of placing Debbie Fletcher back in Scaraway Woods? Had he already decided to take his own life and wanted to make one last futile overblown gesture? Harlan knew the investigation would be closed down as quickly as possible, answers or no answers. Simon Dolman's brother might have lost his position as Scottish Justice Minister, but he was still an influential MP, a wheeler and dealer who moved in circles where the big money flowed. He would put pressure on the top brass to shut up shop with all possible haste.

Brock sidled up. 'DI Scanlon is on his way, sir.'

Harlan scowled back at him. 'Aren't you meant to be keeping an eye on the entrance like I told you?'

'Already got half a dozen uniforms securing the church gate. Quite a crowd gathering out there.'

'What about Scanlon? Did he give you a message?'

Brock didn't answer straight away. Instead he slowly gazed around him, taking in the empty pews before settling on the hanging figure of the Reverend Dolman. When he turned back to Harlan that infuriating smirk had returned. 'He did, but nothing I could possibly repeat in a place of worship. Don't think I've ever heard DI Scanlon swear before.'

Only the sudden arrival of a burly figure barging through the entrance and heading directly towards them stopped Harlan from tearing a strip off Brock. The newcomer was a squarely built man, his head covered by a black hoodie worn beneath his scuffed leather jacket, his face mostly concealed by a pair of aviator sunglasses. The man ignored Harlan and pushed Brock aside, making straight for the hanging body of Simon Dolman. He stared long and hard at the body of the minister then muttered, 'Fuck. I don't believe this.'

Before Harlan could demand what this man thought he was doing, the newcomer turned his attention to both detectives, weighing them up, a sour twist on his face seemingly finding them wanting. When he spoke, his voice had a trace of an Edinburgh accent. 'Who the fuck's in charge here?'

Harlan took a step towards the man. 'That would be me, for the time being at least. DI John Scanlon is the SIO running the investigation into the body found in the woods last night, but he's um... dealing with something else at the moment. And you are...?'

The man fleetingly flashed his ID then withdrew it, but not before Harlan's quick eyes managed to catch a glimpse of his name. DCI Ray Talbot. He also saw the ID identified Talbot as belonging to Special Branch, which was puzzling. Those spooky bastards only crawled out of the woodwork when it was a matter of national security; some threat against the government. So what was he doing here? Even more of a mystery was how Talbot had gotten here so quickly? It was barely twenty minutes since Dolman had stepped off the ladder and gone to meet his maker. Unless of course Talbot was already on his way to speak with the Reverend Dolman, a possibility that complicated matters further.

The Special Branch man pulled back his hood, removing the sunglasses to reveal close-cropped grey hair and a grizzled, street-fighter's face full of lumps and long-healed scars; the kind of face that told you when it came to violent confrontations, its owner didn't mind mucking in and getting his hands dirty. Harlan estimated him to be in his late forties.

Talbot scrutinised Harlan more closely. 'You're Harlan, right? I seem to remember seeing your face in the papers a few times.' He paused, then added, 'And usually for all the wrong reasons.'

Out of the corner of his eye Harlan saw Brock smirking again, enjoying his discomfort. He hooked his thumb towards the front entrance. 'DS Brock, I'd be obliged if you could return to your duties outside. There should be more uniforms to deploy by now, and the press will be descending like vultures. I don't want it turning into a three-ring circus.'

Brock sucked in those red cheeks of his as if he'd found something sharp and bitter in his mouth. Giving one last curious look at the Special Branch man, he slouched off towards the entrance. Talbot nodded at Brock's retreating back, 'Bit of a short-arse for a cop, isn't he?' There was a slight hitch in Brock's stride and Harlan knew he'd overheard the remark.

He had expected Cara to be straight over checking out the visitor, but she was still manning her post at the fire exit, head down as she studied a text on her phone. Harlan found this odd. It wasn't like Cara to miss out on the chance to square up to a new potential adversary. He found himself hoping she'd hurry up and get her arse over here. Talbot was spooking him. The man exuded an aura of danger and threat level that he seldom came across, even among the most hardened of the criminal element, but Cara seemed engrossed by what she was reading on her mobile and showed no sign of coming to his aid.

Talbot moved closer than felt comfortable, deliberately invading Harlan's personal space. 'Let's keep this brief, DI Harlan. You were here when Dolman hanged himself?'

'I was.'

Talbot glanced briefly at the corpse. 'You mind telling me exactly what he said?'

Harlan shrugged, 'He went through the usual Holy-Willie stuff, sang a few songs, said a few prayers then he talked about Debbie Fletcher. Preached about forgiveness. The congregation weren't buying it.'

'Then what?'

'He climbed up the ladder and stuck a picture of the girl on top of the tree. Then he confessed to raping and killing her. He wasn't exactly repentant about it. He'd obviously planned all this, had a noose prepared and hidden on top of the cross beam. Once he'd said his piece, he slipped the noose over his head and stepped off the ladder. That's about it really.'

Talbot took another half-step closer to Harlan, bitter coffee breath wafting across his face, his aura of barely restrained violence almost overwhelming. 'That's all he said? You sure about that? Nothing particularly unusual?'

Harlan found himself smiling. 'With all respect, sir, I'm not sure how much more unusual it could have been. It's not every day a minister of the Church confesses to killing a young girl and then jumps to his death from the top of a twenty foot ladder.'

'Don't get smart with me, Harlan. I'm talking specifically about what he said. His sermon for instance; nothing... how shall I say, esoteric? Occultist? References to religious texts not likely to be found in the Bible?'

The question threw Harlan. What was Talbot looking for? Did he really think Simon Dolman was a subversive satanic preacher? 'Um... can't say I'm any expert on the Bible, but it all sounded pretty orthodox to me.' Then Harlan remembered the very last thing Dolman said before taking the long drop.

'There was a phrase he used at the end. Something about a face in the dark. Then something else about the heart of the swarm. Sounded Biblical, but I didn't recognise it.'

For a brief instant there was a flash of alarm in the other man's eyes. Talbot's voice sank to a low whisper. 'Might it have been - *I am the face in the darkness? I am the heart of the swarm?*'

'Now you mention it, that's exactly what he said.'

'You absolutely sure about that?'

Talbot's eyes bored into his, scrutinising him for any sign he might holding something back. Harlan had a flash of inspiration. A chance to kill two birds with one stone. 'Tell you what. There was a journalist in here recording the whole thing. Guy Noonan. I got the impression Dolman arranged for him to attend the service. They exchanged a nod of recognition earlier on. He should still be outside. Sandy hair and buck teeth. Can't miss him. He's likely already uploaded the footage, but I'm sure with a little persuasion you can confiscate the SD card from his phone.'

Talbot blinked twice in quick succession. This was probably as close as he ever looked to expressing shock and surprise. 'Recorded the whole thing, you say?' He took a step back. 'In that case I'll take up no more of your time, DI Harlan.'

Harlan watched Talbot march towards the doors and couldn't help smiling. He had no idea what Simon Dolman could possibly have done to warrant the attentions of Special Branch, but when national security was threatened, civil rights went out the window. With any luck Noonan might take a few solid jabs to the kidneys before handing over the footage. As Talbot exited the church, Harlan realised Cara was finally at his side.

'Who was that?' she asked.

He tried to hide his annoyance, but not too hard. 'Oh, now you decide to come over? I could have done with some backup there. Fucking Special Branch giving me a hard time and you're too busy sending Christmas greetings to your mates.'

She winced, looking guilty. 'Sorry. Got an important message. Had to respond straight away. What was he wanting?'

When Harlan told her, she only shrugged. 'I guess it'll all come out in the wash. Nice work, setting him on that buck-toothed wanker.'

Then everything seemed to happen at once. The ambulance crew finally turned up to cart off the injured parishioners, closely followed by Scanlon, a white-suited team of SOCOs, and in their wake, the pathologist Jo Haney. Scanlon immediately dragged Harlan into a corner, his eyes fixed rigidly on Dolman's body as he talked.

'Bloody hell, Harlan. How could you have let this happen? I mean, just... how could you? I leave you alone for an hour and look what happens.' Scanlon wrung his hands like an aggrieved washerwoman.

'Hang on. This isn't my fault. By the time I realised what he intended doing it was far too late. The bastard was already at the top of the ladder. Even if I'd tried to stop him I'd only have knocked the ladder over and been facing a murder charge this time instead of assault.'

Scanlon pursed his lips together and blew out a compressed breath of air. 'Sorry. I know it's not your fault. I'm just wondering how we're going to explain this to the DCI. Have you spoken to him?'

Harlan held up his phone. 'Left a message. Just said we were dealing with it. Obviously he hasn't read it or he'd have called back. Maybe he's stuck in a bunker at the fourth green. Then again, the suicide will be all over the news like a rash. A journalist recorded the whole thing. So I imagine an edited clip of the Christmas service will be online within the hour.'

'You allowed a journalist to film the service? What were you thinking?'

Harlan let Scanlon moan on a bit longer over his failings to properly police the Christmas service while watching Jo Haney, dressed in jeans and a pink sweater, shin up the ladder and hold her fingers against Simon Dolman's neck. She gave a thumbs down to the SOCOs waiting below and began to slowly descend.

Scanlon had finished lecturing him and seemed to be waiting for an answer. Harlan let out a heavy sigh to let him know he was getting fed up with his attitude. 'What did you really expect me to do about the journalist? Dolman must have invited him along; promised him the scoop of his life. Oh, and something else you should be aware of. Just before you arrived I had a visitor from Special Branch. A heavy-hitter called Ray Talbot. Ever heard of him? He was very interested in what Dolman was preaching before he took the high-jump.'

Scanlon shook his head, looking more worried than ever. 'Special Branch? What's this got to do with them? You don't think the Reverend Dolman was involved in terrorism, do you?'

'Hardly think so. This is Brackenbrae. Not some fundamentalist hotbed of Islamic backpackers.'

Harlan watched Haney jump off the last few rungs of the ladder and walk towards them. She peeled off her Nitrile gloves and shook Scanlon's hand, 'Merry Christmas, John.' Then she wished Harlan a merry Christmas, but he got a hug and a kiss on the lips instead of a handshake.

'So, Will, have you got over your Genghis Khan complex?'

'What you on about?'

Jo Haney's face creased into a wide smile. 'Last night. Brandishing a severed head at your enemies and shouting your defiance to all and sundry.'

Harlan felt his face redden. When he thought about how he'd acted it did seem a bit excessive. 'Oh, that? Just got carried away. You had a chance to examine the girl? Confirm her identity?'

Haney laughed loudly, drawing disapproving looks from the Scene of Crime Officers who were mostly sullen-faced to start with, making no effort to conceal their displeasure at being dragged out again on Christmas morning – and for a case that wasn't even technically a proper crime scene. They were only here to bring Simon Dolman down from his makeshift gibbet.

She slapped at Harlan's arm as if he had told her a hilarious joke. 'Examined the girl? Will, it's still only Christmas morning. You think I had her laid out on my dining room table while I was eating breakfast? It'll be at least the day after tomorrow before I get round to examining her and that head you seemed so fond of waving around.'

'Right, sorry. Wasn't thinking.'

Scanlon made his excuses and left to supervise the SOCOs bringing down the body. Haney lowered her voice and leaned in close. 'So you were actually here when Dolman hanged himself?'

Harlan nodded. 'Scanlon seems to think I used mind control to make him do it.'

The pathologist arched her carefully plucked eyebrows. 'Wouldn't put it past you.' Then her expression became more sympathetic. 'Surely it must feel good knowing you were right and everyone else was wrong.'

He let out a long sigh. 'Not really. Dolman's guilt is still to be proven, no matter what he claimed. And to be honest, too much water has passed under the bridge. No one is going to suddenly start singing my praises. I'll always be damaged goods as far as everyone is concerned.'

Haney's hand slipped into his and gave it a gentle squeeze. 'Not everyone, Will. Some of us have always had faith in you.' Letting go his hand she glanced at her watch and slipped on her coat. 'Have to dash. I've a twenty-pound turkey to cook. See you at the post-mortem?'

'Perhaps. If I'm still involved in the case.'

Jo Haney flashed him one last glorious smile. 'I wouldn't bet against it.'

Harlan watched her leave then looked for Cara, but it seemed she too was gone.

Chapter 5

Harlan made his way along the monoblock driveway of a large detached house in Garrowhill. It was already dark, and although not as cold as earlier in the day, a creeping mist had stolen over the city, adding a finishing touch to the dismal emptiness of the streets. He patted his coat pocket, making certain he still had the small package for Holly. His daughter's new home emanated Christmas cheer from a combination of lights strung beneath the eaves, candles flickering in the windows, and a huge festive wreath adorning the front door. He had to admit Steph had done well for herself since they'd divorced, now married to a computer whizz-kid who owned his own software company.

Reaching the doorway he pressed the bell, hoping Holly herself would greet him at the door, but it was Steph standing there dressed in a shimmering cocktail dress showing lots of tanned cleavage. She'd changed her hairstyle again, gold and amber streaks tinting her naturally blonde locks, all artfully arranged with wax and mousse. The expression on her beautiful face could have frozen fire in its tracks.

'Merry Christmas,' said Harlan, waiting patiently to be invited in. Steph kept him standing on the doorstep for another ten seconds before stepping back silently, her eyes flicking to her right to indicate he should enter. As he took off his coat and hung it over the stair post, he wondered if he should offer a compliment on her new hairstyle, or even the dress, but she'd only think he was taking the piss.

He turned just as Steph narrowed her eyes and hissed, 'You're later than you said you'd be. Rob's parents are due to drop by in twenty minutes for drinks, so we'd both appreciate it if you were gone by then.'

Whenever Harlan had any face-to-face contact with Steph these days, she habitually employed that same old fixed-stare and frosty-tone combination, the same one she'd perfected during their marriage – ice in the eyes, cold steel in the voice. He'd thought she would mellow as the years passed, especially as she'd gone up in the world while his position in the grand scheme of things had diminished. She'd always claimed Harlan's job was like an insatiable mistress, a mistress to whom she always came off second-best. So you would think that now that very same mistress was no longer returning his affections, she might feel avenged and even show a little sympathy. But Steph always did view the world in shades of black and white. If you weren't a friend, you were potentially her mortal enemy.

'Yeah, sorry about that. Got caught up in a case today. Probably been all over the news by now. Simon Dolman hanging himself in front of his congregation.'

For the slightest of moments, Steph's laser-stare softened. She knew how much Dolman had contributed to his downfall. Then the hardness returned. 'You were there? In Brackenbrae?'

'Not exactly a front row seat. More of a back pew. But, yes, I was there when he jumped.'

Steph's lips twisted into a sneer. 'Bet you enjoyed seeing that.'

Even Harlan, well used to Steph's spiteful remarks was shocked by her words. How much of a monster had she turned him into in her head? For a fleeting moment he felt like grabbing hold of her bare arms and shaking her. Then the fierce flush of anger passed and he forced his expression to remain neutral. She always did have a talent for bringing out the worst in him.

'Enjoyed it? No. Not really. Even an evil, twisted copper like me has limits to what passes for entertainment.'

They stood facing each other in silence, each daring the other to say something inflammatory, kicking off an argument that would end badly. Before either of them could commit to such a course of action they were saved by Holly opening her bedroom door and running down the stairs.

'Is that Dad?' she yelled, then screamed in delight when she saw Harlan standing at the side of the stair post, throwing her arms around his waist and hugging him tightly.

'Merry Christmas, Holly. Sorry I'm late.'

'I don't care if you're late. I'm just happy to see you on Christmas Day. Wait till you see what I got you as a present.'

Harlan gently pushed his daughter back, always a little dumbstruck by how pretty she was. She'd definitely inherited Steph's looks, but he liked to think she had more of his personality. 'I've got something for you, too, sweetheart.' He reached out for his coat and withdrew the small package. 'Here you go. Merry Christmas.'

Holly tore open the wrapping, making an overblown show of appreciation as she pulled out the iTunes voucher, then held up the earrings. 'Dad, they're lovely. I'll wear them next time we meet for lunch. Your present is under the tree.'

She grabbed his hand and pulled him into the lounge, Harlan having to brush past Steph, close enough to smell the vodka on her breath, which might explain the excessive venom in her words. He knew Holly was overplaying the enthusiasm to let her mother know that even if she had no time for Harlan, his daughter still loved him.

The lounge seemed as big as a furnished showroom, filled with sofas, lamps, side tables and drapes; everything arranged perfectly to catch the eye. Harlan never failed to feel a touch envious when he compared it to his single room at the Cathedral House Hotel. Rob, Steph's husband, was standing beside a huge Adam fireplace, cradling a glass of whisky and peering nervously from behind thick-lensed spectacles, his free hand rubbing at his ginger beard. He looked like everyone's favourite computer geek. Rob took a step forward and shook hands with Harlan. 'Merry Christmas, Will. Have a fun day?'

Harlan shrugged. 'Had better ones to be honest, Rob.'

From the doorway Steph remarked, 'He's been to a hanging.'

Rob's eyes widened behind the thick lenses, making him look like an alarmed puppy. 'You mean…?' his head nodded in the direction of the giant plasma screen TV, 'the minister who…?'

Harlan drew Steph a cold look then glanced quickly at Holly who was still scrabbling beneath the Christmas tree for his present. The last thing he wanted to talk about in front of his daughter was witnessing Simon Dolman taking his own life. Rob, to his credit winced apologetically and murmured, 'Sorry, not thinking.'

Steph, however, had to push it a little further, doing what she could to spoil Harlan's one solitary bit of Christmas cheer.

'They said on the telly that before he hung himself, Dolman claimed the dead girl found in the woods last night is Debbie Fletcher. How is that possible? I mean, how can you kill the same girl twice?'

Harlan once again felt that old tug of anger that Steph was such an adept at awakening. Didn't this woman he'd once loved have a single shred of fucking decency left in her soul? He saw Holly was now staring up at him, mouth open, and dismay in her eyes. Holly had been the exact same age as Debbie Fletcher when the girl was murdered, making the investigation all the more stressful for him. When he'd stood in those woods five years ago, he hadn't been able to stop seeing Holly up there draped in green tinsel.

He swallowed his anger, feeling it burn deep down in his belly and managed a shrug. 'I'm not allowed to discuss the investigation. You should know that by now, Steph.' Harlan moved over to the tree where Holly was still kneeling, clutching at a small square gift box. He sat on the edge of the leather settee nearest the tree, smiled and held out his hand. 'So what have you got me this year? Another Homer Simpson tie? A new police whistle? Or is it a Terry's Chocolate Orange?'

Holly seemed to visibly relax and handed the gift-wrapped box to him. 'You'll have to open it to find out.'

Harlan carefully unwrapped the small box, not wanting to rip apart the paper. He couldn't help remembering a similar gift-wrapped box from last night, half wondering if this one contained a tiny shrunken head. Instead what he found was a solid cube of lucite with a tarantula spider suspended inside. He pulled Holly to him and kissed the top of her head. 'Brilliant. Absolutely love it.'

Rob came over for a closer look and said, 'Wow, Really cool. All I got was socks.' When Holly glared at him, he added, 'But really cool socks.'

'Where on earth did you get that horrible thing, Holly?' asked Steph, still standing sentry duty at the door.

'The internet. I always remember that Dad caught spiders in a matchbox then let them run out the door before you could stomp on them.'

Steph made a disgusted sound and announced she was going to make herself a drink in the kitchen. Holly grinned at Harlan and said, 'You have to name it before you leave.'

Rob looked over his shoulder, making sure his wife had definitely left the room. Even so he kept his voice low as he chinked his glass against the cube of lucite. 'I hereby christen this tarantula, Steph.'

Cathedral House Hotel possibly had the smallest car park in the country. It had previously been a tiny beer garden with two trestle tables before Lenny, the hotel owner, decided to chop up the tables. It held two cars, three if the third vehicle completely blocked in the other two. Normally only Harlan and Lenny himself parked here, except when some hotel guest didn't see the sign saying 'Parking for Staff Only'. Technically Harlan didn't work for the hotel, but he'd been in residence so long he felt he qualified for tenancy rights.

There was never any shortage of people who liked to make comments over his choice of accommodation, as if his living arrangements were fair game for public judgement, but it wasn't like he was lodging in a soulless modern hotel with cloned rooms and insipid decor. Just like it said in the tourist brochure; *Cathedral House is a 19th-century Scottish baronial-style boutique hotel, complete with turrets, crow-stepped gables and its very own ghost.* Harlan thought the description was bang on the nail, although he'd yet to see the ghost. Solidly constructed from faded red sandstone blocks, it sat like a sturdy fortress directly off the busy junction of Castle Street and John Knox Street, only a short stroll from the thriving bars and restaurants in Merchant City.

Taking great care to avoid denting Lenny's huge Ranger Rover, Harlan parked his Astra, squeezing himself out the vehicle carefully so as not to damage the door's paintwork against the wall. He left the car park, following the curve of the hill until he reached the side door and let himself in. His room at the top of the spiral stairway was an historian's wet dream, with the north-facing window directly overlooking the 800-year-old medieval Glasgow Cathedral, and if he craned his neck to look west, he had Provand's Lordship, the oldest dwelling house in the city staring back him. It was the east-facing window he liked best, giving a perfect view on to the City Necropolis where the steep grassy mound was heavily populated with elaborately carved Victorian tombs, mausoleums, weeping angels and obelisks.

He didn't keep many personal things in the room. Just his clothes, books, laptop and an iPod docking station. Any other stuff he owned was packed in boxes down in the hotel cellar. Harlan took the lucite cube holding Steph the Spider from his coat pocket, placing it on the windowsill. Hopefully Elsie the cleaner wouldn't have a screaming fit when she came in to do his room in the morning. After a quick wash in the bathroom sink, he changed his shirt and headed downstairs. He realised he hadn't eaten for most of the day, hunger pangs making themselves known as the smell of cooking wafted up the stairs from the restaurant below, along with some rowdy singing.

He'd forgotten the hotel was always full of drunk diners on Christmas Day. They'd have finished eating hours ago and now enjoying a spirited sing-song backed on the piano by Archie the resident entertainment. He wondered if he should order a takeaway, if he could find one that was open, but just as he passed the restaurant door, Lenny's wife, Marilyn, bustled out and grabbed hold of him, planting a huge wet kiss on his cheek. She was a plump black woman in her sixties who had once been Lenny's housekeeper in London. When he moved north, the old villain had married her and brought her with him.

'Will Harlan! Haven't seen you around all day. You been out wining and dining with that skinny little girlfriend of yours? Surprised she's still talking to you after the way you left her high and dry last night. She called you some nasty names.'

Harlan returned the kiss and gave Marilyn a hug. 'Been working all day. And Cara calls me nasty names even when she is talking to me.'

Marilyn rolled her eyes in exaggerated parody of feigned disbelief. 'You eaten yet? If not I can rustle something up in a trice.'

Harlan's stomach answered for him, giving out a low rumble, making Marilyn honk with laughter. 'Sounds like someone missed out on Christmas dinner. You get yourself down to the bar and I'll root through the rubbish bin to see if anything is still edible.'

Harlan laughed and gave Marilyn another squeeze. 'Don't know what I'd do without you, Marilyn. If Lenny ever dumps you, you're always welcome to shack up with me.'

The big woman hee-hawed and swatted at Harlan's backside with the flat of her hand. 'Be off with you. You won't be adding this clean-living lady to your harem of loose women. And I'll let Lenny know you're here. He's skulking in the flat, watching the telly. You know he always makes himself scarce when the guests get too rowdy.'

As if on cue, the diners in the restaurant launched into what sounded like a death-metal version of the hokey cokey. Harlan placed his hands over his ears. 'Can't say I blame him.'

And so it was that Harlan tucked into Christmas dinner in the bar of Cathedral House Hotel. There was heavily seasoned Scotch broth followed by a heaped plate of turkey, mashed and roast potatoes and honey-glazed vegetables. Marilyn had obviously got lucky rooting through her rubbish bin. The bar was closed to the public, which meant he could eat his dinner in relative peace and quiet if he ignored the muffled chaos from upstairs.

Before taking up residence in the hotel, Harlan had been a regular here. The Cathedral House bar felt like a proper pub. A place a bloke could sit and have a pint and take time out from the world. From the outside the building looked traditionally Scottish from its foundations to the topmost turret, but inside it resembled something elegant from the old world. A sense of time perfectly preserved. Victorian craftsmanship overlain with an echo of European café society.

The lower level was furnished with soft sofas and chairs, the floor laid in a diamond pattern with small black and white tiles. Wide steps took you to a raised area with tables, and from there a wooden staircase led to a small mezzanine level where Harlan was sitting now. From this vantage point he could look down upon the long mahogany bar as if he were a theatregoer high up in the balcony gazing down on a brightly lit stage with its backdrop of optics and carefully arranged glass bottles. When drinking alone he enjoyed watching the different actors who performed on this stage. Doctors and nurses from the nearby Glasgow Royal Infirmary, students from Strathclyde University, tourists and staff from the cathedral and museum across the road, as well as the regular overspill from the Merchant City drinking crowd. They would drift in, speak their lines and exit stage left through the public doors.

The flat-screen television on the wall next to the bar was turned on, but muted. It was showing a carefully edited montage of clips from the morning's excitement at the church. Harlan bit into a roast potato as the TV showed Simon Dolman enter the church, proving Noonan wasn't there by chance. The image shifted to the minister standing in the centre aisle, and finally a brief shot of Dolman up the ladder hanging Debbie Fletcher's photo from the top of the tree. The images were low-res and not quite stable, taken as they were from Noonan's phone.

The next few clips were from the exterior of the church. They showed a large crowd gathered at the church gates, the medics hurrying inside with stretchers; a clip that unfortunately caught the bulky figure of Scanlon slipping in behind them, his face turned towards the camera for an instant looking like a guilty schoolboy. The next image was of the SOCOs wheeling out the body of Simon Dolman in a plastic body bag and loading it into a van.

Harlan cringed as he saw himself walking out behind them, captured grim-faced, talking into his phone at the time, leaving a message on Cara's voicemail. It wasn't like her to have left him in the lurch like that. He wondered what had spooked her so badly she'd disappeared without so much as a word. Then again, she had been acting oddly ever since that old woman spoke to her outside the mini-market. It got him thinking it was also odd that when the Special Branch officer stormed into the church she'd been conspicuously engrossed with her phone. Harlan speared a sausage wrapped in bacon and wondered if he was making something out of nothing. Cara was unpredictable at the best of times.

On screen there was now an image of Kyle Kelly, his golfing attire swapped for a suit and tie, giving a statement to the press. Harlan didn't need the volume up to know what he was saying. His DCI had given the usual old guff about how the police would be looking into Dolman's claims he was the child-killer, blah, blah, blah, and he couldn't possibly speculate on the identity of the dead girl until a post-mortem was carried out.

After the TV people and reporters finally left, Harlan expected to have been involved in a search of the church and Dolman's home, hunting for evidence to back up the minister's confession of murder and rape, but Kyle Kelly had left him sitting on his hands for hours in Brackenbrae village hall which had been commandeered by the police for the duration of the investigation. Kelly had finally sent a brief text message saying Harlan's assistance would no longer be required on the investigation. Now it looked as though they had their man, albeit a dead one, his expertise on the case was considered to be redundant.

Harlan pushed a last morsel of turkey through the remains of the gravy on his plate and popped it into his mouth, washing it down with lager. The combination of a large meal and no sleep the previous night had him feeling stupidly torpid and fit for nothing more than retiring to his room. Before he could make a move, a large man with a pronounced beer-gut entered stage-right at the bar and waved at Harlan before proceeding to pull two pints and carry them up to the mezzanine level.

Harlan accepted the glass, raising it in a toast. 'Merry Christmas, Lenny.'

'Compliments of the season to you too, Harlan. Seen you on the old goggle box earlier. Lurking around in the background like a bad smell. The reporter said that vicar claimed to have murdered the little girl before offing himself.'

'Minister, Lenny. Not vicar.'

Lenny shrugged his massive shoulders. 'Yeah, whatever. Same fucker you smacked in the mush that time, yeah?'

'Same fucker.'

Lenny Baker was the owner of the Cathedral House Hotel. He was in his seventies, bald as a billiard ball, and sported an untidy white moustache and beard, tinged yellow from all the cigarillos he smoked. He'd once been a lower-league player in the London underworld, up to his bull-like neck in murky dealings south of the Thames where he ran a string of pubs where knock-off booze, cigarettes, and all manner of luxury white goods changed hands if you had the readies. He'd done prison time on several occasions, once for aggravated assault, the second time for VAT fraud. That had been when Lenny decided it was time to hand over the reins of his criminal enterprise to a younger contender and move north of the border to Glasgow.

'So, you still think he was a nonce, yeah?'

'That was the impression I got five years ago, and now he seems to have confirmed it.'

Lenny sipped at his pint then wiped his lips, a sardonic smile in place. 'Nonces – hanging's too good for 'em.'

'Did the trick for Simon Dolman.'

Lenny laughed, a phlegm-coated croak of mirth. 'Just a pity we still don't go in for the old drawing and quartering along with the hanging. I mean, what was so wrong about a bit of public disembowelment? Sent out a proper message, so it did.'

'Actually, you'd be wrong there. My mate, Jo Haney, will be carrying out the disembowelling. She'll have his guts on a tray all nicely weighed and measured. I could always arrange a front row seat if you want to watch.'

'Fuck, no. I was never one for relishing the sight of blood. Sometimes there would be some uppity little fuckwit who needed a smack or two to keep 'em in line, but as you know, I wasn't in the business of nailing folk to the wall. Violence was usually a last resort, yeah?'

When Harlan started drinking in the Cathedral House bar he was aware of Lenny's past form. He'd checked him out on the police database and came to the conclusion Lenny was an old-school criminal simply looking for a quiet life in his twilight years. He knew serving police officers who'd committed worse crimes. In turn, Lenny had recognised him for a cop straight away and asked if he was keeping tabs on him. When Harlan told him he was only interested in a decent pint, Lenny had stared hard into his eyes for a long moment and then shook his hand, accepting Harlan as a police officer with no axe to grind.

There was however a certain DCI in the Met who still had a sharp axe aimed at Lenny's neck. Lenny had run rings around him too many times, and this DCI hated to see his old adversary flee into the sunset with his ill-gotten gains. This grudge-bearing DCI called in a favour with a mate in Strathclyde CID who arranged for a crate of whisky, on which no excise duties had been paid, to be discovered in the Cathedral House beer cellar. It was a petty gesture, but one which would have seen Lenny and Marilyn lose their licence and have to close down the hotel.

Lenny never said a word to Harlan, but the story quickly became the source of much amusement at the station. Cops are never particularly good at keeping their big traps shut when it comes to sticking one right up the dastardly criminal element. So Harlan did what he thought was only fair and just. He waited until there was a retirement party in full swing, an inspector being put out to pasture, then borrowed the key to the temporarily unmanned evidence lock-up, removing the whisky and distributing it freely throughout the already well-oiled revellers. When he told Lenny he no longer had to worry about the impending charges as the police themselves had pissed away all the evidence, Lenny had lumbered out from behind the bar and almost broke Harlan's ribs in a crushing bear hug. Which was why when his marriage went tits-up, Lenny offered him the room at a very generous cut-price rate for as long as he needed it. In saying that, he didn't think Lenny expected his words to be taken quite so literally.

Lenny headed back down to the bar where he retrieved an ashtray and an instantly recognisable blue tin. Returning, he laid down the ashtray and offered a cigarillo from the blue tin. Harlan was one of those off and on smokers, forever trying to break the habit. Sometimes he'd go for weeks without a puff, then slip back to twenty a day for a time. Thinking on what a shit day it had been, he decided to break a five-day abstinence and accept the small cigar.

They smoked in silence for a few minutes, watching the muted TV set, a rescreening of a classic Morecambe and Wise show. Retro Christmas at its best.

'Does no one ever mention the smell of tobacco in here? It does linger, you know.'

Lenny blew out a smoke ring held together by air friction and contempt. 'Wouldn't give a toss if they did. Pubs should always have a slight whiff of tobacco about them. Traditional ain't it?'

Harlan tried blowing a smoke ring back at him; his however looked more like a mushroom cloud hovering over Hiroshima. 'Yeah, just like it's traditional for pub toilets to have that faintest hint of piss.'

Another croaky rasp from Lenny. 'That's what I've always liked about you, Harlan. Soul of a poet.'

Upstairs, Archie was pounding out a ragtime version of 'Little Ole Wine Drinker Me'; the Christmas diners struggling to sing along, always lagging way behind the beat. It was Archie's speciality to bamboozle his audience by playing well-known favourites in a style ill-suited to the composition. The worst Harlan had heard so far was Archie's ska rendition of Leonard Cohen's 'Hallelujah'.

'Anyhow, you go see that little princess of yours today?'

Harlan nodded. 'I got a whole twenty minutes. Steph couldn't push me out the door fast enough.'

'No sign of the ex-wife easing up a bit? Still going full-throttle with the old hostilities act?'

'And then some. She gets worse with time.'

Lenny gave him a consoling look. 'Women, eh? Still, I bet the little princess was pleased to see you.'

'Practically threw herself at me. Sometimes I think she overdoes the welcome just to spite Steph.'

'She's a good kid, Harlan. Hope you gave her my love.'

Lenny and Marilyn always made a big deal of Holly on the occasions he brought her to the hotel for lunch. Steph would have thrown a screaming fit if she'd known Lenny had allowed Holly to pull Harlan a pint behind the bar.

'I did, and she said she hopes you're taking good care of your reindeer this Christmas.'

Lenny croaked another laugh, rubbing at his straggly white beard and patting his ample belly. 'Cheeky little bleeder. Tell her poor old Donner and Blitzen got served up as venison steaks to our guests upstairs.'

Lenny stirred himself, slipping back down to the bar to fetch Harlan a gin and tonic while pouring himself a generous measure of brandy. 'You look all done in,' he said setting the drinks on the table.

'No sleep last night. Spent half of it in Scaraway Woods. The other half reading though the old case notes.'

Lenny nodded at the gin glass. 'Get that down your neck, then grab yourself some well-earned shut-eye.'

Upstairs the revellers now sounded like they were line-dancing to a countrified rendition of Sinatra's 'My Way'. Tonight even Archie's mutilated piano karaoke wouldn't keep him awake.

'Before you head off though, how about unburdening yourself? Give me the low-down on what's what. I'm dying to know. Or do I need to send Marilyn along to your room tonight to get the truth out of you?'

Harlan almost choked on his gin. 'Marilyn thinks I have a harem of loose women at my beck and call.'

Lenny's bushy eyebrows shot up. 'Fuck me, you might as well as done for a time. Even I couldn't keep track of how many women you sneaked upstairs. Thought you was going to fuck yourself to death at one point. Come to think of it, wasn't that pathologist woman you mentioned earlier one of your old conquests? Seem to remember a certain Hogmanay ceilidh when…'

'Don't go there, Lenny. That was a one-off.'

'She was a real screamer. You could hear her even when the band were playing.'

Harlan felt himself redden. Jo Haney certainly hadn't reminded him of Enid Blyton that particular night.

Lenny was staring at him. 'So, are you going to tell me about today, or what?'

Harlan downed the remainder of the gin and handed the empty glass to his landlord. 'Pour me a double Hendricks and I'll spill my guts.'

Once his drink was refreshed, he told Lenny about the girl in Scaraway Woods being the same young girl as last time. He talked of Derek Drake's head in the box, Kyle Kelly throwing him into the investigation, and lastly, how it had ended in the church with Simon Dolman hanging himself, and Kelly kicking him back off the case.

Lenny was grimacing and rubbing at his beard. 'No wonder you look completely fucked over, matey. But at least it's all done and dusted. Maybe it'll give you a bit of closure.'

Harlan wasn't so sure. He was convinced Dolman must have been working with someone else. How else could Debbie Fletcher have been snatched off the street when witnesses swore he'd still been at the church after the carol singing rehearsal? He was too tired to think about it much more tonight. He needed sleep. Lots of it. Then something dropped into his mind.

'Lenny, when you were in London, did you ever come across a copper called Ray Talbot?'

'Talbot? You mean that Scottish bastard from the Serious Crime Squad?'

'Might be. Only we had a scary-looking bloke from Special Branch force his way into the church right after Dolman killed himself. Just wondered if you knew him.'

Lenny smiled indulgently. 'I remember a real pain in the arse named Talbot when I was doing business with some lads over the river in Islington. He was nothing but a violent thug with a warrant card. I did hear he later transferred to Special Branch, but obviously he can't be the same bloke.'

'Why's that?'

Lenny's smile was wolfish. 'Because that particular bastard's been dead for the last ten years.'

Chapter 6

Someone was banging on the door. Heavy flesh against wood. The noise filtered into Harlan's dream where he was playing golf with Kyle Kelly, the shaft of the DCI's putter wrapped around with green Christmas tinsel. Even the golf ball was tightly wound with the stuff, making it difficult for Harlan to follow the progress of the ball as it rolled across the green. Kelly handed the putter to his caddy, Debbie Fletcher, her eyes and mouth stitched shut, grey flesh marbled with blue veins. She took the club and used it to pound the grass as if to summon the man who had killed her. *Thump. Thump. Thump.*

Harlan opened one bleary eye and shouted, 'Too early, Elsie. Come back later.' Trust the old cleaner to wake him up. At least she had knocked this time. Sometimes she just unlocked the door and dragged in her hoover while he was still naked and wet from the shower. Instead of going away and letting him grab another few hours of sleep, Elsie continued hammering on the bedroom door. *Fucking hell*, this was uncalled for. Harlan squirmed into a sitting position as a voice shouted through the door, and it wasn't Elsie's.

'Oi! Harlan! Get your arse out of bed and switch on the telly. News channel. Any one you like.' It was Lenny.

Harlan blinked and rubbed his eyes. What did Lenny say about the news channel? Stumbling out of bed, he pulled the door open a few inches and there was Lenny, his huge fist cocked and ready for another spot of door thumping. Seeing Harlan peering blearily out through the gap, he said, 'Oh, you're up then? Like I said, switch on the telly. Some big news you might be interested in. Then get yourself downstairs for breakfast. If you've still got any appetite, that is.'

Harlan pushed the door shut and crawled on his hands and knees until he found the TV remote under the bed. It took a few moments to find a news channel, but when he tuned into what the presenters were talking about, all vestiges of sleep disappeared like rainwater from a steep slate roof. The images were of the exterior of Brackenbrae Church, this time lit by bright lights, driving back the darkness. Harlan dumbly realised this footage must have been shot last night, probably while he was eating his turkey and roast potatoes.

In the shot he could see scene of crime officers carrying body bags from the church entrance and load them into a van. The news commentator's voice drifted over the disturbing image – *Police have tonight confirmed six bodies, believed to be that of young girls, were discovered in the basement of Brackenbrae Church where earlier today the Reverend Simon Dolman, brother of MP, Stuart Dolman, confessed to murdering schoolgirl Debbie Fletcher before hanging himself.* A picture of a smiling Dolman flashed momentarily onto the screen before the picture once more returned to the front of the church as yet another body was transported out. That was when Harlan spotted a figure standing in the shadows at the side of the van. It was Cara.

He sat down on the bed with shock. Six bodies found in the church? *Simon Dolman's fucking church.* And no one had bothered letting him know? They must have found the bodies while he'd been sitting like a spare prick in the village hall. He remembered Kyle Kelly's text telling him to piss off home. *Your assistance is no longer required in this investigation.* The bastard hadn't cracked a light about the bodies. No one had. Surely Scanlon could have called him.

As for Cara, that was a different story. Harlan couldn't have felt more betrayed if he'd come back to Cathedral House and discovered Lenny had dumped all his possessions on the pavement. She was his only real ally. His friend. Technically, his lover. What was she doing in Brackenbrae last night? It made her vanishing act in the church all the worse. Harlan reached for his phone; maybe she had texted him or tried calling while he was asleep, but there were no missed calls or texts on his phone apart from a message from Holly, thanking him again for the earrings and reminding him to feed the spider.

He slumped forward, his head sinking to his knees. Over the past five years he'd been marginalised, alienated, overlooked, ignored – and now when there was overwhelming evidence against Dolman that should have vindicated him – they'd cut him out the loop. Stuck him in a village hall to stew in his own juices, then sent him home. Perhaps it was time to resign, just turn his back on the whole stinking mess. He could get a job as a security consultant, sell his story to the press and get a tidy sum. That would teach the fuckers.

Slowly, as if he had aged fifty years in the last five minutes, Harlan levered himself to his feet and plodded towards the shower.

'Oh for fuck's sake give it a rest, will you. You're starting to sound like a little kid who didn't get picked for a game of footie. And if you're not going to eat those sausages, give 'em over here.'

Lenny's normally placid face was frowning at Harlan across the bar where Marilyn had served him breakfast. Before Lenny could make a grab for a sausage, Harlan speared one with his fork and stuck it in his mouth. Only trouble was, he now couldn't respond to Lenny's remark.

'See here, Harlan. You've spent the past ten minutes whinging on about how unfair it all is. Sometimes you just got to suck it up.' Lenny hooked his thumb at the TV set showing more clips of Brackenbrae Church. 'Your main gripe is you want to be there, in the thick of things, centre stage grabbing all the glory. And fair play, maybe you should be. But you ain't, so accept it.'

Harlan grabbed for his coffee mug to help dislodge the huge chunk of sausage threatening to block his windpipe. Once his airway was free and clear, he said, 'Well, thanks for the sympathy. Always good to know you can rely on your friends for a bit of support.'

'You're very welcome. Any time.' Lenny gave Harlan a withering look before returning to his laptop where he'd been reading the latest reports concerning the bodies found in the church.

'Any chance of at least turning up the sound on the telly?'

Lenny shook his head. 'Nope. No point. All they've been doing is going over the same old stuff, stretching it out like they usually do when they've got a huge story and very little detail. They even had your face up there earlier on. Shows how desperate they are.'

'Me? What were they saying?'

'No idea. I had the sound down. Probably just pointing out that you and Dolman had a bit of a lovers' tiff last time you met.'

Harlan returned to his breakfast, cutting into a fried potato scone and wishing it was Kyle Kelly's face. He wouldn't get anything sensible out of Lenny for the foreseeable future when he was in this mood. Maybe he had whinged on a bit, but who could blame him? As Lenny himself had said, this was the biggest criminal investigation in Scotland since Howie Danks killed all those young girls, and he was sidelined, not even considered as a substitute all ready to get kitted up and steal the glory.

Lenny spun the laptop around to show Harlan a picture of a clean-shaven, broad-shouldered man with short brown hair wearing a parade ground police uniform. 'This the bloke you were asking about last night? Ray Talbot?'

Harlan leaned in closer to get a better look. The Special Branch man he'd met yesterday was older and had more lumps and bumps, but it was definitely the same face. 'That's him. I'd swear on it.'

Lenny tapped the screen with a meaty forefinger. 'In that case you definitely have a problem. Talbot was involved in a high-speed car chase and came to grief when his car overturned and caught fire. Had to identify him by his dental records. And yet, you claim he turned up yesterday, right after Dolman topped himself.'

Harlan gulped down more coffee. His brain was finally cranking into gear. He'd already come to the conclusion Dolman wasn't working alone. So where did Talbot, a supposedly deceased police officer fit into the picture?

'Anyone else see him? Talk to him?'

'Just Adam Brock and Cara, although I'm not sure Cara was even paying much attention at the time. Brock will probably deny seeing Talbot if he thinks I might use this to get a foot in the door of the investigation.'

'In that case, I bet no one is even looking into his resurrection. Could be something for you to dig into behind the scenes. Run a little investigation off the books, so to speak.'

Harlan found himself smiling for the first time that morning. Lenny was right. He could look further into Talbot's visit to the church. He thought of how it would look if Kelly mopped up the investigation, heaping all the blame onto Dolman, and then Harlan blew the whole thing to pieces with evidence that Talbot was Dolman's accomplice. Suddenly he felt invigorated, his internal engine revving up. Talbot might even have been caught on the video footage from the church. It wasn't much to go on, but it would be a start. Still smiling, he tried spearing his other sausage with the fork and found that while he'd been distracted looking at the laptop, Lenny had stolen it.

Looking up from his plate, he saw Lenny give an apologetic shrug. 'Hate to see good food go cold. Especially when my Marilyn went to the trouble of cooking it.'

'Sometimes I can see why the Met hated you so much.'

Lenny grinned through his beard. 'Just keeping me hand in. And there's something else that might cheer you up. I was reading about some scandal-rag journalist who got his head kicked in last night. Probably snooping where he shouldn't have. Ended up in hospital. Now if that don't put a smile on your face, nothing will.'

'They give a name?'

Lenny took back the laptop and paged back. 'Here it is. Guy Noonan. You know him?'

Harlan almost stopped breathing. He'd been the one who'd directed Talbot straight to Noonan. Was it possible Noonan hadn't been so keen to hand over the SD card and it all got a bit nasty? This was definitely worth following up.

Wiping his mouth with a napkin, Harlan slipped off the bar stool.

Lenny looked surprised. 'Where you off to in such a rush then? It's Boxing Day, remember?'

Harlan winked at his landlord. 'Just remembered I've got a hospital appointment.'

Sadie rose later than planned and got herself ready. Her arthritis was playing up, slowing her down and making every little task that much harder. A small pan of milk on the stove was simmering and had to be watched carefully or else it would boil over and make a mess. She waited until the milk frothed then quickly switched off the gas. Spooning hot chocolate into her favourite mug, she added the milk, then rinsed the pan and left it steeping in a basin of water. Stirring her drink she took a small sip and thought of what her unexpected visitor had told by her the day before.

Derek hadn't been able to stay long, but he'd told her plenty of things while he could. Shocking things. Terrible things. When he'd left, she'd been able to do nothing but sit in her armchair and absorb the information. If she'd been younger she'd have dashed out straight away and told a policeman what she knew. But she wasn't young. She was old and afraid. So she'd sat there, unable to make herself rise, her heart fluttering in her chest, until eventually she'd drifted off into a deep sleep. She hadn't woken until much later, the room in darkness except for the glow from the television. What she saw on the small screen had brought everything Derek said flooding back.

There he was, right in front of her eyes, the Reverend Simon Dolman. Sadie had strained to hear what the newsreader was saying and could scarcely believe her ears when she heard the man say Dolman had confessed to murdering the little Fletcher girl right before hanging himself in the church in front of the whole congregation. She would have listened to more if her bladder hadn't urgently told her to go pee.

When she got back from the toilet, the news had finished, so Sadie had turned off the television and gone to bed. Derek had been right about Dolman being an evil man. Not that anything could be done about him now. He was way past any sort of punishment the authorities could dole out. But Sadie had another two names. Names she would make sure would be called to account for their actions.

Finishing the hot chocolate, she considered simply phoning the police and having them send someone around, but the police had to deal with lots of crank calls and they might easily write off her allegations as the ramblings of a deluded old woman. Knowing through experience her queer spells were always more likely to occur when she forgot to eat, she boiled herself an egg and toasted some stale bread. She'd meant to buy another loaf from that awful Mike McBrearty's shop yesterday, but the checkout girl's grandmother had started chatting to her in the aisle and she'd clean forgot.

When breakfast was finished she got her coat and walking stick. The police had taken over the village hall, directly across the road from her house, and she could pick up that loaf while she was out. The weather wasn't too bad and the low winter sun had cleared away the remains of the snow on the pavements, but she'd be careful all the same. A broken hip at her age usually meant you never came out the hospital. She seen it happen to more than few people she knew.

There was a crowd of people milling around outside the village hall, mostly those who lived right here in the village. Some of them looked angry and maybe even a little scared. There were also a few with cameras around their necks who had to be reporters for the newspapers. Two uniformed policemen were keeping them away from the doors, and one was saying loudly, 'The Assistant Chief Constable will be giving a statement later on this morning, so please disperse unless you have information relating to the investigation.'

In return, some of the crowd shouted back at the policemen. She heard one man scream loudly, 'How many more did the bastard kill? Tell us that?' Obviously they were talking about the Reverend Dolman. A woman was shouting about why the police had never arrested Dolman five years ago. The two policemen ignored the shouters and stared blankly ahead. Sadie felt sorry for them. She knew what people were like. Yesterday not one of them would have said a bad word about Dolman, and now they'd all claim to have known there was something wrong about him. Sadie saw Mike McBrearty, still wearing that ridiculous Santa hat, at the edge of the crowd. He looked like he was enjoying himself as he handed out leaflets. A man next to Sadie was reading one and she saw it had a grainy picture of a cup of coffee and the words 2 for 1. That was McBrearty for you. Never one to miss a trick.

Sadie slowly pushed her way through the crowd, most people recognising her and letting her past, but one man glared and deliberately bumped her, making her stagger, and without the stick she'd have toppled over. One of the policemen spotted her and moved forward to take her arm. 'Can I help you, madam?' he asked.

Sadie took a deep breath. 'I know who the other killers are,' she said in as a loud a voice as she could manage. The noise surrounding her faded to almost nothing and then clamoured up again twice as loud. One of the reporters was pointing his camera at her. From behind her she recognised Mike McBrearty's voice yelling, 'Psychic Sadie strikes again,' and someone else burst into laughter. The policeman looked at his colleague. 'We better let her speak to the DI. You never know.'

Then Sadie was being helped inside and taken through into the hall. Inside there wasn't much to see. Tables with kettles and polystyrene cups and jars of coffee. At the top end where dance bands sometimes played was a desk where a large man was sitting, talking to another man, neither of them in uniform. The police officer still holding onto Sadie's arm said, 'Sorry to disturb you, sir. But this lady says she has information about… the killers…?'

The larger of the two men stood up. He looked weary and haggard. He said something to the other detective who pulled over a chair and ushered Sadie into it.

'I'm Detective Inspector John Scanlon, and this is Detective Sergeant Adam Brock. I understand you have some information you'd like to pass on. I'm afraid we're rather busy right now with the new developments in the case, so if…' He waved his hand to let Sadie know she could speak.

'Thank you for seeing me,' she said. 'My name is Sadie Goldridge. I've lived here more than sixty years ever since I married my husband George. I know this might all seem odd, but I've been given important information about the murder of the Fletcher girl.'

The man who'd introduced himself as John Scanlon lifted a pen and held it poised above a sheet of paper. 'Please go on,' he said.

'Obviously you now know about the Reverend Dolman as it was on the television last night, but I had a visitor and he told me all about two more people involved. You have to arrest them straight away.'

Scanlon's pen remained poised above the paper. 'You said you had a visitor. Can you tell us who this visitor was?'

'Oh yes, it was Derek Drake. I sometimes get his name muddled up with Donald Duck. We always used to laugh about it if I called him Donald by mistake.'

Scanlon gave the other man a funny look, and Sadie knew they didn't believe her.

'You're certain this visitor was Derek Drake?'

'Yes, I've known Derek since he was a wee boy. I was a friend of his mother. He said he's been trying for ages to contact me and…'

Scanlon laid his pen down. 'Mrs Goldridge. As I said, we're very busy here. Perhaps it's possible you had a dream about Mr Drake, and…'

Sadie got to her feet, feeling a sense of fluttering panic in her breast. Were they going to throw her out before she could even tell them the names?

'It wasn't a dream! It was Derek. I saw him as clear as I can see you right now.' A soft fuzziness was coming over her. *The names. What were the names?* It was all drifting away from her. The smaller man, *Brick? Brock?* put his hand on her shoulder. 'Perhaps we ought to get you home, Mrs Goldridge,' he said solicitously. Sadie felt like screaming at him.

Then there was someone else in the hall. A woman with a baking apron and a bosom like the prow of a ship. The woman was standing next to the big policeman, Detective Inspector *Scallop?* She ruffled his hair and said to Sadie, 'You'll have to forgive my John. Always so impatient. Especially with women.'

Scallop was following Sadie's gaze over his shoulder. When he spoke his tone was gentle. 'Mrs Goldridge. What are you looking at right now?'

Sadie's mouth had gone very dry. The fuzziness was getting worse, and she knew she would be compelled to pass on any message she received from the dead. 'I can see your mother. She's wearing her apron. Dark hair, bushy just like yours, and big in the bust.'

Dimly she heard the second policeman snigger. Sadie ignored him and listened to what the woman had to say. Then she turned back to John Scallop, or whatever his name was, 'Your mother says she's very proud of you, but she thinks you should lose some of that weight before you need to buy a bigger pair of trousers.'

Then the fuzziness closed in from all sides and Sadie began to cry.

Harlan sat in his room poring over an A4 notebook. On the page was scrawled jottings, dates, names linked by arrows; complete gibberish to anyone who looked at it; including himself at times. It always helped him make connections even though all the pen was doing was echoing a much more precise system of annotation inside his head. This was how he communicated with his subconscious. Not that he had much to communicate yet, but it was always best to create a baseline, a foundation to build upon. Eventually his hand stopped writing and he stared out the window at Glasgow Cathedral with its distinctive green copper roof. It wasn't technically a cathedral anymore, not since the Reformation kicked out the Catholic bishops in the sixteenth century, claiming it for the Protestants. Despite staying right next door to the Cathedral, Harlan had never once crossed its hallowed threshold. Churches had never been of much interest to him – unless there were fresh bodies in the basement.

He'd already tried calling Scanlon for an update on Brackenbrae and got no answer. Looking again at the Cathedral, he allowed himself a small smile. This was definitely a minor form of excommunication. He'd also tried once again to get Cara, but she too was keeping her head down. He didn't blame her; she must have realised he'd be demanding an explanation for her treachery. If she wanted to work for Scanlon so badly, she could fucking well stay there and see how her moody strops were tolerated.

Picking up his phone, Harlan decided to get some info on Guy Noonan. Find out who had taken his statement. This time he called Pete Cooper, the same detective constable whose lack of punctuality had contributed to Harlan being left alone with Dolman five years ago. Cooper still exhibited a sense of guilt over that incident and it may well have contributed to his own lack of ambition where promotion was concerned. Cooper was the longest serving DC in the department and showed no sign of ever moving upwards.

Cooper's phone rang twice before it was answered. The detective constable sounded furtive, keeping his voice low. 'Sir? Sorry, we've all been told not to speak to you. DCI's orders.'

'Look, Pete, I'm not on to get the low-down on Brackenbrae. It's something else. You in the office right now?'

'I'm at the village hall, which is why I'm whispering.'

'Fine. I need you to look up who took Guy Noonan's statement last night.'

'What, the journalist who got mugged?'

'The very same.'

'Hang on.' There came the sound of Pete's scatter-fire typing. 'Hello? Looks like it was Jinty Shields.'

'Honeytrap?'

'Yup. You got her number?'

'Fuck, no. How desperate do you think I am, Pete?'

Pete sniggered like a schoolboy. 'I'll read it off for you.'

Harlan jotted down the number and hung up. Honeytrap Shields was a uniformed constable with an addiction to internet dating sites. She was short, squat and had a face like a bloodhound with ruptured testicles. She'd earned her nickname after volunteering to work undercover as a street prostitute when there was a clampdown on kerb crawlers. Her offer was politely declined. Honeytrap was quite happy to boast she had sex with each and every man she dated via the internet; justifying her rampant promiscuity on merely wanting to get full value from the dating site fees.

Harlan got through straight away. Obviously Kyle Kelly's orders not to speak with him hadn't reached the lower ranks.

'Jinty. DI Harlan here. I understand you had dealings with a certain reporter last night. Guy Noonan.'

Honeytrap's voice was flat and nasal. 'Noonan? That I did, sir. He won't be pokin' his Dictaphone in anyone's face any time soon. Or anythin' else for that matter.'

'You mind telling me what he said, regarding the mugging. Did he give a description of his attacker?'

'Naw, he did not, sir. Says he was jumped from behind on his way home. Didn't seem too bothered about whether we catch his assailant or no. Then again, his face was aw bashed up. Hard to make out what he was sayin' properly.'

'Which hospital treated him?'

'The Royal. Might still be there. Might no.'

'Er… that's really helpful, Jinty. Shame you being stuck in work over Christmas.'

'Ah, don't mind, sir. Gives me somethin' to do. The datin' scene is always quiet over Christmas. All those guys who pretend to be divorced havin' to spend time with their families. You know how it's like.'

'I do indeed, Jinty. I do indeed. Thanks for the help.'

'No bother, sir.'

Harlan cut the connection and grinned out the window.

The Glasgow Royal Infirmary was only a short walk past the cathedral. Harlan found his way to reception and enquired about Guy Noonan, being told the journalist was on the fourth floor of the new wing. He bought some grapes then took the lift up to the ward. At the nurses station, a tall nursing sister with dark hair, very prominent breasts and green eyes smiled at him. 'Well, well. If it's not Will Harlan himself.'

Harlan did a double take and realised he knew the woman. *Intimately*. She'd been one of his special overnight guests during that period he'd split with Steph and gone a bit mad. He reached for a name, and it was only when his gaze flickered over her breasts that it came to him.

'Izzy. Bloody hell, I forgot all about you saying you worked here.'

The nurse's smile took on a hint of mischief. 'You also forgot to phone.'

Harlan felt himself blush. How many times had he said that with no intention of ever doing so? It had become just another ritual, taking their number and promising to call. Something you did out of politeness, like offering to pay for their taxi home and kissing their cheek as they left.

'About that. I must have lost your number. Really sorry.'

'So you lost your phone as well?'

'What do you mean?'

'You put my number directly onto your SIM card.'

'I did?'

'You sure did.'

Harlan found himself tongue-tied, not sure how to proceed.

The nurse suddenly brayed with laughter. 'Oh, God. I'm messing with you. If I did you give you my number, which I'm not sure I did, it would have been fake anyway. We had a nice time in your room, but to be honest, you were a bit too intense for my taste. Talked about your job a lot. Well, moaned about it would better description.'

'This is making me feel so much better, Izzy.'

'Goes with the territory, lover boy. Now, what brings you here to my little kingdom of the lame and seriously wounded?'

'Guy Noonan. Got mugged last night. I really need to have a quick chat with him.'

Izzy checked her notes. 'Somehow I don't think Mr Noonan is going to be very chatty today. He suffered serious injuries to his mouth. Got him down for dental surgery later today.'

'How about five minutes? I'm sure he can nod and shake his head.'

Izzy pulled a face, so Harlan reached for his warrant card, hoping it might make the visit appear more official, but the nurse just laughed and shook her head.

'Oh please. I've seen your credentials before. And very nice they were, too.'

'Nice? Not impressive? Or awe-inspiring?'

Her smile became a prim straight line. 'Nice. Now quit while you're ahead. I'll give you those five minutes and not a second more. He's in 4B.'

'Thanks, Izzy. I won't forget this.' Harlan took two steps forward then stopped and looked back, his gaze fixed on her chest. 'Just for the record, your own credentials definitely were awe-inspiring.'

Then he was heading for 4B, Nurse Izzy shouting, 'You cheeky sod,' behind him.

Ward 4B was a single room and Guy Noonan was propped up in bed looking like he'd been dragged along behind a truck for two miles. His white hospital gown was liberally stained with blood. Harlan was quite sure Noonan no longer had to worry over insults about his buck teeth, as the entire front row seemed to be missing. He held up the bag of grapes. 'Brought you a present, Guy.'

Noonan peered through red swollen eyes and whispered, 'Grapeth.'

'Sorry, was all I could get at short notice. Bet you're glad I didn't get the salted peanuts.' He pointed at the chair beside the bed. 'Mind if I sit for a few minutes?'

'Be my gueth.'

Harlan though of all the fun he could have with this conversation, but knew he had very little time before Nurse Izzy would be on the warpath. 'I'll get straight to it, Guy. Someone attacked you, nicked your stuff, and scarpered.'

'Yeth.'

'You see who it was?'

A shake of the head.

'Thing is, Guy. I don't believe that. I think you got a good look at your attacker.'

A look of fear appeared in Noonan's blackened eyes, and red, ropey saliva drooled from the side of his mouth. 'No. Didn't.'

For a minute Harlan actually felt sorry for Guy Noonan, then remembered all the unkind words the journalist had typed about him simply to enliven other people's Sunday morning reading. He pulled out his phone where he'd downloaded the picture of Talbot, holding it directly in front of the journalist's face. 'Is this the man? He'd be older now.'

Noonan said nothing, but Harlan saw his pupils dilate, a classic fear response.

'I'll take that as a yes. Or even a *yeth*. Now listen to me, I'm guessing he was after the footage of Dolman's church service, and you refused, after which he beat you up and threatened that if you gave us his description he'd come back and do some more damage. Am I right?'

A slight nod of the head.

'Fair enough. I promise this won't go any further.' Harlan stood, still holding on to the grapes. 'If it's any consolation you might have a scoop on your hands. You just got mugged by a dead man.'

Chapter 7

Dev was quite literally freezing his bollocks off. He'd heard the expression more than a few times in his life, but now he knew what it really meant. He was lying flat out on a piece of old sacking laid on the roof of the lock-up garages close to where he lived. When he'd planned his drop-off location, it had seemed the perfect plan. Now, having been in this uncomfortable position for over half an hour it didn't seem such a good idea.

The temperature this afternoon had been mild, then dropped sharply away as the winds returned to gust around like a curious beast poking its nose into every nook and cranny. Dev wished for the hundredth time he'd worn a warmer jacket, or better still, a few extra pairs of underpants. He checked the luminous dial of his new watch with and saw it was ten past seven. The pervy bastard was late.

His email had been replied to that morning. There had been no haggling, no threat of police action; just a simple acknowledgement of his demands and a promise the money would be left exactly where and when he'd requested. It had been that easy. Now Dev wished he'd asked for more money. The pervert must be loaded, as he hadn't flinched at coughing up the five grand. He should have asked for ten, but no one was stopping him for going back for more when he needed it, and the pervert probably knew that. But what other choice did he have but to pay up. It was either that or risk public humiliation.

The lock-ups had seemed a good choice for the drop-off as Dev could hide on the flat roof and watch who came and went. There was only one streetlight near the entrance to the dead-end road where they were situated, and they weren't easily overlooked, not when it was dark. In summer someone might have seen him lying up here, but wearing dark clothes at night he was practically invisible.

At quarter-past seven, just when Dev was having doubts over whether the man would show, a car purred into the lock-up space, headlights illuminating the old wooden doors. Dev flattened himself as low as possible in case the pervert saw him peeping over the top. He heard the car door open and footsteps approach the lock-up directly below him. He could actually hear the man breathing as he laid the plastic bag on the ground and then retrace his footsteps back to the car.

It was only when the car reversed and drove off that Dev realised he'd been holding his breath. He let it out with a huge whoosh. He'd done it. He'd fucking done it. Quickly checking the lock-ups were still deserted, he sat on the edge of the roof, turning as he let his weight take him over, hanging by his hands for a few seconds before dropping the last few feet onto the cracked tarmac.

The bag was there. It was really there. All that money just waiting for him. He squatted and felt the weight of the cash inside. He knew he should wait until he was home before checking the contents of the bag, but he was so excited he just had to have one little peek. Ripping a hole in the plastic with his nails, he pulled his phone from his pocket, using it as a torch. Through the tear in the plastic, Dev saw bundles of blank paper tied together.

Disbelief washed over him. The pervert had tricked him, fobbed him off with useless paper. Was he calling Dev's bluff, thinking he wouldn't have the nerve to post the photos on the internet where everyone would see what a disgusting perverted creep he really was? Then another darker thought dropped into Dev's mind. Or did the pervert only intend using the fake bag of money as bait...?

Too late, Dev surged to his feet just as a shadow detached itself from a lock-up door a few yards away and something hard and unyielding smashed into the back of his head.

Harlan was lying on top of his bed listening to Radiohead's 'A Moon Shaped Pool'. Between tracks he could hear Archie doing something strange to 'Red Red Wine' making it sound like a Lonnie Donegan skiffle number. There was a private party in the dining room tonight, a birthday or an anniversary. Marilyn had mentioned it earlier, but he'd already forgotten. Too much going on inside his head. This was what happened when he pandered to his subconscious, let it think it had an equal say in matters. Even when he decided to take a break and switch off the gas for a time, the subconscious kept plodding on; it didn't need to sleep, or eat or take a dump. He'd think he was relaxing, chilling out to a bit of music, then he'd become aware he was still analysing and plotting course changes to his theorems.

The display on his alarm clock told him it was ten o'clock. He tried to let himself sink into the music, allow it to take him somewhere else, but he was already running what little data he had, attempting to knit it into a pattern that made sense. Harlan knew the best way to find answers was to find the right questions. Why was Talbot hiding in the shadows after faking his death ten years ago? Was he the mysterious accomplice who helped Dolman snatch Debbie Fletcher and then shared in the spoils of rape and murder? Why had Dolman frozen the corpse of Debbie Fletcher? Who were the other children found in the church? And maybe more perplexing than everything: why had Dolman blown the whole thing wide open by confessing and killing himself?

Ray Talbot was the key to this. He'd already been rushing to the church before any news of Dolman's death had broken. Did he have prior knowledge that Dolman was going to jump? And asking if Dolman had included any occult references in his sermon? – Did that imply Dolman and Talbot weren't just working on their own, but part of something else?

The data was cycling round and round like damp clothes in a tumble dryer, but nothing emerged from his subconscious think-tank that resembled anything like an educated guess. Harlan slipped off the bed and changed the music to 'World Party', a change of groove sometimes worked wonders for the grey matter; creating an interference wave to knock down old walls while at the same time building new ones. Before he could stretch back out on the bed there was a quiet knock on his door. He wondered if it was Marilyn, come to see if he wanted anything from the bar.

Instead of a gloriously plump black woman, he found himself staring at a gaunt white man five inches shorter than himself. Archie kept his gaze trained on his shoes; a man who permanently avoided eye contact. Harlan had found it an annoying habit at first, but he'd eventually got used to it. Archie had to be in his sixties, dyed his hair jet black and kept it slicked back with some sort of spicy smelling hair oil that almost made your eyes water.

'Archie. What gives?'

'Sorry to disturb, Mr Harlan. It's just, I'm on my break and I was wanting a smoke, you know? And as it's rainin' outside and I know you sometimes have a fag in here with the window open, I just thought…'

'That's taking a bit of a liberty, Archie.'

'I know, son. I know. Was just askin'. If it's a problem I'll vamoose. No offence, eh? Just don't say anythin' to big Lenny.'

'Hang on. Who said I smoked in my room?'

'Elsie, the wee cleanin' woman. Said she could smell it on your curtains.'

'Oh, did she now? Ah, fuck it. In you come, Archie. But this is a one off. Okay?'

'Appreciate it, Mr Harlan. You're a toff, son.'

Harlan couldn't help smiling as Archie pulled the desk chair over to the window, opened the sash a few inches, and proceeded to light up. Archie had played in the hotel restaurant for as long as Harlan had been drinking there. He didn't know much about him other than he'd been a long-term drug addict who managed to get himself clean. His fear of eye contact alone told a sad story of beatings and living rough on the streets.

Now he was settled, Archie made no attempt at conversation, just puffed away on his fag, and when the first one got flicked out the window, he lit another. He never once looked at Harlan, his gaze locked on the spotlit cathedral across the road.

'So then, Archie. Big party downstairs tonight?'

'Aye, Mr Harlan. You're right enough. A twenty-first. Nice people. Aye, son.'

Harlan couldn't think of anything else to say. Archie wasn't renowned as a conversationalist, but once he was sitting at the piano he became something else. He knew thousands of songs and had a pleasant world-weary singing voice that could have given Michael Marra a good run for his money. He always sang in a Glaswegian accent, too, which sounded weird on stuff like 'My Way' and 'Mack the Knife'.

Archie flicked his second fag out the window then pulled it closed. 'Many thanks, Mr Harlan. God bless ye, son.'

As Archie made for the door, Harlan remembered something he'd always wanted to ask the little musician. 'Archie, tell me. Where the hell did you learn to play the piano so well?'

For the first time ever, Archie turned and looked Harlan straight in the eyes. 'I don't play the piano, Mr Harlan. It plays me. Aye, son.'

Then Archie was slipping out the door, leaving only the smell of his spicy hair oil behind. Harlan looked at his own baffled reflection in the mirror, shook his head and shrugged. There was another knock on the door, even quieter than before. Harlan wondered if Archie had left his fags behind. Opening it he found Cara standing there.

'Wake up Sadie, we know you're in there. Wake up!'

A heavy hand slapped Sadie's cheek making her head ring. She struggled to open her eyes but they felt gummed shut.

Another slap landed on her face, this time knocking her head sideways. For some reason her arms weren't working, it felt as though she was floating in thick liquid. She tried to scream out her distress but nothing except a slurred moan escaped from her dry lips. She knew she was in her bed; she had a dim memory of her neighbour sitting with her, waiting for the doctor to come from his surgery in Kilsyth. Why had Mrs Frew put her to bed? Why had she called the doctor?

Slap.

Sadie's head lolled in the opposite direction. She heard hushed laughter as if whoever was tormenting her was being careful not to make too much noise.

'Sadie? Can you hear me? Not playing possum are you?'

She knew that voice although the name escaped her. Once again she attempted to open her eyes and push herself up – still no response. Had she been in an accident and was now paralysed?

Slap.

'What did you say to the police, Sadie? Tell us the truth and we won't have to hurt you. What did you tell them?'

The police. Of course. She had been in the village hall talking to that big policeman who was soon going to need bigger trousers if he didn't stop piling on the weight. Why had she been talking to him?

'Last chance, Sadie. If you don't start taking this seriously I'm going to hurt you very badly. You spoke to the police today. You told everyone outside the village hall you knew who the other killers were. Did you give them my name?'

And then it all came flooding back. Derek Drake visiting her to pass on important information. But she hadn't passed it on, had she? The policeman had kept interrupting her, and then she had started slipping into the twilight zone and getting confused, and to make matters worse the policeman's mother had appeared and distracted her further. She had lost her way and couldn't stop crying.

She remembered stumbling from the village hall, trying to get home, going the wrong way. Mrs Frew had come out the newsagents and took her home. Put her into bed and called the doctor, that tall Indian man with the kind voice. He'd given her some pills and said he would come back tomorrow. Was this why she couldn't open her eyes or move her limbs?

There was a loud crunch and Sadie's head filled with a bright flashing light. She felt agony flood through her face, and warm liquid ran over her tongue. *Blood.* She tried calling for help, but the weak noises coming from her mouth sounded like a foreign language.

'Don't say I didn't warn you, Sadie. Now, don't make a fuss. It's only a broken nose. Next time I might have to snap your arms. Did you, or did you not, give my name to the police?'

What was happening to her? Why couldn't she move? Why couldn't she even scream? The pain was so bad. Down below she felt her bladder give way, warmth spreading over her thighs. She wanted to die.

A second voice was saying something. She knew that voice, too.

'You know something? I think the old cunt has had a stroke. Look at the way one side of face is all frozen up.'

'Actually, you could be right. And here was me thinking she was just ugly.'

Both intruders laughed into their hands to muffle the noise.

'Fuck. No wonder she can't tell us anything. But we do need to know what she said.'

'You think so? If she had given the police our names, they'd have already contacted us. Taken us in for questioning. I don't think she told them anything.'

'In that case...'

'We just kill her. Set things up like we agreed. Unless you're going to fuck her first. You do like them a bit on the geriatric side.'

'Not when they've just pissed themselves. Smell that?'

'Now you mention it, I think your date has sprung a leak.'

More muffled laughter.

'Right, I suppose we better get on with it.'

Sadie, now barely aware what was happening, felt her duvet pulled away, and then the sound of tearing as her nightdress was ripped open. Rough hands hauled at her underwear.

'Fucking hell, Sadie, I've never seen so many wrinkles on one person. Maybe we should iron you first. Make you all nice and smooth.'

The second voice didn't sound pleased. 'Not enough time for that stuff tonight. Just get the boy onto the bed.'

A dead weight fell upon Sadie. A naked body. Cold flesh against her own burning skin. Dear God, had they brought a dead body with them? Her legs were wrenched apart and positioned around the hips of the corpse. None of this was real. It couldn't be. But the pain in her face and the weight of the body positioned between her thighs told her differently.

'Excellent. A job well done. The Reverend would be proud of us.'

'Aren't you forgetting something? She's still alive.'

'Oh. So she is. Oops. I'll soon put that right. Where's my knife?'

Sadie was drifting away on a strange tide. The voices barely audible now, the pain gone. She felt weightless, tethered only by the slimmest of threads. She hoped George wouldn't drop by and see her like this. She'd be so embarrassed.

As just by thinking of him, she felt George slip his hand into hers and whisper in her ear. '*It's time to go, Sadie.*'

'*Yes. But where are we going?*'

'*Anywhere you like, love.*'

Harlan stared at Cara, not sure what to say. If she thought she could casually drop by and offer to fuck and make up, she was making a big mistake.

'What do you want, Cara?'

'To talk.'

Talk? That would be a first. Cara's previous visits had never involved much talking unless it was to give instructions. Harlan decided he wasn't going to be swayed by Cara's new approach.

'Surprised you could spare me the time. Thought you'd be out socialising with your new friends, Scanlon and Brock.'

He expected a stinging comeback. Even took a step back in case she punched him. Surprisingly, she did neither. Instead she mirrored Archie's default mien and stared down at her feet. Harlan wondered if she was ill.

'Please, Harlan. I really need to talk. It's important.'

Maybe it was because this was the first time he'd ever heard Cara say please, but he found himself letting her into the room. Cara took off her leather jacket, letting it drop to the floor, then perched nervously on the edge on the bed. She was dressed in black jeans and a black sweater. Her dark corkscrew hair was damp as if she'd been walking for hours in the drizzle. She looked unfocused, and not a little scared. Harlan stared at her, perplexed by this sea change in her manner. The fact Cara looked scared frightened him. Had she finally killed someone? Brock, maybe?

He cleared his throat, unsure of how to act with this strange, new Cara. 'You want something to drink? Tea? Coffee? Something from the bar?'

She shook her head. 'I just need you to hear me out, okay?'

Harlan sat down in the chair Archie had used for his smoke break. 'I'm listening. You in trouble?'

'Maybe. I don't really know. Something happened yesterday that's really fucked up my head and I don't know how to deal with it.'

'Is it something to do with that old woman outside the shop? The one who passed on the message from someone named Susan?'

Cara looked directly at Harlan, her eyes glistening, and he realised with a shock she was on the verge of tears.

'Susan was my twin sister. When we were eight years old our parents died in a house fire. Susan and I were rescued, but Mum and Dad suffocated from the smoke. They said it was a faulty electrical heater that started the fire. We had no close relatives, so we ended up in the system. Children's home to start with, then a series of foster homes.'

'Fuck, Cara. I had no idea.'

'Why should you? It's not something I ever talk about.'

'What happened to Susan?'

Cara closed her eyes, said nothing for a moment then took a deep breath. 'She died when we were thirteen. Fell down the stairs and broke her neck. It was recorded as accidental death, but I know it wasn't. I'm convinced Susan killed herself. It was a bad time for me. I did a lot of stupid destructive stuff, ended up back in the care home when my foster parents couldn't cope any longer.'

'What makes you think she threw herself down the stairs? Was your foster-dad, you know… abusive?'

'No, he never touched us. Looking back he was a fucking saint for putting up with my shit as long as he did. It was a neighbour who did the damage. He was a policeman, respected by everyone in the neighbourhood. People went to him when they had problems and he sorted everything out. People trusted him. Wouldn't hear a word against him.'

From downstairs Harlan heard Archie back playing his piano. Something operatic, played as boogie-woogie.

'He took an interest in me and Susan, offered to take us to the seaside, the zoo, to the fucking pictures. But these trips always ended in a quiet country lane where he would make us expose ourselves on the back seat while he took photographs. After he finished taking pictures he made us watch him masturbate. He'd be kneeling between the gap in the front seats so we could see what he was doing, and he always made sure his semen landed on our legs, or sometimes worse. When he was finished he'd hand us a packet of hankies to clean up.'

Harlan found himself wishing Archie had left him a couple of cigarettes. He'd always guessed Cara had a dark secret in her past, but not this. 'Did you ever threaten to report him?'

She gave him a bitter smile. 'Harlan, we were thirteen, foster kids with no one in the big wide world we could trust except each other. This man told us that if we ever blabbed, ever said a word to anyone, he had friends who would do much worse things to us. He said we would just disappear one day and never be seen again.'

'Jeez, Cara. I'm so sorry. That's just so…' he faltered to a halt, unable to find a suitable word.

'Thing is, Harlan, when that old woman told me Susan said to watch my step, I thought it was stairs she talking about. Like the stairs she threw herself down, but I was wrong. She really did mean for me to be careful. She knew I was in danger.'

Harlan wasn't sure what she meant. At no point yesterday was Cara in any danger, other than the threat of being stampeded by the church congregation. 'Cara, this policeman, did you ever see him again?'

Cara's hands twisted in her lap, long fingers entwining and releasing like fronds of grass beneath the surface of a pond. She swallowed hard before speaking. 'I saw him yesterday, Harlan. He was at the church. I know that's sounds crazy because the bastard is dead.'

Finally the penny dropped and Harlan found himself on his feet, fists bunched at his sides. Cara's behaviour had annoyed him yesterday. Standing hunched over her phone, not providing him with any moral support when he needed it. Disappearing without a word. And now he knew why.

'Talbot? You mean Ray Talbot?'

She nodded. 'Did he actually tell you his real name? Shows how confident he is.'

'I saw it on his warrant card. He flashed it at me so briefly I don't think he expected me to read it. I also recognised the Special Branch logo. I asked Lenny last night if he knew anything about him, and Lenny thought I was mistaken, as Talbot was long dead. I read his obituary on the web. Burned to death in a car chase. Given a posthumous award for bravery.'

There was still something Harlan didn't understand and it must have showed on his face as Cara said, 'You're wondering why I didn't tear his balls off. A chance to get revenge after all these years?'

Harlan stared back. 'It did cross my mind. What stopped you?'

'Because I was scared. Just seeing him again made me feel like I was thirteen and helpless. Sorry, I know that doesn't make a lot of sense.'

'To be honest, he scared the shit out of me as well. It was like, I don't know, meeting the devil or something. If people really do have auras, his would be black, like a big thundercloud with lightning flickering inside and bats flying around the edges.'

'Yeah, that about sums up Ray Talbot. All I could do yesterday was hang back and keep my head down in case he recognised me. Did he look in my direction at all?'

Harlan thought back. Talbot had only briefly glanced at Cara when he was scoping out the church. 'Don't think so, he was too focused on Dolman's body. I've been sitting here all night trying to figure out what connects them. If they were working together or not. I think we have to assume they were. That's our starting point.'

'Harlan, you're not part of the investigation any longer. Scanlon told me last night when I asked where you were.'

'But you are involved.'

'How do you know that?'

'Saw you on TV this morning. That was the first I'd heard about the bodies in the church. I was a little hurt to say the least.'

Cara looked confused. 'I thought you were involved with the search of the church after I left yesterday. You really didn't know?'

'Nope. Kelly told me to report to the village hall and write up my report, after which I sat around doing nothing until I got a text saying I was surplus to requirement and to sod off home. So where had Dolman stashed the bodies?'

'In the basement. Access was from the vestry accessed from the reception hallway. It was fucking horrible down there, Harlan. All white tiles like a morgue, if you ignored the manacles and the bloodstained mattress. The girls were kept inside a row of freezer chests – and this is the part that's being kept strictly under wraps for now – bits were missing from the bodies. Organs removed, cuts made on the thighs and buttocks like…'

Harlan couldn't stop himself butting in. 'Someone was eating them? You mean Dolman was a real-life Hannibal Lecter? Fuck, it gets worse and worse. And I bet they close the whole thing down with little or no attempt at finding out who else is involved. Dolman couldn't possibly have taken Debbie Fletcher off the street. It was someone local. Someone she knew.'

'Maybe Derek Drake played a part after all.'

'Can't see it, Cara. He wasn't clever enough to have lied so convincingly when I questioned him. I mean, he was falling to bits in the interview room. Cried like a baby. If he'd been involved I'd have known. Anyway, I'll fill in Scanlon with what I've discovered about Talbot. If that doesn't force Kyle Kelly into putting me back on the investigation, nothing will.'

They sat in silence for a few minutes, each lost in their own private thoughts. Harlan knew he hadn't really processed what had happened to Cara as a child. He'd even taken the punchline and used it to neatly segue into a discussion about the investigation. It was hard to think of any words of comfort that wouldn't cause further distress, but if he said nothing it would look like he didn't give a shit.

'How did you get yourself together after going back into care? I suppose most victims of abuse simply plod on until it hurts less. I bet you didn't.'

Cara tilted her head like a wary animal. 'I became what I am, Harlan. I learned how to shape-shift. That's all you can do. Hide yourself in plain sight.' Then she gave the smallest of smiles. 'It's funny, most women abused as children grow up emotionally needy and suffer from retarded libidos. My wires must have got twisted pretty badly.'

This time Harlan smiled along with her. 'So what now? About us, I mean. Are we good?'

Cara peeled off her sweater, she had nothing on underneath. 'You want to fuck?'

Moira made her way home from her friend Tracey's house, warmed inside by six Bacardi Breezers. She didn't normally drink and felt more than a little drunk. It had rained earlier and the pavements were wet and slick, reflecting distorted orange fractals from the streetlights. There had only been one real subject of conversation. The Reverend Simon Dolman. Despite the internal insulation of the Bacardi, Moira shivered to think how many times she'd been in the man's company, thankfully never alone. It had been horrible enough what he did on Christmas Day, but then to have the police find all those dead bodies under the church? It was just awful. If that sort of thing happened in a movie it was deliciously creepy, in real life it only made you feel sick.

Moira halted by a parked car, steadying herself against the rain-spotted metal, thinking she really might puke. After a few deep breaths she continued walking, steeling herself for passing the church. She had thought of calling her dad for a lift, but it was only a ten-minute walk, and she'd thought the fresh air might clear her head. She hoped there might still be lots of police officers standing guard outside the church like last night, but the closer she got, the less hopeful she became. There was no sign of activity other than the flapping crime scene tape.

The junction of New Road and Main Street loomed up and Moira tried not to look at the church, sitting there dark and brooding, no longer a place of peaceful worship; transformed within the space of a single day to a haunted temple where the ghosts of dead children walked. Moira mentally slapped herself. Why did she always have to spook herself so badly? Next she would be imagining the ghost of Simon Dolman appearing to drag her inside.

Even as she half-smiled at the thought, a figure appeared at the mouth of the lane separating the church from the elevated rise of the cemetery behind it. There were no lights in the lane and the figure was nothing more than a black outline as it lurched towards her like one of those zombies in *The Walking Dead*. A small whimper of fear escaped from Moira's lips as the figure lifted its arm and waved at her from the opposite side of the road.

'Moira. What you doing out at this time of night?'

The figure moved a few steps closer to the street light and Moira saw it was only Thom Wilson, his limp worse than usual. She found herself giggling through sheer relief as she crossed the road to where he stood regarding her outbreak of mirth with mild bemusement. 'Thom, you gave me a fright. For a minute I thought you were…'

He changed his face into a nasty Halloween leer, his voice a deep growl. 'The evil ghost of dastardly devil-worshipping Reverend Dolman?'

'Oh my God, you think he was a satanist?'

Thom relaxed his face back to its normal shape, and Moira couldn't help thinking once again what a good-looking guy he was. What had he been thinking in marrying dog-faced Stella?

'Nah, he was just a sick, twisted pervert. Still shocking though when you think how long he'd been fooling everyone. But what are you doing out so late? Especially after the terrible stuff in there.' He hooked his thumb back over his shoulder in the direction of the church.

'I was at my friend's house. Tracey McArthur. You know her?'

Thom looked thoughtful. 'She the one who dresses up like Amy Winehouse when you two are waiting for the Kirkintilloch bus on a Saturday?'

'That's her. She didn't even like Amy Winehouse until she died, now she's always playing her music and pinning her hair up.'

Thom shrugged. 'Aye, well, people are like that. I bet when Beethoven died everyone ran out and bought an ear trumpet and a couple of his CDs.'

Moira found herself giggling again. 'Stupid. They didn't have CDs back then.'

It was strange to think a few moments ago she'd been scared stiff and now she was having a lovely chat with an older guy she'd had a crush on for ages. She might even be flirting. If she was she didn't care. The alcohol in her system was making her feel pleasantly chatty. She moved another step closer to Thom without even realising it. She thought he looked really good in his denim jacket and black jeans. If only he had been fifteen years younger it might have been her going out with Thom instead of his bitchwife.

'Listen, Moira, I'm glad I bumped into you. I really need to apologise for yesterday. Stella, making that big scene in the minimarket. Sometimes she gets something in her head and there's no shifting it. If I'd contradicted her she'd have gone off like a rocket.'

'It's fine, honest. Apart from that dickhead, Mike, deducting those mince pies out of my wages.'

'You're joking?'

'Am not. He really did.'

Thom put his hand in his pocket and brought out some loose change. He picked out a couple of pound coins, thrusting them at her. 'Here, consider yourself reimbursed.'

Moira laughingly pushed his hand away causing the money to drop into the gutter. She heard Thom swear quietly as he bent to pick them up, saw him almost lose his balance as he straightened up. He was almost as drunk as she was. For some reason this made her giggle again.

'So what were you doing down the back lane? Weren't trying to break into Mike's shop for more mince pies, were you?'

Thom grinned. 'Better than that. Stella's visiting her mum tonight, so I nipped down to the Golden Oak for a few pints. It's normally shut on Boxing Day, but Billy Grant opened up thinking he'd get a decent trade out of all the traumatised locals wanting to drown their sorrows and gossip about the minister. But it was mostly empty apart from a few bored journalists hanging about in case anything else exciting happens. I had a pint with a mate of mine and when he buggered off early I had another few on my own. Anyway, when I got to this corner I realised I should have visited the little boys' room before I left, and rather than walk all the way back, I nipped up the lane. Guess whose back gate I peed against?'

Moira had to stuff her hand into her mouth to stop from screeching with stupid laughter. When the fit passed she managed to say, 'Oh God, Mike's always moaning about people doing that. Serves him right. But were you not scared up that dark lane, after what's happened?'

'What? You think an old soldier like me is scared of the dark? Once you've served a few tours in the backstreets of Kabul, nothing much frightens you after that.'

At this mention of his military service, Moira couldn't help herself glancing down at his lame leg, then felt horrified at what she was doing and started apologising.

Thom shrugged. 'It's okay. Just one of those things. It was a ricochet, a bit of bad luck. Bullet went straight through my knee. Hurt like buggery at the time. Still does to be honest.'

Moira reached out and took hold of Thom's hand. It felt nice. Warm and dry. No sweaty palms like the boys from school when they practised Scottish country dancing for the sixth year prom. 'You must have been very brave.'

He let out a short bark of laughter. 'Not as brave as when I got hitched to Stella.' Then his smile soured. 'Sometimes I think she only married me for my disability pension.'

'So why did you marry her?'

'Dunno. She sort of attached herself to me when I came out the army. Like a limpet mine only twice as deadly. Anyway, I'm not exactly spoiled for choice where women are concerned with this leg, am I? I feel like the village gimp.'

Moira withdrew her hand from Thom's and slapped at his arm. 'You shouldn't say that. You're a lovely guy. And I'm not the only one who thinks it.'

'Well, thanks. I think you're lovely too, Moira. It's been nice talking to you. Really nice.'

Moira felt a warm glow inside her. It was like Thom saw her as an adult. Not a silly teenager only interested in pop music and make-up. The glow faded somewhat as he checked his watch and pulled at his jacket collar, a sure sign he was preparing to head home. As if to confirm this he said, 'Got to be getting back. Call of duty and all that.'

'You really have to go? I've enjoyed talking to you, too.' She knew she must sound like a needy little girl, but couldn't call the words back.

Thom looked as though he was debating with himself. 'I suppose another ten minutes wouldn't hurt, but let's not stand here. The police have a patrol car going up and down Main Street every half an hour or so. Letting people know they're still about. Might not look too good if I'm spotted talking to a young lassie like yourself. Sends out all the wrong signals. Even worse, if Stella drives by on the way back from her mum's, she'd go ballistic.'

'Where else is there to go?'

Thom took hold of her hand and pulled her towards the lane. 'Let's take a little stroll.'

Moira wasn't so sure about this, but she allowed herself to be pulled along anyway. Thom wasn't limping as badly as he'd been when she first spotted him, and she wondered if he was making an effort for her sake.

'Thom, it's dark.'

He laughed quietly. 'You'll be quite safe with me beside you. Anyway, doesn't your house back onto the lane at the other end? I can walk you straight to your back gate. I'd feel better knowing you got home safely. There's a lot of weirdos in this village no matter how many policemen are crammed into the village hall drinking tea and playing cards.'

The lane was darker than she'd imagined and Moira wondered if she was doing the right thing. But they were only going to talk, weren't they? Thom wouldn't let any harm come to her. Besides, there was something exciting walking along the dark lane with Thom holding her hand. They'd just passed the back gate to Mike's Mini-Market and Moira was telling Thom about the fabrics and design course she was doing at college, when he stumbled and almost fell over, just managing to steady himself against the high wall that separated the lane from the graveyard above their heads.

As Thom bent over, rubbing at his leg and swearing under his breath, Moira leaned back against the wall. The effects of the alcohol once again crashing over her in a wave. In near pitch darkness with Thom no longer holding her hand, she experienced a strange sense of dislocation and panic. She heard herself say in a small voice, 'Are you okay? Did you hurt your leg?'

Thom straightened up with a grunt. 'I'm fine. Jarred my knee. How about you? Your breathing sounds a bit funny.'

'Just felt a bit weird. I'm okay now. I think.' Thom's arm moved in the darkness and she felt his hand land on her shoulder. The contact was comforting.

'Sure you're okay? We can stop for a bit if you like.'

Moira relaxed, letting the wall take her weight. Thom's fingers were kneading at her shoulder, massaging the tense muscles. She was about to tell him how nice it felt when his lips descended upon her own, cutting off all need for words. In the back of her mind she knew this was wrong. Thom was at least fifteen years older than she was. And he was married. But it all felt so right. She put her arms around him, pulling him closer, enjoying the feel of his warm tongue against her own. It was like his kisses were igniting something inside her, making her want to grind her pelvis against him. His hand crept inside her jacket, cupping a breast, his thumb lightly brushing her nipple. There was something so tender about the way he caressed her, so unlike the *snatch-grab-squeeze* approach of the boys she'd snogged at parties. She could feel him hardening against her.

Thom lifted his mouth away from hers, his breathing harsh and urgent, murmuring into her ear, 'Moira, you're so beautiful. Just so beautiful.'

She was beautiful. Thom had told her she was beautiful. Moira's heart was beating so hard she knew he must feel it pumping against his palm as he increased the pressure on her breast. She removed her hand from his waist to the front of his trousers, feeling his hardness, pressing against it, rewarded by a moan of pleasure. Then, barely thinking about what she was doing, she undid the buttons on his jeans, releasing him into her hand, amazed at the heat of him, the silky texture of his skin. His tongue was frantic in her mouth as Moira encircled him with her fingers, tentatively moving her hand up and down. She'd never done this before, wasn't sure if she was doing it properly. His whole body went rigid, then spasmed as if an electrical current was passing through him. At the same time she became aware of warm wetness on her palm and wrist. She only realised what must have happened when he recoiled away from her, groaning softly.

'Fuck! Look what you made me do.' His breath came in ragged sobs. Moira wanted to hold him against her, but Thom was moving out of reach.

'Fuck. Fuck. Fuck.'

She heard him slap at the wall in frustration. 'Thom, honestly it's fine. There's no harm done.'

In the darkness his tone sounded bitter as cloves. 'You think so? Here I am making an arse of myself with a stupid wee girl like you, and you think no harm's done?'

Moira felt tears well up. Why was he spoiling it like this? Hadn't she made him feel good? Made him... *come*? She had no experience of this. He was the first man she'd ever touched in that way. What had she done that was so wrong? She felt his semen cooling on her hand and pulled a paper hankie from her pocket to wipe it off, dropping the soiled tissue at her feet.

'I suppose you'll get a good laugh about this when you tell all your mates? Poor old gimpy Thom. Couldn't even last two seconds before shooting his load.'

'Please, Thom. Don't be like this. If I've done something wrong, I'm sorry.' Tears were tracking down her cheeks, hearing that hitch in her voice she so hated when she cried.

Thom scooped his arms above his head as if casting something unwelcome and unwanted from him. 'Fuck. This was all a big mistake. And if I were you, I'd keep my mouth shut. Because if Stella ever hears about what we did, it won't just be my guts she'll want to see hanging out. Understand?'

Even as Moira tried once more to placate him, Thom was lurching along the lane, back the way they'd come. She stood where she was, confused beyond belief. Now the heat of passion was gone, she found herself shivering. She couldn't think what to do for a few moments, then decided all she could do was carry on along the lane until she reached her back gate. She'd have to get herself together before going in or her parents would want to know why she was upset. Worse still, maybe they'd phoned Tracey's house, wondering why she was taking so long to get back.

Suddenly Moira felt almost sober. Thom Wilson was right about it being a mistake, but it was her mistake, not his. Anger and resentment welled up inside her. How dare he manipulate her the way he had and then act like a child because he couldn't control himself? It was his problem not hers. Feeling a tiny bit better, she wiped at her wet face with her sleeve then realised some of him must have landed on her jacket cuff. She gave a sob of disgust and found another tissue in her pocket, wiping at her face, then scrubbed at her cuff, desperate to remove all traces of Thom Wilson from her.

Satisfied she'd done all she could, she pulled her phone from her pocket wondering why she was standing in the dark when her phone had a flashlight App. Thumbing the screen, she stabbed at the little torch icon and instantly a bright beam of light lit up the lane in front of her. It also illuminated a grinning face only three feet away. Before she could even draw a breath to scream, Moira's world plunged into an all-encompassing darkness no phone App could ever hope to dispel.

Chapter 8

Lorna Frew hadn't slept well. She'd been worrying about Sadie next door. The poor old dear had been in a right state the day before, breaking down like that in the village hall. Lorna had a good mind to ask those policemen what they had done to upset her so. She hoped they hadn't been shouting questions at Sadie like they did on the telly. Not that she would have slept well anyway with the goings-on up at the church. She'd never trusted that minister. As a Catholic she could probably say the same for most Protestant men of the cloth. At least it made a nice change from Catholic priests scandalising the country by touching up wee boys.

She was up, washed and dressed before the clock reached seven. She thought about having breakfast before checking on Sadie, but she was sure she'd heard her neighbour bumping around a few times in the night. That nice Dr Amjit had given Sadie a strong sedative and said she'd probably sleep all the way through the night, but maybe she'd had to empty her bladder and knocked something over. The poor old soul might have hurt herself. Lorna put on her coat and checked herself in the mirror before leaving the house. She smiled, thinking how she always considered Sadie to be old, but never herself, even though only seven years separated them.

Making sure she had her door key, she slipped outside into the dark, cold morning. The biting wind scoured right through her coat, making her shiver as she walked down the path and turned left, pushing Sadie's gate open. She had her own set of keys for Sadie's house just in case of emergencies. Lorna really hoped today wouldn't be an emergency. All being well, Sadie would be feeling much better and happy for Lorna to make her a cup of tea and maybe a slice of toast.

Closing the door behind her, Lorna climbed the stairs to the Sadie's bedroom. She called out her neighbour's name as she stood outside the room. Getting no answer, she knocked lightly with her knuckles. When this still didn't elicit a response, Lorna took hold of the doorknob and opened the door a crack, reluctant to barge in uninvited unless there was no other choice.

Again she called Sadie's name, straining her ears for any response, even the soft rasp of snoring would have reassured her. When she heard nothing, Lorna prepared to enter the room then stopped as she noticed a strange smell escaping from the gap between the door and the frame. It reminded her of a boy she'd once dated when she was a young woman. He'd been a butcher's apprentice and wasn't exactly overzealous about his personal hygiene. When he turned up for their date she'd sometimes caught that same smell on his hair.

Now expecting the worst, Lorna pushed open the door and found that her expectations of a worst-case scenario fell so short of reality it took a full ten seconds for her mind to comprehend what she was looking at. Only then did she let out a scream so loud it might have woken the dead people inside the room.

Harlan was in his office just after seven o'clock and already it seemed something wasn't quite right. He hadn't seen many people, but the handful he did pass looked uncomfortable, barely making eye contact. He was long used to being the detective inspector that time forgot, but the way they glanced after him made him feel radioactive. He remembered Brock's sly expression outside the church and wondered what new misery might be heading his way. Whatever mischief the DS was up to, Kyle Kelly would be pulling the strings in the background.

He decided to check the online news reports. See what new rubbish they were writing about the events in Brackenbrae, and reached under his desk to turn on his computer. After a few fruitless attempts at finding the power button, or even the computer for that matter, he realised there was nothing below his desk except dust and a few stray paper clips.

His monitor was still there staring blankly at him, a disembodied blind eye; cables trailing free like severed optic nerves. Where was his fucking computer? How was he supposed to work without it? Harlan damped down his annoyance. He had to keep a lid on things, no displays of temper, no shouting the odds. If he wanted to get himself back on the investigation he had to stay calm and controlled, no matter how many obstacles the Kyle Kelly put in his way.

What he'd do while considering the implications of the missing computer was make a brew, and none of that machine muck. In the locked bottom drawer of his desk he kept a small travel kettle along with a jar of half-decent coffee, tea bags and biscuits. The lock was to stop every thieving bastard in the building from helping themselves. When he pointed the key towards the lock however, he noticed the drawer was already open half an inch. Grabbing at the handle, he pulled it out, finding everything gone. This was too fucking much. Kicking the drawer closed, he made to push his chair away from the desk, and only then noticed an A4 sheet of paper on top of the piled reports littering his desktop. The message read simply, HARLAN, REPORT TO MY OFFICE – DCI KYLE KELLY.

He grimaced as he screwed the paper into a tightly compressed ball, dumping it into the bin. Charming. Just fucking charming. His computer stolen, desk drawer broken into and now a haughty demand from the DCI. Seeing as there were no smiley faces or kisses added after Kelly's name, he could only assume his presence was required for something other than a cosy chat over tea and scones. So what now? Kelly was usually in his office at eight a.m. sharp, so that gave him almost an hour to kill. It might be a good idea to go have a peek in the OPs room, see what they had so far regarding the Brackenbrae slayings.

He left his office and jogged up the stairs at the end of the corridor, finding what he was looking for in Room 1. The large whiteboard was cluttered with photographs with arrows linking the connections between the pictures. Centre of the board belonged to Simon Dolman. It was a recent press shot, the Reverend Dolman smiling at the camera, hands firmly clasped around a large Bible. An arrow connected this to another picture where Dolman definitely wasn't looking his best; eyes bulging, slack jaw, skin tone the colour of washed-out linen, a tinsel-wrapped rope cutting deeply into his broken neck.

Debbie Fletcher was up there. Derek Drake, too. There were also six girls with no names as yet. It was difficult to tell from the photographs, but Harlan estimated their ages to range between twelve and fourteen. He shook his head at the senseless destruction of so many young lives. Then another photo jumped out at him. It was a small-sized shot, which was why he hadn't noticed it straight away. The picture showed a serious-faced man with short dark hair, narrowed eyes staring challengingly into the camera lens, looking as if he'd be happier punching the photographer in the face than pose for the shot. It was Harlan's own ID photograph. The same one adorning his warrant card. And there was an arrow directly linking this picture with Simon Dolman.

Someone coughed behind Harlan. He spun around to see the hulking figure of DI Scanlon blocking the door. 'Harlan, you shouldn't be in here. I'll have to ask you to leave.'

Harlan jabbed at the whiteboard with a rigid finger. 'Why is my picture up there?'

Scanlon looked away, embarrassment on his tired-looking face. 'Sorry, Harlan. I really can't discuss anything to do with the investigation.'

Harlan fought the urge to topple the whiteboard to the floor and scatter everything around the room. 'For fuck's sake, Scanlon. This is ridiculous. Am I a suspect now? Is this Kelly's attempt to brand me as some kind of accomplice?'

Scanlon's shoulders sagged. Harlan thought the man looked awful. Lack of sleep and too much pressure. 'Please, Harlan. Don't put me in this position.'

'I can think of a few positions you might find even more uncomfortable. I thought you were a straight arrow, Scanlon. A good samaritan. Not just another foot soldier in Kelly's propaganda unit.'

The other man sucked in his cheeks, his eyes baleful. 'You have no idea, Harlan. No idea.'

'No idea about what exactly?'

'Not here. My office.'

Then Scanlon was exiting the room, leaving Harlan no other choice but to follow. Downstairs, Scanlon almost pushed Harlan into his office, firmly closing the door, then leaning his back against the wood as if fearing someone might try to force their way in. Harlan sat in Scanlon's chair, swivelling back and forth as he waited for an explanation.

'First things first. Your picture is on the whiteboard because it was suggested the only reason Dolman escaped closer investigation first time round was through your own actions.

We've already talked about this. Remember? Dolman had the police by the balls after you broke his nose. It could have led to a high level enquiry, especially as his brother was Justice Minister at the time. Dolman's decision not to press charges against you, and the police, forced the DCI to tread softly where your allegations over his involvement were concerned.'

'Tell me something new.'

A sad smile creased Scanlon's haggard face. 'The new part is that someone has now suggested, you knew exactly what you were doing. That the assault was premeditated, a plan hatched between you and Dolman specifically to stop any further investigation into his activities.'

Harlan stopped swivelling. 'You aren't fucking serious? Me? Working with Dolman?'

'I know it's absolute rubbish, but this time round the DCI wants to leave no stone unturned. So until such times as we can rule you out, your picture stays up there. Besides, that's not all you have to worry about.'

Harlan thought of his missing PC and his broken desk drawer. 'Kelly's really gunning for me this time, isn't he?'

Scanlon nodded. 'It looks that way. Not sure there's anything I can do to stop it. I'm sorry.'

Harlan stood up, looking out the window, finding it odd not to see a stream of headlights sweeping past in both directions, this lack of early morning traffic down to most people still being on holiday. He considered holding back what he knew about Talbot. Use it to his advantage later on, but by then Talbot could have vanished back into the ether leaving no trace to follow. He owed it to Cara to at least try to put a spoke in the bastard's wheels.

'Fine. I'll deal with Kelly when he arrives. Right now there's a few things you need to know. Remember me saying someone from Special Branch came snooping about in the church? I told you his name was Ray Talbot. Well, you're going to love this. Talbot faked his own death ten years ago, and he has a history of sexual abuse against young girls.'

'You can corroborate this?'

Harlan thought of Cara and the secret she'd carried with her for most of her life. 'You'll just have to take my word on the sex abuse part, but it does indicate a solid connection between Talbot and

Dolman. If I were you I'd put out his description and hope he gets careless. Anyone who can stay out of sight for so long must be pretty good at becoming invisible.'

Scanlon nodded. 'Thank you, Harlan. It's probably the first strong lead we've had. No one knows where to start with this mess.'

The phone on Scanlon's desk rang. He picked it up and listened, then said, 'No, sir. Not sure if DI Harlan's arrived yet. Yes, I will. Thank you, sir.'

He put down the phone. 'That was Kelly. Seems he's in early today. Wanted to know if I'd seen you.'

Harlan moved round the desk. He patted Scanlon's shoulder on the way past. 'Best I go face the music.'

DC Pete Cooper sheltered behind a tree outside the village hall, shielding himself from the wind and any early birds who might frown upon him enjoying a fly smoke. He was looking forward to the end of his double shift. Sixteen hours now he'd been on duty, and he felt like he could drop down where he stood and doze off no matter how cold it was. He'd been part of the search party combing Scaraway Woods after two teenagers were reported missing late last night. Many of the search team had grumbled at the duty, assuming both teenagers to have gone clubbing in Glasgow and likely to turn up red-faced and hungover in the morning.

Cooper didn't believe this. The boy, Devlin O'Hara, was last seen leaving his house to go visit a friend in the early part of the evening. The girl's disappearance was even more suspect; seventeen-year-old Moira Harris having vanished while walking home from the opposite end of Main Street. So far there was no trace of either teenager, and their mobile phones were either out of charge or had their batteries removed. Cooper had a bad feeling the story of the missing teenagers wouldn't have a happy ending. It was like the slumbering spirit of Brackenbrae had been roused into wakefulness and was devouring its young.

Cooper yawned. When he finally did get home to bed, he hoped he wouldn't dream of the girls found in the church basement. Those ghostly faces dusted with permafrost would haunt him for the rest of his life. Almost as bad was how they'd been filleted like beasts in an abattoir. He shook away the image as a front door opened across the road, an elderly lady emerging to make her way to the house next door, letting herself inside with a key.

He knew whose house the woman had entered. The one they called Psychic Sadie. Cooper had heard DS Brock make a group of uniformed constables laugh over what she'd said to John Scanlon. Of how the DI's dead mother had returned from the grave to scold her son for having a fat arse. On the face of it, it was funny. But Cooper had sympathy for the old woman. His own grandmother had suffered from dementia in the last years of her life, and she'd said a lot of odd things before she finally passed on. Cooper thought it was nice Sadie's neighbour was keeping an eye on her.

He was stubbing out his cigarette on the grass when the screaming began. He stood frozen for a few seconds then sprinted towards the house, banging on the door with his fist, shouting 'Police!' As the screams gave way to silence, Cooper kicked hard at the door, busting the flimsy Yale lock. At the top of the stairs he saw the crumpled form of the old lady he'd seen entering the property. He rushed towards her, taking two steps at time, dropping to his knees and checking for any obvious injury. Her eyes were wide and staring, not at him, but at something beyond him. Her mouth moved as if she were still trying to scream, but nothing emerged except a weak gasp of air.

Cooper used his airwaves set to call for assistance, then turned to look through the open door of the bedroom. What he saw made him rise like a sleepwalker and enter the room, forgetting all the ingrained protocols regarding contaminating the crime scene. He knew without doubt those dead girls from the church now had a major rival when it came to haunting his dreams. The scene before him was something out of his worst nightmare.

Sadie Goldridge was naked on her bed, scrawny legs wrapped around the slim hips of a young naked male. Their faces seemed welded together as if they had been frozen in the act of a last dying kiss, their empty eye sockets gazing blindly into the crimson depths of eternity. Despite the damage to the boy's face, Cooper instantly recognised Devlin O'Hara from the picture the boy's mother had given the search team. Both bodies were liberally streaked with crusted blood, stiff limbs entwined with glittering green Christmas tinsel.

On the other side of the bed was the missing girl. Like the couple on the bed, she too had been stripped and left slumped in a wicker chair. Her once pretty face was a mask of congealed blood from a terrible wound in her forehead where something like a metal bar had been used to shatter her skull wide open. She had one hand pinned to her breast with a sharp kitchen knife; the other similarly impaled between her legs, transforming her into a terrible parody of a voyeur pleasuring herself while the lovers on the bed frolicked for her amusement. The girl's body was also draped liberally with green tinsel.

Cooper backed out the room, stepping over the prone woman on the landing without another glance; half-running, half-slipping down the stairs until he stumbled out the front door and vomited into the frozen bushes.

Kyle Kelly had discarded his golfing attire in favour of a tweed jacket, starched white shirt and woollen tartan tie. His bald head gleamed as if he'd polished it with soft cloth. 'DI Harlan, take a seat. There are some serious matters we have to discuss.'

Harlan stood where he was by the door. 'I've few important things to get off my chest as well.' He waited a few seconds then added, 'Sir.'

The DCI pointed to the chair. 'I do believe I invited you to sit down. Please don't make this meeting any more unpleasant than it has to be.'

Harlan sat down. 'I think I've got a positive lead on who Simon Dolman was working with. His name is…'

Kelly pushed his chair back and sprang to his feet, his upper body looming over the desk. 'Not another bloody word about Brackenbrae! You hear me? I knew it was a mistake allowing you to tag along with Scanlon. I told him so, but he thought you might prove to be a valuable asset in the investigation, and look where that's got us.'

Harlan had known he had his work cut out convincing Kelly that Ray Talbot might be the key to unlocking Dolman's motives, but already the situation was sliding out of his control. 'What's that meant to mean? Are you blaming me for Dolman's confession and suicide? If anything, you should be asking yourself if those six girls might still be alive today if only you'd listened to me five years ago.'

Kelly's face was a dull puce colour as he slammed his hands on the desk. 'How dare you imply those deaths rest with me? You were the arsehole who thumped the minister. The question is, was it all part of an arrangement between you and Dolman to ensure he got a free pass?'

Now Harlan was on his feet, his face only inches away from Kelly's. 'That's a fucking preposterous accusation, and you know it.'

For a few seconds he thought Kelly might actually haul him bodily across the desk and wrestle him to the floor, so intense was his look of rage. Then the DCI's expression changed so suddenly, Harlan was caught wrong-footed. Kelly's snarl relaxed and became a gloating smile. He backed off, straightened his tie, taking his seat once more. 'I'm sure you'll get every chance to refute that possibility in due course, Harlan. Right now we have a different matter to discuss. I'm placing you on suspension from this moment forward.'

'What?' Harlan was so surprised he retook his seat without even being ordered to. He thought of his missing computer, feeling an acute sense of foreboding. What was the conniving bastard up to?

Kyle Kelly leaned down and picked up a cardboard box from the floor. 'Perhaps you might like to explain why you were in possession of these items.'

Harlan stared at the box. Whatever was in there wasn't good news. He leaned forward to look in the box, but Kelly snatched it away, a teasing smile on his face.

'Not so fast. Maybe it's best if I explain why these items are now in my possession.'

Harlan slumped back in his seat. 'I can hardly wait.'

'Yesterday I needed to sign off some paperwork you were dealing with, and I asked DS Brock to go check in your office.'

Adam Brock? Rooting about in his office? Harlan once again remembered Brock's sly smile outside the church. This raid had been planned days in advance. For now he had to play it cool. Not let Kelly see he was rattled.

'And what paperwork would that be?'

Kelly airily waved his hand in a see-saw fashion. 'Doesn't really matter. What does matter is that when Brock couldn't find it on your desk, he tried the drawer and…'

'That drawer was locked. The bastard burst the lock.'

'Not according to DS Brock. He assured me the drawer was unlocked.' Kelly was openly grinning now, enjoying himself. 'As I was saying, he checked the drawer, and found these items hidden inside.'

The box was firmly pushed across the desk. Harlan reached in and pulled out a handful of DVDs bagged in cellophane. The top one was titled, *Granny's Wet Gusset*. On the cover was a colour photograph of a well-preserved elderly woman, naked and down on all fours, smiling alluringly over her shoulder at the camera.

Harlan couldn't stop himself. He burst out laughing. 'You've got to be fucking well joking. This is your sophisticated plan to get shot of me? Have Brock plant some pensioner porn in my drawer?' He skimmed through the pile of DVDs. *Farmyard Frolics, Mothers and Daughters, Pissing Lesbians.* If this was Brock's own personal filth collection, it wouldn't surprise him.

Kelly pointed to the DVDs. 'Extremely distasteful, but in all probability not even illegal.' The DCI lifted a plastic bag full of white powder from the box. 'But this undoubtedly is.' Kelly hefted the bag from hand to hand. 'Cocaine would be my educated guess.'

Harlan swallowed hard. Were Kelly and Brock actually going as far as to plant drugs on him? This was serious shit. Then he relaxed. Kelly wouldn't take the risk of ordering Brock to plant real drugs in case his pet worm turned on him. Whatever was in the bag wasn't cocaine. It would be icing sugar or baking soda, but until the powder was analysed properly, it could be anything Kelly wanted it to be. All it took was a discreet call to a friendly journalist to mention a senior police officer was currently suspended pending an investigation with regard to possession of pornography and drugs. Shit, as he knew all too well, had a nasty habit of sticking and stinking the place out.

Kelly dropped the bag of white powder back into the cardboard box. 'Well, Harlan? Got anything to say for yourself?'

'Where's the rest of it?'

'What?' the DCI looked momentarily flummoxed. 'What do you mean by the rest of it? Isn't this damning enough?'

'I'm talking about my coffee and tea bags. They were locked in that drawer, now they're gone. And where's my computer?'

Kelly shook his gleaming bald head as if dealing with an imbecile. 'Unbelievable. As for your computer, I asked the IT department to scrutinise it for any drugs-related emails, or downloads of a sexual nature.'

The phone on Kelly's desk rang, but he ignored it. 'Now, if you wouldn't mind handing over your warrant card, we can conclude this interview.'

Harlan kept his tone casual. 'I suppose you want my gun as well.'

The DCI's eyes widened to huge circles of surprise. 'You have a gun? Are you crazy, Harlan?'

'Of course I don't have a fucking gun. And you might want to answer that phone. It might be the vice squad reporting me for kerb crawling.'

Kelly snatched at the phone, but the caller had already hung up. He slammed down the receiver, his fake veneer of civility stripped away to naked hate. 'You're finished, Harlan. Dead in the water. By the time you fight this disciplinary charge, not to mention being dragged back here as many times as I see fit to answer questions over your possible collusion with Dolman, your reputation will be so tarnished no one will work with you again. Not even that psycho lesbian bitch who follows you around like a shadow. Now, your warrant card. Hand it over or I'll…'

A loud knocking on the door interrupted Kelly. He shouted, 'Not now! I'm busy!' But the knocking continued. Kelly put his hands to his head and squeezed so hard his fingertips left white indentations when he removed them. 'Come in, but this had better be damn well important!'

The door opened and Harlan was surprised to see Scanlon standing there. The bear-like detective inspector's face was grim. 'Sorry to disturb, sir. Just had a call from DC Cooper. Those missing teenagers in Brackenbrae have been found. Both of them are dead, along with an elderly lady. I'm heading out there right now.'

Harlan spun around in his seat. 'What missing teenagers? What old lady?'

Kelly practically screamed at him. 'None of your fucking business, Harlan! This investigation is nothing to do with you any longer other than to judge your involvement.' To Scanlon, the DCI said, 'Call and brief me on the details later, Scanlon. I need to get this idiot to see sense and hand over his warrant card before I call in half a dozen uniforms to hold him down and remove it from him forcibly.'

Scanlon backed out the room, unable to look Harlan in the eye. When the door closed, Kelly stared down at Harlan, his teeth bared like a dog. 'Last chance, Harlan. The warrant card or...' Once again there came a loud knocking on the door. 'For fuck's sake! What is it now?' bellowed Kelly.

The door opened a second time, and Detective Chief Superintendent William Walker walked in. Harlan could see he wasn't looking at all pleased. 'God damn it, Kyle. Been trying to get you on the blasted phone. And what the hell is all this shouting about?'

Harlan had to bite the inside of his cheek to stop himself from smiling. The expression of sheer frustration on Kelly's face was worth a month's salary.

'It's nothing, sir. Just an internal disciplinary matter,' Kelly muttered, fighting to get himself back under control. The DCI had managed to mask the feral snarl, but Harlan saw his fist was tightly gripping the tartan tie, knuckles white with pressure.

Walker patted Harlan on the shoulder. 'DI Harlan, just the man I was hoping to speak with this morning. I'm sure the Kyle won't mind if I interrupt your dressing down for a few moments.'

Harlan could only stare back blankly at Walker, a trim, businesslike man with grey-streaked hair. It had been Walker who had blocked Harlan's demotion on two separate occasions when Kyle Kelly was gunning for him. Harlan had never quite figured out why Walker had taken it upon himself to play the part of fairy godfather. He'd barely spoken to the man apart from small talk at official functions where Walker always acted like a kindly uncle, offering advice and encouragement.

As Kelly continued to exert pressure on his tie, Walker became distracted by what lay on the desk. He picked up the copy of *Granny's Wet Gusset*. 'Good God, that woman looks like my mother-in-law.' Dropping the DVD, Walker reached into the box and pulled out the bag of white powder. To Harlan's amazement, the chief superintendent used his thumbnail to slit through the plastic, then dipped his finger inside before touching the tip to his tongue. 'Icing sugar,' he said, almost to himself. 'I think I'm beginning to see what all the shouting is about. We used to get up to this type of lark all the time back in the day. You been pranking one of your fellow officers, DI Harlan?'

Harlan shook his head. He could barely believe how the situation had changed in the space of a few minutes. Maybe there was a God after all. 'Um… no, sir. I'm afraid I'm the one being… pranked.'

The chief super actually guffawed with laughter. 'And now here you are getting your ear chewed off for possession of icing sugar and pornographic DVDs.' Walker tossed the bag into the box, raising a fine white cloud of powder. He rested his hand on Harlan's shoulder. 'Probably best all round if this rubbish found its way into the bin. Wouldn't you agree, Kyle?'

Kelly had been pulling at his tie so much the knot was barely visible and now in danger of cutting off his air supply, but he managed a strangled, 'Yes, sir.'

'Now, the reason I wished to speak with you, Harlan. I had a call from the solicitor acting for our old friend, Howie Danks.'

Harlan, already stunned by the surreal turnaround in events, gaped open-mouthed at Walker, who was now perched on the edge of Kelly's desk. 'Howie Danks, sir?'

Walker smiled and rubbed at a slight crease in his trousers. 'Yes, Howie Danks. Strangled ten young girls, and you, as I recall, were the officer who brought him in.'

Out the corner of his eye, Harlan could see Kyle Kelly now attempting to extricate his bulging Adam's apple from the death-grip of the woollen tie. He wasn't sure where the chief super was going with this Howie Danks stuff. Why would Danks' solicitor be getting in touch with Walker?

'I do remember, sir. Not the sort thing you tend to forget.'

Walker continued, 'Danks claims he's willing to reveal the locations of where he buried more bodies. The only thing is, he's insisting on speaking to the arresting officer. In other words, you, DI Harlan. So I'd be obliged if you get yourself over to Barlinnie prison this morning and see what information you can squeeze out the evil bastard.'

Walker stood up, but before leaving the room, he turned and addressed Kelly, his kindly uncle act abandoned. 'By the way, I've just heard we have three new murders in Brackenbrae, directly across the road from the village hall full of police officers where we've set up our mobile command post. It makes us look a laughing stock, Kyle. Do something about it or I'll put someone else in charge. Someone who is up to the job.'

When the door closed behind the chief super, Harlan slipped his warrant card from his pocket, silently offering it to Kyle Kelly.

The DCI stared at him as if he wanted to rip Harlan's throat out with his bare teeth. 'Get the fuck out of here.'

Harlan left Kelly's office feeling like he'd won the national lottery.

Chapter 9

Driving along the motorway, Harlan was still smiling. It had been like a miracle, the way Kyle Kelly had him bang in his sights, then the chief superintendent riding to his rescue. How often did you get a break like that? Kelly would be like a raging bull when he returned, but it was unlikely the DCI would mount another dirty tricks campaign any time soon as it would stink of personal harassment. Besides, Kelly now had his hands full dealing with another helping of corrosive fallout from Brackenbrae. Three new murders, and right under the noses of the mobile command post. DCS Walker was absolutely correct. It did make the police look like bumbling fools. The media would go crazy once the news filtered out.

As he drove further, his good mood faltered, remembering where he was going, and the reason for doing so. Having a cosy chat with Howie Danks about dead girls wasn't his idea of a pleasurable day out. Harlan hadn't seen Danks in the flesh since the courtroom trial, when the child-killer had been sentenced to life with no hope of parole. What he couldn't understand – why wait so long to give up the location of these new victims? And the very fact the bodies were buried meant Danks must have changed his killing pattern at some point.

Danks killed ten girls by strangling them, then laying them out carefully posed, arms folded across their chests, a spray of blue larkspur tucked beneath where their wrists crossed. He placed pennies on their eyes and tied ribbons in their hair, making their deaths look peaceful and serene. Some journalists had daubed him the *Sleeping Beauty Killer*. There was no evidence of a sexual motive. No penetration. No torn underwear. Danks had left no trace of himself whatsoever. He posed them in public places where they were certain to be found, so why were these other girls buried in unmarked graves? Had he still been experimenting to discover what sort of ritual fulfilled him? Or had he simply lost any fear of getting caught?

Back then, Harlan had been a DS already making a name for himself but only involved on the outside fringes of the investigation. The murders had been spread across Scotland. The first in Dundee, the next two bodies discovered in Edinburgh. Then Danks moved his work to Glasgow, harvesting five more girls for his twisted gratification. The last two bodies were found in Perth and Stirling. This widespread pattern of kills added to the difficulty of mounting a focused investigation with detectives from neighbouring divisions working on different theories and not communicating properly. Questions were raised in the Scottish parliament resulting in a dedicated team being tasked to collate and act upon the skimpy amount of data available. It was like Danks was a ghost who moved among his victims without ever leaving a trace of himself behind. Until Harlan arrested him, that was.

At the prison, Harlan was escorted to the high-security wing by the assistant governor and ushered into a small, blue-painted room devoid of anything except for a small table and two plastic chairs. This was where prisoners were allowed to speak with their solicitors, leaving behind the bitter stink of crushed hopes and cigarette smoke. He didn't have long to wait till Howie Danks was brought in, the prison officer guiding the child-killer to the empty chair. Danks nodded his thanks to the guard, who briskly left the room, closing the door behind him.

It perturbed Harlan that Danks was sitting across the table with his hands free. This was a man not only driven to kill, but also highly trained to do so. Danks had spent twelve years in the army, seeing action in both Iraq wars, Afghanistan and Bosnia. Harlan tried to remember what he'd read of Danks' assessment culled from his military reports. The army was never keen on giving anything away to civilian law enforcement. If there had been evidence of psychotic behaviour while Danks was a serving soldier, it was never revealed. The reports did state Danks had been a solid, reliable soldier, decorated twice for bravery. Calm under fire, he had a reputation for carrying out his orders regardless of collateral damage. Much of the already limited report had been redacted to spare the blushes of his superior officers who thought so highly of him.

He and Danks stared at each other for a full minute in silence. Danks had barely changed in appearance. He was a slim, compact man in his forties, with the sinewy build of a dancer. His hair was cropped to an even fuzz, accentuating a sensual face framing deep-set dark eyes that fixed upon you like a bird of prey. He wore loose-fitting grey cargo pants and a black cotton sweatshirt. What struck Harlan most about the man sitting across the table was his absolute stillness. Most people, even when they tried to be motionless, displayed small involuntary muscular tics, blinks of the eye, or a twitch of the lips. Danks was like an image burned into the air.

It was Danks who tired of the game first. 'DI Harlan. Nice to see you after all this time.' His voice was soft with barely any trace of accent, each word enunciated clearly.

'Hello, Howie. I'm told you want to give me some information.'

Danks looked down at his hands before returning his gaze to Harlan. 'I do. Maybe just not the information you expect to receive. If you'd like tea or coffee, just say and I'll ring for service.'

Harlan smiled, thinking the comment was made in jest, but Danks appeared so comfortable and confident he got the feeling the man might actually be serious about the offer. 'Um, no thanks. Perhaps best if we get down to it.' Harlan pulled his notebook from his pocket along with a pen. 'Now, these buried bodies of yours?'

Danks shook his head. 'Sorry, no more bodies. Only a proposition from an interested party that might be to your advantage.'

Harlan was thrown off-balance by the child-killer's statement. 'You want to make me an offer? Regarding what?'

'Brackenbrae.'

Harlan's heart jumped in his chest. *Brackenbrae.* Why was everything suddenly about Brackenbrae? What was he getting into here? Did Danks have a direct connection with Dolman? Both of them were child-killers, but how far did it go?

'And this interested party you mentioned, who would they be?'

Danks smiled for the first time. 'If I told you that... well, you know how the rest of it goes.'

'You'd have to kill me?'

'Someone would.'

'Fucking hell, it's not the Masonic Lodge we're dealing with, is it?'

Danks grinned, showing small tobacco-stained teeth. 'Masonic Lodge. Very good, DI Harlan. A pity you don't even understand how funny that is.'

Harlan stared back at the grinning face. He hated not getting the joke, especially when it was his joke. Rather than ask Danks to explain, he said, 'Tell you what. Maybe I'll take you up on that offer of coffee after all.'

He still half-expected Danks to admit he'd been joking, but the other man rose from his chair and walked towards the door. Harlan fought against the urge to flinch as Danks passed close enough to touch, but the prisoner made no attempt to assault him, instead doing nothing more threatening than pulling the door open and saying to the guard outside, 'Coffee for DI Harlan, please. I'll have tea. Camomile, if you don't mind.'

Danks closed the door and retook his seat, appearing amused at Harlan's expression of surprise. 'We have an arrangement, the governor and I,' he replied to Harlan's unspoken question. 'I keep this wing under control. Not always an easy task given the unstable psychology of the inmates. Murderers, serial rapists, deeply violent men who'd think nothing of cutting your face off and making you eat it if it took their fancy. I ensure these inmates behave themselves, and if disciplinary measures are called for, I see it's taken care of quietly and discreetly. For this service I am extended certain courtesies. One of which is refreshments when entertaining guests.'

Harlan could hardly believe his ears. His day was becoming stranger as the minutes ticked away. The only way it could possibly surprise him now was if Kyle Kelly himself served up the coffee wearing a French maid's outfit.

From his sweatshirt pocket Danks took a plastic wallet of rolling tobacco and a tin foil ashtray, which had been crushed flat. Removing cigarette papers and filters from the wallet, he rolled himself a smoke. Harlan studied the other man's carefully manicured hands as they busied themselves with the ritual of rolling and pinching at the tobacco-filled paper, bringing it to his mouth where his tongue applied a lick of spit to the gummed edge of the paper. Harlan couldn't help think what those hands had done to ten young girls, holding them by the neck and slowly cutting off their air until they suffocated, terror in their bulging eyes.

Danks pushed the wallet across the table to Harlan. 'You still smoke, DI Harlan?'

Harlan looked down at the green Golden Virginia wallet, considering if he really wanted to share this man's tobacco. It seemed like a betrayal of some kind. After a moment, he picked it up anyway.

Danks waited until Harlan managed to roll a smoke, a much cruder version than the perfect slim cylinder Danks himself had produced, then pulled out a disposable lighter and lit both cigarettes. The door opened and the same prison officer who had escorted Danks into the room now appeared with a tray holding two steaming mugs, along with a milk jug and sugar bowl.

'Many thanks, Gavin,' said Danks as the man placed the tray on the table. Before he left, the prison officer said, 'Any trouble, just give us a shout.'

'Don't worry', said Harlan, 'I will.'

The prison officer threw him a confused frown before closing the door.

Danks barked out a small laugh. 'I think he was talking to me. Not you.'

Trying to hide his embarrassment, Harlan helped himself to milk and sugar, taking a sip and finding himself surprised at how good the coffee was. You didn't get coffee this good back at HQ.

'Now we're nice and settled, let's get back to the matter of that proposition, DI Harlan.'

Harlan's old intuition, that ephemeral engine which had catapulted him way ahead of everyone else prior to Brackenbrae, was making itself known again, purring away beneath the surface as if it had never been away. Right now it was warning him he was in danger and should step carefully. Nothing this man told him was what it would appear to be, but what harm could it do to sit back and listen? Unless of course, the coffee was drugged, and he'd wake up in a cell with a bunch of hairy-arsed psychopathic criminals waiting their turn to sodomise him.

'And what if I simply get up and walk out the door?'

Instead of answering, Danks inhaled steam from his tea, then sipped from the mug. 'Camomile tea. I've been drinking it ever since I passed a kidney stone two years ago. Ever suffered a kidney stone, DI Harlan?'

'Not that I've noticed.'

'Oh, you'd notice. The pain is like entering another dimension. Feels like you've opened a doorway into hell, if truth be told. That's the sort of pain you'll experience when you wake up one night in your hotel room and someone is cutting out your kidney.'

Harlan had been threatened by more people in his job than he cared to remember. They'd frothed at the mouth and promised all manner of painful endings to his life, but it had been like water off a duck's back; meaningless verbal static. Howie Danks' words, however, slipped beneath his skin and chilled him.

'Personally I've nothing against you, DI Harlan. I'm just making you aware that a proposition has been put on the table. I'd advise you to at least give me ten minutes of your time.'

The coffee in Harlan's mouth now tasted bitter. 'I'll hear you out. Say what you have to say.'

'Thank you,' said Danks, looking genuinely pleased at Harlan's compliance on the matter. He paused to relight his cigarette, blowing smoke towards the ceiling. 'It's like this. Simon Dolman was privy to some highly sensitive information belonging to this interested party I referred to. They are convinced that Dolman intends for that information to be put into the hands of the authorities. That information could be damaging to their business interests.'

'Seeing as he's dead, how is he going to manage that? Has he left something in trust with his solicitor? One of those letters that start off with – In the event of my death etc etc?'

Danks looked away as if deliberating how much he could say on the matter. After a few moments he seemed to come to a decision. 'Dolman liked to play the long game. You already know he was involved in the killing of Debbie Fletcher, and that he arranged for her body to be stolen prior to the burial. My friends are convinced that Dolman placed something incriminating in the coffin before it was put in the ground. It's why he gave you back Debbie Fletcher two nights ago. He knew you would have no choice other than to exhume the grave.'

Harlan shook his head. 'That makes no sense at all. Why would he go to so much trouble? Come to that, why kill himself in the first place if he was so keen to cause trouble for these friends of yours?'

'I can't go into that. It's a complex matter. You'll have to take this proposition at face value.'

Despite himself, Harlan couldn't help being intrigued. 'Okay, so if Dolman did hide something in the coffin, what sort of thing would it be?'

'Possibly a list of names.'

'Fuck sake, Danks. Is this nothing more than a paedophile ring trying to protect themselves from exposure?'

'If only it were that simple, DI Harlan.'

Grabbing hold of the Golden Virginia wallet, Harlan helped himself to another smoke. 'I'm still not sure what your interested party thinks I can do to help. I'm no longer part of the investigation. Come to that, why would I help, even if I could? Do I look like the patron saint of kiddie-fiddlers?'

As Harlan picked up the lighter, Danks' hand shot out and grabbed his wrist. The man's grip was like iron. 'Because this interested party will not only ensure you are back on the investigation, they will put you in charge of it. You'll get your career back. Become what you were meant to be.'

Danks released his grip, leaning back in his chair, studying Harlan as he rubbed gingerly at his wrist. The bastard was strong, probably been pumping iron since he was sent to prison. Harlan wondered what fucking idiot first sanctioned the idea of giving violent criminals gym equipment to make themselves more dangerous than they already were.

'So how are these friends of yours going to arrange for me to be given the investigation? Write a letter of recommendation to the Chief Constable?'

'No need for you to know that, DI Harlan. Let's just say they have sufficient leverage over several senior officers to make it happen. The exhumation will take place tonight. You have to be there. You have to see if Dolman left anything behind as a leaving gift. So what's your answer? Yes or no?'

Harlan's head was a disaster zone. He'd been offered bribes before to look the other way, and never had a moment's hesitation in refusing. It wasn't the type of policeman he was. But, being handed the chance to lead up the Brackenbrae investigation? It sounded ridiculous. Too far-fetched for words. Yet, Howie Danks wasn't the sort of man to play practical jokes. Harlan thought of how it would feel being handed the chance to run the case, not just a peripheral figure on the sidelines taking orders from Kelly and Scanlon. Brackenbrae was a scab he'd picked at for years. How could he refuse?

He breathed in deeply, then exhaled as if expelling his tarnished conscience. 'Look, I'm not exactly saying yes… but what if there is something in that grave, and I'm in a position to do something about it?'

Danks smiled, knowing he'd hooked Harlan through the balls. 'You keep hold of it. Someone will collect it in due time. End of story. Everyone's happy. Oh, and as a token of my friends' good faith, I have something for you. Give me your pen and notepad.'

Harlan slid the items across the table. If Danks had wanted to grab the pen and stick it through his eye he could have done it at any time. He watched as Danks scrawled some numbers on the pad and pushed it back.

'What's this?'

'An IP address. You type it into your internet browser.'

'I know what an IP address is. But where will it take me?'

Danks got up and moved towards the door. 'The answer to where Debbie Fletcher has been for the last five years.'

Harlan stared at the numbers on the notepad. 'This had better not be a joke. If it takes me to Iceland's online shopping page, I'm going to be a bit pissed off.'

'Ah, DI Harlan. Always got a smart answer in your top pocket.' Danks pulled the door open and said something in a low voice to the guard outside.

Harlan couldn't help himself. Maybe it was his wounded pride at the way Danks had dangled something too precious for him to refuse in front of his nose, perhaps leading him into a swamp where he would sink to the bottom of the mud and vanish forever. Maybe he just needed to have one token swipe at the man.

As Danks walked through the door, Harlan called after him. 'Smart? I was smart enough to catch you.'

Danks took a half step back into the room, his expression unreadable. 'Are you really sure about that, DI Harlan? I seem to remember it somewhat differently. Didn't those blue larkspurs ever bother you?'

Softly falling drizzle smeared the windshield as Harlan sat brooding in the prison car park, his emotions in conflict. He was unable to shake off the feeling he'd just made a deal with the devil. He remembered feeling the exact same way the first time he cheated on Steph. The thrill of getting something he desired jarring against a stomach-clenching roil of guilt. Was he really going to let a bunch of paedophiles off the hook in return for taking charge of the investigation? That's if it wasn't all a huge practical joke. Viewed objectively, what were the chances he'd be allowed anywhere near the Brackenbrae case given his own DCI had accused him of being complicit with Dolman? But if Danks really was serious about his friends having leverage over senior police officers... It made his head hurt thinking about it.

He was also troubled by Danks' jibe about the blue larkspurs. Even now, Harlan had to admit the capture and arrest of Howie Danks had been a complete fluke. He had stopped off that day at a small supermarket to grab a bottle of water and a sandwich for lunch. As he joined the queue, another shopper tried cutting in front of him, the collision causing the man to drop the bunch of cellophane-wrapped blooms he held. The flowers strewn across the supermarket floor were bright blue in colour; *larkspurs*, the same flowers the Sleeping Beauty Killer left behind at each of his slayings. Harlan had looked into the man's eyes and knew instantly who he was. Dropping his water and sandwich, he'd readied himself for a struggle, but Danks had moved first, not to attack, instead dropping to his knees and holding his hands out to be cuffed. He had smiled sadly at Harlan. The smile of a man who knew the game was at an end. A martyr's smile.

Danks was right. Those larkspurs had bothered him. They weren't the sort of bloom commonly found in small supermarkets. He'd even gone back and asked the owner about them, only to be told the flowers hadn't been on sale in the shop. And if that were true – why had Danks pushed his way into the queue, as he had no other purchases? Was Danks admitting he'd deliberately staged the collision to get himself caught? If so, why choose himself as the arresting officer?

So many unanswered questions were driving him crazy. From his pocket he took out his notebook and looked at the IP address Danks had written down. What should he do with this? Hand it over to the computer crime department to see if it really did explain where Debbie Fletcher's body had been for five years? The same bastards who were right now combing through his hard drive for porn? Harlan wanted to know what the website contained before submitting it as evidence against Dolman – but no way was he typing that IP address into his own laptop. Instead, he would take it to someone who in all likelihood knew their way around the dark web.

His phone pinged. A text from DCS Walker. He opened the message. *Report to my office when you return from Barlinnie.* He closed the message and started the car. Walker would be wanting to know if Danks had coughed up the locations for the non-existent dead girls. But what if…? Harlan shook his head. No point even thinking it. It was only ten thirty in the morning and already it seemed a long day. He switched on the windscreen wipers to clear the drizzle and headed back to work.

Harlan hadn't been in Walker's office for some time. He remembered the last visit, right after Kyle Kelly had recommended him for demotion; Walker had asked him up for chat. The DCS had basically put a fatherly arm around him and given a pep talk, telling him to keep plugging away and try to rekindle his old knack of solving cases other detectives couldn't get a handle on. Harlan had appreciated the gesture, but it was difficult to make any headway when all you got was the dross no one else wanted; domestic violence, petty theft, muggings, nothing to cause a stir of excitement and get you noticed.

Harlan knocked on the door and heard Walker shout, 'Enter.' The chief super was nursing a cup of coffee while gazing out the window. He turned and gestured for Harlan to sit. He felt nervous as he sat down, unable to help wondering if Walker was one of those senior officers Danks had referred to.

'So, how was our old friend Howie Danks?' asked Walker, still staring out the window. 'Did he sing like the proverbial canary?'

'Afraid not, sir. He was yanking our chain. The boredom of prison life must be getting to him.' Harlan thought of the IP address in his pocket and decided not to mention it.

Walker finally turned from the window. There was a wary expression on his face. 'You're a puzzling bugger, Harlan. Best detective to break through the ranks in years, and look at you now. A paper shuffler. Dead wood. So wrapped up in your cocoon of self-pity, you wouldn't spot a decent clue if it sat in your lap and wriggled its arse against your balls.'

'Sir, if I can…'

'Don't interrupt, Harlan. I realise Brackenbrae has been a millstone around your neck, and you partially have yourself to blame for that. However, that was five years ago. I know Kyle Kelly has ground you down to cover for his own bad judgement in the Debbie Fletcher investigation, but what I fail to understand is why you let him do it. I've kept waiting for you to pull something out of the hat. Muscle your way into someone else's investigation and make a spectacular arrest, but it's like you don't even care.'

Harlan sat with his face burning. Walker was right. He could have fought back, but something had been left behind in Brackenbrae five years ago. He'd been going through the motions ever since, making it easy for Kelly to undermine him, keep him cowed and lacking the self-belief to make a fight of it.

Meeting Walker's gaze, he mumbled, 'I could make a thousand excuses, but that's all they would be. Perhaps I've simply lost it.'

Walker closed his eyes, shaking his head slowly. 'Then God help us all, because I've had a call from the assistant chief constable insisting he wants you to take over the Brackenbrae investigation. Can you think of any reason why that might be?'

Walker's eyes were full of angry suspicion. That alone told Harlan the chief super wasn't under the yoke of Danks' friends. As for the assistant chief constable, who knew?

'Haven't a clue, sir.'

'Neither do I, but what I do find strange is you getting invited on a wild goose chase to Barlinnie for a chat with Howie Danks and soon after I get a call instructing me to put you in charge of the most sensitive and high profile investigation we've had in years. An investigation already making Police Scotland look like a bunch of bungling PC Plods. Odd in the extreme, wouldn't you say?'

'Very odd, indeed, sir.' Harlan felt ashamed. Walker had been an ally, even if he hadn't intervened directly in the office politics between himself and Kelly. Now it seemed that bond had been broken. Walker knew something rotten was going on behind the scenes, something ripe and stinking to high heaven, and naturally he assumed Harlan knew more than he was letting on.

Drinking the last of his coffee, Walker placed the cup on his desk then checked his watch. 'I've called a meeting in the Operations room. The gang should all be there. Let's go.'

As Harlan followed Walker out the door he wondered where this journey down the left-hand path would take him. He felt like Judas; he'd sold himself, not for silver, but for the chance to become a proper functioning detective again. What did that say about his integrity or his morals? When you thought about it, deals were made every day between the prosecution services and defence lawyers, dickering back and forth over what went to court depending on what the guilty party could offer in return. Even so, Harlan still felt like he'd betrayed his own principles, but if it meant catching Dolman's accomplice, and those responsible for these three latest murders, well, that would be a good thing, wouldn't it? At least that was what he could keep telling himself.

Kelly and Scanlon, along with DS Brock and Cara, were waiting in the Ops room when Walker marched in, Harlan trailing behind him like an afterthought. Kyle Kelly's face crumpled in disbelief when he spotted Harlan. Scanlon merely looked confused, while Brock actually had the cheek to smirk, mistakenly thinking he was still protected from Harlan's wrath over the stitch-up. Cara met Harlan's nod with no expression at all.

Walker strode to the front of the room. Harlan could see three new pictures had been added to the whiteboard since earlier this morning. He was shocked to find he recognised two of the faces. One was the old lady the mini-market owner called Psychic Sadie. He knew the girl, too. She'd been working at the checkout in Mike's Mini-Market. The teenage boy he didn't know.

Walker cleared his throat and addressed the room. 'We have a change of strategy regarding Brackenbrae. The top brass are not happy at the way this investigation has been handled so far. We have one dead girl returned to us from the grave. A well-known minister hanging himself in public. Six as-yet unidentified young girls discovered beneath the church, and now three new murders, the bodies discovered directly across the road from our mobile incident command post in the village hall. The media are already kicking up a shit-storm. Which is why from this point forward, DI Harlan will be taking over the investigation.'

There were a few gasps of disbelief, then Kyle Kelly was on his feet, his face bright red. 'This is outrageous! That man isn't fit to run the office sweepstake. I demand…'

Walker cut him off in mid-sentence. 'You're in no position to demand anything, Kyle. Here we are in the middle of a sensationalist case with the eyes of the world scrutinising our every move, and you think it's wise to waste time and resources playing nasty pranks on DI Harlan?'

Kelly's bald head was already gleaming with sweat. 'Sir, with all respect, I can assure you those items were discovered…'

'Save your bullshit for someone more gullible, Kyle. I have my own eyes and ears on the ground. Just be grateful I don't decide to take this further.'

Kelly flashed a look of hatred at Harlan before lowering his gaze. Brock too was looking elsewhere, his smirk now replaced with a look of apprehension.

'Let me be clear about this, Kyle. DI Harlan will be reporting directly to myself, just in case the personal enmity between you causes any further fuck-ups. DI Scanlon, you will continue working on the investigation, assisting DI Harlan. Perhaps you could update him on what has taken place this morning.'

Scanlon moved forward and Harlan thought he looked relieved at having the responsibility of the investigation taken from him. 'Yes, sir.' Scanlon pointed to the three new pictures. 'Sadie Goldridge, Moira Harris and Devlin O'Hara were all discovered in Mrs Goldridge's home this morning by a neighbour. DC Cooper was alerted by the neighbour screaming and entered the house to offer assistance.' Scanlon picked up a sheaf of A4-sized colour photographs from a desk and handed them to Harlan.

He flicked through the high resolution pictures, his eyes wide. They showed the old woman and the boy posed in a sexual embrace, their blood-streaked naked bodies decorated with green tinsel. Close-up shots revealed their lips had somehow been sewn together to simulate a lover's kiss. Needlework as intricate as that would have taken time and sheer nerve. He tried to imagine how cool and confident this killer must be to indulge in such time-consuming mockery considering the house was directly across the road from a village hall occupied by a dozen or so police officers.

He flicked through the photographs until he found the checkout girl, Moira Harris, wincing at the sight of the gaping wound in the middle of her forehead, her once pretty face mostly hidden behind a death-mask of crusted blood. She had been posed upright in a wicker chair, one hand impaled to her breast, the other between her legs. Like the two bodies on the bed, she too had been adorned with strands of green tinsel. Scanlon began to speak but Harlan waved him to silence. He needed to think about what he was looking at.

He wondered briefly if the scene was a grisly recreation of some obscure work of art; the tableaux painstakingly arranged to send the police a hidden message; a *memento mori* from the sort of erudite serial killer with delusions of culture who appeared with irritating regularity in the pages of crime fiction. The removal of the victims' eyes however, told him otherwise. Compared to the care and attention required in stitching two peoples' mouths together, gouging out their eyes was a cheap theatrical gesture. A quick flick with a dessertspoon would have sufficed.

There was no secret message hidden within the murder scene. All this killer was concerned with was creating a shock wave. It was all about generating a reaction. Almost as childish as a small boy grossing out his classmates by brandishing a fistful of worms. Debbie Fletcher's body hanging from a tree on the fifth anniversary of her death had been a similar gesture, but if Howie Danks had spoken the truth, there was more to it than simple shock tactics. And if Debbie Fletcher's return had been designed to unmask a paedophile ring then what was the purpose of these latest deaths? What need did they serve? Unless someone else was deliberately muddying the waters to create confusion and perhaps delay the exhumation. Had the ex-Special Branch man Ray Talbot been responsible for the new carnage? If so, why? The more Harlan struggled to make the connections, the more tangled the threads became. He decided to let it go for now and nodded to John Scanlon to carry on.

Scanlon cleared his throat. 'We're working on the assumption Mrs Goldridge was already in bed when her assailant broke in. She'd been sedated by the doctor yesterday after taking a funny turn. Her killer must have brought the other victims with him either by persuasion or force. The back door was jemmied open and the clothes belonging to both teenagers were left dumped in the room. Forensics are checking them to see if they yield any incriminating DNA.'

'Were the teenagers reported missing?'

'Devlin O'Hara's parents called us just after ten o'clock. He said he was going to a friend's house, but when his stepdad called him on his mobile it went straight to voicemail. He tried calling the friend's house and discovered Devlin hadn't been there at any point that evening. The girl's parents reported her missing not long after. She left her friend's house at ten thirty and only had a ten-minute walk home. Her father went out looking for her and when it was obvious she was missing, he called the police. The girl stays only two doors away from Mrs Goldridge. The boy comes from the council flats further up New Road.'

Harlan put the photographs down. 'Have you interviewed the parents yet?'

'Not yet. There's a family liaison officer at both houses. I was on my way to speak to them when I got the call from DCS Walker to get back here for this meeting.'

'Any obvious suspects? Ideas on motive? I mean, why would the killer have chosen those three in particular?' Harlan realised he was more talking out loud to himself than asking a direct question, but Scanlon's expression and the quick look he exchanged with Brock told him there was something he hadn't been informed of yet.

'Out with it, John. Tell the truth and shame the devil.'

Scanlon sighed heavily. 'The old lady. Sadie Goldridge. She came to see me in the village hall yesterday and claimed she had a visit from the ghost of Derek Drake and knew the name of the other killers.'

Harlan flashed a look at Cara who glowered back as if daring him to share the story of Psychic Sadie passing on a message from her dead twin sister. To do so would open a can of worms so fat and juicy that Cara would likely rip his tongue out before he'd got half way through the story. To Scanlon he said, 'Killers? As in plural? And did she give you names?'

'No, she got confused and left in tears. I feel so guilty about not at least appearing to take her seriously. We all know that psychic stuff is complete bunkum, the dead passing on messages from beyond the grave, but I feel, as a good Christian, I could have acted more charitably.'

'Did anyone else know she was planning on grassing up these killers?'

'There was a crowd outside the village hall at the time. A protest group of locals blaming the police for their troubles as usual. Mrs Goldridge told the uniforms at the door what she was planning on doing when she arrived, so I imagine the story is halfway around Brackenbrae by now.'

'I'm told she did have a reputation for being accurate with her information from the spirit world.'

Scanlon looked incredulous. 'For goodness sake, don't tell me you take that kind of thing seriously?'

DCS Walker spoke up. 'I think where DI Harlan is going with this is that doesn't matter whether we take it seriously or not. If the real killer got to hear about it, he might think it made good sense to shut her up permanently just to be on the safe side.'

As his colleague's face flushed a deep shade of red at having been found wanting in front of the DCS, Harlan asked him, 'What about the other two? Anything I should know about?'

Scanlon shook his head. 'We're doing more door-to-door enquiries. The village was very quiet last night, people still recovering from the Christmas day festivities, not to mention the communal shock the village must be suffering at what we found beneath the church. We did have a patrol car making a routine circuit around the village as well as the housing estates, but nothing appeared out of the ordinary. We never expected this…' Scanlon, seemed momentarily lost for words, 'this… atrocity. With Dolman dead, the focus of the investigation was centred on the bodies in the church.'

Harlan felt a surge of dull anger. How many times did he have to make this point? 'Even though it was obvious Dolman must have been working with an accomplice?'

'What are you taking about, DI Harlan?' asked Walker. 'What accomplice?'

'Dolman might have killed Debbie Fletcher five years ago, but he couldn't possibly have abducted her as his movements at the time are accounted for. Witnesses gave sworn statements he was still in the church for at least half an hour after the carol singing rehearsal broke up. The Fletcher girl must have been snatched barely ten minutes after leaving the church. And now we have this!'

Harlan waved the photographs of the bedroom massacre in the air. 'Another grotesque murder scene all wrapped in green tinsel. We still don't actually know if Dolman killed Debbie Fletcher. It could have been his partner. Maybe Dolman killed himself to protect someone else.'

Walker was giving Kyle Kelly a hard stare. 'Why has this theory been ignored?'

Kelly looked distinctly sheepish. 'Sir, with so much conjecture over the six girls discovered in the church basement, we simply didn't get round to making further enquiries…'

'Try Ray Talbot,' cut in Harlan. 'He might have something to tell us.'

'Who the fuck is Ray Talbot?' demanded Kelly.

A glance at Scanlon's guilty face told Harlan his colleague hadn't as yet acted upon his information. He found himself once again relating how an officer from Special Branch had gatecrashed the church wanting information on what Dolman had said prior to hanging himself. Harlan nodded to Brock. 'Both DS Brock and DS McAullay will back me up regarding Talbot.'

Brock said nothing, simply nodded his head, still not willing to meet Harlan's stare. Cara said, 'I did see the individual, DI Harlan described, but I didn't hear any of the conversation.'

Harlan knew the last thing Cara wanted was to admit to recognising Talbot, and he had no intention of pushing her on that.

'So, this Talbot,' asked Walker, 'did he actually explain his interest in Dolman?'

'No, sir.'

'Then we contact his department and demand answers.'

Harlan winced. 'Might have a spot of trouble doing that, sir. I'm afraid Talbot died ten years ago.'

Waiting until the inevitable hue and cry died down, Harlan explained how Talbot had supposedly perished in a high-speed car chase in London. 'Right now, my money is on Talbot working with Dolman in some capacity. It's vital we find him. He assaulted a journalist called Guy Noonan after he left the church, and he took Noonan's SD card containing footage of the church service. I suggest we contact the media for images taken outside the church. They probably captured Talbot leaving just before the SOCOs turned up.'

Walker was staring intently at Harlan. 'How do you know all this, DI Harlan, considering you were kicked off the investigation?'

'Just followed my instincts, sir. There was a news item on Noonan's assault. I visited him in hospital and showed him an old picture of Talbot. He verified it was the same man who kicked his teeth in and stole his SD card.' Harlan thought it wise not to mention it was he himself who had unleashed Talbot upon Noonan.

'Impressive,' said Walker. 'Maybe you are the man for this investigation after all. Wouldn't you agree, Kyle?'

Kelly's look would have soured a pint of milk from fifty paces. 'If you say so, sir.'

Walker rubbed his hands together. 'Right, I'll leave you all to it. I'm sure DI Harlan has his own ideas on how this investigation should move forward. Keep me updated with any new developments.' With that, Walker left the room.

Kelly was first to speak. 'I've no idea how the fuck you pulled off this stunt, Harlan. Just don't think it's finished between us, no matter how this turns out.'

Harlan reached out to his own photograph stuck to the whiteboard, ripping it off. 'With all respect, sir. As DCS Walker stated, this case no longer belongs to you. So if you don't mind getting back to your duties, I have an investigation to run.'

Kyle Kelly's head turned so red Harlan worried it might explode and shower the room with his brains and bloodied scraps of scalp.

He prepared himself for a tirade of threats and general insults, but Kelly abruptly wheeled away and vanished out the door. Harlan rounded on Brock. 'You. Give me one fucking reason why I shouldn't drag you into an empty interview room and kick your arse until I drop dead from exhaustion.'

Brock's red cheeks were now so suffused with blood his face was almost dark purple. 'Might be best if you remove me from this case. I'll get DCI Kelly to assign me to another team for the time being.'

'What? You think I'm going to pass up the opportunity to give you every dirty task I can think of for as long as this investigation lasts? You're going nowhere except over to the IT workshop where you can collect my computer and put it back where it belongs. Why are you still standing there? Move it.'

Brock scuttled from the room as Harlan turned to Scanlon. 'Sorry for nicking your investigation, John. Believe me when I say it's come as much as a surprise to me than everyone else.'

Scanlon raised his eyebrows, a look of resignation on his face. 'To be honest, you're welcome to it. It's a poisoned chalice. Brackenbrae is cursed.'

'Look, here's what we'll do. You contact the TV people and ask for a copy of the footage outside the church. I want a shot of Ray Talbot. Something we can show people. Then head out to Brackenbrae, I'll meet you there in about an hour. I've got something important to do first.'

Scanlon raised his eyebrows but didn't enquire any further. With a curt nod he left the room.

Now it was only Harlan and Cara. He wondered if their relationship would be any different from here on in, now that she had shared her darkest secret with him. It couldn't have been easy for her telling him all that stuff about Talbot abusing her and Susan, and how her sister had dealt with the abuse by throwing herself down a flight of stairs.

'You okay?' he asked. 'About last night I mean.'

Cara stared back at him, pale face impassive. Instead of answering his question, she said, 'What the fuck is going on, Harlan? When I arrived this morning all anyone was talking about was how you were being suspended after being caught with porn and drugs in your desk.'

'It was a stitch-up. Kelly and Brock, the dynamic duo. Walker must have got wind of it and intervened.'

'That so? How about the other story doing the rounds of how you were at Barlinnie visiting Howie Danks?'

'Um… strange but true. Danks wanted to give us the locations of where he'd buried more girls. It was all bollocks.'

Cara kept her impassive face on. 'Really? And now instead of getting kicked off the force in disgrace, you're suddenly in charge of the investigation. I'll ask you again, Harlan. What the fuck is going on?'

What could he say? Tell Cara that he'd struck a bargain with Danks, whose friends were most likely a group of high-profile paedophiles, in return for being handed the case? He couldn't see Cara taking that very well seeing as she was a victim of another such paedophile. She'd view it as a personal betrayal.

'Cara, right now you have to trust me. If this whole thing goes tits-up, I'll be the only one culpable. I won't drag you down with me. All you have to know is that I'm going to catch that bastard Ray Talbot.'

She stared back as if trying to mesmerise him, draw out his secrets like pus from an infected wound, but eventually she dropped her gaze. 'So what's this important thing you have to do?'

Harlan smiled. He'd at least postponed an explosive confrontation for now.

'Follow me,' he said. 'I've got to go see a man about an IP address.'

Chapter 10

Screwtop Software was situated in Queenslie industrial estate, just off the eastbound M8. From outside it looked nothing more than another identikit unit, but once you stepped into the reception area you realised this place made serious money. Soft carpets, ambient lighting, leather sofas and a curved marble reception desk that resembled an ergonomic computer keyboard. Harlan walked up to the desk and spoke with the young woman behind it.

'I'm hoping to speak with Rob Scott.'

The young woman smiled sincerely. 'Do you have an appointment?'

Harlan brought out his warrant card. 'Please tell him Detective Inspector Will Harlan wants a quick word.'

The smile dropped from the woman's face. She picked up a phone behind the desk and passed on Harlan's message. When she hung up, she said, 'Mr Scott will be out shortly. Please take a seat while you're waiting.'

Harlan and Cara sat on two sofas angled towards each other, an arrow-shaped glass table between them. Cara leaned forward, speaking quietly, 'Do you actually intend telling me what we're doing here?'

He took out his notebook and showed her the IP address. 'Danks gave me this. Said it shows where Debbie Fletcher has been for the past five years. I thought I'd like to see it before the geeks get their grubby hands on it.'

Cara's eyes went wide. 'Danks gave you this? Why?'

Danks had called it a token of good faith. Harlan thought better of mentioning this to Cara. 'He didn't say. I'm guessing he's playing some kind of game we'll never understand.'

'So why bring it here? *Screwtop Software* mainly design games, shoot-'em-ups, survival horror, adventure quests. Got to admit, I never realised they were based in a grotty Glasgow industrial estate.'

Harlan smiled. 'Let's say it's a family connection.'

'You? Related to Rob Scott? You kidding me?'

'In a way. He's Holly's stepdad.'

Cara took a moment to digest this. 'What? He's your ex-wife's husband?'

At that moment Rob came through the doors, a nervy look on his face. He probably thought Harlan was here to arrest him for not giving Holly enough pocket money. Standing up, Harlan shook hands with Rob then introduced Cara.

'So, Will, how's the tarantula? Not escaped has it?'

When Cara looked puzzled, Harlan explained how Holly had given him the spider in a lucite block as a Christmas present. 'Rob even named it for me.'

Rob looked even nervier than he had before. 'Best we never mention that again in case Steph hears about it. I'd had a few drinks. Feeling brave, you know? So why are you here? Is this an official visit?'

'Not exactly. I've got an IP address I need checked and I'm too scared to use my own laptop in case it catches fire.'

Rob slowly scratched at his beard. 'And you want to put my machines at risk instead of yours?'

'Also because it might need a password.'

'Okay.' Rob looked wary. 'I can probably crack it, but I hope I'm not breaking the law doing this.'

'Trust me, Rob. I'm a policeman.'

Rob thought about it, then shrugged. 'That's what I'm worried about. Oh hell. Let's do it.'

He ushered Harlan and Cara into a large office space where a dozen or so young men and women were busy doing strange things on large twin-screen monitors. No one was chatting or hanging around the water cooler.

'Hell, Rob, you run a tight ship. Don't you give anyone time off for Christmas?'

'Couldn't keep them out if I tried. They're all gamers at heart. We're working to a tight timescale to get a new game on the market before the end of the month. Ironing out all the last minute glitches and bugs.'

Cara asked, 'What's the game called?'

Rob looked sideways at Harlan before replying. '*Serial Killer Sam*. Strictly for the over 18s market. Holly will never play this, Will. I promise.'

They entered a smaller though still very large office, where Rob ran his business. He had several desks covered with monitors, all running different programs.

'Hey, forgot to say, you guys want coffee or anything?'

Cara shook her head, and Harlan declined saying he'd already had too much caffeine. He didn't want to admit he'd already been served coffee by a real serial killer that morning. Rob took the IP address and entered the numbers into a computer attached to several black boxes with cables snaking from them. When Cara inspected them, Rob said, 'One of them filters out any nasty viruses, the second one is a password generator.'

Cara looked impressed. 'Wow. Neat.'

Rob laughed. 'Nah, just kidding. That's my speaker system. Everything I need is on my machine.'

Harlan held his breath, anxious Cara might take offence but she actually smiled. Obviously she was a bigger gaming freak that she made out.

On-screen an image was forming, red letters against a black background. Rob glanced at Harlan. '*Dead Darlings*. What the hell is this, Will?'

Harlan shook his head. His mind was already forming an idea, but he couldn't speak the words out loud. A white flashing box requested a password. Rob began typing commands into his machine and his second screen showed what looked like a set of algorithms flashing past.

'Maybe it's going to be one of those crazy zombie porn sites.'

Cara seemed interested. 'For real? They make zombie porn?'

'Oh yeah,' Rob was grinning. 'Everybody loves zombies right now. Films, games, TV shows, comic books. The public can't get enough of them. It was vampires for a while, now it's zombies. It was only a matter of time before the hardcore fan base demanded something more, erm, hardcore.'

A chime sounded and Rob scribbled down a password. 'Right here we go.' He typed the password into the box and the intro screen vanished to show Debbie Fletcher'snaked corpse on a stained mattress. A masked man with a straining erection lay beside her, his hands running over the girl's pallid and mottled flesh.

Rob stood up so suddenly he sent his chair spinning. He was holding his hand to his mouth. 'Oh dear God. Please tell me that isn't what I think it is.'

'You can log off now, Rob. I've seen enough.'

Cara's face was deathly pale, her eyes burning with rage. 'If we catch the bastards who made this I'll fucking kill them.'

Rob was hitting buttons like a man swatting at wasps. 'I was happy to do you a favour, Will, but never bring anything like that into my office again. Understood?'

Harlan rubbed at his face. The people who had made that video were probably the same ones he was protecting. He tasted a sourness in his mouth that made him want to spit. 'Rob, I'm so sorry. I never knew. Never even thought…' He stood up, lifting the scrap of paper with the password. 'Cara, we better go.'

They left Rob standing there, still staring at the blank screen. Harlan wondered if he would say anything to Steph about his visit. It would make things more awkward than usual next time he picked up Holly. Once out the building Cara slapped at his arm. 'You let Danks subject us to that filth?'

Harlan rubbed at his arm. 'I didn't know what we would see. But it's knowledge. We now know why Dolman stole her body; what he was using it for.'

'And where does that get us? Other than me seeing those images in my fucking sleep for the next month.'

Cara was right. Sometimes knowledge wasn't worth shit. Just a burden to be carried around. Trying to snap Cara out of her glowering rage, he said, 'Cheer up. We've still got an exhumation to look forward to later on.'

This time she didn't slap at his arm. She punched it.

Harlan found Scanlon in Brackenbrae village hall drinking tea and looking morose. He'd dropped Cara off at HQ, instructing her to pass the IP address and password to the new Paedophile and Child Pornography unit, then head out to Brackenbrae. He didn't envy the poor bastard who got the job of wading through the *Dead Darlings* website.

'Any word from scene of crime?'

Scanlon shook his head. 'They're still going through Sadie Goldridge's house with their dusting powders and vacuum cleaners.'

'Brock showed up yet?'

'He did. I thought I'd keep him out your way by having him help out with door-to-door enquires. I paired him up with PC Jinty Shields.'

'Honeytrap?'

'You shouldn't call her that, Harlan. Just because…'

'She's as ugly as an elephant's arse and more than a bit free with her sexual favours?'

Scanlon sighed and sipped his tea. 'Harlan, I have to apologise for Brock's behaviour. After all, he is one of my team and…'

Harlan waved away the apology. 'He was always a nasty little shit. Hardly think you need apologise for him. Anyway, we better go talk to the parents of the dead kids.'

'You think we should do this together?'

'No, you talk to the Harris family, I'll take the boy's parents. I get the feeling we're up against the clock. Has anyone interviewed the undertaker yet?'

'Hughes? No, we got sidetracked by the dead girls in the church basement. Checking back on the old case file didn't seem much of a priority once we knew Dolman was the guilty party.'

Harlan felt like shaking Scanlon. 'Dolman wasn't doing it on his own, was he? It could even be more than one person. Stands to reason whoever helped him is the same person who committed the murders last night. Green tinsel? Bodies posed in a grotesque fashion? Notice a pattern emerging?'

'No need for sarcasm, Harlan. No one expected this to happen.'

'I need to know who apart from Hughes and his staff had access to Debbie Fletcher's coffin. Oh, and before I forget, what's the time for the exhumation tonight?'

Scanlon picked up a memo from the desk. Eleven o'clock. We've got an emergency licence from the Sherriff court. Normally these things take a considerable amount of time, but under the circumstances when we know the girl isn't actually buried there, they've agreed to let us go ahead.'

'Good. By that I take it Debbie Fletcher has been positively identified?'

'Dr Haney has confirmed the body we found on Christmas Eve is definitely the Fletcher girl. Positive DNA match. She said it looks like the body has been frozen and thawed out multiple times. She gave me a lot of technical stuff about cell damage caused by the defrosting process. Why would Dolman defrost the poor girl so many times?'

Harlan thought of the images he'd seen in Rob Scott's office. The masked man sliding his hands over the skin of Debbie Fletcher. 'I think I know the answer to that, but I'll explain later. What about Derek Drake? Was that definitely his head Dolman left me in the box?'

Scanlon nodded. 'You still think it was Dolman's way of letting you know Drake was innocent?'

'I imagine it amused him to rub salt into the wound. His way of telling me he'd stolen five years of my career from me. I still don't understand why he would top himself. I mean, it was hardly a bad case of a guilty conscience. And why wait five years? There's a lot we still don't know about this.'

Scanlon finished off his tea and put his mug down. 'Poor Dr Haney will have her work cut out again today, I'm thinking. She had to work Boxing Day because of Debbie Fletcher, Derek Drake and Simon Dolman.'

'Hardly think Drake would have taken up much of her time. It was only his head, after all.'

'Maybe so, but she was also overseeing the autopsies of those six girls from the church, and today she's got three new bodies. I wouldn't do her job for all the tea in China.'

Harlan checked his watch. 'Hell, I suppose I'll need to check in with Jo Haney as well. It's going to be a busy day. See you back here in an hour. And send Brock a text. I need him for something.'

'You want him to accompany you to the O'Hara's house?'

'Fuck, no. I want him to pick up sandwiches for our lunch.'

Steve and Maureen O'Hara stayed in tenement flats originally built as council dwellings, although many of the occupiers now owned them outright. These flats had a common close with two houses to each landing, which meant eight families to a block. The O'Haras were on the second floor. The family liaison officer babysitting the bereaved parents was a pretty dark-haired detective constable by the name of Sheila Brown. She looked flustered on opening the door to find Harlan standing there. Obviously Scanlon hadn't got around to informing everyone on the team he was now in charge of things.

'Oh, DI Harlan. Can I ask why you're here?'

'I'm here to interview Devlin O'Hara's parents. Now, if you don't mind moving aside.'

DC Brown stood her ground. 'Very sorry, sir. I can't let you enter without DI Scanlon's direct permission. Aren't you meant to be...?'

'Rumours of my suspension on drugs and granny-porn charges have been greatly exaggerated, DC Brown.'

Brown flushed deep red. Harlan stared down at the FLO, considering getting into an argument, but with two distraught parents probably able to hear every word, it wasn't the best time to kick off a lively debate. Pulling out his phone, he quickly found Scanlon's number on speed dial.

Scanlon sounded irate, speaking in a hushed whisper. 'Harlan, for goodness sake I've just started speaking to Mr and Mrs Harris. Can't this wait?'

'Not really. Have a word with DC Brown please. She seems to think I shouldn't be here.'

Harlan handed the phone to Brown, whose face reddened even further as Scanlon put matters right. She hung up and handed back the phone. 'Sorry, sir. It was just...'

'Not your fault. Scanlon should have forewarned you I've taken over the investigation. Now, if we can proceed?'

Brown quickly guided Harlan into the living room where the O'Haras sat together on the couch, the husband with an arm around his weeping wife. The cheery Christmas decorations and tree in the corner only served to mock their distress.

'Really sorry about your loss, Mr and Mrs O'Hara. I'm Detective Inspector Will Harlan. I have to ask you some questions.'

The man removed his arm from his wife's shoulders and stood up. He looked to be in his mid-thirties, his muscular physique showing he was the sort of man who kept himself fit. His dirty blonde hair was receding away from his temples and cut short. He held his hand out for Harlan to shake.

'Steve O'Hara. Dev was my stepson. This is my wife, Maureen.'

The woman barely looked up, her face a mask of mute grief, eyes bloodshot from crying. Her blonde hair hadn't been brushed, and the way she was dressed, wrinkled T-shirt and jeans, suggested she had been up all night, waiting for news of her son. Steve O'Hara pointed to an armchair, indicating Harlan should be seated. He took off his coat, draping it over the back of the chair, and sat down. When he saw DC Brown still hovering at the door he said, 'Maybe you could make us a cuppa, Sheila. I'll have a coffee. Milk and two sugars.'

Brown offered to make the bereaved parents a drink, but both declined.

Harlan decided to focus on Steve O'Hara. 'You called your son Dev?'

'Everyone called him Dev. Never Devlin. He hated that.' This brought a fresh bout of weeping from his wife.

'Look, I know this is hard, but I have to ask, did Dev mention any trouble he was having with anybody from around here?'

Steve O'Hara shook his head. 'Never said a word. You know what seventeen-year-olds are like. Keep themselves to themselves. I was the same at that age, but if there had been a problem I'd have noticed.'

'Who was the friend he claimed to be seeing last night?'

'A kid called Sammy Bestle. Stays along the street. Dev was over there on a regular basis. He left the house at half six. When he didn't get back by ten, I called his mobile and it went straight to voicemail. I thought maybe his battery had run out, so I called Sammy's house and discovered Dev had never been there. Sammy said there had been no arrangement for Dev to go over.'

Harlan took out his notepad and wrote down Sammy Bestle's name, then asked for a contact number. 'Did Dev maybe have a girlfriend, perhaps not wanted you to know about it? That's why he lied about where he was headed?'

'Can't see it,' said O'Hara. 'If there was a girlfriend he'd have changed his shirt and reeked of Lynx deodorant.'

'Dev was discovered at the home of Sadie Goldridge, just across from the village hall. Did he have any reason to be there?'

O'Hara rubbed at his unshaven cheeks. 'No idea. Obviously he'd know who Sadie was. She was quite a character. Everyone said she could talk to the dea…' O'Hara broke off, aware of his poor choice of phrase, glancing down at his wife to see if he'd upset her further, but Maureen O'Hara was hunched forward, head in hands, lost in her own world of hurt.

DC Brown appeared with Harlan's coffee, handing it to him with a cautious expression. He thanked her, then asked O'Hara, 'Steve, we still haven't recovered Dev's phone. Did he have a laptop? It's possible we might find some answers in his email account.'

O'Hara nodded. 'I'll go get it. It'll be in his bedroom. I've got his password.' The man looked slightly embarrassed. 'Sometimes I check up on what he was browsing on the web. Just in case of... You know?'

Harlan nodded in agreement, silently thinking to himself that O'Hara snooping through his seventeen-year-old stepson's laptop smacked of nosiness. DC Brown took O'Hara's place on the couch beside his wife and put a comforting hand on the woman's arm. A few moments later Steve O'Hara returned looking puzzled.

'Sorry, I can't find it. I know he didn't take it out with him last night. Come have a look for yourself.'

Harlan put down his coffee and followed O'Hara into Dev's room. It was tidier than most teenage boy's bedrooms he'd seen. There was a small television with an X-Box 360 attached, a pile of games stacked neatly at the side. A few posters on the walls – Kasabian and the Arctic Monkeys. A DVD collection on a shelf along with a dusty lava lamp. A metallic blue baseball bat was propped in the corner next to a pair of Converse sneakers. Just an ordinary teenager's bedroom full of ordinary teenage possessions.

He asked O'Hara if it was okay to have a poke around the room and the man nodded. There didn't seem many places a laptop could be concealed, but Harlan ran his hands over the duvet, lifted the mattress, checked beneath the pillow and even got down on his hands and knees to look under the bed itself. Nothing. He tried the wardrobe, the chest of drawers and down behind the television unit. As Steve O'Hara had said, the laptop was missing.

'Would Dev have loaned it out? Maybe one of his mates has it.'

O'Hara looked doubtful. 'Can't see him doing that. He'd hate the thought of anyone prying through his files.'

Harlan suppressed a cynical smile. *Didn't stop you snooping.* A quick check of his watch told him he had to move on. This was a dead end for now. Then a folded sheet of paper caught his eye. He picked it up and found a list of names and addresses. He showed it to O'Hara. 'What's this?'

O'Hara squinted at the list. 'That? Just Dev's paper round customers. He delivers the *Evening Times*.'

'Was he out on his rounds yesterday?'

'No. The *Evening Times* doesn't run on Boxing Day.'

'Might he have been out collecting money from those customers he missed before Christmas?'

'No idea, but if he was, why lie about going to see Sammy?'

Harlan glanced at the list. 'He didn't deliver to Sadie Goldridge, did he?'

O'Hara shook his head. 'Just did this estate, and a few up at Brackenbrae Meadows, the private houses. Used to moan about walking up there to deliver two or three papers.'

Harlan refolded the sheet of paper and stuck it in his pocket. 'Many thanks for your time, Steve. I really am sorry about Dev. I know it sounds like an empty soundbite, but I will catch the bastard who murdered him.'

O'Hara said nothing, just stood there, his fists clenching and unclenching.

When Harlan returned to the living room to pick up his coat, he asked DC Brown to step outside for a quick word. On the landing he said, 'If you get the chance, have a look in the parents' bedroom for that laptop. It's got to be somewhere.'

Brown looked mortified. 'I can't go searching through their bedroom while they're in there.'

'Persuade Mrs O'Hara to go for a lie down. Take her through and get her comfy. Then have a snoop around.'

'Isn't that a bit unethical, sir?'

Harlan gave her a withering look. 'Yeah, well, you know me. Drugs and porn are the least of my sins.'

Leaning against his car, Harlan took out the tin of Café Crème cigarillos he'd nicked from behind Lenny's bar that morning and lit one up. There was always something that felt good about smoking outside in the cold air. He deserved this. It had already been a harrowing day, and he felt certain it wasn't about to get any easier. He was thankful no journalists were gathered outside the

O'Hara home. They were still encamped outside Sadie Goldridge's house where all the action had taken place. He called Scanlon and found him back in the village hall. Scanlon told him the interview with the dead girl's parents had gone much the same as his own. No obvious enemies, although Moira told her parents she'd had words with a difficult customer over a packet of mince pies while working in the mini-market on Christmas Day. Harlan thought that was hardly a motive for murdering the girl.

Scanlon however had succeeded where Harlan himself had failed. He had collected the girl's laptop, now already on its way to HQ. Harlan asked if Cara had turned up, and when Scanlon affirmed she had, he asked for his detective sergeant to be put on the line.

'You hand over that IP address and password?'

'Gladly. Just having that bit of paper in my pocket was making me feel soiled. Where are you?' Then probably because Scanlon was listening, she added, 'Sir.'

'Outside the dead boy's house. I've just spoken with his parents.'

'Get anything useful?'

'Not really, but the boy's laptop is missing. That could be significant. I'm heading straight up to have a chat with the funeral director, Tim Hughes. You fancy coming along?'

'Be better than kicking my heels down here. What's the address?'

Harlan riffled through his notebook and gave her the house number. 'It's the posh houses out beyond the council estate. Oh, and before you drive up there, get hold of Brock and tell him to go buy sandwiches from the mini-market. I'm starving, haven't had a bite to eat all day. Now put Scanlon back on.'

Cara signed off with a crisp and sarcastic, 'Yes, sir. Of course, sir.'

When Scanlon came back on the line, Harlan told him, 'I'm on my way to talk with Tim Hughes. Shouldn't be too long. Then I want a look at that church basement, so I'll call you when I'm on my way back. You can meet me outside the church. Hopefully by then forensics might have come up with something from the Goldridge house.'

Harlan hung up, dropped the remains of his small cigar into the gutter, then climbed into his car and drove towards the funeral director's home. A minute after he'd pulled in at the kerbside, Cara's car parked behind his own. He got out and surveyed the houses on this estate; far different from the council flats. All the houses here were of detached four and five bedroom design, with integral garages and large front gardens.

'How the other half live,' sneered Cara as she joined him on the pavement.

Harlan shrugged. 'Not a crime to live in a nice house. No need to get all judgemental just because you live in a grotty tenement in Shawlands.'

'At least I actually stay in a real house. Unlike some folk I could mention.'

'I live in a hotel out of choice, not of necessity.'

Cara shrugged, dismissing his argument. 'Let's get this done, Harlan. It's freezing out here.'

The door of number twenty-four was answered by a tall, soft-faced man with curly black hair. He wore an expensive black suit with a discreet white pinstripe. Beneath the suit he wore a white shirt and black tie. The last time Harlan had spoken to Tim Hughes he'd been at least three stone lighter. By the looks of things business was good enough for Hughes to have developed a taste for good food and fine wines.

Hughes looked at Harlan and Cara quizzically before a look of recognition filtered across his face.

'Ah, Detective Inspector Harlan. 'You just caught me. I was heading into the office.'

'I'm sure you could spare us ten minutes of your time, Mr Hughes.'

Hughes chewed at the corner of his mouth before standing aside. 'As long as you're brief about it. We've had two bodies delivered unexpectedly from Stobhill Hospital that require preparation.'

'I'm sure they won't complain too loudly if you're a few minutes late,' commented Harlan as they entered the hallway.

Hughes drew him a haughty look as he ushered them into an expensively furnished lounge, dominated by chintzy sofas and brocaded pastel-coloured drapes. 'I wouldn't have thought the police would have much to joke about considering the tragedies this village has endured over the past forty-eight hours.'

Harlan allowed himself a wry smile. 'I guess in jobs like we have, Mr Hughes, we have to find our amusement where we can. By the way, this is Detective Sergeant Cara McAullay.'

Hughes nodded to Cara but didn't extend the hand of friendship. 'Please be seated both of you. I'd offer refreshments, but as I said, I'm in a bit of a rush.'

Harlan sat down and felt himself sink slowly into the soft cushions. It was possible he might have to ask Cara for assistance in getting up again. Although it had been five years since he had last met Hughes, he found he instinctively still didn't like the man. He remembered Hughes' bubbling enthusiasm for prettifying Debbie Fletcher back then. He'd been like a young boy with a new train set. To Hughes, the girl's death had been nothing more than an opportunity to show off his skills at the mortician's table.

Hughes hadn't taken a seat and now loomed over both Harlan and Cara. 'What exactly can I help you with today?'

'For a start you can tell me who the last person was to be left alone with Debbie Fletcher in your funeral parlour before her coffin was loaded into the hearse on the day of her burial.'

Hughes put a podgy hand to his mouth as if genuinely shocked by the question. 'What on earth are you suggesting? That I had something to do with Debbie Fletcher's body being stolen? I can assure you the girl was safely in her coffin when I screwed down the lid. If you think otherwise, I'd like my lawyer present.'

Before Harlan could reply, Cara decided to intervene. She stood up and laid a placating hand on Hughes' arm. 'Now, now, Mr Hughes. DI Harlan was suggesting nothing of the sort. We do however need to establish who had access to the coffin before it was taken to the cemetery.'

Harlan saw Cara's fingers probe the edge of the funeral director's elbow seeking the sensitive nerve at the joint and knew what was coming next.

Hughes yelped with pain, jerking his arm upwards. 'Ow! You're hurting me!'

Cara's face was the picture of innocence. 'Was I? Sorry, Mr Hughes. I really didn't mean any harm.'

Hughes took a few steps back, rubbing at his elbow and looking aggrieved. Harlan knew the purpose of Cara's nerve pinch wasn't to torture a confession from Hughes, it was to simply knock him off his stride: rattle him a little. Perhaps make him say something he hadn't meant to.

Struggling against the soft cushions, Harlan got to his feet. 'Answer the question, Mr Hughes. Can you swear you were the last person to set eyes on the body of Debbie Fletcher before she was put in the ground?'

Hughes voice was pitched higher than before. 'I can't say for sure. It might have been the Reverend Dolman.'

'Explain.'

'We brought her body from the parlour to the church. Usually the coffin goes on a bier in front of the altar, but the minister asked us bring the deceased to the church early and put her in the vestry. He said he wanted to pray with Debbie privately. Claimed he felt partly responsible for her death, as she'd attended his carol singing rehearsal that night. The night she...' Hughes faltered to a halt.

'And is that normal? Having the body in the vestry before the service?'

Hughes looked embarrassed and ill at ease. 'It's not an entirely orthodox procedure, but everyone trusted the Reverend. He was alone with her for maybe ten minutes at most. When he came out of the vestry, the pallbearers carried the coffin straight to the bier. The lid was screwed closed.' Hughes struck a ham-actor pose with his hands clenched together like a penitent. 'I'd swear my life on it.'

Harlan sighed. It looked like Dolman had danced his way around everyone. He had raped, murdered and then brazenly stolen the girl's corpse for future defilement. Cara's body language suggested she was maybe hoping to inflict some more pain upon the hapless undertaker, so Harlan moved between them. 'Thank you for your time, Mr Hughes. I may have to ask you to come in and give a formal statement over the next days. For now, enjoy your embalming.'

Hughes dropped his hands and looked about to say something waspish, but at that moment the lounge door opened and an elderly woman entered, looking confused and frightened. She wore only a long cotton nightgown, her feet bare, hair flattened on one side of her head as if she'd been sleeping.

'Tim. Who are these people? Do I have to put my make-up on?'

Hughes moved swiftly to put his arm around the old lady's shoulder. 'Hush now, Mother. No need to be alarmed. These are police officers. They're here to ask me few questions. Nothing to worry about.'

The old lady stared at Cara, then Harlan. 'Are they here to lock me away? Don't let them take me, Tim.' She started to cry, burying her face against Hughes' arm.

Hughes looked coldly at Harlan. 'This is my mother. She suffers from dementia. Normally her medication makes her sleep right through till teatime, when I have a private nurse come to sit with her. All your commotion must have woken her up.'

'Sorry about that, Mr Hughes.' Harlan actually found himself feeling guilty. It wasn't the old woman's fault she had such an arse of a son. He gestured to Cara. 'We'll be leaving, but I will call you about that statement. Thanks again for your time.'

He and Cara let themselves out the house and walked to the car. Cara looked back over her shoulder. 'Just hope he doesn't embalm his mum by mistake.'

Harlan didn't answer. Something was niggling at him. No, not niggling. *Gnawing.*

'What's wrong, Harlan? You look like you've got piles.'

He shook his head. 'Mrs Hughes. Could swear I know her from somewhere.'

'Didn't you meet her last time you interviewed Hughes? Five years ago?'

Harlan shook his head. 'Didn't get introduced that time.' Then the memory came to him and he slapped at the roof of his car with the flat of his hand.

'Fuck. Fuck. Fucking fuck.'

'Harlan, you're scaring me. Are you going mental?'

'Cara, get back in there and arrest Tim Hughes. Then arrange for someone to sit with his mother until social services get here.'

'What the hell are you on about?'

'Don't argue. Just do it.'

'Why can't you do it yourself?'

'Because I'll break his fucking jaw if I step back into that house right now.'

Cara finally seemed to get the message he was serious. 'So what am I arresting Hughes for? Unlawful possession of an old woman? Being a fat, pompous twat?'

Harlan closed his eyes, unable to stop himself seeing the image on the DVD in Kelly's office. An old lady, naked, down on her hands and knees, staring coyly back over her liver-spotted shoulder at the camera.

'For pimping out his dementia-ridden old mother. That's what fucking for.'

Chapter 11

Two bites into the chicken sandwich made Harlan realise just how hungry he was. He'd never eaten a sandwich in a church before. Scanlon had shown his disapproval by saying it was disrespectful to eat your lunch in God's house, to which Harlan had replied that for the next five minutes he should consider it God's snack bar. That had shut Scanlon up for a few moments, long enough to get the sandwich open and start eating it. Brock, as instructed, brought the sandwiches and then sat himself on a pew keeping very quiet. Harlan expected he was praying for divine intervention.

Now Scanlon was demanding to know why Harlan had arrested Tim Hughes. Through a mouthful of bread, roast chicken and mayo, he mumbled, 'Not yet, Scanlon. Sensory overload,' then took another huge bite from the sandwich. It was left to Cara to explain that her DI was convinced Hughes had been casting his mentally ill mother in hardcore porn videos.

Scanlon was shocked rigid, his big face freezing like the Edvard Munch painting *The Scream*. 'Dear Lord, Harlan. Are you out of your mind? What if you're wrong? It'll be another high-profile own goal for us. You'll look like a raving lunatic. Walker will kick you back off the case.'

Cara pointed to Brock. 'We'll need that granny-porn DVD back. It's important evidence.'

Brock continued to skulk on the pew, his narrow shoulders hunched as if expecting a blow to come at any moment. Harlan swallowed the last bit of chicken sandwich then washed it down with a swig of Coke. 'Brock, I'll need you to jot down any distinguishing marks.'

Brock gaped silently back at him.

'She's an old lady. She must have a few. Birth marks, colostomy scars, tattoos, warts, stretch marks. Stuff like that. I mean, you have watched it, Brock? Yes?'

Brock nodded, eyes cast down, humiliation seeping from every pore.

'Good. In that case write down what you remember, or maybe best if you have another look to refresh your memory. We might have to insist on a physical examination of Mrs Hughes. That sort of visual identification is vital when it gets to court.'

Scanlon butted in. 'Baiting Brock isn't going to save your arse if you're wrong about this, Harlan.'

'Probably not. But I'm right. A hundred per cent right.' Harlan realised he really was absolutely sure of his accusation. True, he'd only had a brief look at the DVD cover, and many elderly women did look alike when posed naked on their hands and knees, or so he imagined, but – he was trusting in his gut instinct again. No questions asked. His lost faith had returned.

'Brock, best you call Kelly right away to get hold of that DVD. I want it entered as evidence. Don't take any excuses from him, even if he's in the middle of watching it. Oh, and here's something else useful you can do.' Harlan took from his pocket Dev O'Hara's list of paper round customers. 'The O'Hara boy had a paper round. All the names and addresses are on here. Go ask every one of them if Dev was at their door last night collecting paper money. There's only about thirty people on the list so it shouldn't take you long.'

Brock's face looked even more miserable as he perused the long list. 'What about this one? Will you be doing it yourself back at HQ?'

'What?'

'Tim Hughes is on the list.'

Harlan took a look. He hadn't bothered studying it closely so had been unaware of this fact. 'Fuck. Well spotted, Brock. I'll be speaking to Hughes later, so strike him off for the time being. Now, get going.'

Brock left the church quickly before Harlan could task him with something worse than a long walk around the housing estate.

'Scanlon, how about showing me this basement?'

Scanlon led him back out to the reception hallway where a side door led into the vestry. Most of the small space was taken up with a desk, bare except for a monitor and cables left coiled where a computer had been removed, and shelving full of hymn books and paperwork. 'Not much to look at in here,' Scanlon said, 'but in this closet…' He pulled open what looked like a normal cupboard door and yanked on a light cord inside. 'We have a staircase down to the basement. If you don't mind I'll wait up here.'

Harlan made his way down the narrow concrete steps, emerging into a large space that smelled of damp and something more unpleasant. The floor and walls were all tiled white, almost camouflaging the bank of five freezer units at the far end of the room. The whole basement looked like a sterile area until you noticed the manacles set into the wall and a filthy bloodstained stained mattress on the floor. He realised Cara had followed him down.

'Fucking hell. This is where the bastard was storing the bodies?'

Cara pointed to the freezer units. 'Every single one had a young girl inside, except the last one where he'd stacked one on top of the other.'

It was cold down here and not all of it attributable to the temperature. Harlan could feel a deeper coldness eating into him, the sense of coldness one associated with the evil acts of men. He looked at the iron manacles and wondered what despicable things Dolman and whoever else had acted out in this basement. He checked his watch, surprised to find out it was already three o'clock. Where had the day gone?

Scanlon's voice echoed down the stairwell. 'Harlan. You better come up. We've got some news.'

Harlan raced back up the stairs to find Scanlon waving his phone excitedly. 'Lab just called. They found semen on the cuff of the Moira Harris' jacket, as well as traces on her hand, wrist and face. They've rushed through the DNA test and a match came up on the database. We might just have caught the bastard.'

Harlan felt his hopes soar. 'Who is it?'

'A local man, Thom Wilson. Stays on the council estate, close to where Devlin O'Hara lived. He's on the database because of his army service. Shall we go pick him up?'

'Radio it in. Pack a couple of police cars full of uniforms and descend upon the bastard. Have them put on their lights and sirens, make a big show of it. Get someone to tip off the press and let them know where we're headed. Then have the uniforms keep him there until the press get a chance to hotfoot it along. Gives us maximum exposure when we pick him up. It's all about making an impact these days, yeah?'

Scanlon smiled broadly. 'I'll get right on to it.'

Harlan left the vestry and wandered back into the church, heading towards the altar, looking up at where Simon Dolman had dangled from his rope only two days ago. It seemed much longer than that. Cara followed him out and said, 'Wow, look at you. Just back on the job a few hours and already made two arrests. Walker will be giving you a gold star.'

Harlan shrugged. 'Can't claim any credit for Thom Wilson. DNA would have come through anyway. And Hughes isn't anything to do with this. Just a nasty pervert caught up in the web. Still, looks good, doesn't it?'

Cara surprised him by reaching out and brushing his hand. 'Maybe you'll get your reward later on tonight.'

'Would that be before or after the exhumation?'

She frowned and withdrew her hand. 'Shit. Forgot about that.'

Harlan gazed around the church, troubled. 'You know, there's something not right about all this.'

'What do you mean?'

'This church, look at it. Last time I was here five years ago it was run-down. Old carpets, decrepit wood panelling, needed painting, replastering. Now look at it. New floors, suspended ceiling, new pews, designer lighting, top-of-the-range sound system, underfloor heating. This must have cost a fucking fortune. So where was the money coming from?'

Cara only shrugged. 'Maybe he was fiddling the collection box.'

Scanlon appeared in the central aisle. 'All arranged. How long do you think we should wait until making our grand entrance?'

'Actually, I meant to ask. Where did Dolman live? Is it far from here?'

'Dolman's house? It's right next door to the church. Not much to see. Lots of books on his shelves. Scene of crime dusted it down, but all we found out the ordinary were several small bottles of morphine in his fridge along with sealed packets of hypodermic needles. We think he may have used the morphine on his victims to subdue them. Bloodwork from the autopsies will give us a clearer picture.'

'Fancy giving me a quick look? Just a couple of minutes. Should give the press enough time to camp outside Thom Wilson's flat.'

As they left the church, two police cars screamed past, lights flashing and sirens wailing as instructed. They could already see a group of reporters much further behind, jogging along Main Street trying to catch up. Stupid bastards likely hadn't realised they'd be running up a steep hill to Wilson's flat. With a bit of luck one or two might drop dead of a coronary on the way.

As Scanlon had said, the first terraced house after the church was Dolman's. Scanlon jangled the key ring then opened the door, ushering Harlan and Cara inside before closing it again. The inside of the house was much smaller than Harlan had expected for a minister's residence. As if picking up on his thoughts, Scanlon said, 'Apparently the church offered to install Dolman in one of those detached houses up the hill, but he preferred staying next door to the church. Now we know why, I suppose.'

Harlan walked into the living room and let out a low whistle. The room was practically empty except for a single armchair, some tightly packed bookcases and a small television in the corner. What drew the eye immediately was a huge oil painting taking up most of one wall. It appeared to show some sort of astronomy scene; a massive black globe against a background of nebulous gases, and orbiting the dark globe was a series of starburst flares of white light. Harlan had seen similar images before; artistic renderings from data captured off the Hubble space telescope. For some reason he couldn't explain, the oil painting made him feel uneasy. Now that he examined the dark globe more carefully he saw it wasn't devoid of detail. The artist, assuming it wasn't Dolman himself, had used a knife to ridge and shape the oil paint, creating a feeling of depth. He almost felt as if he could lean forward and fall into the painting.

'What the hell is that? The cover of Dolman's favourite sci-fi novel?'

Scanlon shook his head. 'No idea. Maybe he just liked astronomy.'

Cara moved closer to the painting. 'I think I know what this is.' She ran her finger over a blob of paint that Harlan had assumed to be the artist's signature in the corner of the frame. 'See here. It originally said *Sagittarius A*, but someone has scored a line through it and written *Heart Swarm* beneath.' Cara used her fingernail to scratch at the canvas. 'And If I'm not mistaken, the new addition might be daubed in blood.'

'*Sagittarius A*? *Heart Swarm*? What the hell does that mean?'

'No idea what *Heart Swarm* means, but *Sagittarius A* is theorised to be a massive black hole at the centre of our galaxy, orbited by thirteen stars whirling around at more than fifty thousand kilometres per second.'

Harlan stared at her. 'How the hell do you know that?'

'I saw it in a documentary. I like all that shit.'

'It obviously meant something to Dolman. We'll have to get forensics to check out the blood if it actually is blood.' Harlan wracked his brains trying to think of what might attract a man like Simon Dolman to own such an image. No one hung a painting of that size inside a small terraced cottage. Possibly it held a clue to the man's behaviour. Harlan pulled out his phone and took a snapshot of the painting.

Scanlon clapped his hands and then rubbed them together briskly. 'What say, we walk back to the village hall, drive to the housing estate and arrest our suspect.'

The three of them walked up the pathway leading into Thom Wilson's close. Already a group of locals were gathering around the garden gate, alerted by the police vehicles that an arrest was imminent. The four constables standing guard duty at the close entrance straightened up, nodding to Harlan as he passed through. On the way here they had passed the last of the stragglers from the media, most having given up running and now doing nothing more than a brisk walk. Harlan was sure they'd get there by the time Wilson was brought out in handcuffs. Walking up the stairs, Harlan could hear a woman, presumably Wilson's wife, shrieking abuse at someone.

The front door was open so they marched straight in, passing more uniformed constables in the hallway. Inside the living room Harlan saw the source of the shrieking was a small, heavy-built woman, her face twisted into a mask of rage. She was being restrained by a burly sergeant, and a much shorter, but equally bulky PC Honeytrap Shields.

'You fucking scumbag evil bastard cunt!'

The object of the woman's wrath sat quivering in an armchair with two more uniformed officers either side of him. Whether they were there to stop him escaping or to protect him if the woman broke free was anyone's guess. Harlan had to admit

Wilson didn't exactly look like a blood-crazed killer. He was of medium build, dark hair and if he hadn't looked so terrified, he'd probably be handsome in his own way.

'I'll fucking rip your fucking balls off you fucking pervert!' screamed the woman.

Harlan stood directly in front of her. 'Enough!'

Surprisingly she paused, her wide mouth still open, flecks of spit on her lips, baring misshapen teeth in a frozen snarl. The tops of her breasts were exposed and heaving like she'd just run a ten-mile race. She reminded Harlan of a frenzied dog. 'You'll get your chance to speak, but if you interrupt me I'll have you removed.'

Harlan turned to the man in the chair. 'Thom Wilson?'

The man nodded, eyes wide with fear.

'You know why we're here?'

Thom Wilson nodded again, his mouth trembling as if he was trying not to cry.

'I am placing you under arrest on suspicion of the murder of Moira Harris.'

Wilson closed his eyes and began whispering under his breath. Harlan nodded to the constables who dragged Wilson to his feet, cuffing his hands behind his back.

'Scanlon, would you mind reading Mr Wilson his rights.' When Scanlon raised his eyebrows, Harlan said quietly. 'It's been a while. I don't want to fuck it up.'

While Scanlon informed Wilson of his rights, Harlan turned to Wilson's wife, still held securely by the two officers. 'Mrs Wilson, I'm presuming.'

'Stella. That's me.'

'Stella, I'll have to ask you some questions. It would be better if we do this down at the station.'

Stella Wilson lunged forward as if she intended taking a bite from Harlan's face. 'I'm going to no fucking police station. I know my fucking rights. I'm staying right here.'

'In that case, I'll have no choice but to place you under arrest, too.'

Suddenly all the fight evaporated from Stella Wilson and she sagged in the officers' arms, fat tears rolling down her cheeks. They manhandled her into an armchair where she buried her face in her hands, her shoulders quivering. Harlan felt a bit of sympathy for her. It was never easy when your husband was being dragged away on a murder charge.

He had half turned away when the woman sprang from the chair with a snarl, hands extended like claws, attempting to reach her husband. Honeytrap Shields reacted faster than anyone, catching Stella Wilson in a choke hold, then kicking her legs away and rolling her onto her front with her arms twisted behind her back. In the blink of an eye Honeytrap had the woman cuffed. The other officers seemed most impressed. Even Cara, no slouch herself when it came to slam-dunking suspects to the ground, gave Honeytrap a tacit nod of approval. Harlan couldn't help wondering if this was the same technique Honeytrap used on any reluctant internet-dating partners.

Keeping her weight on Stella Wilson's legs to stop her kicking, PC Shields grinned up at Harlan. 'Another dangerous prisoner aw ready for transportation, sir.'

'Um… thanks for that, Jinty.' He walked towards the door, all set to take his bow for the press outside. He halted at the door, half-turned, then said, 'I hate telling people how to do their own jobs, but maybe best if we put those two in different cars.'

The Cathedral House bar was quiet when Harlan stopped by for an hour's break, with only a few lone drinkers propping up the bar. Lenny put down the glass he was polishing when Harlan walked in.

'So, the wanderer returns. Couldn't help noticing there's been a few more bodies turning up in that little village of yours. I take it you've been asked to play with the big boys again.'

Harlan slumped down at a table. 'Any chance of a pint? Maybe get Marilyn to fix me up a plate of chips?'

Lenny scratched his beard. 'Definitely a bad day at the office then? Give me a few minutes and you can tell Uncle Lenny all about it.'

Harlan leaned back in the seat feeling tired, but happy enough with the arrest. Wilson had been led out to a volley of camera flashes. Something for the front pages of tomorrow's newspapers and the six o'clock news bulletin. There had been a small incident when Steve O'Hara made an appearance, lunging for Wilson as they bundled him into the police car. It had taken two police officers to restrain the man. Obviously there was no evidence directly linking Wilson to Dev O'Hara, but as all the bodies were found in one location, it stood reason if he was involved with the death of Moira Harris, then he was also involved in the deaths of the teenage boy and Sadie Goldridge.

He felt his phone vibrate in his jacket pocket. It was a text from Steph, all in shouting-in-your-face capital letters – CALL ME!!! He checked his phone log and saw he'd missed three calls from her. He considered ignoring the text, but sometimes it was best to get it over with. Bracing himself, he hit call-back. It was picked up straight away.

'Steph.'

'What the hell were you thinking of? How could you traumatise Rob like that? Exposing him to that sort of filth? He came home early from work, all upset. I've a good mind to put in a complaint to your boss.'

So Rob had grassed him up after all. So much for solidarity between those who had suffered from Steph's demanding ways. Maybe he should casually mention what Rob had suggested naming the tarantula, but that would be downright petty. To be fair he couldn't really blame Rob after what he'd forced the guy to look at.

'Look, Steph, I didn't know what we were going to see. If I'd known I'd never have asked for his help.'

'Men having sex with dead children? If that's the sort of thing you're working on right now, perhaps it's best if you skip your next visitation with Holly.'

'Whoa, hang on a minute. What's my job got to do with anything where Holly is concerned?'

'Because those images will still be in your head.'

'That's rubbish, Steph. Complete bullshit.' But Harlan knew there actually a grain of truth in her accusation. 'Steph, why don't I…'

But Steph had already hung up. Lenny placed a pint glass on the table before him, a sympathetic look on his face. 'More grief from the old trouble and strife?'

Harlan nodded. 'All my own fault this time.' He picked up the pint and took a long swig.

'Marilyn's got your chips in hand. So what's the latest? Anything more on Talbot?'

'Nothing as yet, but it's been one strange fucker of a day.'

'I'm all ears.'

Harlan began with how Kelly and Brock had worked as a tag-team to stitch him up with porn DVDs and fake cocaine. Lenny laughed and slapped at his thigh. 'Granny porn? They fitted you up with Granny porn?'

Harlan smiled back. 'You've not heard the best part yet. I'll get to that later.'

He went on to tell Lenny of how DCS Walker had saved his bacon before sending him to Barlinnie to speak with Howie Danks, and how Danks had given him a mysterious IP address. Naturally he omitted the part where Danks recruited him to do a small favour for a nameless group of people who were in all likelihood an organised paedophile ring in return for getting handed the investigation. Somehow he didn't think Lenny would understand.

'So you checked out this website?'

Harlan took another gulp of lager. 'It was a necrophilia site involving children. Debbie Fletcher to be exact.'

'Jesus fucking Christ. How sick can you get? But why would Danks hand this over to you? Was he involved with that Dolman character?'

'No idea. Obviously he's playing some sort of deep game. Dare say I'll find out at some point.'

'So you're back working on the case?'

Harlan could barely meet Lenny's gaze. 'Um... I'm actually running the whole show.'

'What? One minute they're fitting you up, the next they put you in charge? How did that come about?' Lenny was giving Harlan the hard stare.

'Orders from the high command. Someone thinks my time has come back round. I can't really explain it.'

'Bet you fucking well can. You're up to something devious. I'm not completely stupid.'

'Lenny, leave it. Maybe once it's all done and dusted. But not now, okay?'

Lenny didn't look pleased. 'Whatever. But you be careful where you tread. Sometimes the water ain't as shallow as you might think it is. So you managed to arrest anyone yet?'

'Two as a matter of fact.'

He told Lenny of the interview with Tim Hughes, the funeral director, and how his old mum had shown up just as they were leaving.

Lenny looked incredulous. 'You mean you arrested this bloke on the strength of a seeing some old wrinkly's arse on a DVD cover? Are you pulling my leg?'

'It was her, Lenny. I know it. I've got a crew looking through the guy's phone, laptop and personal DVD collection right now. By the time I get back to question him, I expect it to be confirmed beyond all doubt.'

'Hope you're right or you'll look like a real tosser. And this other bloke you arrested? What you accusing him of?'

'Murder. Got a DNA match from semen on the clothing of the girl they found this morning. Looks like an open and shut case. I might even learn where Ray Talbot fits into all of this.'

Marilyn bustled down the stairs and placed a huge plate of chips in front of Harlan. 'Chips ain't a proper meal, Will Harlan. So I've given you some healthy veg to go along with them.'

Harlan stared down at the pile of steaming vegetables accompanying his chips. 'Sprouts, Marilyn? Really?'

'Had some left over from Christmas. They're good for you. Get them all eaten up.' She slapped at Lenny's shoulder. 'And you. There's a man waiting to be served at the bar.'

One of the drinkers raised his empty glass with an apologetic shrug. Lenny heaved himself up from his seat. 'Enjoy the sprouts, Harlan.' He took two steps towards the bar, then stopped. 'And before I forget, you owe me a tin of cigarillos. Thieving git.'

Harlan wolfed into the chips, wondering if he could ask Lenny for a plastic bag to tip the sprouts into, but he got the feeling Lenny might not be so helpful right now. Just like Cara, Lenny knew he was involved up to his neck in something murky. He could only hope once the exhumation was over he could wash his hands of the whole deal, but he had a nasty feeling Danks' friends might feel they owned him now; maybe expect a few more favours in the future. On the table his phone trilled and Jo Haney's name appeared on the screen. He had meant to call her and forgot.

'Hi, Jo. Sorry, meant to get in touch with you earlier.'

'Don't fret about it, Will. I'm hearing you've had quite the busy day. I also hear congratulations are in order. Back in the hot seat and already bagged yourself a prime suspect. Well done, you. Are you still in Brackenbrae?'

'No. I nipped back to the hotel for a bite to eat. Got a long night ahead of me.'

Haney's voice took on a teasing tone. 'You're at Cathedral House? Mmmm. Brings back a few nice memories.'

Harlan wasn't sure how to reply. His one night stand with Jo Haney happened three years ago. Lenny had organised a New Year ceilidh and Haney came along due to her husband being out the country on business. Both of them had been more than a little drunk, but he remembered it was definitely her idea to slip upstairs to his room. The pathologist, normally so staid and sensible and ever so *nice*, had surprised him with the sheer exuberance of her sexual appetite. She'd made such a racket that Lenny had complaints from his other guests about the noise, some of whom were still dancing their socks off at the ceilidh.

'Definitely a night to remember, Jo.'

Haney giggled. 'Is your landlord still annoyed at me?'

'He did mention I should foot the bill for soundproofing next time you stayed over.'

'Next time? Are you hinting we should enjoy a repeat performance?'

Harlan didn't know what to say. The sex with Haney had been wild and uninhibited, but once was probably enough, especially as they still had to work together, and the fact Haney's husband was a barrister he might have to face across the courtroom one day didn't help. Sleeping with Cara was already dicing with danger without bringing Jo Haney back into the equation.

'Jo, I…'

Haney laughed down the phone. 'I'm just teasing, Will. I realise your life is complicated enough right now. I was calling to let you know how the autopsies were progressing. I've already filed the official reports, but thought you'd like the brief version.'

'I definitely would. Scanlon already told me we've got positive DNA matches on both Debbie Fletcher and Derek Drake. What about the girls found beneath the church?'

'The cause of death in each case was strangulation. Hyoid bones broken and all show signs they'd been beaten and raped. We're running DNA tests to try and establish their identities. Most of them show signs of poor diet, definitely undernourished, which could mean they were runaways living on the streets.'

'What about their other injuries?'

'Definitely carried out post mortem. Each girl had her heart, liver and kidneys removed. Very neat work I have to say, although the removal of flesh from their thighs and buttocks was much more amateurish. Looked like nothing more than a sharp kitchen knife was used for that.'

'What about the three bodies discovered in Brackenbrae this morning? You had a chance to examine them yet?'

'I have. Sadie Goldridge died from blood loss after having her throat cut with a sharp serrated blade. It's likely the attack only hastened her death as she had suffered a massive stroke. Both Devlin O'Hara and Moira Harris died from fatal blows to the head with a blunt object. Most probably something like an aluminium baseball bat. I found tiny splinters of the metal inside the wounds of both victims. Flecks of paint, too. All the other injuries such as the removal of their eyes and nailing the girl's hands were carried out post mortem.'

'Whoa. Back up. Did you say an aluminium baseball bat?'

'Or something similar.'

'What colour were the flakes of paint?'

'Metallic blue.'

'Fuck.' Harlan thought back to Devlin O'Hara's bedroom. The baseball bat propped in the corner.

'From that response, Will, I'm guessing I might have just given you a lead.'

'Could be very useful. I need to go make a phone call. Thanks for the info, Jo. I'll read through the reports tomorrow.'

'Not so fast. Aren't you interested in the result of Simon Dolman's autopsy?'

Harlan snorted. 'Don't think they'll be any surprises there. Broken neck due to hanging is my professional guess.'

'True. But bet you didn't know Dolman was suffering from pancreatic cancer. Quite advanced. Bloodwork also shows large amounts of morphine in his system. He was obviously self-medicating to keep the pain at bay. It might also explain why he decided to confess his sins and commit suicide.'

Harlan remembered Scanlon saying they'd found morphine in Dolman's fridge. So it wasn't for subduing the victims after all. Dolman had been dosing himself up.

'I get that, Jo. But if Dolman was dying and in pain, why not just overdose on morphine? Why put on a big show of hanging himself in front of his congregation? Why even confess to the crimes for that matter?'

'I suppose we'll never know the answer to that, Will. However, given how much pain he must have been in, and the effects of the morphine, it's possible Dolman might have been clinically insane when he took his own life.'

Harlan didn't think so. He remembered the way Dolman had acted at the Christmas service. He certainly didn't look or sound insane. He looked in control. A man who knew exactly what he was doing, but he didn't want to waste any more time speculating about Dolman right now.

'You might be right, Jo. I doubt it will make any difference to anything now. Anyway, got to get moving. Got a call to make, then at least two interviews to take care of, and then the exhumation later tonight.'

Haney laughed lightly. 'God, yes. Probably more work for me to fit into my schedule tomorrow, depending on what's in that coffin. The last thing I need is a five-year-old corpse to dissect first thing in the morning.'

After a few more pleasantries, Harlan hung up, then immediately called Scanlon. 'Who's holding the fort in Brackenbrae right now?'

Scanlon sounded as if he too were in the middle of his dinner. 'I left Adam Brock in charge for a few hours. You left so quickly I never had the chance to run it past you. I take it you disapprove?'

'Doesn't matter. I've got a job for him. Tell him to get a few uniforms in tow and arrest Steve O'Hara on suspicion of murder. There's a blue baseball bat in the dead boy's bedroom. Tell him to bag it as evidence. Also, get back onto scene of crime, I want the flat picked over, that missing laptop must be somewhere in the house. Get them to pull the place apart. That includes rooting through the rubbish bins outside. Maybe Mrs O'Hara could go stay with a relative for a few days. I'll deal with Steve O'Hara when I get back.'

Harlan cut the connection just as the phone rang again. He didn't recognise the number.

'DI Harlan?'

'That's me.'

'This is DC Montrelle Rigg. I was involved in the search of Tim Hughes' house.'

Harlan hadn't had too many dealings with Rigg, a young black detective constable, but remembered he was the budding artist who had drawn the Little Miss Frosty Fud caricature of Cara.

'You find anything that's going to make me happy, DC Rigg?'

'Oh, sir. I'm about to make you the happiest man alive.'

When Harlan finally hung up, the remains of the chips were now cold, as were the sprouts. Marilyn wasn't going to be pleased with him. He carried the plate to the bar. 'Lenny, you couldn't do me a favour and dispose of the evidence?'

Lenny looked at the food left on the plate, a slow grin forming on his face. 'You know something, Harlan? Never thought I'd see the day when a copper put that particular question to me.'

Tim Hughes and his solicitor sat across from Harlan and Cara in interview room number two. The room was never designed to give its visitors a feeling of welcome; all it had to be was functional. Beige painted walls, cheap nylon carpet, CD recording equipment, a TV on a stand and a two-way mirror for when third party observation was required. Scanlon was keen to interview Thom Wilson straight away, but Harlan wanted Wilson to sweat some more in his cell before dragging him in here. Also, it meant Harlan had a chance to warm up his interviewing technique, which had been badly neglected of late.

He let Cara take care of the recording protocols then took the DVD of *Granny's Wet Gusset* from a folder, placing it on the table in front of the accused. If he had been playing poker, this would have been like throwing in an ace as your opening card.

The solicitor, Jonathan Broomfield, was old school. Three piece suit, white wavy hair and gold-rimmed spectacles. When he saw the DVD he immediately got to his feet. 'Before this ridiculous interview goes ahead, I am instructed to say that my client, Mr Hughes, is already filing a complaint of personal harassment and unlawful arrest. He intends fighting this preposterous charge through every court in the land until the police are forced to pay out a substantial sum of damages for besmirching his character and any loss of business incurred.'

'Sit down, Mr Broomfield. Your job is to advise your client, not to make speeches on his behalf.' Harlan picked up the DVD and showed it to Hughes. 'Mr Hughes, do you deny the woman on the cover is your mother?'

'I most certainly do.' Hughes was doing his utmost best to present a face of indignation and disgust. 'What an outrageous question.'

Harlan handed the DVD box to Cara who removed the disk and inserted it into the side of the television. When the picture appeared on the screen, Cara hit fast forward until the screen showed a close-up shot of an elderly woman performing fellatio.

Hughes' solicitor surged once more to his feet, this time Hughes joining him. 'This is intolerable. You cannot force my client to watch this filth. I am removing him at once from this interview.'

Cara reacted before Harlan could say a word. 'Sit down, you pair of arseholes. If either of you takes so much as a step towards that door, I'll consider it an organised jail break and take appropriate action. You, Mr Broomfield, will be charged as an accessory. Perhaps a night in the cells might teach you some sense.'

Harlan nodded amicably. 'I've seen DS McAullay take appropriate action on more than a few occasions, and believe me gentlemen, it hurts a great deal.'

Broomfield stared Cara down, but must have seen something in her face that frightened him. He took his seat again, pulling Hughes with him. He pointed to the television screen where the elderly lady was now flat on her back and engaging in vigorous sexual intercourse with her partner. 'This is unacceptable. Completely beyond the pale.'

Harlan nodded to Cara who paused the DVD. 'I think we've seen enough anyway. Now, Mr Hughes, have you got anything you'd like to get off your chest at this point in time?'

Broomfield laid his hand on his client's arm, cautioning silence, but Hughes leaned across the table and snarled, 'I want to know how my mother is, and who is taking care of her. If any harm has befallen her I'll be holding you personally responsible, DI Harlan.'

'Your mother is being well looked after. We called in social services who took her into care this evening. You do realise that if you force my hand, I'll have to interview your mother and ask her about these... *activities* you've been subjecting her to.'

Broomfield snapped, 'That's rubbish. Mrs Hughes is suffering from dementia, and nothing she says can possibly carry any weight in a court of law. Now, if you have any proof whatsoever that the woman in that DVD is my client's mother please get to it.'

Harlan reached into the cardboard folder and this time produced Tim Hughes' phone. Another ace, this time courtesy of DC Montrelle Rigg. Hughes turned to his solicitor. 'That's my bloody phone. Can they do this?'

Harlan held up the phone. 'Of course I can. I had a search warrant issued, all signed, sealed and delivered with much haste due to the possibility of a vulnerable, elderly person being in danger. This phone had something very interesting on it. In particular, a certain email.'

The funeral director's mouth dropped open and for the first time there was an expression of real concern. 'You can't read through my emails. Those are private.'

Harlan smiled happily. 'You were being blackmailed.' He reached again into the folder and produced three blown-up photographs. 'I'd say the blackmailer snapped these on their own phone, thinking they could squeeze some easy cash from you. Sorry, the quality isn't the best, but every picture, as they say, does tell a story.'

Harlan laid the blow-ups on the table for Hughes and his solicitor to see. All three pictures showed Mrs Hughes having sex with an unknown man. In the last photo Tim Hughes was clearly visible standing beside a camera mounted on a tripod.

'I would like to add that during a search of your home, we found a professional quality digital camcorder, along with a large selection of DVDs, all apparently featuring Mrs Hughes. We also found a selection of sex toys, vibrators, dildos and a few dozen jars of lubricating gel. You still have nothing to say, Mr Hughes?'

Broomfield stared at the pictures with an anxious look on his face. 'At this point in time I strongly urge my client to say nothing at all.'

Tim Hughes let out a wail. 'It was Dolman. Simon Dolman forced me into it.'

Harlan sat up straight. 'What?'

The funeral director rubbed at his face, now red and glistening with sweat. 'My business was in trouble. Too many debts and bad investments. Dolman was a friend I confided in. He said he knew a way we could both make a lot of money. I was horrified when he suggested using Mother to make adult films, but he said she would enjoy it. We'd be doing her a favour. You've no idea how persuasive Dolman could be. He could talk anyone into anything. I wanted to stop after the first time, but Dolman wouldn't let me. I thought when he killed himself the nightmare would be over. But it's only got worse.'

Cara asked, 'Who was blackmailing you?'

'I don't know. They told me to leave the money at the lock-ups beside the council estate. I never saw who picked it up.'

'You gave the blackmailer five thousand pounds in cash?'

Hughes nodded, his face a mask of misery. 'I had no choice. I couldn't very well go to the police, could I?'

'When did you drop off the money?'

'Last night. Around seven o'clock.'

Harlan checked his watch. He had lots more to do tonight. No point in dragging this out any further. It was only a sideshow anyway. He put the photos and phone back into the folder along with the DVD. Standing, he said, 'Timothy Hughes, I am charging you with…'

There was a knock at the door and DC Montrelle Rigg burst in, his face full of excitement. 'Sir, really sorry to interrupt, but I think you might want to hear this.'

'Won't this wait another few minutes, DC Rigg?'

The young detective constable shook his head. 'Don't think so, sir.'

Harlan shrugged and followed Rigg outside the room. 'What's so important you have to come crashing into my interview? We've already got everything we need to put Hughes away.'

Rigg shook his head, 'Actually, you don't, sir. I was speaking with a systems admin at Google. Trying to find out who sent the blackmail email and pictures to Hughes. You know what they're like, always hiding behind their customer's privacy rights, but once I mentioned it was connected with the Brackenbrae investigation, he changed his mind and said he'd help out so they wouldn't get bad publicity over non-cooperation.'

Harlan smiled. 'In other words you lied to Google. This case is nothing to do with the murders.'

DC Rigg grinned right back. 'Perhaps it does.'

'What?'

'You see, they traced the email account and found the personal information was obviously fake. Thing is, when the admin chased down the IP address the email was sent from, it matched another Gmail account they have. It was Devlin O'Hara who sent the email. I'd say that gives Tim Hughes a pretty good motive for murder.'

Harlan felt like kicking himself up the arse. He'd completely forgotten that Dev O'Hara delivered the *Evening Times* to Hughes.

'Well done, DC Rigg. A fine piece of work. As a reward I promise never to let DS McAullay know about that drawing you did. Little Miss Frosty Fud.'

Rigg's dark skin actually seemed to pale a little. 'You knew that was me, sir?'

'If I were you, I'd stick to landscapes in future. Safer for your health. Maybe even do a few still lifes. If you like I can ask Tim Hughes if his mother is available for posing.'

Rigg smiled. 'No thanks, sir. Got my reputation to think of.'

Harlan patted him on the shoulder. 'Don't we all, DC Rigg. Don't we all.'

Chapter 12

Adam Brock had a black eye. The best one Harlan had seen for some time. They were sitting in the empty canteen drinking coffee along with Scanlon and Cara.

'What happened to you, Brock? Kyle Kelly get mad because you took away his DVD?'

Brock kept his eyes downcast, exuding the air of a man in purgatory. 'Steve O'Hara resisted arrest. Took three of us to bring him in.'

Harlan tried to look sympathetic, but his heart wasn't in it. 'Ah, well, just think of it as taking one for the team. Any sign of the boy's missing laptop?'

'Not in the house. We found it in the rubbish bin in the back gardens. Someone had prised it open and ripped out the hard drive.'

Harlan slapped his hand on the table. 'Which means someone knew Dev had incriminating pictures of Tim Hughes and wanted to destroy the evidence. Obviously they never anticipated us arresting Hughes himself and looking through his emails. So how does this fit in with what we already know?'

Brock muttered in a tired voice, 'I've no idea.'

Scanlon said, 'I really think we should send DS Brock home. I know we've all been on duty since early this morning, but Adam has been physically assaulted. He should really go to A&E and make sure his eye socket isn't fractured.'

Brock looked up, a glint of hope in his expression. Harlan quashed that without a second thought. 'Sure he can go home, but only after one more little job.' Brock sighed in resignation. He knew it wasn't going to be pleasant. 'Is Stella Wilson still downstairs?'

Scanlon said, 'Yes, after Brock and I took her statement, I told her to sit tight in case you wanted a word.'

'I don't, so Brock can run her home.'

Brock gulped on his coffee, then said, 'Do I really have to? She's scary.'

Harlan agreed. 'God help Thom Wilson when he gets out of prison in thirty years or so and finds Stella waiting for him with her rolling pin. But tonight, consider yourself her designated chauffeur, Brock. Off you go.'

Brock wearily pushed himself to his feet and trudged away. Scanlon shook his head in a disapproving fashion. 'I think you're being very hard on him. I know he's badly blotted his copybook, but as a Christian I believe in forgiveness and giving people a second chance.'

Cara smirked. 'Ever think you might in the wrong job, sir?'

Scanlon ignored the remark and turned to Harlan. 'So Tim Hughes is now officially implicated in Devlin O'Hara's murder?'

Harlan grimaced and rubbed at his stubble. He should probably have shaved while he was back at the hotel, but all those phone calls had eaten up what little time he'd had. 'I'd say we have a lot of threads to untangle. Dev O'Hara delivered the *Evening Times* to Hughes. Possibly what might have happened is that young Dev got too nosy for his own good, and got an eyeful through the window. He took a few snapshots thinking he could blackmail Hughes into parting with five thousand quid.'

'And got killed for his trouble?' said Scanlon.

'This is where it all gets rather murky. Hughes claims he paid out the blackmail demand, but never saw who collected it. When I challenged him on it, he denied everything, as you'd expect. I charged him with the in-family porn movie stuff, then rearrested him on suspicion of murder. We can interview him again in the morning. We also have Thom Wilson whose semen was found on Moira Harris' clothing, but the weapon possibly used to murder both Moira and Dev was found in Dev O'Hara's bedroom. Is this fucked up or what?'

Cara asked, 'And how do any of them connect to Sadie Goldridge?'

'Mrs Goldridge told everyone outside the village hall she knew the names of the killers,' said Scanlon swirling the dregs of his coffee around the bottom of his plastic cup. 'I know everyone thinks she was slightly mad and eccentric, but whoever killed her wanted her out the way just in case she really did know something. She did have a reputation for getting things right.'

'But how does that tie in with Moira Harris and Dev O'Hara? Why dump all three bodies in Sadie's house then mutilate and pose them the way they did? It's completely crazy.' Harlan wasn't sure if he was talking to his colleagues or to himself. 'Sadie Goldridge thought she knew the killers' names. Dev O'Hara was blackmailing Hughes. So if Hughes is part of Dolman's little murder club and discovered Sadie was mouthing off, it does give him a motive for both Sadie and Dev. I just don't see where Moira Harris fits in. Scanlon, what did you get from the lovely Stella Wilson? Anything remotely useful?'

'She shouted a lot at first, then calmed down and said she was visiting her mother last night. Didn't get home till after eleven. Thom Wilson was at home watching the telly when she returned.'

'So not much of an alibi for Thom.'

Scanlon stood up. 'Time we spoke to him.'

Harlan checked his watch. Three hours till the exhumation. Three hours until he might have to conceal evidence of a paedophile ring under the noses of scene of crime officers and whoever else was present. The very thought was making him feel ill. But when you danced with the devil…

He stood up and faced Scanlon. 'Yeah, let's go speak with Thom Wilson.'

Thom Wilson's duty solicitor looked young enough to have only recently qualified for the job. He introduced himself as Richard Birnie, and looked nervous seated next to Thom Wilson across the table from Harlan and Scanlon. Cara had taken up a standing position at the back of the room. Harlan knew he really should have been better prepared for this interview and read the background notes on Wilson, but there hadn't been enough time. He quickly flipped through the pages he'd been handed by Cara as Scanlon took care of the introductions for the benefit of the recording.

He knew Wilson had been in the army, which is why they had his DNA on file, but didn't realise Wilson had been medically discharged after having a bullet shatter his knee. It crossed his mind that Wilson perhaps had a connection to Howie Danks. Possibly serving together at some point. Harlan studied the man across from him, seeing how pale his face was, deep shadows already forming under his eyes. His hands constantly fidgeted with each other on top of the table, fingers knotting and twisting themselves around each other. He knew instinctively it would not take much pressure to break this man.

Once everyone in the room had identified themselves for the recording, Harlan said, 'Hello, Thom. I don't see any point in beating around the bush. Did you kill Moira Harris by smashing her head in with a blunt object?'

Wilson's eyes went wide as he blurted out, 'No. I didn't hurt Moira. She was fine when I left her.'

'So you do admit to being with her last night?'

'Yes.'

'What time was this?'

Wilson glanced at his legal brief who nodded. 'I met Moira around half ten. At the corner of Main Street and New Road.'

'Where were you before that?'

Wilson took a deep breath. 'I was in the pub. The Golden Oak.'

'Anyone that could verify that?'

'Billy Grant behind the bar. A few journalists. And I had a pint with my neighbour, Steve O'Hara.'

'You met Steve O'Hara last night?' Harlan couldn't help but be surprised. Out of his three suspects, two of them had been drinking together. How did that fit into the puzzle?

'What time did you meet him?'

'Nine o'clock. Steve was already in the pub when I got there. It wasn't as if we planned on meeting up.'

'How well do you know Steve O'Hara, Thom?'

'Steve? Been out with him and his wife as a foursome a few times. Stella is friendly with Maureen, Steve's wife.' Wilson's face twisted into a rueful smile. 'I guess we won't be doing that any more. Steve seems to think I've something to do with Dev getting murdered. I thought he was going to batter me when you arrested me today.'

'And do you have anything to do with Devlin O'Hara's death?' This was Scanlon.

'Of course I don't! I didn't kill Moira either. This is a complete fucking nightmare. Why won't anyone believe me?'

Harlan studied Thom Wilson closely. He was scared, that much was obvious, but who wouldn't be after getting dragged into a police station on a murder charge?

'Tell me, Thom. What happened when you left the pub?'

From the way Wilson folded his arms, gripping at his elbows, Harlan knew this was the part he dreaded talking about.

'When I left the pub I got to the corner of New Road and realised I needed to piss. I thought about walking back to the pub, then decided to nip into the lane that runs behind the church. On the way back, Moira was standing across the road. She'd been at her pal's house. We sort of got talking.'

'Talking about what exactly?'

'Just stuff. The minister hanging himself. The bodies found in the church basement. What else are people talking about in Brackenbrae right now?'

'Was Moira acting naturally? Nothing odd about her behaviour?'

Wilson stared back at Harlan. He knew where this was going.

'She'd had a few drinks, okay? Like I had. She was, you know, a bit flirty.'

'I expect you must have been flattered. A young, attractive girl like Moira showing interest in an older bloke like yourself.'

A spark of anger, with maybe a touch of shame, flared in Wilson's eyes. 'Of course I was flattered. What guy my age wouldn't be?'

'How's your marriage, Thom? Everything hunky-dory there?'

Another flash of anger. 'What the hell's that to do with anything?'

'Just answer the question.'

Wilson looked at his legal brief who only shrugged. 'You've met Stella. Probably formed your own opinion. She's not the easiest woman in the world to live with, but we rub along most of the time. Just like most people.'

'So when Moira stared flirting, how did you react?'

Wilson rolled his eyes upwards as if seeking help from above. 'I was uncomfortable. I knew it wasn't right. I made my excuses and told her I was heading home.'

'But you didn't go home, did you?'

'No.' Wilson's voice was almost a whisper.

Harlan pointed at the recorder. 'Can you speak up a bit, Thom.'

'I said, no. I didn't go home, not then.'

'So what happened? How did Moira persuade you to stay?'

'She just… she talked me round. Said she was having a good time. Having a laugh. That's when I decided to go with the flow, just let things happen.'

'Go on.'

'I said I'd walk her home the back way, along the lane. I wouldn't have made a move on her, it had to be her choice.'

'So she made a move, then?'

'Not at first, we just talked, then I took a stumble, almost fell on my arse.' Wilson looked down at his knee. 'This fucking thing, always betrays me when I least expect it. Next thing I know we're kissing, up against the wall. That was it. It's not as if we had sex or anything.'

Harlan glanced at Scanlon. Wilson wasn't going to volunteer the rest without a bit of a push. Time to apply the thumbscrews.

'So this kissing where nothing really happened – how come your semen ended up on the cuff of her jacket? Traces on her hand and wrist, too.'

Wilson seemed to crumble in front of Harlan. Colour flooding into his pale cheeks, arms held tight against his chest, his shoulders dropping; all signs of someone trying to vanish from plain sight. Shame did that to you.

'Thom, answer the question.'

'She touched me.'

'Touched you?'

'We were kissing, and she put her hand on the front of my trousers. She pulled me out, stroked me and… and…' Wilson halted, shaking his head. There were tears on his cheeks. 'I couldn't control it. I tried not to, but… fuck, one touch and I shot my load all over her hand. I was just so fucking mortified. I knew she would tell all her mates. I'd be the big fucking joke around the village. Peg-leg Wilson with the hair-trigger cock. I've always suffered from premature ejaculation. It's why Stella…'

Harlan leaned forward, his voice quiet. 'Why Stella what?'

Wilson stared back. Utter misery in his eyes. 'She goes with other men. I thought maybe that's where she was last night.'

'You know this for certain? About the other men?'

'She makes sure I know it. Never names anyone. Just likes to humiliate me, saying things like what a great fuck she's just had.

It's why I kissed Moira. I was trying to find my own self-esteem. Can you possibly understand that?'

'I can understand that, Thom. But tell me, what happened after you ejaculated?' Harlan knew there was something more eating away at Wilson. One last bit of venom to extract.

Wilson sighed loudly, despair and self-loathing flavouring his breath. 'I blamed her. Can you believe that? I was angry with myself and I blamed Moira. She tried to be nice about it, and that made it worse, more shameful. That's when I walked off and left her in that dark lane. And now she's dead.'

Wilson started to cry. Great heaving sobs that sounded like he was tearing his lungs apart.

Harlan stood and spoke into the recorder. 'Detective Inspector Harlan terminating interview.' He walked out the room and stood in the corridor, cooling his head against the wall. So much for an open and closed case. Unless Thom Wilson was the best actor he'd met in his life, the man was innocent of killing Moira Harris. So where did that leave them?

He was back in the canteen, this time with only Cara for company. Scanlon had gone home, as there was no real need for him to attend the exhumation. They had spoken briefly after interviewing Thom Wilson and decided to leave Steve O'Hara until morning when everyone felt less jaded.

Cara was drinking black tea, blowing across the top of the cup to cool it down. 'So Wilson isn't our man then?'

'Nope. Never in a million years. I'll probably release him tomorrow.'

'You really think the lovely Stella is shagging her way through the available men in Brackenbrae? She's not exactly got much in the looks and charm department.'

Harlan smiled. 'Hell, it's never stopped Honeytrap Shields. She's probably getting more sex than anyone else around here.'

An evil grin formed across Cara's face. 'I just hope Brock managed to take Stella home without getting molested. I mean, she's got an *empty* tonight with poor hubby locked up.'

Harlan made a disgusted face. The thought of Brock and Stella Wilson romping in the back seat of his car wasn't a pleasant one.

'Even she must have her standards to keep up. Little Adam would be a mere morsel for a woman like her.'

Cara stopped grinning and became more serious. 'So what about Hughes, our mother-pimping undertaker? He's definitely far more involved in everything than he'd like us to think. The kid who was blackmailing him ends up dead right after he picks up the money? That stinks.'

'I'm with you on that one, but we need proof, Cara. Maybe forensics will come up with something from Hughes' car. What I do need as quickly as possible is for the lock-ups to be examined for any blood. The lane, too.'

'Harlan, it was raining last night. Complete waste of time. And the SOCOs are already on the verge of mutiny, the amount of hours they've put in over Christmas.'

Harlan grunted seeing her point. 'Still, a quick look wouldn't harm anyone.'

Cara began flicking through a few sheets of paper she'd been carrying around.

'What you got there?'

'Steve O'Hara's extensive criminal record. I printed it off when I was getting you Thom Wilson's background notes. May as well prep up for tomorrow's interview. There's loads of stuff from when he was a teenage gang-member. Theft, assault, nicking cars, breach of the peace, more assault, more thieving and…' Cara's face went stiff. 'Oh fuck. How did we miss this?'

'What is it?'

'Steve O'Hara did eight years for manslaughter.'

'You're joking?'

Cara waved her hand at him impatiently. 'Let me read this. Hang on.' After a few moments she looked up, eyes shining. 'We might be on to something here. When he was twenty-two, O'Hara killed his girlfriend during a sex game that went badly wrong. In his statement he said both of them had been drinking and snorting coke while experimenting with cutting off each other's air using scarves during sex. O'Hara claimed that he passed out and must have fallen forward, cutting off his girlfriend's air for good with his forearm. When he regained consciousness, the girlfriend was dead and he immediately called the police. Initially they charged him with murder, but the procurator fiscal's office accepted a plea of manslaughter.'

Cara was right. How the hell had they missed something like that? Background checks should have been carried out on the parents of both dead teenagers. But with everything else going on it had simply been overlooked.

'It does fit the pattern, Cara. We have Dolman, now exposed as a serial killer involved in weird sexual practices. Tim Hughes, filming his mother for granny porn, and likely connected with Dev O'Hara's death. Now Steve O'Hara, another killer linked to kinky sex who possibly may have killed Moira Harris and Dev with the baseball bat. So how do we tie all that together? And we still don't have a clue where fucking Ray Talbot fits into this mess.'

Cara had her eyes closed, concentrating. When she opened them she said, 'What if O'Hara, Hughes and Dolman were all in it together; a little murder club with a taste for the sexually macabre, making deviant porn movies and killing when they felt like it. Then Dev sends his blackmail demand to Hughes just before Christmas. Dolman sees it all falling apart and decides to go out with a bang, leaving just O'Hara and Hughes. They keep their nerve, and when Hughes drops off the blackmail money, O'Hara is there to kill Dev, probably not expecting it to be his own stepson. Also, they're nervous about Sadie Goldridge shouting her mouth off. So they kill her and use her house to dump Dev's body, setting up the scene up as a grotesque porn tableaux. On the way out they hear Thom Wilson in the back lane with Moira, wait until Wilson storms off, then add Moira to their pornographic freak show. O'Hara then gets rid of Dev's laptop because the incriminating photos of Hughes are on there. How does that sound?' Cara sat back looking pleased with herself.

'Timings don't work.'

'What?'

'We know Steve O'Hara did leave the house to go for a drink. Wilson said he met him at nine o'clock. Dev left the house at six thirty, and if Hughes dropped off the money at seven, that gave O'Hara just under two hours to kill Dev, dump him off at Sadie's, then get to the pub. Although going for a few pints right after killing your stepson and a helpless old woman, you'd have to be one cold-hearted bastard. Thing is, we know O'Hara got home before ten, because that's when he called the police to report Dev missing. That means he can't have been in the lane to whack Moira on the head with his baseball bat.'

'But what if O'Hara left Hughes on his own, and it was Hughes who killed Moira, then carried her into Sadie's house?'

Harlan shook his head. 'So how did the baseball bat end up back at O'Hara's house? Unlikely Hughes would have dropped by with the murder weapon. Especially not after O'Hara calling the police to report Dev missing.' Cara was frowning, clearly annoyed at herself for missing that small fact. 'But I think you're on the right lines. We just need to get the configuration right. By the way, forgot to tell you, Dolman was dying of pancreatic cancer. I imagine that was a major reason why, as you said, he wanted to go out with a bang.'

'When did you learn about Dolman's cancer?'

'When I went back to the hotel for something to eat. Jo Haney called me.'

Cara arched her brows. 'Oh, did she?'

'What's that meant to mean?'

'Oh come off it, Harlan. You've fucked her, haven't you? I saw the way she was all kissy-feely with you in the church. Women only ever act that way when they've done the dirty deed.'

Harlan wasn't sure how to react. Surely Cara wasn't jealous? 'It was only once. A few years ago,' he admitted. 'And we were both drunk.' He looked at his watch. Supervising a coffin being pulled from the earth after five years of decay and rot was actually preferable to Cara quizzing him on his past conquests. 'I think it's time we left for Brackenbrae. The exhumation is due in just under an hour.'

Cara said nothing as she stood up, folded Steve O'Hara's paperwork and stuck it in her jacket pocket. But just as Harlan thought the subject of Jo Haney was safely in the past, she said, 'I just hope she washed her hands, Harlan. You never know whose guts she had them in that day.'

Brackenbrae Cemetery was on the small side compared to the sprawling landscape of the Glasgow Necropolis. Harlan had never attended an exhumation before and wasn't sure what to expect. What he hadn't anticipated was to be confined within a large polythene tent watching a small JCB excavate Debbie Fletcher's grave at the open end of the enclosure. The tent was floodlit, the lights powered by a generator. The headstone had already been removed and laid to the side like a misplaced marble paving slab.

Inside the tent was a folding trestle table, where the coffin, once removed from the earth, would set down for examination. That was the part Harlan dreaded most. Not because he feared whatever horror might reside within the coffin. The source of his dread was the list of names Danks' friends suspected had been hidden to create some sort of major scandal. Harlan wondered whose names might be on the list. Politicians? TV personalities? Senior members of the legal profession? Royalty? Obviously they must be powerful people, as how else could they have arranged for Harlan to be handed the investigation with such speed and ease?

What worried him most was how he was supposed to spirit this evidence away from under the noses of those attending the exhumation. The tent was actually pretty crowded right now. Besides himself and Cara, there were a handful of scene of crime officers, already booted and suited, three blokes from the specialist firm hired to carry out the exhumation and a stern-faced representative from the borough council, present to see no rules and regulations were breached. There were also a dozen uniforms deployed within the grounds of the cemetery to ensure no interlopers such as the media or the morbidly curious managed to gain access.

Dave Campbell, the senior SOCO, approached Harlan, his white polythene suit making him look like an under-the-weather Smurf. 'Surprised to see you back in charge Detective Inspector Harlan.' There was no implied judgement in his tone, just a sense of professional curiosity.

'Not half as much as I am, if truth be told.'

The corners of Campbell's mouth twitched in a mischievous smile. 'Especially after your stunt with the severed head a few nights ago.'

Harlan shrugged, 'Heat of the moment, Dave. Derek Drake would have understood.'

'Hopefully we won't have a repeat performance tonight, eh?'

'You have my word on it.'

Campbell scratched his bushy moustache. 'All this must be costing your bosses a bloody fortune.'

'You mean the exhumation?'

Campbell gave a soft laugh. 'No, the whole bloody shebang. Brackenbrae since Christmas Eve. All the bodies, trace evidence to sift through, DNA, dusting for fingerprints, autopsies and everything processed as quickly as possible at premium rates. I've had to call my people back off their Christmas break and pay them double time.'

'Talking of which, Dave. Any updates you think I might find useful, seeing as we're paying you so much.'

'Anything in particular?'

'Identifying the baseball bat as the weapon used to murder Moira Harris and Dev O'Hara would be useful.'

'Someone's working on that as we speak. Should have a result by morning.'

Harlan gave a non-committal grunt. He hadn't expected anything so soon anyway.

'And we ran the blood sample we got from the painting in Dolman's home. From the words *Heart Swarm*? It's Dolman's own blood. You any idea what the words refer to?'

'I wish I did, Dave. It might explain a lot of things.'

The mini-JCB had finished excavating the grave, and now two men from the specialist firm were in the grave itself, using small spades to remove the last of the soil. The tent smelled strongly of damp earth and exhaust fumes from the JCB. Dave Campbell wandered over to supervise as they tied ropes around the small coffin, before climbing out of the hole and looping the ropes over the blade of the JCB. Harlan watched transfixed as the blade slowly rose upwards bringing the coffin with it.

Cara moved up close beside Harlan. 'So what do you think we'll find? Another body? Or just a bag of bricks?'

'We'll soon find out.' Harlan found he didn't much care what they found. All he could think of was the list of names Dolman might have hidden away, and how to get his hands on it before Dave Campbell and his SOCOs claimed it. Then again, there might be nothing at all. Danks' friends could just be ultra-paranoid, in which case he'd have fulfilled his obligations and have nothing to worry about.

As the coffin came clear of the ground, four pairs of hands steadied the wooden box, then slipped it free of the ropes and carried it to the trestle table. The small coffin looked surprisingly well preserved for being underground for five years. Everyone stayed silent as Campbell hammered a wedge between the top and the side of the coffin, then used a crowbar to prise open the lid. Harlan was surprised to see a thin metal wire dangling from the underside of the lid, a rusted ring dangling from the end.

Campbell shouted, 'Grenade! Everyone down! Now!' and threw himself flat to the ground. Instinctively, Harlan spun and hit the ground, his hands covering the back of his head. There came a muffled *crump* – followed by screams of pain and the sound of breaking glass as the lights shattered. The entire tent lifted up, then settled back, the torn polythene collapsing over everyone inside.

For a few moments Harlan stayed perfectly still, wondering if he'd been injured, before realising he was fine. By some fluke, one of the lights was still giving off a stuttering dim glow, although it was now on the wrong side of the ruined tent. He could hear several people moaning in pain. His first thought was for Cara. She'd been standing close to him when the coffin exploded. He felt a surge of relief when he heard her shouting instructions to the uniformed police officers in the cemetery grounds, screaming at them to bring their torches.

He groped his way on hands and knees through the clinging polythene in the direction he thought the coffin had been. He found the remains of the table, mostly splintered wood now, and amongst the debris, what was left of the coffin. In the murky light he caught sight of a grinning skull and scattered bones; they were small, belonging to a child. Harlan ignored them, spotting a flat metal box, dented and twisted out of shape by the explosion. The lid was already half open as he grasped the corner of a white envelope exposed within, managing to tug it free and slip it into his coat pocket just as the helpers outside the tent pulled the remains of the polythene away. Then a pair of hands were grabbing at him.

'Harlan, are you okay?'

He squinted into a bright beam of torchlight. It was Cara's voice. He pushed himself into a squatting position, ignoring the brittle human remains scattered around him as he reached for

Cara's hand, pulling himself upright. Her face was dirty and a trickle of blood ran down her cheek. She grinned and said 'I'm guessing it wasn't a bag of bricks then.'

It was least an hour before the last of the injured had been taken to hospital – and what little could be salvaged from the wreck of the coffin bagged and loaded into the SOCO's van. The slim metal box that had protected the envelope now nestling in his coat pocket had attracted a few puzzled comments, but it would remain a mystery to everyone except himself. Dave Campbell, who'd badly wrenched his knee diving for cover, had remarked they'd got off lucky. Five years underground had weakened whatever made up the explosive charge of the grenade, otherwise they might all be either dead or in intensive care. As it was, one of the specialists, the JCB driver, had lost an eye and most the fingers on his left hand, while a SOCO had been peppered along his spine with exploding fragments from the grenade casing. There were other less serious injuries that required hospital treatment, but nothing major. Cara herself had caught a flying splinter of wood in her cheek from either the table or the coffin. Even Harlan who'd thought himself unscathed, discovered he'd taken a hit when he'd taken Lenny's cigarillo tin from his back pocket and found a sharp fragment of cast iron from the grenade casing stuck through the tin.

'Where did you keep the tin?' asked Cara, a look of amazement in her face. 'Wasn't over your heart was it?'

'Back pocket,' he replied, still staring stupidly at the quarter inch fragment of cast iron.

'In that case it definitely saved your arse.'

Harlan took out a cigarillo and lit it up. 'I'm going to buy Lenny a whole caseload of these when this is over.'

A new tent had been erected over the open grave to prevent any idiots from falling in before it was back-filled in the morning. The small JCB, its glass window blown in, sat there alone and unattended like a sleeping iron velociraptor. No doubt it would be picked up as soon as the specialist company's men recovered from their near-death experience. The cemetery was eerily quiet. Even the press photographers had vanished into the night.

Cara plucked the cigarillo from between Harlan's fingers and took a draw from it. 'Can you believe that bastard Dolman actually booby-trapped a coffin? It means he planned all along to return Debbie Fletcher's body, right?'

Harlan took back the smoke. As he'd already had a similar conversation with Howie Danks earlier that morning, it didn't come as that much of a surprise. 'Seems like he did. A real bag of tricks wasn't he?' Harlan surprised himself by yawning. 'Christ, I'm all done in. I need to get some sleep. This has been one of the most fucked-up days in my entire life.'

Cara playfully elbowed him in the ribs. 'And here was me thinking you might enjoy a nightcap back in your room.'

Harlan was about to tell her exactly what he thought of her idea when a uniformed policeman approached. It was the same sergeant who had helped bring in Thom Wilson earlier that day. Harlan was expecting the man to report everything was now secure and he could bugger off home.

'Everything okay, sergeant? Um, sorry the name's gone. Been a long day.'

'Sergeant Ian Lawrie, sir. And no, I'm afraid to say nothing's exactly okay. We've got a serious incident just down the road. Another body. You better come have a look.'

Harlan dropped the cigarillo and ground the embers under his heel. 'Lead on, Sergeant Lawrie.'

As he and Cara accompanied Lawrie down the hill, Harlan could see the press milling around the junction of New Road and Main Street. Exactly where Thom Wilson said he met Moira Harris the night before. There were police vehicles blocking off the road in both directions to any traffic, and scene of crime tape was stopping anyone from entering the lane running behind Main Street, the same lane that bordered the cemetery.

Harlan ignored the flashing cameras as he and Cara stooped under the tape and were led twenty feet or so along the lane to where temporary plastic sheeting blocked the lane from public view. A uniformed PC held the barrier aside and Harlan's breath caught in his throat. There was a body suspended halfway up the wall that separated the cemetery from the lane. Looking closer he could see a rope had been looped over the cemetery railings fifteen feet above their heads, the other end tied around the neck of the dead man. The rope was decorated with green Christmas tinsel.

The body had been stripped naked, the feet and hands crudely hacked off. The worst of it was that Harlan recognised the man.

It was Adam Brock.

The drive back to Cathedral House seemed to take longer than it really was. Harlan's head was pounding from sheer exhaustion and the weight of yet another horrific death – this one maybe indirectly attributable to him. He shouldn't have ordered Brock out to Brackenbrae as Stella Wilson's designated driver. At the time he'd viewed it simply as a punishment detail, yet another cheap kick up the arse for Brock's complicity in Kelly's dirty tricks campaign. And now Brock was horribly dead.

But how could it have happened in the first place? All Brock had to do was drop the bloody woman off and go home. Harlan wondered if he'd pushed Brock too far. Had the DS decided to show everyone he wasn't the idiot they assumed him to be? Tried to prove Harlan wrong by going it alone and cracking the case wide open through his own efforts? And where had it got him? Strung up by the neck with his hands and feet missing.

Harlan ran a red light coming off the dual carriageway at the Royal Infirmary. He wasn't looking forward to the early morning briefing with DCS Walker. With Tim Hughes and Steve O'Hara already in custody, who else was out there killing people? Had Dolman recruited a small army of sexual predators to carry on the good work after his death? This thought caused the ache in his head to edge up another notch. The only thing he intended doing before sleeping was to examine the letter in his coat pocket.

Parking in the tiny car park at Cathedral House he turned off the engine and pulled out the envelope. It was made from expensive vellum and was completely unscathed. On the front of the envelope two words had been written in a flowery script with a fountain pen: *Heart Swarm*. What the hell? It was the same phrase Dolman had daubed in blood on the oil painting in his home. What did it mean? Harlan turned the envelope over and saw it was sealed with a blob of red wax. He ran his finger over the seal, hesitating to open the envelope. Did he really want to see what was inside? Breaking the seal would mean invalidating the deal he'd made with Howie Danks.

With a groan he performed his usual contortionist act squeezing out the car before walking around the hotel to the side door. Climbing the spiral stairway made his tired legs ache, and when he finally opened his room door and spotted a hunched silhouette smoking at the open window he decided he might bodily throw Archie down the stairs. The only trouble was, when he kicked the door closed and switched on the light, he saw the figure sitting by the window wasn't Archie.

'I'll have that if you don't mind, DI Harlan,' said Ray Talbot using a combat knife to indicate the envelope Harlan still held in his hand. 'Nice and easy now, no stupid moves.'

Very slowly, unable to take his eyes from the knife, Harlan stepped forward and handed the envelope to Talbot before retreating back a few steps.

Talbot took a quick look at the unbroken seal on the envelope and smiled as he slipped it inside his leather jacket. 'Good lad. If you'd gotten a bit nosy and peeked in there I'd have no other choice than to stick a few holes in you. Even I wouldn't dare read what's in there. Personally I'd be more than happy to cut your throat whether you peeked or not, but my employers have given implicit instructions where you're concerned. You've done what they asked so they'll keep their side of the bargain.'

Harlan dimly realised he'd got it all wrong about Talbot. He hadn't been working with the Reverend Simon Dolman after all; he was with the other side – Danks' friends.

Talbot flicked his cigarette out the window. 'My employers are going to be very pleased. You've saved them a great deal of embarrassment.'

Harlan took a deep breath. *Employers?* Talbot wasn't even part of this mysterious group. Just the hired muscle. 'So we're finished then?'

Talbot gave a nasty chuckle and picked up the lucite cube holding the tarantula, hefting it in his hand. 'Not by a longshot, my friend. My employers need you to perform one last small favour. These people causing havoc in Brackenbrae. They want them handed over for questioning. Dolman may have told them things my employers don't want being repeated in court. So you carry on with your investigation, arrest the guilty parties, then drop the charges and let them walk. We'll pick them up and do the rest.'

Harlan couldn't believe what he was hearing. 'What? How am I supposed to do that?'

'You're a very resourceful man, Harlan. You'll find a way. I hear you already have three persons of interest in your loving care. I'll expect them to be released tomorrow.'

'But I don't even know if they're guilty yet.'

Talbot began scoring the tip of his blade across the lucite cube. 'No need to worry about that. I like knives, I'm very good at using them, but to me it's all about a quick slash across the jugular or a thrust into a vital organ. No finesse, if you get my meaning. But I've got a friend who's a real artist with a blade. This friend of mine can tease any amount of secrets from a man no matter how determined he is keep his trap shut.'

'And if I don't release them? What then? You going to kill me?'

'That would stupid. First we have to try some friendly persuasion.' Talbot slipped his hand through the open window and placed the tarantula on the window ledge, then casually nudged it off. Harlan heard the lucite cube strike the pavement below. 'Oops. Sorry about that. I hate spiders.'

Talbot fished inside his jacket and removed a small cellophane bag, which he tossed on to the bed before standing and moving towards the door. 'I'll leave you with a token of our strong resolve. Sleep tight, DI Harlan.' And then Talbot was slipping out of the door, quickly vanishing down the spiral staircase.

Harlan briefly thought about following him, chasing him down the stairs; but Talbot was a killer, and Harlan was exhausted and unarmed. It would only end badly. Instead he locked the door, then examined the small cellophane bag Talbot had left behind. Inside the bag was a pair of gold earrings. The same pair he'd given Holly as a Christmas present.

Chapter 13

Steph's voice was like a thermal lance burrowing a scorched channel directly into his brain.

'I don't believe this! What sort of stupid fucked up thing have you gone and done now? You put all our lives in danger and then have the barefaced cheek to say you can't even comment on what it's about? I want a twenty-four hour police guard outside our house right now. If you don't arrange it I'll call 999 and do it myself!'

The last sentence was screamed at him in such a high pitch that Harlan had to fight against placing his hands over his ears.

'You can't, Steph. It'll only make things worse.'

'Worse! How much fucking worse can it be? A psychopath tramping through our house? In our daughter's bedroom?' Steph suddenly clutched her dressing gown around her and burst into tears.

On the couch a pale-faced Holly sat silently staring at him with big frightened eyes. Harlan rubbed at his cheeks unsure how things had taken such a bad turn. It would be easy to tell himself all this was out of his control, but he had only himself to blame getting involved with Danks' friends, accepting their tainted offer to resurrect his career and in doing so he'd put Holly's life in danger. Why hadn't he seen this coming?

He'd driven straight over the house in Garrowhill, waking them all up hammering on the door, then tried explaining the position they were in. Holly had confirmed her earring was missing which meant Talbot had definitely been here.

Rob came into the lounge and handed Harlan a black coffee. 'You look awful, Will. When was the last time you slept properly?'

Harlan sipped at the brew, wincing as it burned his lips and tongue. 'I'm fine. Did you check the windows to see if that's how he got in? Any left open?'

'Nothing to report. It's possible he managed to pick the lock on the back door, but how he managed to disable the alarm? I mean, it's a state of the art system. Thank God we were out this evening.'

'The alarm probably wouldn't trouble this guy.'

'Will, please run this past me again. I know you say you can't go into details, but is it tied in with that IP address you made me access?'

He felt Steph's glare laser its way from the armchair she was slumped in. 'Um… well, yes, in a manner of speaking. Look, as I've already tried to explain, it's very complicated.'

Rob crouched down in front of him. 'On the late night news it said there was a police officer murdered in Brackenbrae this evening, as well as some sort of explosion in the cemetery. Is this all connected with the break-in?'

He had trouble meeting Rob's gaze. 'It might be. Look, I'm so sorry about all this. I really am.'

'And why can't we get police protection? Not sure I fully understand that bit.'

Because if you did, I'd have to explain what Ray Talbot was doing in my room and why he thinks he has enough leverage to order me around. And if I get fired and sent to prison there's nothing to stop these people making good on their threat to kill Holly just to punish me further.

'Like I said. I can't really explain yet. It would just be safer if you didn't.'

Rob laid his hand on Harlan's arm, forcing him to meet his stare. 'Will, Steph is right, we can't just sit here waiting for this intruder to return. You have to give us something. Anything. Otherwise we will contact the police and report the break-in and the threat on Holly's life.'

Harlan shook his head. Not in refusal, just to clear some of the tiredness. 'All I can say is that the same intruder broke into my room at the hotel. He wants me to do something for him. Something very wrong. Then he gave me the earrings. He didn't actually threaten Holly's life. It was implied.'

Steph leapt from the armchair. 'What? He was in your room? Why didn't you arrest him there and then! Isn't that what your fucking job is?'

Even through the heavy layer of guilt Harlan felt his own anger rise. 'Because he had a huge knife he was going to gut me with. That's fucking why.'

He immediately regretted his harsh words as across the room Holly began to cry. Even Steph lost some of her fury and went across to comfort their daughter.

Rob straightened up. 'So what do we do? We can't stay here with a knife-wielding madman lurking in the shadows.'

Harlan placed his coffee mug on the carpet and stood too. 'I want you all to jump on a flight first thing tomorrow, or later this morning, I mean. Book a short holiday somewhere. Anywhere. This will all be over in a few days. I promise you. If it's not, do what you think needs done.'

Rob sighed. 'I guess my programmers will get by without me for a short time.' He turned to where Steph cradled Holly against her chest. 'We need to go pack, girls.'

Harlan moved towards Holly, intending to murmur some assurances and maybe, if she let him, give her a kiss, but Steph's hissed snarl was so like that of a she-cat defending her young that he backed away in case her claws decided to rake down his face.

With a last few muttered apologies to Rob, he left the house and walked into the bleak night.

'If nothing else, Harlan, you do appear to have made some progress, although I'm not sure if we're any closer to solving this investigation.' DCS Walker tapped his fingers on his desk. Percussive punctuation. 'On the plus side we have three men in custody, while the down side is we've lost Detective Sergeant Adam Brock in brutal and horrendous circumstances. Somehow I don't think the scales quite balance out. Wouldn't you agree?'

Harlan kept his eyes firmly fixed on Walker's desk. 'Yes, sir.'

Beside him, he could feel Scanlon drawing him a cold look. Scanlon thought Harlan had blood all over his hands regarding Brock's death, and while he hadn't directly accused him of sending Brock to the execution block, Scanlon had forcibly reminded him that he'd recommended Brock be sent straight home instead of being ordered out to Brackenbrae on a fool's errand. They already had a statement from Stella Wilson who claimed Brock had dropped her off and then driven away, but no one knew where he'd gone or why. His burned out car had been found in a muddy field a mile outside Brackenbrae.

'If you don't mind me saying so, Harlan. You look like shit.'

In truth Harlan had barely closed his eyes, wondering how he could see justice done, and at the same time protect his daughter against Talbot's implied threat. Rob had texted him saying they were booked on a ten o'clock flight, but didn't say to where. He found he didn't believe Talbot would really go after Holly. Whoever Talbot worked for wanted these high-profile killings to go away as much as the police did. Murdering another child wouldn't be in their interests. It would only draw more attention to their existence. Therefore Talbot was bluffing. A scare tactic to make him cooperate.

Aware Walker was waiting for an answer, he said, 'Had a bad night, sir. Didn't sleep much.'

The DCS peered closely into Harlan's face. 'No. I suppose you didn't. Tell me about the explosion in the cemetery.'

'I'm sure Dave Campbell will have a full report for us soon enough, but basically Dolman planted a grenade in the coffin with the firing pin attached to a wire. When the lid was removed the grenade went bang. We were lucky no one was killed. It proves conclusively Dolman planned ahead for the exhumation. At this moment in time I can't speculate why, however.'

'And while this was taking place, Brock's killer took advantage of the diversion to hang him up like a side of beef in a butcher's window.'

'Seems like it, sir.'

Walker lifted his coffee cup and took a sip. He hadn't offered either Harlan or Scanlon a refreshment. 'So where do we go from here? These men who are currently in custody. Do we think they're involved in all this carnage?'

Scanlon said, 'Tim Hughes is definitely in this up to his armpits. We'll be stripping down his car this morning to search for forensic evidence tying him to Devlin O'Hara's murder. We're also waiting for a report on materials found in his home. DVDs and suchlike. It's possible Hughes may also be involved in uploading videos to the website showing men having sex with dead children.'

Walker looked at Harlan. 'This was the website Howie Danks gifted to us? The one you never thought worth mentioning to me when you returned from Barlinnie?'

Harlan squirmed in his seat. 'It was. I, ah… wanted to check it out first in case it was nothing but a bad joke. We still haven't figured out why Danks passed it on.'

The DCS continued staring at Harlan a moment or two longer than was comfortable. His fingers drummed another tattoo on the desk. 'What about Mr O'Hara?'

'Very likely, sir,' Scanlon said. 'Just had an email from the lab stating the baseball bat found in his home is definitely the weapon used to bludgeon both teenagers. The killer wiped down the bat, but the force of impact created small stress fractures that held minute traces of both victims' blood. The metallic paint on the bat also matches fragments found in the wounds. No fingerprints, just glove marks, but I'll be interested to see how O'Hara tries explaining how the bat came to be in his home.'

'Good work. Let me know how it goes. And this third man you've already interviewed, Thom Wilson. Harlan, your memo seemed to infer you believe he's not involved, although he did have a sexual liaison with the murdered girl.'

Before Harlan could reply, again it was Scanlon butting in, as if actively reasserting himself as the chief investigator, wanting Walker to think that although the task had been handed to Harlan, it was really Scanlon driving things along. 'We've more or less ruled him out, sir. Probably release him later this morning.'

'No!' Too late, Harlan realised he had reacted too strongly. Both Walker and Scanlon were staring at him. How could he tell them that Talbot would be waiting outside for Wilson, ready to spirit him away to a dark room where he'd be tortured and disposed of like a piece of unwanted trash.

'I just think… maybe we should hold Wilson a bit longer. He'll likely head straight home and feelings are running high in Brackenbrae right now. For all we know we might be releasing him into the hands of a lynch mob.' He knew this sounded an unlikely scenario, but it was best he could come up with for now.

Scanlon gave him a patronising smile. 'I think DI Harlan is overreacting a little. A lynch mob in Brackenbrae? A slight exaggeration surely.'

Even Walker found it amusing. 'Indeed. I think DI Harlan needs a proper bit of shut-eye more than he thinks he does.'

Inside, Harlan was seething. How dare these smug bastards treat him like a hysterical scaremonger? But what else could he say? If Wilson were released he'd just have to come up with a plan B.

'Anything else I should know about?' asked Walker.

Harlan shook his head, but once again Scanlon was eager to push himself forward.

'I had an email this morning from a contact in the media. They sent over some footage from outside Brackenbrae church on Christmas Day, and I've grabbed a screenshot of the man we believe to be Ray Talbot. I'll have copies printed off and distributed to the officers in Brackenbrae in case he's still in the vicinity.'

Walker looked pleased. 'Excellent. Well done, DI Scanlon.'

Harlan ground his teeth. He was the one who had pointed them in the direction of Talbot. He was the one who had suggested asking the media for the footage. And he was the one who had delegated the task to Scanlon who was now getting all the praise.

Walker rubbed his hands together. 'Gentlemen, I'll leave you to it.'

Realising they were dismissed, Harlan and Scanlon left the superintendent's office. In the corridor Harlan said in a low voice, 'Fuck sake. What was all that in there? Acting like you're back in charge.'

Scanlon gave him a steely look. 'Perhaps I should be.'

'And what's that supposed to mean?'

'Maybe if I was running this investigation Adam Brock would still be alive. You really couldn't resist twisting the knife, could you? And now look where that's got us.'

Harlan felt his old dull rage rear up inside him and he barely restrained himself from smacking Scanlon in his big, fat mouth. 'Scanlon, you do realise while you were snoozing in your bed last night, Cara and me were dodging shrapnel from a live fucking grenade. Or is that somehow my fault as well?'

At this, Scanlon did have the decency to look abashed. 'I am sorry about that, Harlan. It must have been a frightening experience. But when all is said and done, both of you are safe and unscathed while poor Adam Brock is dead.'

With that, Scanlon stiffly marched away towards the stairs leaving Harlan to trail behind in his wake.

A night in the cells didn't seem to have abated Steve O'Hara's show of belligerence any. He sat across the table from Harlan and Scanlon, heavily muscled arms folded, eyes blazing with rage.

Scanlon was saying, 'Just for the recording, can you confirm you are Steve O'Hara, resident of Brackenbrae?'

'And who else would I fucking well be?' spat O'Hara.

His duty solicitor, a thirty-something woman with bright orange hair and large glasses, laid a calming hand on his arm. Harlan saw O'Hara's forearm muscles tense as she made contact. The bloke was really wired and set to go off if pushed the wrong way. He was glad both Cara and Jinty Shields were in the room in case things kicked off. Cara's cheek was red and swollen from where the splinter had lodged in her face. She'd be meaner than usual and love it if O'Hara tried anything.

'Just answer the question please,' said Scanlon.

There was long pause, then, 'Yes, that's me,' O'Hara finally responded through gritted teeth.

'Could you run us through your movements on the night of the twenty-sixth, the night your stepson Devlin went missing?'

'Dev.'

'What?' Scanlon looked confused.

'I said his name was Dev. No one called him Devlin.'

Scanlon shook his head. 'Whatever. Just run us through where you were that night.'

Harlan saw O'Hara breathe heavily through his nostrils as if willing himself not to leap over the table and take a swing at Scanlon.

'Like I already told your friend there,' his eyes swivelled to Harlan, 'Dev left the house about half six to go to his mate's. I left the house around seven to go for a few pints.'

Scanlon ruffled his notes. 'Would that have been before seven or after seven? I have a statement from your wife who thought it was maybe about ten to seven.'

O'Hara bared his teeth. 'I don't fucking remember. This is ridiculous. My stepson has been murdered, and you're wasting time pulling me in instead of finding the fucker who done it.'

'How long did you stay at the pub, Mr O'Hara?' Scanlon continued, ignoring the outburst.

'Dunno, about two and a half hours, probably. Billy the barman will testify to that.'

'You remember meeting Thom Wilson?'

'That crippled cunt. Yes, I did. How that bastard had the nerve to sit there and talk about football after what he'd just done. I'll kill him if I get my hands on him.'

'What makes you think Wilson is the guilty party?'

'Because you fucking arrested him, didn't you? The whole street saw you take him away.'

A smug smile appeared on Scanlon's face. 'We arrested you as well, Mr O'Hara. Does that mean you're guilty too?'

O'Hara turned his head and asked his solicitor, 'Do I have to sit here and listen to this shit?'

The woman gave him a sympathetic look, but urged him to carry on.

'So why did you arrest him then?'

Scanlon was smiling again. 'I'm afraid I'm not at liberty to reveal why we thought Mr Wilson might have been of help to our enquiries, but I can tell you he'll be released without charge sometime later this morning.'

Steve O'Hara looked stunned. 'What? So he's out there while I'm in here? That's fucking crazy.'

Scanlon only responded with another infuriatingly smug smile. It dawned on Harlan that Scanlon was deliberately baiting the man, attempting to make him lose his temper, not Scanlon's usual interviewing technique. Then he realised it was because of Adam Brock. O'Hara had decked Brock during the arrest and given him a black eye. What Scanlon was doing was nothing more than goading O'Hara as a form of petty revenge. He knew at some point he would have to step in and take over before O'Hara's inner rage spilled over into outright violence.

O'Hara's anger wasn't sitting right with Harlan. He'd interviewed many guilty men, but none had ever kept up this level of rage. The guilty ones either came across as nervous and frightened, or even appeared icy cool, but never were they this angry.

'What time did you leave the pub?' continued Scanlon.

'Half nine, or thereabouts. When Dev didn't show at ten I tried calling him. Then I phoned his pal and found out he was never there. That's when we got worried and called you lot. Fat lot of fucking good that did. Out searching the woods while he was lying dead right across the road from your fucking gang-hut.'

'And you didn't leave the house after that?'

'No. Look, I already told you all this stuff. I'm not stupid, I know the family are always the first ones to get questioned, but you don't normally lock them up overnight. So what gives, eh?'

Scanlon reached down and from a cardboard box picked up the baseball bat sealed in a transparent plastic bag. 'Can you tell me what this is, Mr O'Hara?'

O'Hara shrugged. 'It's a baseball bat. What of it?'

'Ever seen it before?'

O'Hara looked confused. 'It was in Dev's room yesterday. In the corner. I'd never seen it before. I assumed one of his mates gave it to him as a Christmas present.'

'Would it surprise you to know this bat was used to smash in the heads of both Moira Harris and your stepson?'

O'Hara looked worried. He glanced to his solicitor for advice, but she had nothing to offer.

'What are you saying? That I murdered Dev and that girl? This is fucking madness.'

'What about this, Mr O'Hara?' Scanlon put a polythene-wrapped laptop on the table. 'We found it in your rubbish bin. The casing is cracked open and the hard drive has been ripped out. You told DI Harlan that Dev's laptop was missing. Yet here it is.' Scanlon sat back, arms folded, like a contented man after a fine meal.

O'Hara was now shaking his head. 'I don't understand. I looked for it. Looked everywhere.'

Scanlon leaned forward, steepling his hands beneath his chin. 'It wouldn't be the first time you've killed someone, Mr O'Hara. You did eight years for choking your girlfriend to death. I believe Tim Hughes told you he was being blackmailed and asked for your help. Hughes dropped the money at the lock-ups and drove off while you waited nearby to deal with the blackmailer. When you realised it was Dev you knew you'd have to destroy the hard drive in case it held copies of the incriminating photographs.

'After killing your stepson, you handed the body and the murder weapon over to Hughes and then calmly went to the pub so you'd have an alibi. Then after reporting your stepson missing you left the house again. Perhaps went to Mrs Goldridge's home to check with Hughes that everything was taken care of. Or maybe just to retrieve the baseball bat. On the way back home you ended up in the lane and saw Thom Wilson with Moira Harris. You saw them kissing. You waited until Wilson left and then you murdered the girl. Maybe it was a fit of jealousy. Were you having an affair with Moira, Mr O'Hara? Or did you just enjoy smashing her skull for the sheer hell of it?'

Harlan stared at Scanlon in surprise. This was a variation on what Cara had speculated. What was the bastard playing at? Trying to score brownie points, so he would look like the best man for the job in Walker's eyes?

O'Hara had surged to his feet, despite the efforts of his solicitor to drag him back down. His eyes were practically bulging out of his head, jaw muscles twitching as he shouted, 'You fucking filth! You're fitting me up! What do you mean Dev was blackmailing Tim Hughes? I've no idea what you're fucking talking about. And what's this stuff about Thom Wilson being with Moira? Is he the bastard who planted that bat? Him and that little troll of a wife coming over pretending they were giving us moral fucking support?' Spit was now flying from his bloodless lips. His fists clenched tight.

Harlan saw O'Hara was about to explode and quickly got to his feet. 'Steve. Sit down. I don't believe you killed either Dev or Moira.'

O'Hara stared at him like someone possessed by a demon, but Harlan held the man's crazed gaze, forced him through sheer force of will to step back from the abyss. Harlan sensed both Cara and Jinty Shields had moved forward, ready to spring if O'Hara attacked. They stood that way for almost a full minute and then something dwindled and died in O'Hara's eyes. He slumped back into his seat with his head in his hands.

As Harlan sat back down, sighing with relief, Scanlon snapped at him, 'What the hell you are playing at? I think we should step outside and have a few words in private.'

Harlan ignored Scanlon. 'Steve, what did you mean by the Wilsons coming over to give you a bit of moral support?'

O'Hara peered through his fingers. He looked like a broken version of the man who began this interview. 'They came over, didn't they? Heard Dev was missing. Maureen is friends with Stella. Never understood why. Got a mouth on her like sewer.'

'What time would this be, Steve?' Harlan was keeping his voice low and gentle.

'Sometime after eleven. Can't remember.'

'How long did they stay?'

'About half an hour. Drank a cup of tea and went home.'

'Think carefully, Steve. Were they in your sight all the time?'

O'Hara looked like he didn't understand the question. Then he said, 'They were in the living room with us the whole time.'

'You absolutely sure about that?'

O'Hara nodded, then seemed to remember something. 'When they arrived, Stella asked to use the toilet. She was only in there a few minutes.'

Harlan sat back considering this. Was it possible Stella Wilson had brought the murder weapon with her? Maybe under her coat? Pretended to go to the toilet then slipped into Dev's room and planted the bat? But how would she have got the laptop out? He looked again at the sealed bag on the table, then ripped open the polythene for a better look without touching the casing.

'Harlan, have you gone mad?' said Scanlon. 'That's evidence!'

Harlan tuned Scanlon out, his eyes roving over the laptop. He could see where someone had used something like a screwdriver to prise open the casing and brutally snap back the plastic, but the broken corner of the machine didn't look like it had been damaged by a tool. It looked crushed, the sort of damage caused by the impact of having been dropped from a height. In his head he saw Stella place the baseball bat in the corner then pick up the laptop and drop it out the window.

'Oh, fuck. We've got it all wrong.'

Scanlon was staring at him as if he'd lost his marbles. Harlan turned to Cara. 'I need to speak with Thom Wilson. Right now.'

Five minutes later, Harlan, with Cara beside him, sat across from Wilson in the adjoining interview room. Wilson was looking a wreck; hair sticking up all ways, dark eyes set in a pasty white face, his co-ordination jerky.

'Shouldn't my lawyer be here?' he asked. 'You're not supposed to talk to me without my lawyer.'

Harlan shook his head. 'You don't need one, Thom. We won't be bringing any charges against you. I just need a bit of information. About when you and Stella went to visit the O'Haras the night Dev was reported missing.'

'You're not sending me to prison?' Wilson looked astounded. 'I thought...'

'Look, Thom. It was a real shitty thing you did to Moira. Abandoning her in that dark lane. But it doesn't mean I'm going to lump you in with those evil bastards who killed her and turned her into some kind of grotesque peep show. Tell me about your visit to Steve O'Hara's house.'

Wilson clasped his hands in front of him. 'I didn't want to go. I was in a bit of a state. I couldn't stop thinking about what happened with Moira, but Stella insisted we go see Steve and Maureen. Give them a bit of support in their time of need. When Stella's in that sort of mood you don't argue with her.'

'What happened when you first arrived? Did Stella need the loo?'

'How the hell do you know that? Why are you even asking something like that?'

'Yes or no, Thom.'

'Aye, she did. But...'

'And when you left, did Stella go straight home with you?'

'Not right away. When she was washing her hands in the bathroom she'd looked out the window and seen a fox tearing at a rubbish bag in the back court. Said she was going to put it in the bin and kick the fox's arse if it was still there. What's this got to do with anything?'

'One more thing. Do you or Stella own a baseball bat?'

Wilson nodded. 'Stella kept one in her car. She said it was in case she ever broke down and someone tried to take advantage of a woman stranded on her own.'

'Was the bat made of wood?

A shake of the head. 'I think it was one of those aluminium ones. I had to move it a few times when I was putting stuff in the boot. It felt lightweight.'

'Colour?'

Wilson scratched at his unkempt hair. 'Blue, I think. Yes, definitely blue.'

A voice from the door said. 'Detective Inspector Harlan. You cannot interview my client without me being here. You must know that. I'm going to insist…'

Harlan jumped to his feet, grinning at the young duty solicitor. 'He's all yours, Mr Birnie.' He turned back to Wilson. 'Thom, you're free to leave, but I need a quick word before you go. It's really important for your own safety.'

Birnie eyed Harlan suspiciously. 'Is that a threat to my client?'

Harlan brushed past the solicitor at the doorway. 'Believe me, I'm not the one making the threats.'

Once outside the room with the door firmly closed, he said to Cara. 'Get Pete Cooper on the phone. I want him to arrest Stella Wilson for the murder of Adam Brock, Moira Harris, Devlin O'Hara, and Sadie Goldridge. Tell him to take backup. We've no idea what that dangerous little bitch is truly capable of.'

'Can't I go arrest her? I think I might enjoy that.'

'Not enough time. She might already be packing a bag. Let Pete deal with it. I'll let Scanlon know what's going on. Meet me in my office in ten minutes.'

Cara gave a sarcastic curtsy. 'Anything else, *sir*?'

Harlan ignored the jibe. 'Yeah, while you're at it, see if you can find some decent coffee to replace the stuff Brock nicked.'

Striding down the corridor, he knew without looking back that Cara was giving him the finger.

He found Scanlon in the canteen nursing a mug of tea. The big DI didn't look pleased as Harlan sat across from him.

'What the hell were you playing at in there, Harlan? Steve O'Hara was about to break. I'd rattled his cage and he was there for the taking. Then you jumped in with your bloody size nines and killed the interview stone dead. I'm going to have to speak with DCS Walker about this. I'm even starting to think Kyle Kelly may have been right about you. You're a liability.'

Harlan felt like pouring Scanlon's tea over his head to wipe that righteous expression from his face. 'Spare me the sermon, Scanlon. Just listen. We had the wrong Wilson locked up. It was Stella, not Thom we should have been looking at. The baseball bat belonged to her. She planted it in Steve O'Hara's house, and while she was in Dev's room she tossed the laptop out the window into the back gardens. When the Wilsons left, Stella nipped round the back and jemmied it open to get the hard drive, then dumped the casing in the bin.'

Scanlon looked bewildered. 'How do you know all this?'

'Because it's the only way any of it fits. I just asked Thom Wilson about the baseball bat and he told me Stella kept one in her car.'

'He might be lying. It could be his.'

'Thom Wilson didn't kill Moira Harris. It was Stella. I'll have one of the DCs check out the story for her whereabouts on Boxing Day. Bet she was nowhere near her mum's house.' Harlan rubbed at his face. 'This means she was probably responsible for killing Adam Brock. And before you point the finger of blame again, yes, I was the one who put Brock in that car with her. I sent him to his death, okay. I feel bad enough about it without you making it worse.'

Scanlon looked as if he still wanted to say it again anyway, but pursed his lips and stayed silent on the matter. Eventually he said, 'So, what now? Do we go back to Brackenbrae and arrest Stella Wilson?'

'Already in hand. I've instructed Cara to get hold of Pete Cooper and go in mob-handed.'

'What about Tim Hughes? You still think he was involved in all three murders?'

Harlan nodded. 'Definitely. But we need more evidence than just the fact Dev O'Hara was blackmailing him. Hopefully forensics will find something in his house or his car. I'm thinking Stella was the one waiting to bop Dev over the head when Hughes dropped off the money. Then she called Hughes to return and help her transport the body to Sadie Goldridge's house.'

Scanlon sighed. 'I just took a call from Dave Campbell. Hughes' car is clean as a whistle. No blood or even any evidence it had been cleaned recently. The stuff they took from the house only further incriminates Hughes as having used his mother to make sex videos.' Scanlon looked over his shoulder as if to check if anyone was listening, then dropped his voice to a low whisper, making Harlan lean forward to hear.

'They even found a digital tape where he must have left the camera running, and it filmed Hughes joining in the fun.'

The expression of outright incredulity on Scanlon's face was so comical Harlan had to fight off the urge to laugh. He glanced at his watch and the urge to laugh instantly vanished. If he wasn't quick, Thom Wilson might leave and walk straight into the arms of Ray Talbot. Talbot might even have an informer inside the police telling him who to expect.

'Scanlon, why don't you get Hughes' stiff-arsed solicitor back out here and try nibbling around the edges. Confront him with the evidence of his motherfucking. Tell him we've got Stella and she's already blaming everything on him. Make him look at the pictures of the murder scene. Every single one of them. You never know, he might panic and tell you stuff he'd otherwise have kept tight-lipped about.'

Scanlon slurped down the remainder of his tea and stood up. He seemed invigorated. A man with a mission. 'That definitely sounds like a plan. But what about O'Hara? I've left him sitting in the interview room with his duty solicitor.'

'I'll deal with him.'

Just as Scanlon made to move off, DC Montrelle Rigg, the kamikaze artist, came into the canteen and made for their table. He looked from Scanlon to Harlan as if unsure who to report to.

To Harlan's surprise, Scanlon moved off, saying over his shoulder, 'Whatever it is, give it to DI Harlan. He's in charge of this investigation.'

Rigg had a manila folder in his hand. He opened it and removed a single sheet of paper. 'Thought you might find this interesting, sir. It's a list of Simon Dolman's finances and business interests.' Rigg handed the paper to Harlan then pointed to a particular item on the list. 'I was just thinking this might be of significance.'

Harlan stared at what Rigg was pointing at. It might be nothing, but it was worth giving the reels a spin. 'Montrelle, give Pete Cooper a call. Tell him if he's not left Brackenbrae yet, I want him to nip into the mini-market and bring in Mike McBrearty for questioning.'

After quickly checking to see if Thom Wilson was still waiting in the interview room, Harlan said he'd only be a few minutes and quickly went next door where Steve O'Hara sat with his duty solicitor. O'Hara seemed to have regained his composure and was back to sitting with his arms folded and glaring at Harlan with sheer defiance. PC Jinty Shields was still standing sentry duty beside the door in case O'Hara decided to make a break for it. His solicitor, the woman with the orange hair, stood and said, 'When can we expect this interview to resume? This is most irregular. We've been kept sitting here for almost half an hour.'

Harlan ignored the question and said to Steve O'Hara. 'Speaking hypothetically, Steve. If I said that no charges were being brought against you, but that it might be in your best interests to remain in custody for another day, what would you say?'

'I'd tell you to go fuck yourself.'

Harlan nodded. 'Thought as much. In that case I'll have PC Shields escort you back to your cell.' Then, oblivious to O'Hara's shouts of anger, Harlan returned next door to Thom Wilson.

'Thom, listen to me. We're arresting Stella. I think she's deeply involved in all the Brackenbrae murders.'

'Stella?' Thom Wilson looked shocked. 'Jesus fucking Christ, I know Stella is a bit of a tyrant at times, but to actually murder people?' He ran his hands through his hair, trying to absorb the implications of his wife being arrested.

Harlan might have been mistaken, but he thought he saw a flicker of relief kindle in the man's eyes. 'Thing is, Thom. Feelings are running high in Brackenbrae. You might not get a very warm welcome home. I don't want to scare you, but I've received a direct death threat against you.'

Wilson face turned a few shades paler. 'A death threat? From who?'

'Still working on that one,' he lied. 'What I'm getting at, it might be in your best interests to stay here for another day or two, just until everything calms down.'

Wilson's shoulders shook as he buried his face in his hands. 'I can't. I really can't. I'm going insane in here. Cracking up.'

Harlan sighed. He'd half expected this. 'What if I found you somewhere safe? Somewhere nice and comfy. Good food and a TV. It would be like witness protection.'

Wilson nodded. 'Okay, I just can't stay here. I feel like I'm having a breakdown.'

Harlan pulled out his phone. 'Give me a minute.'

He stepped outside and hit speed dial. 'Lenny, I'm looking for a big favour. I need you to put someone up for a night or two. All very hush hush. This guest will have to eat in his room and not poke his nose out the door for any reason.'

Lenny sounded cautious. 'This got anything to do with Brackenbrae?'

'Um… might be.'

Lenny sighed. 'And you'll be footing the bill, yeah?'

'I'll pay for the room,' agreed Harlan.

'Fine then. You bringing him over yourself?'

'Can't. I'll have an officer drop him off. Really appreciate this, mate.'

'Yeah, whatever. Oh, and by the way, Archie needs a word with you. Seemed a bit agitated. You know what that's about?'

'No idea. Maybe he wants some advice on piano arrangements. I'll be in later to make sure my guest is settling in. See you.'

Scrolling through his list of numbers he found the one he wanted.

'Jinty. You manage to escort Steve O'Hara safely to his cell? Yes? Excellent. In that case come and meet me in interview room number two.'

Harlan found Cara in his office reading through the post-mortem reports. On his desk was a jar of instant coffee, a half pint of milk and a kettle. He decided the tide was turning in his favour. He'd just left PC Shields, watching as she smuggled Thom Wilson out the rear car park, Wilson having been instructed to keep his head down until they were well clear of HQ in case Talbot had anyone loitering around the area to monitor all cars and their occupants. And now Harlan had coffee.

He pointed to the items on his desk. 'Where did you steal these from?'

Cara didn't lift her eyes from the reports. 'Scanlon's office. I'd have taken his tea bags as well, but thought I should leave something behind.'

'Very thoughtful of you. You fancy making us both a coffee?'

This time she raised her head to flash a scowl at him. 'I'm not your fucking housemaid. Make one yourself.'

He lifted the kettle to find no water in it, almost complained, then thought better of it. 'So what you doing?'

'Reading your girlfriend's reports.'

'Cara, she's not my girlfriend. Never was. It was a one night stand, okay. I just had too much drink and bad dancing in my system to fight her off.'

'I'll take your word for it.' Cara had returned to reading the report she held. 'What took you so long to get here anyway?'

'Had to bring Scanlon up to speed with the Stella Wilson situation. Bastard was being all sanctimonious with me at first, soon changed his tune however. I've also got Mike McBrearty coming in for a chat. Might be nothing, but worth a punt.'

'Who's McBrearty?'

'The annoying guy in the mini-market where Moira Harris worked. Remember him from Christmas Day?'

Cara looked thoughtful. 'The twat in the hat?'

'That's him.'

'What was all that stuff you were saying to Thom Wilson earlier about needing to speak with him before he left? Something to do with his safety.'

Harlan paused, aware he hadn't told Cara about Talbot's visit the night before. But how could he explain without telling her of his deal with Howie Danks? How would she feel knowing he was in cahoots with a paedophile ring with occult leanings that employed Talbot as an enforcer? It didn't bear thinking about, so instead he told her the same sanitised version he'd given Thom Wilson.

'There was a death threat. Probably some bampot from Brackenbrae. People believe he's the killer because we arrested him. Probably be even worse now we're nicking Stella. They'll likely take to the streets with flaming brands and pitchforks if they discover Wilson's back in his flat. So I got Jinty Shields to drop him off at Cathedral House. He can stay there for a few days.'

Cara looked astonished. 'You sent him off alone with Honeytrap? Are you a fucking idiot? She'll already have him in some underground parking garage and be gobbling him to death.'

Harlan grinned at the thought. 'She's to deposit Wilson into Lenny's protective custody, then go shopping at Primark. I gave her thirty quid for T-shirts, socks and pants. Enough to get him by for a few days.'

'*Primark*? For thirty quid you could have outfitted him for a two-month holiday in Benidorm. Make sure you get your change.'

'Anyway, once she hands the clothes over, she'll call and let me know everything is cool.'

He pointed to the report she was holding. 'Anything out of the ordinary that helps us in there?'

Cara shrugged. 'Not much, only a tiny detail that conclusively puts Hughes in the frame for at least two of the murders.'

Harlan realised he was still holding the empty kettle. He dropped it on the desk with a clatter. 'What? And you were going to tell me this when?'

'Well, you kept me waiting to go off socialising with Scanlon and Honeytrap. I was beginning to think you'd stood me up. And besides, that body-snatching girlfriend of yours should have pointed this detail out. Maybe not half as clever as she thinks she is.'

'Cara, she is not my fucking girlfriend. Anyway Jo Haney has been run ragged these past few days, examining all those bodies.'

'See? Now you're defending her. How gallant.'

Harlan dropped into his seat. 'Cara…' he said in a warning tone. 'Tell me what you found.'

Five minutes later both he and Cara burst into interview room number one where Scanlon was interviewing Tim Hughes. The murder scene pictures were scattered across the desk and Hughes' solicitor, Jonathan Broomfield, was saying to Scanlon, 'This is unwarranted. You have no evidence my client is directly linked to these murders. Showing Mr Hughes these vile and disgusting photographs is a pointless exercise.'

'Actually, you're wrong there, Mr Broomfield,' said Harlan snatching at a close-up shot of Dev O'Hara and Sadie Goldridge's mouths stitched together.

Scanlon said, 'For the benefit of the recording, DI Harlan and DS McAullay have just entered the room.' He drew Harlan a pained look.

Harlan ignored Scanlon and waved the photo in Broomfield's face. 'Proof of your client's guilt is right here.' He dropped the photo directly in from of Tim Hughes. 'Tell him what the post-mortem reports says, Cara.'

Cara flipped open the report and read, 'The sutures used on the mouths of both Devlin O'Hara and Sadie Goldridge were unusual in respect that they passed through the nasal septum and were tied off on the lower lip.' Cara closed the report.

'Thank you for that, Cara. You see, what is described in that report is a specialist cosmetic technique used only by trained morticians and embalmers. It's to keep the mouths of their deceased subjects from dropping open. If you'll pardon the pun, Mr Hughes – you've stitched yourself up.'

Tim Hughes could have made good use of the same embalming trick when his jaw dramatically dropped open. His eyes were blinking rapidly, a sign his mind was spinning the reels and coming up with nothing each time. Scanlon took the report from Cara to read over what it said, while Broomfield got to his feet shouting this still didn't constitute proper proof.

'What's the betting Mr Hughes, that when we conduct a search of your business premises, we find materials exactly matching the sutures used on Dev O'Hara and Mrs Goldridge?'

Harlan's phone vibrated in his pocket. He read the text then patted Scanlon on the shoulder. 'I think I can leave you to formally charge the suspect, DI Scanlon. It seems Stella Wilson has arrived to help us with our enquiries.'

Chapter 14

Cara was leaning across the interview table, perilously well inside Stella Wilson's grab-zone. 'Your husband told us you were shagging other men. Lots of them. This true, Stella?'

Stella Wilson only grinned back, her jutting lower jaw reminding Harlan of a species of barb-toothed scavenger fish. Cara wasn't fazed by the non-communication. 'I wouldn't have thought that many blind men with no sense of smell lived in Brackenbrae.'

The grin faded for only a second before returning full strength, those slanting teeth bared in mute defiance. It had been this way for the last ten minutes. Cara baiting Stella, hoping to wear her down, Stella grinning right back. She had used this tactic since being escorted in with her appointed duty solicitor, a skinny man with grey skin who looked like he'd rather be in a pub or an AA meeting. He'd already given up objecting to Cara's taunts.

Harlan had already walked Stella through what he believed was her part in things, piecing together his facts then threading bits of guesswork into a sequence he felt was true. He'd told her she was the one who'd struck down Dev with the bat. How both she and Hughes had collaborated in the killing of Sadie Goldridge. How on the way out she couldn't resist adding Moira Harris, who'd simply been in the wrong place at the wrong time, to their tally of murder victims. He then described how she'd managed to plant the baseball bat in Dev's room and chucked the laptop from the window.

Stella had merely grinned.

DC Rigg had checked out Stella's story about visiting her mum on the night of the murders, discovering she hadn't visited that particular old woman for at least a year. When Harlan informed Stella he knew she was lying – she had kept grinning. Harlan had moved onto the killing of Adam Brock; how he believed she had persuaded him to drive to a lonely spot where she had either killed or incapacitated him, driven him back to Brackenbrae in his own car, and when everyone's attention was focused on the exhumation, hacked off his hands and feet, then strung him up.

Stella grinned on.

Harlan was convinced there had to have been at least one other person aiding her. Initially they had assumed Brock's killer was male, as strength was required to hoist Brock up the wall. Stella was bare-sleeved and her arms were flabby. No great muscle strength there. When he'd asked who had helped her with Brock, she had continued grinning. That was the point Harlan handed over to Cara. He didn't think they needed a confession. They would find trace evidence to link her to the bodies, no matter how much time it took. Also Thom Wilson would testify the bat belonged to Stella.

With a jolt, Harlan realised Jinty Shields hadn't called him. It wouldn't have taken her that long to get to Primark and then back to Cathedral House. He felt for his phone and found it wasn't there. He cursed himself inwardly, remembering leaving it down on his office desk after the Hughes interview. Whispering to Cara to keep up the good work, he slipped out the door. The last thing he heard before pulling it closed was, 'Wow, Stella. Great bingo wings. You must really work on those…'

In his office Harlan found the phone exactly where he'd left it. Checking, he saw Honeytrap had tried calling him six times. Before he could even attempt to call her back, there was a sharp rap on his door and PC Shields herself entered, her short, squat frame seeming to fill the entire width of the doorframe. She was holding a plastic bag with Primark printed on the front.

'Been tryin' to call you, sir.'

Harlan held up his phone. 'Sorry, my fault, Jinty. Left this in here while I was interviewing Stella Wilson.' He pointed at the plastic bag she was holding. 'Why have you still got that? You were meant to drop it off at the hotel.'

Honeytrap's hangdog face shook in the negative. 'Bit of a problem. As instructed, I left Wilson outside the hotel and went to get his knickers and socks like you asked. Thing is, when I got back, your landlord said he saw Wilson gettin' approached by a man who'd been waitin' in a parked car across the road. He told me the man might have been Ray Talbot, the ex-cop whose picture got handed out at our briefin' this mornin'.'

Harlan sat down, a feeling of horror sweeping over him. He thought of how scared Wilson had been, and he had sent him straight into the hands of Talbot and his torturer friend. What they would do to him didn't bear thinking about.

Honeytrap dropped the bag onto his desk. 'Maybe you can still get some use from these. They're medium size, so they should fit okay.'

Harlan stared at her, mouth gaping, unable to respond to her practical offer of a dead man's pants and socks. He felt like yelling at her, but it wasn't her fault. She had no way of knowing what Talbot planned to do with Thom Wilson. *This friend of mine can tease any amount of secrets from a man no matter how determined he is to keep his fucking trap shut.*

Numbly he heard himself say. 'Thanks, Jinty. That'll be all for now.'

PC Shields smiled, transforming herself in a gurning caricature. 'I've got your change as well, sir. You always get a good bargain in Primark.'

Harlan waved his hand her. 'Keep it. Buy your next internet date a pint on me.'

'Thanks, sir. Will do, sir.' Shields actually saluted as she left him to his misery and closed the door.

Harlan sat motionless at his desk for five minutes then decided to go talk directly to Lenny. He grabbed his phone and headed back down to the interview room.

Walking in the door he heard Cara say, 'You think Thom only married you because he thought your ugly face might be a miracle cure for premature ejaculation?'

Stella grinned at Harlan as he approached the table, then spoke up for the first time since she'd been brought in. 'I just peed myself.'

The grey-skinned duty solicitor immediately moved his chair away, wrinkling his nose. 'I think my client speaks truly, detectives.'

'Seems a good time to take a break,' Harlan said. 'Cara, you want to wind things up and have Mrs Wilson taken to her cell to get cleaned up? Maybe find some clean clothing for her. Actually, there's a Primark bag on my desk with new underwear and T-shirts. Give her that. Then go get yourself lunch. I've got an errand to run. Tell you about it later.'

Cara didn't seem happy with the arrangement, but nodded her assent. Then, knowing he was already far too late to save Thom Wilson, Harlan headed for Cathedral House.

Lenny was serving two old ladies gin and tonics when Harlan pushed his way into the hotel. He leaned on the end of the bar, waiting impatiently as Lenny bantered with his customers, all smiles and cockney charm, seeming to take an age before he finally came across to have a word.

'Good to see you're still with us, Harlan. Saw on the morning news there was an explosion in Brackenbrae last night. Elsie the cleaner said your bed had been slept in and there was no blood stains on the sheets, so we knew you was probably still in one piece.'

'Dolman booby-trapped the coffin. Stuck an old grenade in there, rigged to go off when the lid was removed. Cara and me were lucky not to get our heads blown off. Actually, I've got a souvenir for you.' He stuck his hand in his pocket, pulling out the *Café Crème* tin with the fragment of grenade casing sticking out. 'Thought maybe you could stick it behind the bar.'

Lenny took the tin, examining it, looking impressed. 'So which part of your anatomy did this save? And don't say it was your heart, I know you ain't got one.'

'My arse.'

Lenny gave a great big belly laugh, then his expression turned serious. 'Sorry, shouldn't laugh, especially now there's a copper dead. They gave his name on the lunchtime news. Brock? Wasn't that the geezer who was fitting you up with the dirty movies?'

'Brock was involved with the stitch-up, but he was only acting as the DCI's errand boy. I feel awful about it. I was the one who ordered Brock to give his killer a run home last night. I may as well have wrapped him up in Christmas paper for the nasty little bitch.'

Lenny laid his hand on Harlan's arm. 'You're not serious are you? How did that come about?'

Harlan shook the hand away. This wasn't the time for tea and sympathy. 'Look, Lenny, I'll explain all this in great detail later. Right now I need to know what went down with Thom Wilson, the guy I wanted looking after.'

Lenny picked up a glass from under the bar and started polishing it. 'It was like I told that uniformed sumo wrestler who brought him here. I was out in the car park having a smoke when she dropped him off. Once she drove away, he stood outside the front doors having a look about. I was about to give him a shout, when suddenly this big geezer with a leather jacket gets out his car and makes a beeline for the guy. Never heard what was said, but the big guy flashes a warrant card and proceeds to lead your bloke to his car and off they go. It wasn't till they pulled away that I got a clear view of his face, and that's when I realised it might have been Ray Talbot. Looks much older now, but it definitely looked like him.'

'You get his registration plate, Lenny? Or even the make of the car? Anything at all.'

Lenny gave a rueful shrug. 'All I can tell you is the car was a dark blue Ford Mondeo. Not much to go on is it?'

Harlan hadn't held out much hope, but still felt a keen lance of disappointment stab at his gut. Thom Wilson would almost certainly be a dead man by the end of the day, if he even lasted that long. Harlan was so busy blaming himself that he almost missed what Lenny said next.

'Sorry… what? Say that again.'

'Just said I thought I recognised who was in the car that pulled out right behind the Mondeo. Only caught a glimpse, mind you, but I'm good with faces. Once seen, never forgotten.'

'Who was it?'

Lenny's answer had Harlan scampering for the door.

He was squeezing into his car when the hunched figure of Archie scurried into the car park after him.

'Mr Harlan. Need to talk to you.'

Harlan groaned. He didn't have time for whatever Archie thought was important enough to seek him out. Especially not after what Lenny had said. Slipping sideways back out the car, he leaned on the top of the door. 'Archie. Sorry, I'm pushed for time right now. Won't this wait?'

Archie stood in front of the car, his gaze as usual on his shoes. He seemed more gaunt and haunted than normal. Harlan thought if a strong breeze came gusting through the car park it would blow Archie all the way across the road into the Necropolis. When he spoke again, Harlan had to strain to make him out.

'It's about Talbot. Somethin' I thought you should know.'

Harlan closed his car door and moved around to where Archie stood. What the hell would the little piano player know about someone like Ray Talbot?

'Talbot?'

Archie shuffled his feet awkwardly. 'I saw him.'

'You mean earlier today?'

A shake of the head. 'Last night. I was stayin' over at the hotel as a room was goin' spare. More comfy than the hostel. Went out for a smoke late on, aye? Was a bit windy so I walked across the road to the old Cathedral gatehouse. I saw him sittin' at your window. He's bad news, Mr Harlan. You need to be careful, son.'

Archie rummaged in his jacket pocket and brought out the lucite cube. 'Thought you might want this back, aye?'

Harlan took the cube, noticing a corner was broken off and a big crack ran across one face of the cube, but the spider inside seemed undamaged by the fall.

'How come you know Talbot?'

'Used to work with him. Years ago, this was.'

'What? You were a cop?'

Archie kept his eyes averted. 'Not a cop, son. I was a *Gamekeeper*, but no' the sort of gamekeeper that catches poachers and the like.'

Harlan rubbed at his eyes, stinging and red from sheer tiredness. Archie wasn't making any real sense and he would have stalled him until later but for the fact Talbot's name was involved.

'Archie, I've not a clue what you're talking about. You want to go inside, it's freezing out here.'

'No' inside, son. They might be listenin'.'

'They? Who are they, Archie?'

'People I need to tell you about.'

Harlan frowned. Did Archie actually think Talbot had bugged the hotel? That was crazy. Or was it? He pointed across to the rising spires of Glasgow Cathedral. 'How about in there? No one's going to be listening in that place.'

Archie raised his eyes and Harlan saw a look of anguish on the little man's face. 'God will be listenin', son.'

'Oh, for fuck's sake, Archie. I'm trying to work with you here. You won't talk to me in the hotel, and now the cathedral is out of bounds. You got any other suggestions?'

Archie inclined his head towards the Necropolis. 'Over there. The dead don't care what anyone has to say.' And without waiting to see if Harlan was agreeable to this, Archie shuffled off towards the Cathedral gatehouse where an iron gate bypassed the main entrance to the cemetery.

Harlan quickly caught up and tried a few times to get Archie talking as they walked, but the little man simply stonewalled him. They crossed the Bridge of Sighs that spanned the ravine where the Molendinar Burn once flowed before it was paved over and renamed as Wishart Street, then followed the winding pathway up the hill of the Victorian garden cemetery until Archie found a bench that afforded a good vantage point where no one could approach them from any direction without being seen. Taking a dust-rag from his coat pocket, Archie wiped a smattering of raindrops from the bench and sat down, indicating to Harlan that he should join him.

From up here the view over Glasgow Cathedral was impressive, although it was disconcerting looking down on the hotel. It seemed toy-like; a tiny play-castle a child had left behind after being called in for supper. Harlan thought one advantage of having this conversation out here in the cold was that he could barely detect the smell from Archie's hair oil.

'Okay, Archie, tell me all about you and Ray Talbot.'

Archie pulled his cigarettes from his pocket and lit one up, then offered the packet to Harlan. It had been a while since Harlan had smoked a proper cigarette, but he accepted as it seemed the right thing to do. A universal gesture of camaraderie.

'Just so you know, Mr Harlan. My real name isn't Archie. That what's they called me at the hostel when I got out the hospital. And that's who I've been ever since.'

Harlan said nothing. He waited to see if Archie would say any more on the subject, but the little man just stared down at the ground, puffing on his cigarette. Harlan guessed if he ever wanted to find out Archie's true identity, his fingerprints would likely be on the system, but what did it matter who he really was?

'I was a bad man once, son. I did bad things. Really bad things, aye?' Archie ground out his cigarette under his shoe, then lit another one. 'I was once employed by a group of people that called themselves the *Circle*.'

Harlan smiled bleakly. 'I take it you're not talking about the Magic Circle?'

The corner of Archie's mouth tugged upwards in acknowledgement of the weak joke. 'It's true enough they did magic, though no' the kind of tricks like Tommy Cooper or Paul Daniels. The Circle were inclined to dabble in much darker stuff, but they do have a habit of makin' folk disappear.'

A woman with a dog on a lead climbed the hill towards them. The dog strained in Archie's direction as the woman drew level with them, maybe attracted to his hair oil, Harlan thought, and the little man reached out to ruffle the dog's shaggy coat. Once the woman and the dog moved on Harlan said, 'Archie, I'm not getting this. Who is this Circle? And what do they have to do with Ray Talbot?'

Harlan saw Archie shiver inside his thin coat. 'Their proper name is the *Circle of the Thirteen Apostles*. A secret society, Mr Harlan.'

Harlan couldn't help smiling to himself. It sounded like something from an outlandish conspiracy novel. Even though Archie didn't so much as glance up, he said, 'It's no' a laughin' matter, son. These people are cruel and dangerous beyond anything you could understand.'

To give himself more time to digest all this information, he asked, 'So is there a hierarchy to this Circle?'

A slight nod of the head. 'The Circle is controlled by an inner sanctum of influential people. Beneath them is the rank and file, followers and believers. I know for a fact there's more than a few senior coppers amongst them. There's maybe a few thousand members of the Circle spread across the country.'

'So how do people find out about this Circle if it's so secretive?'

'Usually by mixin' with the right crowd. They get recruited, but no' the way I was drawn in, I was just a hired thug to start with. These people usually have extreme sexual tastes, they like a bit of violence and blood with their nookie, that's what gets them noticed. Most of them are well-educated professional types. They each pay a tithe to the Circle. It entitles them to certain privileges and protections if they make a mistake. You must have noticed how certain people always seem to be above the law.'

Harlan nodded. There were a few high-profile offenders who constantly flirted with jail time, but whose activities never made it to court. He'd always jokingly ascribed it to Masonic connections. He guessed the list of names he'd retrieved from the exploding coffin must be the ruling members of Archie's mysterious Circle.

'So Talbot is what…? A hit man for this Circle?'

'The top boys have got too much to lose by takin' stupid risks. They enforce their rules over the rank and file by usin' men known as *Gamekeepers*. Men who will stamp out any unsanctioned transgressions and silence wagging tongues. Men who can arrange a steady stream of warm bodies for their rituals and ceremonies, and then dispose of the evidence without shirkin' from their duties. Men who obey without question. Men like Ray Talbot. Men like Howie Danks.'

Danks. A few of the pieces were finally dropping into place.

At last, Harlan saw where all this was leading to. 'You were one of these Gamekeepers, Archie?'

'I was, son.'

'And you… you supplied children for these people to rape and murder?' Harlan could barely believe what he was asking. How could Archie, the likeable little piano player be involved in something so evil and depraved?

'No' just children. Don't go makin' the mistake of thinkin' the Circle is simply another sad bunch of child molesters. Their tastes are much more diverse. Boys, girls, men and women of all ages. As a copper I'm sure you have a rough idea of how many people vanish every year. They just disappear from their lives and are never seen again. Many of them end up in the hands of the Circle. Being sexually savaged by one of the inner sanctum and their friends during a religious ceremony is merely the warm-up act. It's what comes after that would sicken you. Frenzied beatin's, broken limbs, flesh slashed and hacked and bitten, until what's left requires to be put out its misery and buried. That was part of my job description.'

'Was Simon Dolman part of this Circle?'

A nod of the head. 'Aye, son. Their spiritual adviser. He would have been well in with the top boys.'

'Why are you telling me all this, Archie?'

Archie dropped yet another cigarette butt to the ground. 'I'm tryin' to save you, son.'

'Save me?' Harlan felt a ball of anger well up in his throat. 'What the fuck do you mean by that?'

'Whatever you've got goin' on with Talbot. He's bad news. When I worked with him he was still a cop. A cop who believed in the Circle's doctrine. I'm guessin' he's now a Gamekeeper. If you don't take him down, he'll destroy you, son. One way or the other.'

Harlan checked his watch, surprised to see how much time had passed sitting here with this man he'd always thought of as a harmless eccentric. A man who'd just told him of his involvement in kidnap, rape and murder. There was so much he wanted to ask Archie about this Circle of the Thirteen Apostles, but given Archie's long absence from their ranks it was unlikely he would be able to supply the answers he needed. One question however, he had to ask.

'How did you get out, Archie? I'm sure they didn't simply let you walk away.'

Another cigarette was lit. 'No one walks away. They stamp down hard on anyone they think is puttin' them at risk. Even Howie Danks got thrown to the dogs when he started takin' his work home with him. If he hadn't still been useful to them inside the jail, he'd have been squashed like a bug.'

'You know Howie Danks?'

'Aye, he was a Gamekeeper, same as me, one of the best they ever had.'

'Were you still working for this Circle when I caught Danks?'

'No, I was long gone by then. Read it all in the papers though, aye? Realised what must have happened. No disrespect, son, but no one would have caught Danks if he hadn't been told to give himself up. He was far too clever.'

Harlan didn't know whether to feel shocked or disappointed to have it confirmed that his high-profile arrest of Danks had been a sham. He remembered Danks' parting words to him the day before. *Didn't those blue larkspurs ever bother you?* The bastard had been mocking him.

'So how did you manage to get away when a smart-arse like Danks ended up doing life in Barlinnie?'

'Pure fluke, son. I'd got to the point where even a bad wee bastard like me couldn't handle it any longer. I began using drugs to get through the worst of it, heroin mostly at the end. I started fuckin' things up, gettin' sloppy. They had Howie Danks deal with me. They knew about my drug habit so they had Danks dose me up with enough skag to kill a normal user, and then drop me off a bridge into the Clyde. Probably the only job he ever screwed up. I washed up about two miles down the river. I was in a coma for months. When I woke up I told the doctors I'd no idea who I was and when they discharged me I ended up as a homeless junkie livin' rough for the next eight years. The Circle thought I was dead. Forgot all about me. But if Talbot's been hangin' about the hotel he might have recognised me. If he did, sooner or later he'll come back.'

Harlan got to his feet. He'd intended immediately pursuing Lenny's surprising bit of info, but maybe he could stop Talbot in his tracks another way. 'I have to go. Some things won't keep.'

Archie stared up at him, his face impassive. 'You should really arrest me, son.'

Harlan stared down at the little man. He should have felt repulsed at being anywhere near him, but Archie was no longer the violent enforcer who had served this mysterious Circle. The coma and the drugs had changed him, broken him completely. Probably there had been a substantial amount of brain damage incurred into the bargain. All Harlan could feel for Archie right now was a deep sense of pity.

'You're right, I should arrest you, but meaning no disrespect, Archie, I've got bigger fish to fry right now.'

As he walked away, Harlan thought he heard the sound of Archie weeping quietly.

Chapter 15

Arriving at Barlinnie prison, Howie Danks was waiting for him in the same blue-painted room as before. The serial killer regarded Harlan with his usual implacable expression before gesturing to the empty chair across the table. Although it had only been a single day since he'd last sat here facing Danks, so much had happened he felt like weeks or even months had passed.

'I hear congratulations are in order, DI Harlan. You've made some influential people very happy, but I'm sure you're not back here just so I can stick a gold star on your report card.'

'Cut the crap, Danks. I kept my side of the deal and almost got blown up for my trouble, so tell your friends in the Circle to call off their attack dog, or should that be Gamekeeper, Ray Talbot.'

For a brief second Danks' sphinx mask slipped just a fraction, his eyes widening slightly before the shutters slammed back down presenting Harlan once more with an expression that reminded him of a still body of water. Yesterday that mirror-flat countenance had suggested serenity and calmness. Now it felt like something was treading water beneath the surface ready to strike and eat him alive. It occurred to him he may have made a huge mistake coming here and showing his hand.

Danks' voice was low and quiet. 'The Circle? Gamekeepers?'

Too late now to take it back. All he could do was plough ahead and hope for the best. 'The Circle of the Thirteen Apostles. I've heard their name mentioned and how they recruit men called Gamekeepers to act as their enforcers.'

Danks surprised him by smiling widely. 'Somehow I don't believe Mr Talbot was so loose-lipped to have passed on that information. You mind telling me where you heard it?'

For a moment Harlan wondered if he would be doing Archie a favour by throwing him to the wolves and ending his tortured existence, then found he couldn't, even if Archie was guilty of what he claimed he'd done in the past. It would be like strangling a sad-eyed puppy. 'Sorry. Not at liberty to say. But you seriously need to get Talbot off my case before I lose my patience and bring him down. I'm sure your precious Circle wouldn't want that sort of complication.'

Danks softly drummed his fingers on the table. 'DI Harlan. Exactly what is Talbot doing to annoy you so much?'

'He's demanding I drop the charges against my suspects in the Brackenbrae killings then hand them over to be tortured and disposed of. And if I fail to comply he's made it clear my daughter is fair game for whatever punishment he thinks is appropriate. The fucker even broke into her bedroom and stole some personal items so I'd know he was serious.'

Danks' fingertips continued their feather-light rhythm making Harlan think of an execution drum roll. He tensed, ready to put up some sort of a defence when those fingers finally came to a halt. It took a full thirty seconds for them to do so. Harlan braced himself to fight for his life.

'Fine.'

Harlan slumped in his chair feeling cold sweat pool in the small of his back. 'What?'

'I said fine. I'm sure it's all a misunderstanding, but I'll pass on the message.'

So much for Danks leaping across the table and beating him to death.

'So then, DI Harlan. Is that all I can do for you today?' Danks was smiling but there was a distinct tone of mockery in his voice.

What the hell, Danks would probably call the meeting to a halt, but there was no harm in asking. 'Tell me about the Circle. I'm intrigued.'

Instead of immediately calling for the prison guards, Dank's inclined his head to one side and closed his eyes as if conferring with an inner voice only he could hear. When his eyes opened once more he asked, 'Are you sure, DI Harlan? Once something is known it cannot become unknown.'

Unsure if he was being threatened or not Harlan nodded.

Danks pulled out his tobacco pouch and rolled a smoke, today not offering the pouch to Harlan. He lit up, took a few deep puffs and said, '*A great, ever-ravenous mouth in the centre of the heavens, eternally guarded by thirteen apostles fleshed in light.*'

'What?'

Danks' words caused something to resonate in Harlan's head, but he couldn't think what it was.

'It's a quote. Inscribed in stone above the chapel door the Circle worship in. You see it in other places too. On wooden plaques on the walls of the big country estate they use for their get-togethers. Some of them even have it tattooed on their flesh.'

'A quote from what? The Bible?'

Danks sniggered. 'Depends whose Bible we're talking about. Let me explain. The Circle have been around for hundreds of years. A man called John Stearne started everything back in the seventeenth century. He was a wealthy landowner paid by the Church to examine women accused of witchcraft. He was the mentor to Matthew Hopkins, the notorious Witchfinder General, no stranger himself to inflicting a bit of pain and torture upon helpless peasants. Stearne was the one who had this vision of the great mouth in the centre of the heavens guarded by thirteen apostles. This mouth spoke to him in his vision. Told him that men like him were born to rule and control the weak fools they lived amongst. Wolves among sheep, yes? He believed this great mouth was the true face of God, a god of chaos and suffering. He found others like himself, men driven by violence and lust to do terrible things, and they founded The Circle of the Thirteen Apostles. Stearne claimed his God demanded tributes in return for wealth and power.'

'Tributes? You mean human sacrifices?'

'Not just killing people. Any act that involved pain, rape, torture and death. There was usually a major sexual element to the rituals, and they believed their God devoured every drop of misery their acts could wring from the poor souls who fell into their hands.'

An image suddenly sprang into Harlan's head. The painting in Simon Dolman's house. *Sagittarius A* – the super-massive black hole orbited by thirteen stars. *A great ravenous mouth in the centre of the heavens eternally guarded by thirteen apostles fleshed in light.* But how could this John Stearne have a vision of something that wouldn't be theorised about for another three hundred years? It all sounded crazy. Then Harlan remembered something else about the painting.

'What does *Heart Swarm* mean?'

Danks relit his roll-up. 'How do you know about Heart Swarm?'

'Dolman daubed it on a painting he had at home. He also wrote it on the envelope I rescued from Debbie Fletcher's coffin.'

'You have to remember, DI Harlan, the Circle is a religious organisation and as devout about worshiping their God as any Islamic terrorist, but their particular method of worship has almost destroyed them a few times over the years. Always the risk of discovery by the authorities. They learned to modify their behaviour, hatches bolted down fast, controls and protocols becoming as much a part of their culture as the compulsion to dominate and destroy. *Chaos within order.* A paradox that became their motto. They minimise the risks of exposure; keeping everything below the surface. And if something does go wrong, they've long had senior police officers under their thumb, either by recruiting them as believers, or simply blackmailing them. Everyone has a dark, dirty secret, DI Harlan. Even you.'

Harlan squirmed on the inside. Right now his dirty secret was actually working for these deluded bastards.

'The thing is, every religion has its radicals and zealots. Some believe that chaos within order is a slap in the face for their God. These extremists want to have chaos *without* order. Sheer anarchy. Undiluted faith. Every so often they slip the leash and form their own little splinter groups, secretly recruiting from outside the Circle those they feel might be drawn in to their own private vision. Those in the mainstream organisation refer to this hard-line stance as going Heart Swarm. It comes from something Stearne was told in his vision. *I am the face in the dark. I am the heart of the swarm.*'

Harlan flinched. Those had been the last words Dolman said before hanging himself.

'The radicals in particular are fond of that line. Shout it out as a show of defiance when they get caught and executed for heresy. They endanger everything the Circle has striven for. Going out their way to make a public show of their handiwork.'

Harlan was having trouble taking all this in, even though it did possibly explain so much regarding the sheer savagery and grotesque nature of the murders. He thought of the way Debbie Fletcher had been left hanging from a tree, not once but twice. The way the three dead bodies had been posed. And even Brock's murder was deliberately arranged to cause maximum shock value. It also explained why Dolman had left the envelope in the coffin instead of simply emailing the names to the press. He'd tried to expose his peers in the most macabre fashion possible. It was madness, but in all probability the majority of these people were insane.

Danks stubbed out his smoke in the little foil ashtray. 'And that's probably all you need to know for now, DI Harlan.'

'One more thing. Do you really believe in all that stuff about a black hole being some sort of God?'

Danks slipped his tobacco punch back into his shirt pocket. 'In all honesty I've never felt the need of any God's approval to kill.'

'Wouldn't your friends in the Circle be pissed off to know about your lack of faith?'

Danks didn't just smile this time. He grinned. 'My friends in the Circle? Don't you mean *our* friends, DI Harlan? Once you know about the Circle – you're part of the Circle. Otherwise you tend to end up dead.'

'Where the fuck have you been?' Cara was sitting with her Doc Martens up on his desk, hands behind her head.

Harlan gave her an indignant look. 'I was working. What are you doing in my office?'

'Hiding.'

'What? Who the hell are you hiding from?'

Cara's finger tenderly rubbed at her wounded cheek. 'That pompous arsehole Scanlon.'

'That's Detective Inspector Scanlon to you.'

'Fine. I've been hiding from that pompous arsehole Detective Inspector Scanlon.'

Harlan sat behind his desk. He needed to make a phone call, but not one he particularly wanted Cara listening in to. To get rid of her he'd have to play along for a time. 'Okay, so why are you hiding from Scanlon?'

Cara's feet swung off the desk. 'I'll tell you why. He's been ordering me around like I'm his personal skivvy since I got back from lunch. Getting me to call the forensic lab three times an hour to find out if anything new has come up.'

'And do they have anything new?'

'That's not the fucking point. You're supposed to be running this investigation, so if anyone should treat me like a skivvy, it should be you. Not that you'd be stupid enough to try.'

'Cara, I'm dead on my feet. I've so much still to do. Please tell me if forensics have anything useful.'

'They've recovered DNA from Brock's body. Traces of saliva on his cock to be exact.'

'So now we know how Stella managed to lure Brock to his death.'

Cara's face was twisted in disgust. 'Just when I thought Stella Wilson couldn't possibly be any more of a sleazebag. I mean, sucking off Brock? What kind of lowlife skank is she?'

He wanted to tell Cara she should more respectful to the dead, but knew he'd only sound like a hypocrite. 'Once we get a DNA sample from Stella, I bet it ties her directly to Brock. Probably everyone else as well. I don't envy the poor bastard who has to take a DNA swab. She'll bite their fingers off if she gets half a chance.'

Cara's eyes gleamed. 'Already got one.'

He was impressed. 'You managed to talk Stella into giving up a DNA swab? How did you manage that?'

'Didn't need to. I just bagged her pissy knickers and sent them straight to the lab.'

'Um... good work. Rather you than me. So where's Scanlon?'

'Interviewing Stella.'

'Then why aren't you in there with him?'

'It wasn't as much fun as this morning. Scanlon wouldn't let me continue insulting her.'

'To be honest, your bear-baiting tactic wasn't exactly getting us anywhere.'

'It got us a DNA sample.'

He had to concede the point. His phone rang and he found himself speaking to a Sergeant Stark from Kirkintilloch police station.

'How can I help you, Sergeant?'

'Sorry to bother you, but I was told to report anything with a connection to Brackenbrae, and you were the contact given.'

'So what have you got?'

'Probably means nothing. We had some cars broken into on Christmas Eve in the Cowgate car park. One of our boys was running through the CCTV footage and noticed what looked like a possible drugs hand-over around ten thirty p.m. We checked out the registration of the van caught on camera, and the owner happens to be a resident of Brackenbrae. Like I said, probably nothing to do with your investigation, but thought I should pass it on anyway.'

Harlan rolled his eyes at Cara who was staring at him impatiently. 'Who was registered against the vehicle?'

'A Michael McBrearty. I've emailed you the clip if you want to have a look, but the image is grainy and it's hard to make much out.'

Harlan sat bolt upright. 'Thank you, Sergeant Stark. Did you by any chance get the registration of the other car?'

'Sorry, he'd parked in the camera's blind-spot.'

Harlan thanked Stark and hung up, quickly opening his email.

'What is it?' asked Cara.

'Come round and have a look.'

On screen was a grainy black and white clip of McBrearty getting out his van and handing over a package to a man wearing a hoodie.

'So much for McBrearty saying he never left the shop on Christmas Eve.'

Cara's face was screwed up. 'What was McBrearty handing over? Cheap groceries past their sell-by date?'

Harlan grimaced. 'I might have an idea about that. Look, do me a favour. I need McBrearty interviewed, but first I need to speak with him alone. You fancy having him brought up for me? By the time he gets his solicitor sorted out I'll know what I need to know.'

Cara's eyebrows were dark arches of inquisition. 'Which is?'

Harlan broke eye contact, staring down at his desk. 'Best if I tell you later. If I'm wrong I don't want to look like a twat.'

The nasty curl on Cara's lips told him she already had a solid opinion on that subject. She stood up and walked to the door. 'If McBrearty is still wearing that stupid Santa hat I'm going to punch it off his head.'

Once she was gone, Harlan took out his phone. There was a text from an unknown number. He opened it.

Talbot running his own game.
Good luck. You'll need it.
Danks xx

Shit. It seemed Talbot had turned renegade. It only left him one option. It was time to make a call.

Mike McBrearty looked much different without his Santa hat and white dustcoat. He appeared smaller, less cocky. The hat had hidden his bald patch, flaky patches of bare scalp showing through the areas his comb-over didn't cover. McBrearty adjusted his glasses and said, 'Where's my lawyer? I want a lawyer. It's my right.'

Harlan leaned forward across the table between them. Driving back from Barlinnie prison he'd formed a strategy for dealing with McBrearty. He tried to remember as much as he could from what Archie and Danks had passed on. It was possible McBrearty had nothing to do with the murders, but it was definitely worth taking a shot at this. At worst he would only look stupid.

'Mike, let's cut to the chase. Lawyers are only required when you're being interviewed by the police.'

McBrearty looked confused and wary, as if he thought Harlan was playing a trick on him. He waved his arm around him. 'This is a police station. You're a policeman. I want a lawyer.'

'True, I am a policeman. However, right here and now, I'm speaking to you not as an officer of the law, but a friend of the Circle.' He thought he saw a flicker of surprise in McBrearty's eyes behind the spectacles, but couldn't be sure. 'The Circle don't give a fuck about lawyers and legal rights. When the Circle prosecutes those who break its rules, we don't answer to anyone. You understand what I'm saying, Mike?'

This time there was a definite change in McBrearty's demeanour. A small tic above his eye jumped involuntarily, and there was a faint sheen of sweat on the man's forehead. McBrearty however was still trying to play innocent.

'I've got no idea what you're talking about. I still want a lawyer.'

Harlan ignored him. 'How well did you know the Reverend Simon Dolman, Mike? Good mates? Bosom pals? Brothers in arms? Fuck buddies?'

McBrearty forgot about asking again for his lawyer. 'I hardly knew the man. He bought stuff in the shop now and again. That's all.'

'Really? Harlan placed a printout flat on the table, the info given to him given to him by DC Rigg. 'This here says otherwise. It's a list of Dolman's financial dealings. Dolman was a sleeping partner in your mini-market. If I were a betting man I'd venture he put up most of the money when you took over the old Co-op.'

The colour of McBrearty's complexion turned a pasty white shade. He took off his spectacles and rubbed at his eyes. 'It was a loan, that's all. I was to pay him back once the mini-market was up and running. Doesn't mean I was friends with him.'

Harlan sat back and smiled at McBrearty. 'Do the words Heart Swarm mean anything to you, Mike?'

This time McBrearty ran a hand over his mouth and his Adam's apple bobbed as he swallowed nervously. 'No,' he whispered.

'You're a fucking liar, and a bad one at that. Dolman was rebelling against the Circle. He was tired of lurking in the shadows. He wanted to preen and show off his artistic talents to the whole world, and he recruited you and Stella Wilson and Tim Hughes as his private congregation. We know all about it, Mike, what we don't know are the fine details, but I guess we'll get those sooner or later.'

McBrearty's bullish attitude was gone completely. This was a seriously scared man. 'You can't lay a finger on me, Harlan. I'm in a police station. You're not all part of the fucking Circle.'

Harlan laughed. 'Fuck me, Mike. How stupid are you really? By the end of today forensics will have something I can use, I'll have you charged and put in remand. What do you think's going to happen once you're behind bars? And if I don't lock you up then you'll be a free man. Only drawback is, outside this building there's a Gamekeeper waiting for you to walk out the door. I'm sure Dolman explained to you all about the danger of crossing paths with men like them. Both ways you're fucked, Mike.'

McBrearty was opening and closing his mouth but no words emerged. White flecks of spittle appeared at the corner of his mouth. He wasn't like either Hughes or Stella. McBrearty was a weak opportunist, not a feral zealot like the other two members of Dolman's splinter group.

'Thing is, Mike. It doesn't have to end like this. The Circle could use someone like you inside prison. Right now Howie Danks is our main man. He practically runs the high-security wing. I'm sure

Dolman must have mentioned Danks to you? Given you some idea what that man is capable of. Yes?'

McBrearty nodded his head. His eyes were bright with fear.

'Like I said, Danks is our main man, but he could be doing with some proper support. Not just the violent headbangers he's locked up with, but someone who knows the score. Someone who knows the true face of God. A believer. That could be you, Mike. Or it could be Tim Hughes. I made him the same offer, but so far he's not given me an answer. Maybe he'll change his mind later on today when he finds himself in a van heading for Barlinnie and a face-to-face meeting with Danks. But only one of you gets the job. The other one...?' Harlan wore his coldest smile and ran a finger across his throat.

'What do I have to do?' McBrearty's voice was now nothing but a mumbled whisper.

'You have to show contrition, Mike. Confess your sins. Obviously you'll say nothing to my colleagues about the Circle. That would be signing your own death warrant. But we want to know the details of what was going on in Brackenbrae. Can you do that, Mike?'

Sweat ran down McBrearty's pale cheeks, 'But I don't know everything. I was the last to join Simon's special group. Stella and Tim were already doing stuff for him. They thought I was a useless cunt. They sneered at me when Simon wasn't there.'

'When did he recruit you, Mike?'

'Four years ago. I can't remember how we got talking, but he had a way of speaking that made you listen. He could see what made people tick. He picked you up and swept you along with him. He told me about the real God, made me a believer. He even knew about my dreams, said he could make them come true.' McBrearty held his hands out to Harlan as if appealing to his better nature. 'You're part of the Circle, Harlan. You know the sort of thing men like us enjoy. I'll bet you've done much worse.'

Harlan stayed silent. There was only so far he could go with this act. McBrearty seemed to mistake his silence for accord. 'I wasn't a killer like Tim or Stella. I was Simon's pick-up and delivery man. No one noticed me when I made late night runs with my van. If anyone asked, I was on my way back from the cash and carry.'

'So what did you deliver for Dolman, Mike?'

'I delivered, you know, the cuts of meat. There's men who pay a great deal of money for that sort of thing. I didn't kill any of those girls, I was just the butcher's boy.'

Harlan felt sick. He wanted to drag McBrearty across the table and beat his face to a bloody pulp, but he had to see this through to the end.

'Is that what you were doing in a Kirkintilloch car park on Christmas Eve? The night you told me you never left the mini-market?'

McBrearty looked astonished. 'Yes. I was just making a delivery. I was never anywhere near Scaraway Woods. I had nothing to do with hanging up that wee girl.'

'Who did you hand the package over to, Mike?'

A shake of the head. 'Never knew his name. Just a bloke. Simon made all the arrangements. All I did was drop off the merchandise.'

'These girls, Mike. Where did they come from? Any idea?'

McBrearty actually smiled. 'Never any shortage where those kind of girls are concerned, if you know where to look. Most of them have run away from children's homes, end up on the streets selling their arses. I'd pick them up, agree a price for a quick fuck, then once they got in the van I'd chloroform them; take them back to Simon. No one missed them. I always thought it was a shame the way Simon ruined them for anything other than butchery.'

A thought struck Harlan. 'But why did Dolman keep them in the freezer after they'd been gutted? Why not get rid of the evidence?'

McBrearty shrugged. 'It made sense to get rid of them in batches. Simon knew someone, one of your lot, in the Circle, who owned an incinerator. Transportation is always the big risk in getting caught, you know, if the van broke down or crashed or something. So we waited until we had a few stacked up then did the one big run. I should have taken those six girls in the basement last week, but my van was playing up and we missed our slot. Bit of bad luck, that.'

Harlan couldn't believe how matter of fact McBrearty was regarding the disposal of so many dead children. He wondered just how many runs McBrearty had made with his van over the last four years. It reminded him of a documentary he'd watched where a SS guard from Auschwitz casually recounted herding hundreds of women and children into the gas chamber. This man deserved to end up in a cell with an executioner like Howie Danks.

'What about Debbie Fletcher five years ago?'

'Before my time. It was Stella who abducted the girl. She used to boast about how easy it had been. She took the girl to Tim's house where Tim, Stella and Simon all had their bit of fun with her. Then Simon and Stella strung her up in the woods. When the police got involved Stella went to that imbecile Derek Drake and persuaded him to fuck her, made him wear a condom so she could smear his spunk all over the girl's knickers. It was easy for them to kill daft Derek and plant all the stuff in his flat. That's what Stella told me anyway.'

'And Hughes helped Dolman steal her corpse. Yes?'

'That's right. Couldn't have been easier seeing as Tim was the funeral director. But I had nothing to do with any of that.'

'And the videos of Debbie on the *Dead Darlings* website? Were you involved in those, Mike?'

McBrearty shook his head. 'No way. I like my girls young and tender, but not rotting on the bone. That was all Tim's idea. He's real hardcore when it comes to sex. He even filmed his senile old mum getting fucked. Stella wanted to get in on the porn stuff, but Tim said she was too fat and ugly.' McBrearty sniggered. 'That caused a lot of arguments, but Simon always smoothed things out between them.'

Harlan quickly checked his watch. Cara would have arranged for a duty solicitor by now. He had to speed things up.

'The three murders a few nights ago. You involved in those?'

A vehement shake of the head. 'That was all down to Stella and Tim. I did mention to Tim about mad old Sadie shooting her mouth off outside the village hall, claiming she knew the names of the killers. That's probably why they bumped her off, but I don't know why they murdered that boy or wee Moira. I was mad about that. I've had to pay almost twice the money I paid Moira for another woman to do her shift at the cash register.'

Harlan knew he really had to leave this room soon before he beat McBrearty to within an inch of his miserable life. Just breathing the same air was almost unbearable. Hughes and Stella Wilson were undoubtedly depraved beyond belief, but they at least knew exactly what kind of inhuman creatures they were and didn't care what anyone thought. This man in front of him actually believed he held the moral high ground.

'And Detective Sergeant Brock. You were involved with his murder. Stella told me as much.'

Again, McBrearty held his hands out in appeal. 'What could I do? She called me saying she had him in the back lane. Needed a hand to hoist him up the wall so it would make a statement. She said Simon would be proud of us. I couldn't say no.'

'What about his hands and feet?'

'In my stockroom freezer at the mini-market. Right beside the fish fingers and chicken fillets. Come to think of it, there's still some special cuts from those girls Simon kept at the church in there. Maybe you could get rid of it all for me. Move them into Stella's house. She was the one who did the chopping on your mate. Don't see why I should shoulder the blame for anything she did.'

Harlan heard voices in the corridor. He stood up. It was time to leave. 'Listen to me, Mike. I'll have DI Scanlon come in here and take your statement. Tell him everything, except for anything that implicates the Circle. You'll do prison time, no getting away from that, but Danks will take good care of you. You can rest easy on that score. One last question. Why did Dolman use the green tinsel? What was it meant to signify?'

McBrearty smiled. 'Oh that? He was just like me. He absolutely loved Christmas. He wanted to make things look nice and festive.'

The interview room door opened and Richard Birnie stood there giving Harlan a suspicious look. 'You seem to be making a habit of talking to my clients behind my back, DI Harlan.'

Harlan patted Birnie on the shoulder as he passed him on the way out. 'Just making sure Mr McBrearty is nice and comfortable. I won't be sitting in on this interview anyway. I'll have DI Scanlon come down and run through a few routine questions. I'm sure it won't take long.'

Before he closed the door, he heard McBrearty shout after him, 'Thanks for all the help, Mr Harlan.'

He found Scanlon at the coffee machine, scowling as he sipped from a plastic cup filled with what looked like watery human excrement.

'Coffee not to your usual standard, Scanlon?'

Scanlon tipped the entire cup into the drain hole on the machine. 'Some bugger nicked my kettle and jar of coffee. Can you believe it? Who would do a thing like that?'

Harlan made a mental note to have Cara return Scanlon's kettle before it was spotted on his desk. 'Now you know how I felt. Just be grateful whoever nicked it didn't plant drugs and porn in your drawer while they were at it.'

Scanlon shook his head sadly. 'And look how that ended up. Brock lying in the mortuary.'

'That's unfair. I didn't mean for Brock to get himself murdered. And if he hadn't been so stupid as to let Stella Wilson give him a blow job, he'd still be with us.'

Scanlon took a deep breath. 'Sorry, that was unfair. I'm just getting frustrated after spending the last hour with Mrs Wilson. She does nothing but grin back at you no matter what you say.'

'Tell me something new. Thing is, now that Cara has sent Stella's urine sample to the lab, it's only a matter of time before we tie her to the crime scenes.'

Scanlon looked worried. 'But what if we don't? It doesn't bear thinking about.'

'In that case let me ease your mind. I've got Mike McBrearty waiting in interview room three. I want you to go in there and take his statement. You won't have to do anything much at all. Just get the CD recorder up and running then sit back. I have it on good authority McBrearty is going to spill his guts. He'll implicate Stella Wilson and Tim Hughes in the murders, and his own role in Brock's death. He'll also confess to the kidnapping and rape of the girls found in the church, and passing on the cuts of flesh taken from their bodies. When he's finished get a search warrant for the mini-market and raid the freezer in the stock room. Once you've retrieved Brock's hands and feet, send any other suspicious meat packages to the lab for analysis. You'll find they were taken from the victims under the church.'

Scanlon was so shocked he tried taking a sip from his empty plastic cup having forgotten he'd poured it all away. 'How do you know all this? What have you been up to, Harlan?'

Harlan felt his phone vibrate in his pocket. 'Best not to ask. Just get in there and do as I say.'

Leaving a perplexed Scanlon staring after him, Harlan hurried along the corridor while he fished his phone from his pocket. It was Jo Haney.

'Hello there, Will. Sorry I missed your call. Had a long lunch today.'

'You back in the mortuary?'

'I am. Got an old friend of yours on the table. Adam Brock. Always so sad when a policeman gets killed in the line of duty. Your message said you wanted to see me about something.'

Harlan stopped at the bottom of the stairwell. 'Yes, I was going to drop in for a chat. A few things I want to run by you. The human remains found in Debbie Fletcher's grave for starters.'

'Oh, and here was me thinking you were just missing my company. There wasn't too much left to examine from those remains. All I can tell you right now is that it was a young girl. Probably a similar age to Debbie Fletcher. From the skull, which was mostly intact, I'd say her ethnic origin was African.'

'There's a few things I need to ask about Brock, too.'

'Feel free to drop by, but I'd understand if you want to leave things today with Brock being the one under the Stryker saw. You could always wait until I'm finished and take me for a drink.'

'It's fine. You can cover Brock with a sheet. He can't be any more annoying dead than he was alive. I'll be there within the hour, Jo.'

Not waiting to hear her reply, Harlan cut the connection and used speed dial to call Cara. Now came the hard part.

'You fucking treacherous cunt.'

'Cara, wait.'

'You fucking arsehole. All this time you've been working for Ray fucking Talbot?'

Harlan ducked as Scanlon's kettle sailed past his head and hit the wall behind him. 'Fucking hell, Cara. Just wait till I've told you the rest.'

He'd told Cara the full story of what had taken place between him and Howie Danks, and how he'd discovered the same group of people he'd agreed to steal evidence for also happened to be Ray Talbot's employers. He hadn't expected for Cara to take it well, and she hadn't.

She stood glaring at him at him from across the desk. 'Speak,' she hissed.

Still wary of her throwing any other objects to hand, he quickly filled in the gaps of the story, leaving nothing out. Of how Simon Dolman had belonged to a depraved sect known as The Circle of the Thirteen Apostles. How the minister had gone renegade, *Heart Swarm*, as it was known, and formed his own splinter group to create blissful chaos. He told her how he'd retrieved the envelope from the coffin only for Talbot to break into his room and collect it, then threaten to kill Holly if he didn't release any suspects for Talbot's own personal interrogation purposes. He told her of Thom Wilson being snatched off the street despite everything he had done to protect him, and then Archie turning out to be the joker in the pack.

When she still hadn't launched a further attack, he quickly ran through what McBrearty had said in the interview room, and how Scanlon was now taking his statement.

'And that's basically it,' he finished.

'You're still an arsehole, Harlan. Why the fuck didn't you tell me any of this before now?'

He held up his hands, remembering Mike McBrearty had made much the same gesture to him. 'Because I was ashamed at cutting the deal with Danks. I was dead in the water at that point. It would have killed me off completely not to be involved in the investigation, knowing they would shut it down as quickly as possible. Then when I realised Talbot's role in all this, I couldn't possibly say anything. How could I, after what he'd done to you?'

Cara only stared at him coldly. 'So let me get this right. Dolman was a religious nutcase who belonged to a serial killer cult who worship a black hole? How fucked up is that for a start?'

'Actually, what's creepier is how they knew the black hole even existed. I mean, according to Danks, The Circle of the Thirteen Apostles was founded in the seventeenth century. To them it's a God of Chaos.'

'Don't complicate things, Harlan. Stick to the facts. So we have Dolman going all fundamentalist and deciding to make his killings high profile. He and his crew snatch Debbie Fletcher and hang her up like a Christmas fairy. Surely this Circle must have suspected Dolman. After all, he was one of their own.'

Harlan was glad Cara at least seemed to be calming down enough to talk it through with him. 'Because they had dim-witted Derek Drake to act as a scapegoat. Sure, these people in the Circle aren't stupid, they must have kept their eye on him, but Dolman was playing the long game. He hid a list of the top dog's names in the coffin after Hughes helps him switch the body, knowing he could bring back Debbie Fletcher any time he chose to force an exhumation.'

'But why go to so much bother?'

'I asked Danks that same question. The only answer that makes sense is that he was a psychopath with an exhibitionist streak a mile wide. He was showing off. It amused him.'

Cara flopped back into her seat. 'Right, so we know Dolman had cancer, was dosing himself with morphine, must have known the end was coming – so he hits code red, brings Debbie back out of cold storage, confesses to everything and hangs himself in front of the congregation and the press. One last shock-fest fuck-you to the world in general.'

'Then Talbot shows up,' said Harlan. 'When news breaks of another body in the woods on the exact anniversary of Debbie Fletcher's death, the Circle must have known it was Dolman this time for certain. They send Talbot to pull out a few of Dolman's fingernails to discover what other mischief he's planned, but Talbot gets there too late. And that should have been the whole crazy story, until the other bodies turned up.'

Cara was winding strands of her hair around her finger. She still looked troubled. 'What I don't get is why they approached you to help them out. In fact, how did they even guess Dolman had left something behind in the coffin?'

'Dolman's last words: *I am the face in the darkness. I am the heart of the swarm.* I think he was sending them a message, taunting them. Telling them to expect the worst.'

'But that still doesn't answer why they got Howie Danks to approach you. Why you, Harlan?'

Harlan shook his head. 'No idea. Maybe they simply thought I was so desperate for a chance to crack the case I'd do anything to redeem myself.' But inside he had a horrible suspicion what the real reason was. The Circle thought that deep down he was just like them.

'There's also the small detail of what Dolman and his disciples were getting up to for the last five years, Harlan.'

'We'll never know for sure. Not unless our three amigos decide to tell us. But we do know McBrearty was snatching young girls off the streets and taking them back to Brackenbrae. Dolman likely used them to make paedophile necrophilia movies, or carved them up for his specialist diners club.'

Cara stood up and wandered over to the window. 'So that's it? All done and dusted? Case closed?'

'Not quite.'

She spun around. 'What do you mean?'

'There's still Talbot to deal with.'

A feverish light grew in Cara's eyes. 'You know where to find him?'

Harlan stood up and held out his phone. 'No, but I know someone who might be able to tell us.'

Chapter 16

Now that the old Glasgow City mortuary across from the High Courts had being transformed into a lost property office, Harlan had to drive across the city to the Southern General Hospital where the new mortuary was incorporated as part of a ninety million pound laboratory building. After showing their warrant cards to a disinterested woman at the reception desk and telling her they were expected by Dr Haney, he and Cara were directed towards the mortuary wing. Harlan pressed a buzzer on the locked doors and after a few moments, Haney's cheery voice sounded from a small intercom grill.

'Is that you, Will?'

'It's me,' he replied.

'Are you on your own?'

'Yes.'

Haney's voice took on a playful tone. 'Then it's going to really cosy. I'm the only one here. Everyone else has gone home.'

Beside him, Cara kicked Harlan on the ankle hard enough to make him wince in pain.

'I'm in the lab at the end of the corridor, Will. See you in a minute.'

There was an electronic click and Harlan pushed the door open. They found themselves in a smaller reception area, this one with signs leading to the mortuary labs, as well as a sensitively designed area for bereaved families attending the unit to identify loved ones.

Harlan kept his voice low. 'Best if you wait here, Cara.'

Cara didn't look pleased, but she dropped onto a small sofa. 'Don't see why I can't tag along with you.'

'Because there's more chance she'll tell me where Talbot is if I'm on my own.'

'You mean it'll be easier for you to turn on the charm and twist her around your little finger? Sweet-talk her into coming across with the goods?'

'Cara, for pity's sake. This isn't going to be easy for me. I always thought of Jo Haney as a…' He paused, unsure what to say.

'A psychopathic public school shag?' prompted Cara.

'A friend, Cara. She was a friend. How was I to know she was connected to this Circle?'

He thought again of his shock when Lenny told him the driver of the car behind Talbot's might have been Haney. *Talbot's friend with an artistic flair for teasing secrets from someone with a flick of her scalpel.* He had no idea what he was going to do about her. If the Circle was protecting her he couldn't very well just arrest her. That might be like sticking his arm in a hornet's nest. Talbot however was a different story. Archie and Howie Danks were proof the Circle viewed their Gamekeepers as dispensable if the circumstances warranted it.

Leaving Cara behind him, he headed through a double set of doors that led to the labs. The distance between the old and new mortuaries might only be a matter of miles as the crow flies, but the difference in appearance was light years apart. On either side of the corridor, empty labs were open to view through huge glass-walled panels. He saw rows of stainless-steel dissecting tables, all hooked up to state of the art drainage systems. With futuristic lighting modules and banks of electronic gadgets, the labs resembled modern-day operating theatres equipped to save lives rather than somewhere to hack apart dead bodies.

The lab at the bottom of the corridor was the only one not open to public scrutiny. He guessed this was where the more case-sensitive autopsies took place. The door was secured by a key entry pad. He knocked with his knuckles and it was immediately opened by Jo Haney. She was dressed in green protective scrubs and rubber boots, her smiling face covered by a clear plastic face shield. She raised the transparent visor and said, 'Come in, Will. I'm just finishing up in here.'

Entering the room, Harlan saw it was a smaller version of the other labs. On a stainless-steel table in the middle of the room he saw Adam Brock laid out, his chest and abdomen opened up, organs glistening wetly. Harlan instinctively gagged; not so much at the sight of Brock's innards, but from the smell. No amount of high-tech equipment and ventilation systems could completely dispel the stink of a freshly sliced-open cadaver.

Haney handed him a cotton face mask, which he accepted gratefully. She returned to Brock's body and began the process of stitching up his abdomen. Harlan wondered if she had left the dead detective sergeant fully exposed for his benefit, a bit of teasing perhaps. He found his eyes drawn to the bloodied stumps where Brock's hands and feet had been. Stella Wilson had done quite the job on him.

'So then, Will. What's so important you had to come along to my chamber of horrors to visit me in person?'

There was no point in pussyfooting around the matter. Harlan took a deep breath, immediately regretting it as the stench of Brock's guts intensified. Taking a more shallow breath he said, 'Jo, what did you do with Thom Wilson?'

Haney stopped stitching and stuck her curved needle deep into Brock's thigh. He saw her eyes widen in surprise. She didn't even attempt to deny her involvement in torturing Wilson. 'My, you're very well informed. Then again, you always were quite the little smarty-pants. It's good to see you back at your best, Will. You'd become a real dullard over the past few years.'

'Thom Wilson was innocent, Jo. He wasn't any threat to you or your precious Circle.'

Haney shrugged indifferently, pulling up her face shield. 'Well, I know that now, don't I? But we had to be sure. And you know about the Circle? Someone's been talking out of school. Very naughty of them.'

'What did you do? Torture him?'

Haney smiled. 'Oh, for goodness sake. That's a bit of an exaggeration. All I did was open up his injured knee and tickle the exposed nerves a little with my scalpel. After five minutes I was completely satisfied he knew nothing that might put us at risk. If it makes you feel any better, I put him out of his misery without further discomfort.'

Without further discomfort. Harlan could barely believe how casual Haney was acting over the taking of a human life. It was like she was talking about flushing a goldfish down the toilet. He thought back to the night they had fucked with abandon in his bed and felt cold inside. Had he actually slept with this monster?

'How did you and Talbot know I'd be sending Wilson to the hotel? You were both right there waiting for him when he arrived. How could you have known?'

'I'm afraid you made that part rather easy for us. Your ever so helpful PC Shields called Talbot and tipped him off. She's been feeding Talbot with all sorts of useful tit-bits over the past few days. Didn't you ever guess she belonged to us?'

Harlan felt like he'd been smacked on the head by a huge padded boxing glove. *Honeytrap*? *Jinty Shields a member of the Circle*? That was twice within twenty-four hours he'd handed someone over to their certain death. First Brock, now Thom Wilson. How could he have been so stupid? He thought of the way Honeytrap had returned the bag of underwear and socks. She'd played her part perfectly. Never given him so much as a hint to suspect where her true loyalties lay.

A mocking smile stole across Haney's face. 'So are you here to arrest me, Will? Put me in handcuffs and beat a full confession from me? I might actually enjoy a little roughhouse stuff. I think that would get me deliciously wet.'

'I'm here for Talbot. You know where he is.'

Haney continued smiling. 'That's true. I do know exactly where he is. But what makes you think I'll tell you? Or for that matter, what makes you think you're any match for him? He's a very brutal sort of man, Will. He might object to you attempting to put him behind bars. You might like to think you can handle yourself, but Talbot would snap you like a twig.' Haney's smile was replaced by a sad face. 'I'd so hate to have you as the next cadaver on my dissecting table. Walk away from this, Will. While you still can. That's my best advice.'

'You think I'm scared of your Gamekeeper?'

'Gamekeeper? You really have been doing your homework. I'm impressed. Who's been tittle-tattling? Was it Howie Danks? I'd have thought he'd have known better.'

'Not Danks. He was very careful not to mention who his offer came from. He did however let me know his arrest wasn't all it appeared to be. Why did the Circle send him to me? Why not someone else?'

He thought he knew the answer, but wanted it confirmed anyway.

'You haven't guessed by now? Danks messed up. He was always such a controlled man. No one imagined he would develop such an extreme taste in flower arranging. His little presentations could have easily jeopardised the Circle. Normally such a serious breach of the rules would have earned him a quick death, but there were some who thought he could prove ever so useful inside prison, identifying those short-term thugs who might fit the bill as hired muscle.'

Harlan remembered what Archie had said about his own recruitment. Danks had become the Circle's recruiting officer in a place teeming with violent men, filtering out the wheat from the chaff.

'But why me in particular, Jo?'

'Because back then they saw you as an investment. You came to their attention years ago. A young detective with real talent. Destined to scale the ladder of promotion. Someone who fitted their defined model of a natural recruit.'

'They thought I was some sort of fucking sexual sadist?'

'Don't get on your high horse, Will. What I'm saying is that you were already known as being the sexually promiscuous sort. You can hardly deny that.'

Harlan swallowed back a hard lump in his throat. Those times he'd cheated on Steph while they were still married. Justifying it to himself as a way to cope with what the job threw at him. Now the thought that someone had been taking notes made him feel sick with shame.

'You had aggression and drive – you had potential. Not to reach the uppermost levels of the Circle, but as a very useful follower. That's why Danks was given up to you. As a direct result of Danks' arrest, you were promoted to detective inspector. The Circle expected you to go further, and then they would have contacted you, called in their debt.'

'You mean I would have been an asset? There to provide a helping hand to any of their members who got caught red-handed with their fingers in the biscuit tin?'

'Just certain people, Will. When it suited them.' Haney smiled wryly. 'Just like when you helped out your friend when it seemed he might lose his hotel.'

'You know about that?' Harlan was shocked.

Haney shrugged. 'The Circle does have an extensive file on you, like it does many other people, policemen, politicians, journalists, bankers, we're almost like MI5. But Simon Dolman rather blotted your copybook. He made you a lost cause. I always had a soft spot for you. It's why I instigated our little flirtation at your hotel a few years ago. I'd hoped you might still have some fire in your belly, but all you were interested in was drinking and fucking, and even that wasn't all I'd hoped for. Now, perhaps, the Circle will have to revise their options. You have been very resourceful of late.'

'Fucking hell, Jo. Surely you don't really believe in all this mumbo-jumbo crap. Dabbling in occult rituals. Worshipping black holes. Pretending you have magic powers?'

Haney surprised him by replying, 'Not at first. I was never a very religious woman. I got drawn in by the incredible sex. But as Aleister Crowley himself said, it doesn't matter if something is real or not, only that it works. I gradually had my eyes opened to what you might loosely term as a higher power. There are those within the Circle who can do things I can't possibly explain. I mean, John Scanlon is a Christian. Why can you accept his religious beliefs, but sneer at the validity of mine?'

'Maybe because his religion doesn't subscribe to raping and killing.'

Haney snorted with laughter. 'Not so much these days admittedly, but the Christian Church does have buckets of blood and gore on its hands. All in the name of their God naturally. The Circle's use of violence isn't so different from the old fashioned Christian ways, but without the attached hypocrisy. And you can't dispute that as a religion, the Circle is not without its mysteries and miracles. You yourself have been a victim of our so-called *occult dabbling*.'

'Meaning what?'

'Your attack on Simon Dolman. You think that was normal behaviour for a seasoned detective inspector? Or do you normally dish out a vicious beating as a matter of course while questioning people?'

Harlan was confused. What did punching Dolman have to do with any of this? He felt his own anger kindle to life inside him. He didn't have to justify himself to this prissy-voiced monster standing across the dissecting table from him, but he found himself answering anyway. 'I was under a lot of stress. Lack of sleep. I'd been called out on Christmas Eve to go look at the dead body of little girl, a girl much the same age as my own daughter. My wife was threatening me with divorce. Then Dolman told me the killer had only been following his God-given fucking nature. That's why I smacked him in the face.'

Haney gave him a pitying smile. 'I'm quite sure, Will, that at many times in your career you've been faced with similar provocation and managed to avoid losing your temper. And even when you have seen fit to use violence, you were professional enough not to leave any physical evidence.'

Harlan felt himself redden. He had dealt out some rough justice over the years. Punches to the kidneys, blows to the back of the head using rolled up newspapers. It was part and parcel of the job at times. But when he remembered the bloodied mess he'd left Dolman in, he had to admit that had been sloppy work.

'Dolman pushed you. Nudged you. Got you all riled up and took away your self-control. He also took away something else.'

Harlan laughed bitterly. 'You mean like my whole fucking career?'

Haney shook her head. 'He took away whatever it was that made you such a good detective. He took away your gift, Will. He left you blind and stupid. I bet you feel like a new man ever since he killed himself.'

Her words struck a chord. He had been feeling different since Christmas Day. Thinking more clearly, instinctively putting together pieces of the puzzle that would have been beyond him for the last five years. Was it even possible Dolman had neutered him? He found himself asking, 'How well did you know Dolman?'

'I've met him on quite a few occasions. Simon Dolman was a highly respected member of the Circle. He was a true believer in the faith. A talented man. He was expected to make the next step and move into the inner sanctum of the Circle.'

'I imagine you already know that Danks asked me to retrieve that list of names from Debbie Fletcher's grave. What I don't get is what's to stop anyone else exposing the names of your precious inner sanctum.'

'Because, Will, very few people know who they are. Even I know only a few. When we have a high celebration, everyone is masked. Dolman was in a unique position as he was their spiritual adviser. However, Talbot thought there was always a chance he might have shared this information with his group of friends in Brackenbrae, which is why I allowed him to talk me into this.' She sighed wearily. 'Now are you done asking questions? You really should let this go for now. You're already wading in deep waters.'

Harlan flicked a glance at his watch. This was taking far too long. He'd stupidly become sidetracked trying to get answers from Jo Haney. Cara might get impatient and come looking for him, and then it would only become more complicated. Haney was far too calm about everything. He had to make her angry. Knock her off her stride.

'One more and then I'm done. I saw the videos Dolman was uploading onto the internet. The *Dead Darlings* site. Little dead girls being violated and defiled. You really get turned on by that sort of disgusting filth?' He pointed an angry hand at Brock's body. 'Is that why you enjoy doing your job so much? Does rummaging about in a dead man's entrails also get you deliciously wet?'

Haney's smile was no longer benign, now there was a nasty curl to it. 'Don't dare to presume we all have the same tastes.' She took hold of Brock's shrivelled penis and began caressing it, like a wife encouraging an impotent husband. 'Personally I've never found much use for the dead, other than the fun of ferreting out all their secrets. But I wouldn't sneer at anyone else's idea of pleasure. Morality has always been mankind's greatest weakness. It's an artificial construct. Maybe you should break a few taboos, Will. See how it liberates you.'

'Jo, tell me where Ray Talbot is. I might not be able to touch you or your Circle, but Talbot is going down, or I'll die trying.'

There was a noise in the corridor outside, followed by the electronic beeps of someone punching numbers into the keypad. Harlan cursed, assuming Cara had come looking for him after all, then realised she wouldn't know the code for the keypad. The door swung open and Ray Talbot stood there pointing a silenced gun at his face. Talbot grinned as he reached down and dragged an unconscious Cara by the collar into the room. There was a smear of blood on the side of Cara's head where Talbot had struck her with the gun.

'DI Harlan, fancy seeing you here. Did I just hear my name taken in vain?' Talbot glanced at Jo Haney who was still grasping Brock's penis in her gloved hand. 'Oops, sorry. I haven't disturbed a cosy little *ménage à trois*, have I?'

Haney removed her hand from Brock's penis, flashing an angry look at Talbot. 'Be more respectful to whom you're speaking, Gamekeeper.'

Harlan saw a flare of resentment in Talbot's own stare, underlain with a hint of wariness. Obviously Talbot hated being spoken to in this manner, but was wise enough to remember his position in the pecking order.

'Sorry, Dr Haney. That was uncalled for.'

In that brief moment when both Talbot and Haney were locking eyes, Harlan wondered if he could make a grab for the gun, before calculating that Talbot would shoot him before he even took two steps.

'What have you done to Cara?'

Talbot glanced down at the prone Cara, a smirk creeping across his face. 'I was having a quiet nap in the Family Bereavement room when you two turned up. Thought it wise to stay out of sight until you left her all alone, then I slipped out and gave her a little tap on the head.' Still keeping the gun trained on Harlan, Talbot knelt and slipped his hand inside Cara's jacket, removing her warrant card.

'Detective Sergeant Cara McAullay,' he read from the card. 'Seen her with you a few times over the past few days.' He screwed his face up as if thinking hard. 'You know, I seem to recall a Cara McAullay from way back. She had a twin sister. They stayed next door, foster kids my neighbour was taking care of. Lovely girls they were.'

Despite the gun pointing at him, Harlan felt his anger boil over. 'You abused them, you fucking shit. Two little girls who'd lost everything, and you used them to satisfy your sick fantasies.'

Talbot's face was the picture of smiling innocence. 'Honest to God. I never laid a finger on either of them.'

'But you made them expose themselves while you tossed yourself off like a sad old pervert.'

Talbot stopped smiling. 'Better watch your mouth, Harlan. I might take any amount of shit from Dr Haney on account of who her husband is, but you're nothing. A washed-up detective who's been the butt of everyone's jokes for the past five years…'

Talbot stopped suddenly, his eyes shifting to Haney, aware he'd said too much. The pathologist was throwing him a furious look.

'So your husband is one of the inner sanctum?' asked Harlan, taking a guess.

'That,' she said through pursed lips, 'is none of your damned business. And if you've any sense at all you'll forget Talbot ever mentioned it.'

'So what now? Is this where Talbot puts a bullet in my head? Smuggles me down to the incinerator for easy disposal?'

'Don't be stupid. Whether you accept it or not, you've already compromised yourself. The Circle know they can always come back and ask a favour or two. Besides, I really do need you to help me with those you currently hold in custody.'

'What about Cara? She needs medical attention.'

'Bringing DS McAullay with you was stupid. We could have resolved this problem amicably, but now…' She gave a resigned shrug. 'I'm afraid you're going to have to make a hard decision. Talbot will babysit dear little Cara until you give me the people we want.'

Talbot leered at Harlan. 'Just imagine how surprised she'll be when she wakes up to find herself bound and gagged in the back seat of my car. It'll just be like old times.'

'You're not letting that animal have her. No fucking way.' No matter how he tried, Harlan couldn't help imagining what Talbot might do to Cara, purely out of sheer spite.

'The sooner you get me Dolman's playmates, the sooner you get Cara back.'

'But they're being charged with murder! How can I possibly set them loose?'

Haney just smiled pleasantly. 'You've been very resourceful so far, Will. You'll find a way.'

'Fucking hell, Jo! Why do you even need them? They'll be in remand by tomorrow. The Circle must have all sorts of people inside who can deal with them. Howie Danks is probably already sharpening his knife for…'

Harlan stopped dead. Something Danks had said yesterday drifted back into his head.

The pain is like entering another dimension. Feels like you've opened a doorway into hell, if truth be told. That's the sort of pain you'll experience when you wake up one night in your hotel room and someone is cutting out your kidney.

It felt like a silent detonation going off inside his head, the remaining pieces of the puzzle falling into place. Harlan knew exactly what Jo Haney had done. Ignoring the muzzle of Talbot's gun trained upon him, he took a few steps closer to the dissecting table where Haney stood in a relaxed pose, one gloved hand lightly resting Brock's thigh, the other on the edge of his open chest cavity.

'You were working with Dolman, weren't you?'

Haney let out a bark of disbelief. 'Me? Working with Simon Dolman? That's insane. Dolman went *Heart Swarm*. He wanted to bring down the Circle. Why would I ever be party to something like that?'

'But you didn't know that at the time, Jo. Those girls in the church. We thought it was all about cannibalism. Dolman having a bit of fun with them, and when they were too damaged to play with any longer, he tore them apart and turned what was left into cuts of meat. Mike McBrearty verified that. He said he stored the flesh in his freezer. He made no mention of the internal organs that were missing. You took those. Didn't you?'

Haney tried to protest, but Harlan cut her off. 'On the phone you went to great pains to point out the organs had been surgically removed, while the cuts of flesh were carried out by an amateur. That was your stiff-necked pride talking. You couldn't bear for anyone to think the same pair of hands had been responsible for both procedures, even on something as impenetrable as a post-mortem report.'

He felt Talbot place the gun against the back of his head, but at this point Harlan no longer cared. Behind him, Talbot growled, 'Just say the word, Dr Haney.'

Haney held her hand up, her face a cold mask of fury. 'No, let's hear what else the great clever-clogs detective has got to say. So if the organs weren't for consumption, what else would I be doing with them?'

Harlan grinned back at her fiercely. He was a dead man anyway. What did he have to lose?

'You were harvesting the organs for the black market. I couldn't work out how Dolman had managed to renovate and refurbish his entire church. That must have taken serious money. And while he no doubt turned a decent profit on the specialist diner's club and the sick porn, those would generate nowhere close to the amount of hard cash he'd need for that sort of work. You and Dolman were in partnership selling the organs, probably to some rich bastards overseas. And all done without the Circle's blessing, so to speak.'

Talbot prodded Harlan on the back of head with the gun. 'And where do I fit into this fairy tale?'

'You? That's easy. You were Dolman's meat-seller. You and Dolman used McBrearty as the go-between so there was minimal contact between you. We've got CCTV footage of McBrearty handing over a package in a car park on Christmas Eve. I'll bet anything you were the guy with the hoodie receiving the package from McBrearty. Again, I'm sure this little arrangement was strictly off the books. Somehow, one of you must have found out about the other, and when it became known to the Circle that Dolman had gone *Heart Swarm*, you both had to make sure your arses were covered. Anyone discovered having unsanctioned dealings with Dolman, in any capacity, would come under some very close scrutiny. The kind of scrutiny that usually ends with a bullet in the head. That's why you're both so keen to make Dolman's conspirators vanish in case they do know one, or both of you, were connected to Dolman more closely than you want anyone to know.'

Harlan waited for the shot that would turn out his lights permanently. But it never came. Instead he heard Talbot say, 'Dr Haney, we have a serious problem on our hands. It needs to be addressed. Just say the word. And while I'm at it, it might be safer to take care of that fat-arsed bitch PC Shields, who gave us Thom Wilson. Can't have her blabber-mouthing to her handler.'

Haney was no longer looking angry. Instead, there was now a melancholy expression on her face. 'Oh, Will. I really can't have you running around making those sort sof accusations to anyone, can I? You must understand the difficult position you've put me in.'

Incredibly, there was a glint of a tear in Haney's eye. She reminded him of a dog-lover taking her precious pet to the vet to be put to sleep. He even had the urge to laugh out loud when she said, 'Don't worry, Will. You won't actually feel anything. It'll be quick and painless, I promise.'

He saw Haney give Talbot the slightest of nods and braced himself for oblivion. From the floor he heard the sound of Cara stirring. A soft groan, followed by a hitched breath. He hoped Talbot would shoot her before she came to and realised what was happening. Suddenly Haney's eyes snapped to her left and the look of blazing anger returned.

'Wait! Not yet, Talbot! The bloody door isn't closed properly. Can't you do anything right? Anyone could stroll in here!'

The gun muzzle was removed from Harlan's head and he quickly looked over his shoulder to see Haney was right. The toe of Cara's boot had stopped the door from closing all the way shut. Talbot swore and stooped down to haul at her collar. The next second, he simply fell over, his gun hitting the tiled floor with a clatter. Blood pooled around him from a large hole in his head. Harlan wasn't sure he'd even heard the silenced gun go off. Had Talbot somehow shot himself? How could that be possible?

But Talbot hadn't accidentally shot himself. The door swung wide open to reveal a bulky figure in green scrubs, a surgical face mask and hair hidden beneath a protective hairnet. The figure was levelling a much bigger gun than Talbot's, not at Harlan, but at Jo Haney. The shooter's free hand came up slowly and pulled back the face mask.

'Looks like Mr Talbot won't be takin' care of the fat-arsed bitch, after aw,' said Honeytrap.

Chapter 17

Harlan stared at the newcomer in disbelief. '*Honeytrap*? I mean… Jinty?'

Honeytrap smiled at him, her doughy features creasing like a Halloween pumpkin left on a rubbish skip for a few days. 'It's fine, sir. Ah never minded gettin' called that. It always sounded kinda sexy.'

Harlan dropped to his knees and took of Cara's hand in his own. It felt cold and clammy. Her eyes were fluttering, her breathing ragged, but he thought she was definitely regaining consciousness.

'She gonny live?' asked Honeytrap.

He nodded. 'Looks like it.'

'Good. But best you take her to A & E before she sees me, or for that matter, Dr Haney. She's got some explaining to do. Maybe her man will put in a good word for her.'

'You were listening?' he asked.

Honeytrap indicated to an earpiece just visible at the side of the hairnet. 'Every word, sir. It's how I knew where to find you.'

'Where's the transmitter?'

She plucked a tiny object that looked like a tiepin from Harlan's coat. 'Fixed it to your lapel on Mr Talbot's instructions when I brought back the pants and socks. So he'd know the whereabouts of the other suspects.'

Harlan could barely believe he was still alive, never mind having this discussion with Honeytrap. 'But you were working with Talbot. You gave him Thom Wilson. Why… this?' he pointed to Talbot's dead body.

'I was told to give Mr Talbot every help and assistance. Which ah did. Then ah gets a call this afternoon tellin' me Mr Talbot was actin' way beyond his own remit. I was told to keep close to you, sir. Which ah did.'

Harlan offered up a silent thank you to Howie Danks. If the serial killer hadn't intervened in some way then Honeytrap wouldn't be here now to save his and Cara's skins.

'Fucking hell, Jinty. What happens now?'

'First I get Talbot into one of those drawers they store the bodies in. Space for over three hundred in here I was told. Might be weeks before they find him. Dr Haney can help me with that. Also with cleanin' up the blood. Then she's comin' with me.'

Jo Haney looked even paler than Adam Brock on the dissecting table. Harlan thought she might have blustered and denied everything, maybe even try to make a run for it. But she simply peeled off her surgical gloves and dropped them into Brock's chest cavity.

She even smiled at Harlan. 'Maybe one day we'll get that repeat performance after all, Will.'

He shook his head. 'Somehow I doubt that, Jo.'

Honeytrap pointed to Cara. 'Best you carry her over to A & E right now, sir. Just say you left her waiting in reception while you went in to see Dr Haney. When you came out she was lyin' unconscious.'

'What about the receptionist at the front door of the lab?'

'Gone home early. I informed her that her house had been burgled when I arrived.'

'And the security cameras?'

'Disabled. Hard drives will be erased later this evenin', sir.'

Harlan scratched his head. 'You've thought of everything, haven't you?'

Again, Honeytrap's face folded into a gurning smile. She pointed her gun down at Talbot and there was a gleam of sheer pride as she said, 'I hope so, because I've been promised his job if I take care of this situation to a satisfactory conclusion. I'm going to be the Circle's very first lady Gamekeeper.'

Harlan scooped Cara up into his arms and walked out the lab. As the door closed behind him he heard Honeytrap say, 'Get a mop, Dr Haney. You can clean that mess up yourself.'

As January drew to an end, Harlan sat in his office watching huge flakes of snow drift across the window. If this weather kept up he might find it difficult getting into town for Cara's leaving party. He thought back to when he had carried her from the mortuary, driving like a madman to the other side of the Southern General where the A & E was located. The doctors held her overnight for X-rays and observation, but found no sign of a fracture, although she had suffered a nasty concussion from the blow to the head.

He barely saw her for the next two weeks as she was signed off on sick leave, while he was busy writing reports and attending meetings with Walker and Scanlon. He'd stuck to the story of leaving Cara in the empty reception area while he and Haney had a chat. Initially this story had been accepted without question until it was discovered the security hard drive for every camera in the lab had been wiped clean. How Honeytrap had managed that he had no idea. It got trickier when Talbot's body was discovered in a morgue cooler drawer two days later with a bullet in his head. Harlan was questioned again by Walker, but he stuck to his story despite the chief super obviously not believing a word he said.

They were also keen to talk with Jo Haney, but she had already resigned her position as pathologist and was reported to be currently out the country. Her husband, Charles Haney, the distinguished Queen's Counsel, seemed unsure exactly where she was or when she would return. Harlan assumed things hadn't gone well for Jo with the Circle despite any support her husband may have given. He wondered if she might be the next one to turn up in a cooler drawer with a bullet in her head. He found he didn't care too much.

When Cara returned from sick leave, he knew something had changed between them. He'd hoped she might have called in at the hotel for a drink, maybe even ended up in his bed. His calls went to voicemail, his texts unanswered. The morning she showed up for work he'd asked her into his office, but she'd said it was best they talked in the canteen over a coffee. They'd sat in silence for a time, weighing each other up like gun fighters.

Eventually Cara said, 'Walker wants to interview me later today. I imagine he'll ask me why we were at the mortuary.'

'What are you going to say?'

She shrugged, her eyes locked on the tabletop. 'Just like you suggested in your text. We were paying a routine visit to question Haney about Brock's injuries to further incriminate Stella Wilson.'

'Why didn't you answer my calls, Cara? I was worried about you.'

She looked up, met his gaze, and Harlan saw distrust in her eyes.

'Thought it best to let things cool down. Give myself a chance to think things over.'

'Weren't you desperate to know what happened that day in the mortuary?'

A shake of the head. 'Probably best if I never know. It'll be safer that way for everyone.'

Harlan finally realised what conclusion Cara had come to. 'Jesus, you don't think I'm now working for *them*? The fucking Circle?'

'You took their deal. Maybe you thought it was for the right reasons, but you're tainted now. They'll always have their hooks in you.'

Aware of other people sitting close by, Harlan struggled to keep his voice low. 'Bullshit. It's over. And Ray Talbot is dead. What more do you want?'

She looked sad then. 'For me Ray Talbot is never going to be dead. Not unless I was the one to put the fucking bullet in his head. And if you truly think the Circle will leave you be, you're not half as smart as you think you are, Harlan.'

There wasn't much he could say to this. He'd had the same thought himself.

'Cara, please, we have to resolve this. We have to work together. If you think continuing to sleep with me is a bad idea, that's your call, but we're still on the same team. We have to sort this out.'

That had been when she'd told him about the transfer to London.

'I applied for a job in the Met. I start next week.'

'What? When did you apply? You only came back to work this morning.'

'Beginning of December. Thought it best not to say anything in case it fell through.'

'But I thought we were…'

Cara pushed her corkscrew hair back and smiled sadly. 'Fuck buddies?'

'I was going to say… *friends*.'

Cara's smile changed into something more cynical. 'You mean like you and Haney were friends? By the way, how's she doing these days? I've heard she's taking a long holiday somewhere hot. Bet she hasn't sent you a postcard.'

Harlan couldn't think of anything else to say except, 'Well, good luck with the new job.'

Thank you, sir.

And that was when Harlan knew it was really finished between them.

He rose from his desk and stood at the window, watching as the falling snow erased the features of the outside world, thinking if only it was so easy to wipe out the life choices you made; start over again with a fresh page. At least coming to work was very different from what it had been before Christmas. He was reborn, back to his old self. Working on proper cases, and if he was honest, smugly enjoying the looks of respect he now saw in his colleagues' eyes instead of the pity and disdain he'd suffered beforehand.

Even better – Kyle Kelly was gone. He'd handed in his resignation to DCS Walker as a knee-jerk protest over Harlan being given charge of the investigation. It was a stupid gesture to make. Instead of rejecting the resignation out of hand, as Kelly probably expected, Walker had accepted it. Scanlon was now acting DCI, with a better than evens chance of keeping the post permanently, having nicked the lion's share of the credit for the arrests relating to the Brackenbrae murders. Harlan didn't care, he had too much ground to make up on his old job.

The phone rang, breaking his reverie – an internal call from downstairs, he had a visitor. When he heard who it was his heart sank. He'd been expecting something like this ever since that day in the mortuary. The only surprise was the choice of emissary. Charles Haney awaited him in reception. He was a well-groomed man in his late fifties with iron-grey hair. He wore a cashmere coat that must have cost at least a couple of months of Harlan's salary. He'd seen QC dressed in his wig and gown at the High Courts on a few occasions, but never actually spoken to the man.

Haney stood and shook his hand. 'Detective Inspector Harlan. A pleasure to meet you at long last. I was hoping we could have a chat somewhere private.'

In silence, not even pretending to make small talk, Harlan led Haney back to his office and closed the door. Haney took a seat without being asked, shrugging out of his coat, folding it carefully and laying it across his lap. Harlan remembered the aura of raw menace Ray Talbot had given off in poisonous waves that day in the church. Haney might well have raped and murdered children to gratify his sexual tastes, but he exuded nothing more than power and unshakeable confidence. This was a man who knew he was untouchable as far as the law was concerned.

Crossing one smartly tailored leg over the other, Haney said, 'Hope you don't mind me dropping in like this. I would have come sooner, but certain matters had still to be resolved properly. You do understand, yes?'

Harlan nodded. A visit from one of the *inner sanctum* wasn't a good sign. Was this where he would be informed he was now forever shackled to the whims of the Circle? Made an offer he couldn't refuse?

'To be honest, Mr Haney, you were the last person I expected to come calling.'

Haney smiled, showing perfect cosmetic teeth. 'On the contrary, it makes perfect sense having me drop by, seeing as both of us are legal men in every sense. Common ground. My presence here shouldn't raise too many eyebrows.'

'If you say so.'

'Oh, I do. By the way, Jocelyn sends her fondest wishes. Apologises for any misunderstandings that may have arisen.'

'You mean Jo is...?' he almost said, *alive*, but stopped himself in time.

'My wife is in the south of France. In a retreat. Somewhere to contemplate her misjudgement in certain matters.'

Harlan cleared his throat. 'Is that a permanent arrangement?'

'That all depends on how well she responds to her fall from grace. If a certain level of repentance and contrition is shown, who knows? But I'm not here to talk about my recent marriage difficulties.'

Harlan was determined not to show any weakness in front of this man. 'I'm guessing you're not here to discuss legal representation of Stella Wilson, Tim Hughes or Mike McBrearty?'

Haney seemed amused. 'I certainly won't be representing any of those ingrates. I admit the evidence against all three is compelling and would provide a splendid legal challenge, but I doubt anyone will ever be tasked with such a burden.'

Harlan didn't respond to this. He'd never expected any of the accused to actually make it to trial. He was only surprised the Circle hadn't yet taken any action. 'So why are you here, Mr Haney?'

'My friends have asked me to pass on their compliments and appreciation for a job well done. Perhaps we can extend our association and make it a more permanent arrangement. I'm well aware the salary for a detective inspector is pitiable considering the responsibilities and long hours you endure. I imagine you must feel financially inadequate seeing your daughter taken care of by a man to whom money is no object. Becoming a friend of the Circle would see you generously rewarded, DI Harlan, and for very little effort on your part. A favour here, a favour there. A helpful hand in times of need.'

Haney had on his professionally disarming smile. The smile he must use when cajoling a jury into seeing how reasonable his counter arguments were. The sort of smile he'd wear when addressing the media after winning a big case. And probably the same smile he conjured up when destroying the poor bastards his Gamekeepers brought him.

The barrister held out his hand. 'A simple handshake would seal our association.'

'What if I say no?' Despite his best poker face Harlan could hear his heart thumping inside his chest.

The hand dropped and the smile altered just a little, just enough to convey a note of warning. 'In that case, DI Harlan, we could simply threaten to expose you on several counts of misconduct.' The smile turned up the wattage again. 'But we won't do that. You're too small in the grand scheme of things. Those kind of favours we squeeze from people with power. No disrespect intended. You simply wouldn't be worth the effort.'

Haney stood up and put on his coat. He was leaving.

'Is that it?'

The barrister stared coolly back at him. 'Unless you intend being a thorn in our side. We would crush you like a bug, DI Harlan. I'll see myself out. Goodbye.'

When the door closed Harlan let out a long breath and held his hands out before him. There was definitely a tremble. Just a little one, but a distinct tremble all the same. That had been seriously scary. He wondered how Honeytrap was enjoying her new job working for Haney and his friends. She had never returned to duty, sending in her resignation by email. Everyone assumed she had struck lucky with one of her numerous internet dates. She'd never had any close friends in the police for anyone to enquire further.

There came a soft tap on his door, causing him to flinch in alarm. Was this the bit where Haney returned to say he'd changed his mind and then shoot him with a poison dart from the end of his umbrella? Stranger things had happened recently.

DCS Walker entered and leaned nonchalantly against the wall. He looked pleased about something.

'Sir?'

'You turned them down. I was hoping you would.'

'What?' Harlan was thinking he'd gone from the frying pan into the fire. If Walker knew about Haney then he likely knew about the Circle and the deal he'd made with them. But Walker didn't look like he was here to demand his resignation.

'The Circle, DI Harlan. You turned down whatever they were offering.'

'How...'

'Because I just passed Charles Haney in the corridor and he definitely wasn't looking happy.'

'Should I be watching my back?'

Walker stroked his trim little moustache. 'Shouldn't think so. Just don't go tilting at windmills, Harlan. The Circle are what they are. Out of reach. Too well protected. Think of them as a nest of vampires. A different breed of creature, barely human. They prey on the weak and defenceless. Pick off those who won't be missed straight away. These days with so much human trafficking going on it's even easier for them. They can buy in bulk.'

'But you knew I'd gotten... involved with them.'

'It wasn't such a huge leap to make when you returned from meeting Howie Danks and suddenly the Assistant Chief Constable is on the phone demanding you take over the investigation. I imagine you accepted their offer thinking it was for the right reasons. I could only hope that once everything was over, you'd make the right decision.'

Harlan nodded. 'Does that mean the Assistant Chief Constable...?'

Walker shook his head. 'Part of the Circle? I think not. He's a genuinely nice bloke. I've played golf with him once or twice. His one weakness is pretty young ladies with no moral scruples. Left himself wide open to extortion is my guess.'

The DCS pushed himself away from the wall and opened the door. 'I'll leave you to it, DI Harlan.'

'Sir?' Harlan wasn't sure exactly what he wanted to ask. 'How do you know so much about the Circle? If you don't mind me asking.'

Walker's smile was rueful. 'Perhaps I was in a similar position to yourself, DI Harlan. In dire need of a big favour to help bring down the bad guys. It was only later I discovered who the really bad guys were. Have a nice evening and don't forget what I said about those windmills.'

After Walker was gone, Harlan turned off his desk lamp and watched the falling snow for a time, thinking of nothing at all, letting the white drifting flakes lull him into a state of inner calm. He was perhaps only a moment or two away from dozing off when he remembered he still hadn't called Steph. He had to sort out access with Holly. Steph had refused to let him see Holly since the night he advised them to flee the country.

Holly had emailed to say she'd had a great time at Rob's Barcelona holiday flat. Steph had texted telling him to go visit a lawyer if was so keen to see his daughter. She would come round eventually. Maybe best to leave the call for another few days.

He decided he'd had enough for the day, locking up his office then driving slowly through the snowstorm to Cathedral House. The bar was empty, those who regularly dropped in for a drink on their way home from work giving it a wide berth due to the bad weather.

It was still strange to no longer hear Archie's eccentric piano arrangements drifting down from upstairs. The little man had simply packed up and vanished the day after their conversation in the Necropolis. Harlan still wondered if the Circle had finally caught up with him, or if he'd simply scarpered. He'd probably never know.

Lenny was leaning on the bar top watching television. He looked surprised to see Harlan.

'Thought you was heading straight out to Cara's leaving bash?'

Harlan shook his head. 'Decided to give it a miss.'

'Too painful?' Lenny's expression was sympathetic.

'Something like that.'

'Never mind, always thought she was a bit young and flighty for you anyway. You oughta be looking for someone nearer your own age.'

'Thanks, Lenny. You always know how to cheer someone up.'

'Don't mention it. I'll let Marilyn know you'll be wanting some dinner rustled up.'

Harlan nodded his thanks as Lenny slipped out, heading for the kitchen.

Alone, he surveyed the bar, appreciating as always the way the spotlights reflected off the brightly coloured bottles on the gantry, thinking how the bar never failed to remind him of a stage. Tonight he was the only actor left. A performer who had said all his lines and now needed to find himself a new script. He turned and gave a small bow to the empty gallery, then headed upstairs to get changed for dinner.